INCIDENT AT EXETER

THE INTERRUPTED JOURNEY

TWO LANDMARK INVESTIGATIONS OF
UFO ENCOUNTERS
TOGETHER IN ONE VOLUME

JOHN G. FULLER

MJF BOOKS
NEW YORK

Published by MJF Books
Fine Communications
Two Lincoln Square
60 West 66th Street
New York, NY 10023

Library of Congress Catalog Card Number 96-76471
ISBN 1-56731-134-2

Manufactured in the United States of America on acid-free paper ∞

MJF Books and the MJF colophon are trademarks of Fine Creative Media, Inc.

10   9   8   7   6   5   4   3   2   1

INCIDENT AT EXETER

Preface

IT was in mid-September of 1965 I learned of the incident at Exeter, a report which was interesting because it was on the official records of the police department, and verified by two officers of the department whose character, reliability and composure in crisis have been certified firmly by their superior officers. Further, the incident was observed by at least five people, at a distance and over a time period that allowed for clear and unmistakable observation.

Exeter lies in a surpassingly beautiful slice of southern New Hampshire, where the Atlantic, tall pine forests, and pre-Revolutionary homes have joined to create the background for a mystery—a mystery as fantastic and sweeping as the legend of Sleepy Hollow, mixed with the most vivid trappings of science fiction. A dozen miles to the northeast is Portsmouth, home of the naval base since 1800, and now host to the Pease Air Force Base. B-52 and B-47 jet bombers rumble out from the runways here on a constant 24-hour schedule. Off the coast nearby are the ghostly Isles of Shoals, neighbors to the shattered hull of the sunken atomic submarine, the *Thresher*.

Autumn here is brilliant; it hurts the eyes. You approach the town from the east through a colonnade of burnt orange and russet maples, past the Old Harrison House on Water Street, a historical relic of the eighteenth century, and continue on to the center of town. Here, where Front and Water streets merge is a stone bandstand, where the townspeople still gather on a summer evening for a brassy concert. Not far up the hill on Front Street is Phillips Exeter Academy, spawning ground for Ivy League hopefuls. Just past the Academy is the Exeter Inn, a sleepy and docile hostelry, and haven for elderly gentility as well as for well-heeled parents when they come to visit their sons at school.

A dozen parking meters down from the stone bandstand on Water Street, the Exeter Police Department occupies a dwarf-size suite of rooms in a hulking brick monstrosity bearing the architectural scars of the industrial revolution.

There's a friendly informality about the police station, perhaps because its size creates an intimacy all its own. On the daytime shift, the desk is monitored by Mrs. Evelyn Oliver, a congenial and efficient lady who mans the radio microphone, dispatches patrol cars, and handles the office detail briskly and without fuss. Chief Richard Irvine, a handsome and somewhat laconic man, joins her in making the most of the cramped quarters and both have been puzzled and confused by the mystery plaguing the area. For the most part, the desk handles the usual type of routine that any New England town of 6,500 residents might face: high school pranks, an occasional drunk, a tavern brawl, a family fight, an unlocked warehouse, a prowler here and there, and a continuous dribble of automobile accident cases. The townspeople are either of sturdy Yankee yeoman stock, varied racial groups who settled in Exeter during the industrial revolution, or the academic cluster at the Phillips Academy.

It was nearly a month before I could clear my schedule after I learned of the case, and I arrived in New Hampshire on Wednesday, October 20, for an appointment with the officers involved, patrolmen Eugene Bertrand and David Hunt, of the Exeter Police Force. It was the beginning of a search which was to continue for many weeks, sometimes on the basis of an 18- or 20-hour day. The point of the search was to find the most logical possible explanation for a dramatic and unusual circumstance involving an Unidentified Flying Object, or UFO as the Air Force likes to call them.

If it had not been for the transistor tape recorder I carried, I would have had serious misgivings about completing the project. The reports that I recorded seemed so improbable, so other-worldly, that written notes alone might not have been enough to convince both the editors of *Look* Magazine and the publishers that over 60 people testified to what they saw with intensity and conviction.

But anyone listening to the many hours of taped interviews cannot doubt the sincerity or honesty of the people involved. Nor was there opportunity or desire for collusion, for many of those who testified were widely separated from each other. Several who experienced low-level encounters suffered genuine shock. They recalled it during the interviews with unselfconscious conviction which it would have been almost impossible to feign.

While the interviews in cold type cannot convey all this conviction, it is important to remember that it is there, underlining the fact that these conservative New England people are stating what they believe to be the whole truth.

All the dialogue in the book recounting these experiences is taken verbatim from the tapes.

This book was no sooner completed, when UFO reports began to break out in unprecedented numbers all over the country. After my research in Exeter, I was convinced that this would happen, surprised that it had not happened sooner. For the first time, the general press began treating the subject with respect.

I knew that Exeter was only a microcosm, a reflection of a story (the biggest newsbreak in history?) that was taking place, or bound to take place in increasing frequency all over the world. Since one reporter cannot hopscotch everywhere to track down an effective story, I decided to use Exeter because of a well-documented case there involving the police. It could have been any number of other places with similar reports.

When the now-famous Michigan cases broke in March, 1966, House Republican leader Gerald R. Ford formally requested a Congressional Investigation, and the wire services furnished front-page stories for the nationwide press. But when an Air Force investigation indicated that some of the sightings might be attributed to methane, or marsh gas, the press again backtracked and seized on this as a blanket explanation for the UFO phenomenon.

This distortion was deplored by Dr. J. Allen Hynek, head of the Astronomy Department of Northwestern University, who himself had advanced the marsh gas theory.

In a letter to me on March 29, 1966, he wrote:

> I am enclosing the actual press release I gave out at Detroit because I wanted you to have the full story. The release was not handled in the papers as released, which of course it rarely is.
>
> You will note my insistence that the swamp sightings and their highly likely explanation does not constitute a blanket explanation for the UFO phenomenon. I'm afraid this point was missed, too.

In the official release so badly distorted by the press, Dr. Hynek states:

> The Air Force has asked me to make a statement of my findings to date. This I am happy to do, provided it is clearly understood that my statement will refer to two principal events as reported to me. . . . It does not cover the hundreds of unexplained reports. . . . I have not investigated those. . . . I have recommended in my capacity as Scientific Consultant (to the Air Force) that competent scientists quietly study such cases when evidence from responsible people appears to warrant such study. There may be

much of potential value to science in such events. We know a very great deal more about the physical world in 1966 than we did in 1866—but, by the same token, the people in the year 2066 may regard us as very incomplete in our scientific knowledge. . . .

JOHN G. FULLER

Westport, Conn.
April, 1966

CHAPTER I

AT 2:24 A.M. on September 3, 1965, Norman Muscarello, three weeks away from joining the Navy, plunged into the Exeter police station in a state of near shock. He was white, and shaking. Patrolman Reginald "Scratch" Toland, on duty at the desk, helped him light a cigarette before he calmed down enough to talk.

His story came out in bursts. He had been hitchhiking on Route 150 from Amesbury, Massachusetts, to his home in Exeter, a distance of twelve miles. The traffic was sparse, and he was forced to walk most of the way. By two that morning he reached Kensington, a few miles short of his home. Near an open field between two houses, the Thing, as he called it, came out of the sky directly toward him. It was as big as or bigger than a house. It appeared to be 80 to 90 feet in diameter, with brilliant, pulsating red lights around an apparent rim. It wobbled, yawed, and floated toward him. It made no noise whatever. When it seemed as if it was going to hit him, he dove down on the shallow shoulder of the road. Then the object appeared to back off slowly, and hovered directly over the roof of one of the houses. Finally, it backed off far enough for Muscarello to make a run for the house. He pounded on the door, screaming. No one answered.

At that moment, a car came by, moving in the direction of Exeter. He ran to the middle of the road and waved his arms frantically. A middle-aged couple drove him into Exeter and dropped him off at the police station.

The kid had calmed down a little now, although he kept lighting one cigarette after another.

"Look," said Muscarello. "I know you don't believe me. I don't blame you. *But you got to send somebody back out there with me!*"

The kid persisted. Officer Toland, puzzled at first, was impressed by his sincerity. He kicked on the police radio and called in Cruiser #21.

Within five minutes, Patrolman Eugene Bertrand pulled into the station. Bertrand, an Air Force veteran during the Korean War, with air-to-air refueling experience on KC-97 tankers, reported an odd coincidence. An hour or so before, cruising near the overpass on Route 101, about two miles out of Exeter, he had come across a car parked on the bypass, a lone woman at the wheel. Trying to keep her composure, she had said that a huge, silent, airborne object had trailed her from the town of Epping, twelve miles away, only a few feet from her car. It had brilliant, flashing red lights. When she had reached the overpass, it suddenly took off at tremendous speed and disappeared among the stars.

"I thought she was a kook," Bertrand told Toland. "So I didn't even bother to radio in."

Toland turned to the kid with a little more interest. "This sound like the thing you saw?"

"Sounds exactly like it," said Muscarello.

It was nearly 3 A.M. when Patrolman Bertrand, still trying to calm Muscarello down, arrived back at the field along Route 150. The night was clear, moonless, and warm. Visibility was unlimited. There was no wind, and the stars were brilliant. Bertrand parked his cruiser near Tel. & Tel. Pole #668. He picked up the radio mike to call to Toland that he saw nothing at all, but that the youngster was still so tense about the situation he was going to walk out on the field with him to investigate further. "I'll be out of the cruiser for a few minutes," he said, "so if you don't get an answer on the radio, don't worry about it."

Bertrand and Muscarello walked down the sloping field in the dark, Bertrand probing the trees in the distance with his flashlight. About 100 yards away from the roadside was a corral, where the horses of the Carl Dining farm were kept. When they reached the fence, and still saw nothing, Bertrand tried to reassure the kid, explaining that it must have been a helicopter. Muscarello refused to be placated. He insisted that he was familiar with all types of conventional aircraft.

Then, as Bertrand turned his back to the corral to shine his light toward the tree line to the north, the horses at the Dining farm began to kick and whinny and bat at the sides of the barn and fence. Dogs in the nearby houses began howling. Muscarello let out a yell.

"I see it! I see it!" he screamed.

Bertrand reeled and looked toward the trees beyond the corral.

It was rising slowly from behind two tall pines: a brilliant, roundish object, without a sound. It came toward them like a leaf fluttering from a tree, wobbling and yawing as it moved. The entire area was bathed in brilliant red light. The white sides of Carl Dining's pre-Revolutionary saltbox house turned blood-red. The Russell house, a hundred yards away, turned the same color. Bertrand reached for his .38, then thought better of it and shoved it back in its holster. Muscarello froze in his tracks. Bertrand, afraid of infrared rays or radiation, grabbed the youngster, yanked him toward the cruiser.

Back at the Exeter police station, Scratch Toland was nearly blasted out of his chair by Bertrand's radio call. *"My God. I see the damn thing myself!"*

Under the half-protection of the cruiser roof, Bertrand and Muscarello watched the object hover. It was about 100 feet

13

above them, about a football field's distance away. It was rocking back and forth on its axis, still absolutely silent. The pulsating red lights seemed to dim from left to right, then from right to left, in a 5-4-3-2-1, then 1-2-3-4-5 pattern, covering about two seconds for each cycle. It was hard to make out a definite shape because of the brilliance of the lights. "Like trying to describe a car with its headlights coming at you," is the way Bertrand puts it.

It hovered there, 100 feet above the field, for several minutes. Still no noise, except for the horses and dogs. Then, slowly, it began to move away, eastward, toward Hampton. Its movement was erratic, defying all conventional aerodynamic patterns. "It darted," says Bertrand. "It could turn on a dime. Then it would slow down."

At that moment Patrolman David Hunt, in Cruiser #20, pulled up by the pole. He had heard the radio conversations between Bertrand and Toland at the desk, and had scrambled out to the scene. Bertrand jumped out to join Hunt at the edge of the field.

"I could see that fluttering movement," Hunt says. "It was going from left to right, between the tops of two big trees. I could see those pulsating lights. I could hear those horses kicking out in the barn there. Those dogs were really howling. Then it started moving, slow-like, across the tops of the trees, just above the trees. It was rocking when it did this. A creepy type of look. Airplanes don't do this. After it moved out of sight, toward Hampton, toward the ocean, we waited awhile. A B-47 came over. You could tell the difference. There was no comparison."

Within moments after the object slid over the trees and out of sight of Bertrand, Hunt and Muscarello, Scratch Toland took a call at the desk from an Exeter night operator.

"She was all excited," says Toland. "Some man had just called her, and she traced the call to one of them outside

14

booths in Hampton, and he was so hysterical he could hardly talk straight. He told her that a flying saucer came right at him, but before he could finish, he was cut off. I got on the phone and called the Hampton police, and they notified the Pease Air Force Base."

The blotter of the Hampton Police Department covers the story tartly:

> SEPT. 3, 1965: 3 A.M. Exeter Police Dept. reports unidentified flying object in that area. Units 2, 4 and Pease Air Force alerted. At 3:17 A.M., received a call from Exeter operator and Officer Toland. Advised that a male subject called and asked for police department, further stating that call was in re: a large, unidentified flying object, but call was cut off. Call received from a Hampton pay phone, location unknown.

At 4:30 A.M. that morning, Mrs. Dolores Gazda, 205½ Front Street, Exeter, and mother of Norman Muscarello from a previous marriage, was in her own words "pretty shook up." Without a phone, she had had no word from her son since early the previous evening. Nervous and wakeful, she watched the police cruiser pull up outside her second-floor flat, where she keeps a spotlessly clean apartment in the face of a restricted budget. She ran to the outside wooden stairs, and watched officers Bertrand and Hunt escort her son up.

"You know what a shock this could be to a mother," she says. "And of course I could hardly believe this fantastic story. It wasn't until I talked to the two police officers that I knew what they went through. When he came in with the police, he was white. White as a ghost. I knew he couldn't be putting me on. Thank God the police saw it with him. People might never believe him."

By 8 A.M. that morning, Patrolman Bertrand returned to his modest clapboard home on, oddly enough, Pickpocket Road. His attractive young wife, Dorothy, was dressing the children and straightening up the house.

15

"When Gene came in the door," she says, "I knew right away that something unusual had happened. He said that I wouldn't believe what he saw during the night, and then he told me about it. And I still didn't believe him. Until after all the reports came in."

For days afterward, whenever he went to bed Bertrand would think about it. "It's a startling thing," he says, "and you think about it because you wonder what it is. Your mind imagines the impossible. The world is going so fast that it could be something from outer space. It makes you wonder, it really does. Dave and I talk about it often. I get the feeling from him that he doesn't think it belongs to the Air Force. I want to keep my mind open. Look for a reasonable explanation. But then, as I look back in my mind again, I wonder. When I first heard the kid tell about it, I thought it must have been a plane. But the more he talked, I knew it couldn't be one. Then I was sure he was talking about a helicopter. I did ask him on that four-mile ride out to the place, did you feel any wind? I know from a helicopter, he's bound to feel some wind from it. But he said he didn't. I thought he might have got scared, and was mistaken. When we watched it, Dave and I and the kid tried to listen, to hear a motor. We did everything to check it out. We weren't believing our eyes. Your mind is telling you this can't be true, and yet you're seeing it. So you check out your eyes to make sure you're seeing what you're really seeing. We just couldn't come up with an answer. I kept telling Dave, what is that, Dave? What do you think? He'd say, I don't know. I had never seen an aircraft like that before, and I know damn well they haven't changed that much since I was in the service."

Lt. Warren Cottrell was on the desk at 8 o'clock that morning. He read Bertrand's report, a rough piece of yellow manuscript paper hunt-and-pecked as a supplement to the regular blotter. It read:

At 2:27 A.M., Officer Toland on duty at the desk called me into the station. Norman J. Muscarello, 205½ Front Street, was in the station and he was upset.

He had told Officer Toland that on the way home from Amesbury, Mass., in Kensington, N.H., while walking along Rt. 150 an unidentified flying object came out of the sky with red lights on it.

He got down on the road so that it would not get him. Officer Toland sent me to this place where Muscarello had seen this thing.

The place was a field near Tel. and Tel. Pole #668 on Rt. 150. I did not see anything.

I got out of the cruiser and went into the field and all of a sudden this thing came at me at about 100 feet off the ground with red lights going back and forth. Officer Hunt got there and also saw this thing. It had no motor and came through the air like a leaf falling from the tree. By the time Hunt got to this field, the UFO had gone over the trees, but he saw it.

(Signed) PTL. E. BERTRAND

Cottrell called the Pease Air Force Base to reconfirm the incident, and by one in the afternoon, Major Thomas Griffin and Lt. Alan Brandt arrived. They went to the scene of the sighting, interviewed Bertrand, Hunt and Muscarello at length, and returned to the base with little comment. They were interested and serious.

By nightfall that evening, a long series of phone calls began coming into the police station, many from people who had distrusted their own senses in previous sightings before the police report.

Nightfall also marked the beginning of a three-week nightly vigil by Muscarello, his mother, and several friends. In the short time left before he was to go to the Great Lakes Naval Training Station, he was determined to see it again. He did.

17

CHAPTER II

ON the morning of September 14, 1965, some eleven days after officers Bertrand and Hunt had filed their report, I was faced with a deadline for the regular column I write for the *Saturday Review*. At this time, I knew nothing about the incident at Exeter and little, if anything, about Unidentified Flying Objects. At one time several years before, I had helped produce a CBS-TV show which had, as guests, some technicians who had sighted UFOs—but that was the extent of my knowledge. As usual, I began the slow, painful search through the mass of undecipherable notes and clippings, kept in the deep, lower-right desk drawer, in the search for column material.

The material was not very promising: a stack of routine, boiler-plate releases on forthcoming books, a few notes scrawled on the backs of envelopes and match covers, notes on an interview with two authors which had turned out to be insufferably dull, and a pile of news clippings marked for follow-up. Clippings often provide the source material for good copy, solely because news stories come and go fleetingly, and are never heard from again. Yet some of them are tantalizing, whetting the curiosity without satisfying it. Additional investigation often reveals a better story than the original.

One of the clippings in the file was an AP dispatch from *The New York Times* of August 3, 1965, over a month old. The dateline was Oklahoma City:

Authorities in Texas, New Mexico, Oklahoma and Kansas were deluged last night and early today by reports of unidentified objects seen flying in the sky.

The Sedgwick County sheriff's office at Wichita, Kansas, said the Weather Bureau had tracked "several of them at altitudes of 6,000 to 9,000 feet."

The Oklahoma Highway Patrol said that Tinker Air Force Base here had tracked four of the unidentified flying objects on its radar screen at one time, estimating their altitude at about 22,000 feet. A Tinker spokesman refused to confirm or deny the reports of radar observations.

Reports poured in from Pecos, Monahans, Odessa, Midland, Fort Worth, Canyon and Dalhard, Tex.; Hobbs, Carlsbad and Artesia, N. Mex.; Chickasha, Shawnee, Cushing, Buymon and Chandler, Okla.; and Oxford, Belle Plaine, Winfield, Caldwell, Mulvane and Wichita, Kan.

The Oklahoma Highway Patrol said police officers in three different patrol cars had reported watching the objects fly in a diamond-shaped formation for about 30 minutes in the Shawnee area. The patrol said the officers had described the objects as changing in color from red to white to blue-green.

At 3:40 A.M., the Weather Bureau at Wichita said it had tracked one of the objects south and west of Wellington. The bureau said the object had first appeared on its radar at an altitude of about 22,000 feet and had then descended to 4,000 feet.

Descriptions telephoned to the police and other authorities included these:

"I was a disbeliever, but I saw something up there tonight, and so did other observers at the Weather Bureau."

"They were red and exploded in a shower of sparks and at other times, floated like a leaf."

"You could see it with the naked eye. It looked like it was on the ground or hovering just above the ground.

19

It was red, greenish, blue and yellowish white, about 100 yards long and egg-shaped."

Spokesmen at Tinker and McConnell Air Force bases are referring all queries to the Air Force in Washintgon. In the past, the Air Force has said the sightings have turned out to be such things as balloons, birds, searchlights, jet exhaust, kites, meteors, missiles.

As of last July 20, the Air Force had checked out 9,127 such sightings since 1947 with 667 still unidentified.

I had clipped the item, first, because it had appeared in *The New York Times*, which is very reluctant to print stories of Unidentified Flying Objects. Second, the sightings seemed to be much more heavily documented than the usual report of this sort of thing: three different patrol cars, weather observers, Air Force base and Weather Bureau radar. All this would seem to rule out hysteria, illusion, or incompetence in observation. Fourth, I was curious about what the follow-up would be. Certainly with such complete documentation as this, there would be extensive discussion and comment, even in the pages of the august *Times*.

Little or nothing appeared after the original story, however. It was some weeks later that I decided it might make an interesting column to take a single isolated case of a UFO sighting and track it down to prove it out as either an illusion, a mistaken identity, or something which had to remain a mystery. It would, if nothing else, be an interesting space-age ghost story, and it was on this premise that I put in a long-distance call to the National Investigations Committee on Aerial Phenomena in Washington.

NICAP—as the organization is referred to in alphabetical shorthand—was set up in 1956 under the direction of Major Donald E. Keyhoe, USMC (Ret.). It is known for its conservative and technical approach to the subject. Among its Board of Governors and panel of special advisers are former Air Force officers, commercial airline pilots, engineers, technicians, clergymen, astronomers, retired naval officers, and NASA technicians. In the spring of 1964, it issued a scholarly and well-documented book titled *The UFO Evidence* which analyzes 746 reports from among 5,000 signed statements it has in its files. I had received a press copy of this volume when it was first published, well over a year before, but had never bothered to look at it. It was helpful now in locating the organization by phone, but I decided not to study it at this time to avoid developing any preconceived ideas. I wanted the column to be an objective report, uninfluenced by other opinions. I had often found in the past that it is better to come into a story with "intelligent ignorance," if you could call it that, plus a fair measure of friendly skepticism.

On the phone, Richard Hall, the Assistant Director of NICAP, was cooperative and helpful. "We've got a tremendous number of reports on these Southwest sightings," he said, "but the newspapers dropped them fast. The main case —the one involving the Tinker Air Force Base—was at first reported as a confirmed radar-and-visual sighting. Now the Air Force has come along and singled that case out to say that their radar did *not* confirm the visual sightings of the Oklahoma Highway Patrol. But we're used to this."

I asked Hall why.

"The Air Force is constantly trying to knock down all UFO reports," he said. "They've clamped down the lid, and issued denials of reliable reports repeatedly. This is our big battle. For instance, we've got information to contradict the Air Force denial here. It's a nine-page report of the Oklahoma Department of Public Safety, outlining a sighting by the police, and confirmed by the Carswell Air Force Base radar. And the reports are still going on. Reports from all over."

"Could you give me some examples?" I asked.

"Well," he said, "on September third—just a week or so ago—there were two extreme low-level sightings reported to us. One in Exeter, New Hampshire; the other southeast of

Houston, Texas. Both of them are police reports, so we can count on them at least being fairly reliable. In the Texas story, two policemen from Angleton started to investigate a large object which had landed in a field. When it moved toward them, they jumped back in their car and drove off fast."

"What about the Exeter case?" I asked.

He gave me a brief summary of officers Bertrand and Hunt and their story. I made a note to contact their New England subcommittee member, a Mr. Raymond Fowler, who was a technician with Sylvania Electric's Minute Man Program.

"What else have you run into lately?" I asked.

"About a month ago," Hall said, "as a matter of fact, on August fifteenth, two coastguardsmen in Virginia reported an elliptical object hovering near a radio antenna. It was a more-or-less featureless egg-shaped object, according to them, and it took off rapidly after a few moments."

I decided to confine myself to recent reports from competent observers, preferably at low level. This would at least help to rule out mistaken identity as far as high-flying planes, meteors, planets or reflections were concerned. According to Hall, a rash of sightings began in July in Antarctica. Technical and scientific teams from Argentina, Chile, and Great Britain had reported a perfect disk hovering about their stations on July 3. Similar sightings were reported in the Azores. During August, a former Air Force flight instructor, a Costa Rica control tower operator, and a weather observer saw such an object at close range. In the same month, a missile engineering analyst, Francis C. Jennings of Seattle, Washington, filed a detailed report, as well as a U.S. Forest Service officer in a lookout tower in Idaho. On August 3, five police officers in Cocoa, Florida, observed four objects in diamond-shaped formation. And on August 19, in Cherry Creek, New York, near Buffalo, New York State Police thoroughly investigated a landing of a UFO, reliably reported, which left a bluish substance staining the ground.

Hall was obviously intelligent, analytical, and serious. But to adjust from ordinary journalism to the other-worldliness of this subject is not easy. Adjustment is not even desirable, because it would tend to diminish objectivity.

"Tell me something," I asked Hall. "What is NICAP's position on all this?"

"You mean what are our conclusions?"

"Yes."

"Well," he said, "we have carefully considered all the evidence we have, and we support the hypothesis that UFOs are under intelligent control—and that some of them might be of extraterrestrial origin."

I reached Raymond Fowler, the New England subcommittee member, on the phone later in the day. He had, he told me, returned from Exeter, New Hampshire, a few days before, and had just filed an 18-page report to Washington which had probably not arrived there yet. He had obtained signed statements from both policemen involved, surveyed the area, and confirmed as much detail as possible about the sighting.

"I can't seem to find any holes in it," he said. "Both the officers are intelligent, capable, and seem to know what they're talking about. The sighting was near, and it was low. Bertrand's experience in Air Force refueling makes him capable of discriminating between a UFO and anything else in the air, commercial or military."

We talked for nearly an hour as he read me portions of his report and I took down copious notes. For the amount of space in my column—only 1,000 words—I didn't plan to make a trip to Exeter. But I did intend to check out every possible fact by phone to make sure I was reporting material direct from the source, rather than hearsay. The call to Fowler was the first of seven. But the incident still had to be confirmed direct from the source, and it wasn't until after nearly three hours of long distance conversation that I was satisfied that I could report at least the available facts.

23

After confirming with the Exeter police desk that the story was officially on the blotter of September 3, 1965, I talked with Lt. Warren Cottrell, who told me that both Bertrand and Hunt were level-headed and calm, and not at all inclined to exaggerate. What's more, the station had been getting too many reports from too many reliable people to question the fact that *something* was being seen, and being seen regularly. "They're still coming in from all over," the lieutenant said. "And either you believe these people or call them nuts. Well, I know a lot of them, and they definitely are not nuts. They're good, quiet respectable people who wouldn't be inclined to go around making up yarns like this. Now take Bertrand, for instance. He's one of the toughest boys on the force. We send him out on all the rough jobs. Not afraid of anything. But boy, he was scared *this* time. I will say this—if only *one* of these boys saw this thing, I might have taken the live ammunition out of his gun. Or if I had any reason to doubt him and Hunt, I'd put 'em in the back room and give 'em some blocks to play with. And I'll tell you this much—if I had seen this thing, the way they describe it, and I was *alone*—nobody else would've ever heard about it."

A call to the Hampton, New Hampshire, police confirmed their side of the story: the hysterical, unidentified man in the phone booth, the report into the Pease Air Force Base. In addition, the officer on duty at the desk added: "We've been getting an awful lot of calls lately, and they seem to be responsible people. I don't really know what the heck is going on, but something is." Another call to the Manchester *Union Leader*, which covers a large area of New Hampshire, brought me in touch with James Bucknam, managing editor. He said that dozens of people in a wide area around Manchester (some 20 miles west of Exeter) had told him about UFO sightings, most of the reports being corroborated by more than one person. He read me the paper's coverage of the Bertrand-Hunt story, as written by their reporter who

24

arrived in the Exeter police station shortly after the sighting. The details checked in substance with Fowler's more technical account, as did the story from the Exeter *News-Letter*.

I was unable to reach Patrolman David Hunt, but finally got through a call to Patrolman Eugene Bertrand, who patiently went through his story in detail. "I was sure this was a helicopter that the kid was describing. But when it come up from behind the trees, I knew right away that it wasn't a helicopter or any kind of craft I ever ran into. Then when it started coming at us, I kept wondering why we didn't feel any breeze from the blades, and *no sound*. No sound at all, that's what got me. No tail, no wings, no sound. All I can tell you is that it was definitely a craft, a big one, with the lights so bright that you couldn't make out the shape at all. And it was low. Not much over the treetops. . . ."

Muscarello, I learned, did not have a phone, and there was no other way to reach him in time for the deadline on the column. I sat back and went over my notes, scrawled on a dozen pages of yellow foolscap. The elements of the story were so sensational that it was important to document only those facts which had been confirmed first hand. I had talked to the NICAP representatives in both Washington and New England, two newspaper editors, the police lieutenant at Exeter, the Hampton police desk, and Bertrand himself. There was no doubt that these people took this thing seriously, and all seemed of better than average intelligence. Even though I had been warned that I would get little or no information from the Pease Air Force Base in Portsmouth, a dozen or so miles away from Exeter, I put in a call to the Public Information Office there and spoke with Sgt. Robert Szarvas. "About the only thing I can do," he said, "is to confirm the fact that there have been a large number of sightings reported to us. Some of them come from important and influential people, there's no doubt about that. Matter of fact, a wire service reporter for the UPI who's always been ribbing us about UFOs, told me, 'I hate to bring this up, but I saw one myself.'

"The Air Force has a set procedure, and our hands are tied for releasing any specific information. When we get a report on a UFO, we take down the information, send out a rated officer who gathers as much information as possible. This is sent along to Wright-Patterson Air Force Base in Dayton, where they have a team of scientists who evaluate all the reports that come in. They're supposed to come up with the answers, but any release of information is made directly from the Pentagon."

"How much information does the Pentagon release?" I asked him.

"Well," Sergeant Szarvas said, "I don't think it's so much censorship as it is that the local bases aren't able to supply as much competent information on the subject as the Wright-Patterson air base can supply."

As Richard Hall of NICAP had suggested, it looked as if the Air Force position was a one-way street.

CHAPTER III

I WROTE the column with extreme care, giving the exact words of the persons involved in the incident at Exeter who had talked with me on the phone. I pointed out that State Police in Oklahoma, Texas, Kansas and New Mexico had risked their jobs and reputations for sanity in documenting a wide number of observations, as well as the two policemen in Exeter, New Hampshire.

The police aspect seemed significant. It is one thing to start an irresponsible rumor, or to report a fleeting glimpse of some kind of light or object in the sky which may be puzzling. But police officials in widely separated geographical areas are not likely to radio their superiors with detailed descriptions of their observations unless the evidence is almost overwhelming. Nor are weather observers and radar men. The very essence of their jobs depends on reliability for accurate observation. It was only because of the reliability of the witnesses and the extent of their observations that I could even consider writing about them.

In the face of this, it was hard to understand the attitude of the Government and the Air Force, as well as the scientific fraternity in general. Such authorities must maintain a very reserved and conservative approach to the subject. This is fully understandable. But indications seemed to be that the subject was totally ignored, tossed aside with a laugh, or downgraded to the status of mass illusion. And yet if there were even partial demonstrable truth to the reports, and to the theory that the earth was host to extraterrestrial visitors, it would become the biggest newsbreak in history.

Many of the letters from *Saturday Review* readers who read the column reflected puzzlement. A Mr. Ralph Newman, from Darien, Connecticut, wrote:

> Nobody is more bewildered than I am about this flying saucer matter. From the start of reading about strange objects over Sweden in 1946 and off and on in the press, including *The New York Times,* which is generally a believable paper, I keep thinking there must be some kind of *answer!*
>
> I am forever hearing of our government investigation departments on this matter as saying it's all so much mistaken identification (balloons, bright stars, etc.), or just so much hysteria, or plain falsehoods or fiction or hallucinations . . . or malarky.
>
> Your account of "following through to a conclusion" (you

27

didn't seem to come to any conclusion in the column) was interesting. Who can doubt these policemen? And have you heard any more from these police, or sighting of odd objects in the sky from that area since you wrote the article?

It certainly seems to me that if UFOs are hysteria, imaginary, and unreal objects, then why cannot a logical scientific authority *prove* this is so from a completely accepted viewpoint? After almost 20 years, I am unhappily having the growing notion that UFOs are forever going to be in the same category as ghosts, haunted houses: We'll always hear of such vivid accounts, sightings . . . but never get the proof.

But golly, modern-day cops report such things! And so have other cops in recent times, airline pilots, too, sticking their necks out to report seeing the seemingly inexplicable. Though *True* Magazine is not my idea of sober writing, there is an interesting book condensation by Jacques Valée, a French mathematician connected with NASA, in the October issue. He writes so sincerely, as sincerely as your UFO item reads, but dammit, I just don't know what to believe.

All I can say is I urge you to print more, if you learn more on this UFO matter, in *Trade Winds*. Maybe you'll come up with the truth in the matter. . . .

His mood was reflected by many other readers. From North Texas State University, James Davidson wrote:

I was most interested—and depressed—with your article (*Saturday Review*, October 2, 1965). Clearly evident is the public attitude, fostered in part by the Air Force and a host of "scientific" writers, that has long plagued investigation of this interesting and very important subject.

You say the "skepticism is a healthy thing." True. But scientific bigotry is not. Far from being healthily skeptical, we are profoundly convinced that there just is no such thing as a UFO. And starting from this grand, self-evident proposition, we wisely deduce that anyone who does see one is either malicious, foolish, or innocently misguided—and probably feebleminded.

28

No one wants to be like that. Consequently, those who have seen UFOs often remain silent. Exceptions only confirm the wisdom of their decision: I recently saw a young man, who knew no better than to admit that he had seen a UFO, made the fool of the week on a television interview.

Of course national hysteria is a poor alternative. But is it not just possible that we are mature enough to listen to facts for a change?

Another letter, from P. S. Hensel in Cleveland, expressed similar feelings:

> For the past 16 years, especially, thousands of sane humans, just as sane as the many police officers and airplane pilots and scientists around the world, have been seeing these things. But to the Air Force, they are hallucinations, flying stars, and planets. Dozens have seen UFOs of one type or another; many have faith in their fellow-men so that they do not deem them liars, fools.

I was impressed with the quality of the letters, none of them hysterical or crackpot. Madeline Moschenross, writing from Elizabeth, New Jersey, recounted an experience which she, as an obviously intelligent and level-headed person, had gone through:

> I feel much better now that I've read your column on UFOs. For back in 1950 or so, I called a top New Jersey newspaper to report what seemed more than a phenomenon, more than what even were called "flying saucers."
>
> I was looking out a bedroom window in front of my home, after midnight, when my attention was drawn to a perfect circle the size of an extra-large child's balloon. It remained stationary for quite awhile, then moved as though propelled, then stopped again. I went to another bedroom to wake up a member of my family, but changed my mind. Supposing this thing wasn't there? An illusion? Returning to my own room, I noticed The Thing had progressed a little nearer, and possibly slightly lower. It remained a long time. I decided to go to bed after reading a bit. Some-

time later, I moved on to the bathroom in the back of the house, looked out of the window and saw an amazing sight. A great circle of bright red (like a mammoth setting sun) was behind the leafless branches of some trees. How near the area in which I lived, I could not gauge. Again I hurried to waken the member of my family, but he didn't want to be roused. I don't know how long I watched the thing. I began to conjecture: the earth's movements are so mysterious, maybe this is some axis-turning sight only the few—the awake and the curious—are privileged to see. Like another world's setting. I went to bed—and as mentioned before, next morning informed the Newark *Evening News*. And of course, I was probably considered a nut.

From Alfred Rathmann, in Manitowoc, Wisconsin, came these questions:

From a strictly pragmatic point of view, I can't seem to see why scientists doubt the reports on sightings. Our own space program is rather impressive considering the short span of time that Homo sapiens has come out of the caves into the light of a sophisticated world.

I wonder if governments in general are keeping back facts on the total question of flying saucers? Could the fear of mass riots be the reason for the secrecy behind our own Air Force reports on UFOs? Reported radar sightings of UFOs are numerous. Reported sightings by qualified airline pilots, Air Force personnel, etc., are to be found in respected journals. I feel that a great deal of research on the subject would bring out a more logical ground to view all these sightings. Wouldn't you agree?

Frankly, at this point, I didn't know whether to agree or not. I knew that the only research which would satisfy me would be that taken direct from the source, without benefit of hearsay. The checking and rechecking on the incident at Exeter made it seem likely that something definite was to be learned there. But thorough as my inquiry was, it had been done entirely by phone. The mystery was challenging, as challenging as the conquest of Everest.

Early in October, I received a call from a Gordon Evans, an analyst and writer for a leading industrial institution. He had read the column, and was interested because it was a fresh, new case at low-level altitude supported by police testimony. He had spent a good many years analyzing the UFO subject, and offered further information. His call intrigued me because his approach to UFOs seemed literate, informed, and conservative. We arranged to have lunch on October 5.

Evans had some interesting theories. He contended that the Government knew all about UFOs, that they did exist, that they were interplanetary, and that an analysis of the evidence and action of the Government would lead logically to this conclusion.

"During the 1960's our final bill for space exploration could run over seventy billion dollars, and that's a conservative estimate," Evans said. "And when you stop to think about the reasons the Government tries to give for this massive outlay, they just don't add up. The so-called explanation is that it's part military, part economic, part scientific. 'Deep space' is practically useless as a military operation. They'd get much more military advantage from 'near space.' But most of the funds are going to be spent on lunar and planetary projects. Economic value? Another WPA or an increased war on poverty would do a much better job. Scientific? We've got enough problems here on earth to solve before we should take off for deep space—at least at this stepped-up pace, and with these budgets. Yet Congress is voting the funds, and the Government is spending them. And when you look at Russia's gross national product—much less than ours, and with a lot more economic planning—and then figure out how much *they're* spending on deep-space projects, it makes even *less* sense.

"Nobody's trying to say the people running the Government are idiots, or madmen. They're well aware how weak all this reasoning is. But they don't dare say anything else officially. The fact is that the earth is not the first in space by a long shot. And what the situation amounts to is that we're facing a half-voluntary censorship. As soon as any reliable expert begins to catch on, he's squashed on the basis that it's good for the people to be kept in the dark. The whole thing works out pretty neatly. This is what accounts for the paradox—a practically conclusive case for alien spacecraft hovering over the earth, and a seeming—only *seeming,* don't forget—lack of reputable scientific interest in the subject."

Evans also had a hunch—and he labeled it clearly as such —that the C.I.A. was making sure that any real news breakthrough would be very subtly sidetracked in a variety of ways. "There are a lot of really crackpot flying saucer groups in the country, as you know. Absolutely wild and irresponsible. And they put out these ridiculous newsletters which are so absurd you cannot understand how any human being would print them, and still stay out of the Laughing Academy. There are some people who have the sneaking suspicion that the C.I.A. actually creates some of these groups, makes them up out of whole cloth, so that the entire UFO situation becomes a laughing matter. So that a sensible person who gets involved in the subject is forced into sort of a guilt by association with these nuts."

Evans' theories were fascinating, but I had no way of evaluating them. Official silence would, in any case, block any chance of exploring them. If they were worthless, there seemed to be no way of proving that, either.

Evans mentioned that Carl Jung once said that the best way to dispel fear of an unknown is to dispel its mystery. "Jung was interested in the possibility of alien spacecraft coming to the earth, with governments trying to overprotect the population from reality. If a society were not ready for it emotionally, much more alarm might be caused. A grand plan for guarding the public from panic could lead to a greater panic, a greater social dislocation. If they suppress knowledge by state power, by official deception, it becomes an unnatural thing, and it's bound to fail eventually."

He went into the report from the Brookings Institution, which suggested that grave social consequences might follow from contact with highly evolved life beyond the earth. The report had given considerable attention to this possibility. "Anthropological files contain many examples of societies," it said, "sure of their place in the Universe, which have disintegrated when they came to associate with previously unfamiliar societies espousing different ideas and different ways of life. . . . It has been speculated that, of all groups, scientists and engineers might be the most devastated by the discovery of relatively superior creatures, since these professions are most clearly associated with mastery of nature. . . ."

Evans contended that the Brookings Institution took the human spirit for too fragile a structure. "The human spirit is tougher than they think," he said. "A little realistic humility does no harm. How much does civilization owe to cultural borrowing? Of course, if it's proved that man isn't alone in the solar system, the loss of what Harlow Shapley calls our 'cosmic loneliness' will certainly have a profound effect on our consciousness. But do they have to be so negative? Where there's been social collapse in the past, it's usually been the result of greed or brutality. Any UFOs which have been encountered haven't shown any such tendencies yet. They've avoided us, in a sense, in that they haven't shown any attempt to communicate with us directly. Suppose it turns out that socialism is the prevailing principle of these advanced civilizations? How is capitalism going to feel about that? Or suppose they're theologically minded? The Marxist materialists aren't going to be very happy about that. If a change is to come, I think we'd be a lot better off if it came naturally, without lying to the public."

If a civilization were *really* advanced, Evans reasoned, the

33

chances were it wouldn't be destructive. And in spite of the thousands of reports on UFOs, there had been no indication at all of any hostile motives.

But reason and logic seem strangely inadequate for this situation. With detailed documentation of sightings coming from hundreds of technical and expert sources, it would be reasonable and logical to believe without question that UFOs existed. With denials coming from leading scientists, Air Force and government authorities it would be equally logical and believable to deny the existence of the phenomena. Each of the two factions is automatically put in the position of calling the other either a liar or an incompetent. It is of course ridiculous to suggest that a leading scientist is incompetent. It is almost equally ridiculous to assume that hundreds of policemen, airline pilots, technicians and reliable people are liars or incompetent observers. The question could be posed: Are the scientists lying—for the assumed protection of society, and are the observers not lying, but mistaken in their observations? And was it worth time, money and effort to try to find out?

The answer to the last question was important. Aside from the strong lure of an unsolved mystery, the possibility of the existence of interplanetary visitors is of vital importance. The warlike nations of the world might become suddenly more amenable to working out their differences amicably. The suicidal collision course of the Great Powers might be shifted in the interest of overall world welfare. The petty quarrels of man might be submerged in the interest of the wider Universe. The fear of alien visitors would obviously cause a disruption in the pattern of normal life. But what greater fear is there than the potential incineration of the earth by hydrogen bombs? And how could any super-civilized visitors match or exceed man's inhumanity to man? The choice between even total dislocation of civilization (if UFOs were proven real and interplanetary) and total incineration

(Atomic War) would be easy to make. The former is curable, the latter is not.

CHAPTER IV

BEFORE the widespread reports from the Southwest during August of 1965, interest of the press in UFOs had been reasonably dormant for several years. Scattered items had appeared, but for the general public the subject was almost forgotten in contrast to the years following World War II, the early 50's, and especially 1957 when for two weeks headlines across the country reported UFO cases involving electromagnetic effects on automobile ignitions, radios, and lights. In Hammond, Indiana, for instance, police chased an elongated object when a loud, beeping sound interfered with their cruiser radio. A few days before this, James W. Stokes, a high-altitude research engineer at White Sands, saw an elliptical UFO sweep across the highway twice, as his car engine and radio failed. About the same time, a group of electronic technicians and ham radio operators north of Ottawa, Canada, reported seeing a huge brightly lighted sphere, projecting beams of light, hovering above a hill. Two radios failed, except for a rapidly modulated strong single tone picked up on one frequency. The UFO finally disappeared into the clouds.

Most interesting, however, were the recent cases. After my column on the incident at Exeter appeared in the *Saturday Review*, NICAP sent me several interesting reports from Washington noting an increase not only in recent cases, but in extreme low-level, and even landing reports. In chronological order, the cases covered a time period between April, 1964 through August of 1965.

The material seemed sober and well-documented. On April 24, 1964, a New Mexico police officer saw an egg-shaped craft the size of a car blast off from a desert gully. The Air Force, instead of labeling the UFO a delusion or hoax, finally admitted he had seen an "unknown vehicle."

On November 8, 1964, at Montreal, Canada, a Mr. Nelson Lebel sighted a round, luminous craft hovering above the trees some 2,000 feet from his house. Later, the area was searched by a retired Canadian army officer, Lebel, and representatives of a Montreal newspaper. A circular depression was found, with grass and foliage scorched around it. Above the site, investigators found branches of trees broken and blackened.

On November 30, 1964, at Terryville, Connecticut, a medical official saw an unknown flying object with a blinding white light descend toward a nearby woods. When he drove into a clearing where the UFO had landed, the craft took off, rushing over the top of his car. It disappeared at "faster than jet speed," leaving a burned area and definite landing marks.

On December 21, 1964, at Staunton, Virginia, a gun-shop owner saw a huge UFO, shaped like an inverted top, land briefly near Route 250. Later, Geiger counter checks by two Dupont Company engineers showed the landing spot to be highly radioactive.

On January 12, 1965, at Custer, Washington, a round, illuminated craft landed on a farm near the Blaine Air Force Base. Apparently, it was the same 30-foot flying disk which was tracked by Air Force radar as it swooped down to buzz the car of a federal law enforcement officer. Snow melted and the ground was scorched in a circular area where the UFO had landed. One of the witnesses said that the Air Force instructed him not to discuss the case.

On January 25, 1965, at Williamsburg, Virginia, a UFO descending rapidly from the sky caused engine failure in the car of a Richmond real estate executive. The strange craft, aluminum-colored, with an inverted-top shape, hovered just off the ground for 25 seconds. Then it shot straight up, with a swish of air, and disappeared with tremendous speed. On the same night, several miles away, a top-shaped UFO came toward the ground near the car of another Richmond businessman. An electromagnetic effect stopped his car as the UFO touched down.

On January 27, 1965, two NASA engineers, one a former Air Force pilot, saw a UFO with flashing lights descend near Hampton, Virginia. Engineer A. C. Grimmins told NICAP that the flying disk zigzagged to a brief landing, then rapidly climbed out of sight.

On May 24, 1965, an American engineer by the name of Paul Norman, along with J. W. Tilse, a commercial pilot with 11,500 flying hours, watched a brightly glowing object approach them at Eton Range, Australia, 42 miles from Mackay. Two other men were with them. "It was about three hundred yards from the hotel where we were staying," reported Pilot Tilse. "It had a bank of spotlights, twenty or thirty of them, below a circular platform. It was solid, metallic-looking, thirty feet or more in diameter."

As the machine settled on a sparsely timbered ridge, illuminating the trees, the orange glow of the lights diminished. But it was still too bright to tell whether the glow came from inside, through ports, or from lights encircling the craft.

Finally, the craft lifted. As it did, the men saw a massive, tripod-type landing gear which the glow had concealed. Each of the three legs had a bright, pulsating light. But after a few moments, they were no longer visible. As the UFO reached 300 feet, it accelerated rapidly, but no exhaust, no trails, could be seen.

"I had always scoffed at these reports," said Tilse. "But I

saw it. We all saw it. It was under intelligent control, and it certainly was no known aircraft."

The next day, Tilse photographed a circular impression on the ground where the UFO had landed or hovered. As confirmed by local police, it was a perfect circle, its inside diameter, 20 feet. The Regional Director of Civil Aviation has accepted the report as genuine.

NICAP, in assembling these reports, required detailed investigation by their subcommittee members, and signed statements wherever they could be obtained. Wherever possible, their representative would try to punch holes in the story. It was especially true of the case reported by the New York State Police on August 19, 1965 at Cherry Creek, New York, a town tucked in the western corner if the state, some 50 miles south of Niagara Falls.

On Friday, August 20, 1965, Jeffrey Gow, a member of NICAP, went to the Fredonia State Police Barracks to investigate the sighting by Mrs. William Butcher and her three sons, William, Jr., seventeen, Harold, sixteen, and Robert, fourteen. Trooper E. J. Haas had been dispatched to the Butcher farm the previous evening at 9:15 P.M. to check the event, and was impressed with the fact that the Butchers seemed to be a reliable and honest family, not the sort that might be likely to try to create a hoax. Trooper Haas had, in fact, run a background check on the family, and reported that the neighbors confirmed this.

Gow ran down the details of the police report with the trooper, and then visited the farm the next morning. Here he carefully pieced together the story, making maps and sketches as he did so.

He found that Harold Butcher, the sixteen-year-old, was milking the cows in the main barn, near the east window, at about 8:30 Thursday evening, August 19. The boy was listening to Radio Station WKBW, and the 8:15 news had just ended, giving Harold accurate knowledge of the time. At just about this moment the boy heard the three-year-old bull, which was tethered in the field to a metal pipe, let out a noise he describes as "like I have never heard come from an animal before."

Harold looked out the east window, as Gow reports it, and saw that the bull out on the field was in the process of bending the metal pipe, even though the bull was tethered through the nose. Then the boy saw a football-shaped object hovering just above tree level, about 450 feet from the barn.

It was a silver-chromelike object, some 50 feet in length, and approximately 20 feet thick. It seemed to have two vertical seams, with apparent rivets along the edges. When the craft moved vertically, a red vapor was emitted along the bottom. When it moved horizontally, a yellowish tail appeared from one of the points of the "football."

The object went down just behind a large maple tree, and Gow reports that the boy was unable to tell whether or not it touched down, because there was a slight elevation between the object and the barn that partially obstructed the view. As it descended slowly, the red vapor seemed to come "from the edges, not the middle." There was no wind, but the object emitted a *beep-beep* or a *bizz-bizz* noise.

He noted that the radio was making "a heck of a noise like a loud static," even though WKBW has a strong, clear radio signal in the area. Gow gathered that the boy then ran outside toward the object, and just before he reached the place where the bull was tethered, the object shot upward and into the clouds "as fast as the snap of my fingers," as Harold put it. When it rose, the band of red vapor, about 50 inches wide, shot from the edges toward the ground, then bounced back into the ship as it hovered momentarily about 10 feet in the air. As it shot higher, the pitch of the *bizz-bizz* sound increased. Harold claims he heard a sonic boom at the moment the craft disappeared into the clouds, but others in the vicinity were not aware of it. Inside the farmhouse, Mrs. Butcher did notice a definite interference on her radio.

The object pushed into the clouds, leaving a luminous

green glow. Harold ran to the farmhouse, yelling about what he had seen, and darted out again with his brother Robert. The two of them saw the UFO hovering over a pine grove, but Robert saw it only long enough to notice the red vapor as it went up behind the clouds. As the two boys returned to the house, the family, including Mrs. Butcher and Kathleen Brougham, a sixteen-year-old friend, rushed out, but not in time to see either the craft or the luminous cloud. Mrs. Butcher called the Fredonia State Police Barracks and Trooper Haas was ordered to the scene. Mr. Butcher was away from home at the time.

Shortly after the phone call, Kathleen Brougham ran into the house, knocking over the young Butcher daughter as she did so. "It's here again!" she screamed, and ran out as the others followed her. Only Mrs. Butcher remained inside to soothe the youngster who had been knocked down. The four young people, William, Jr., Harold, Robert and Kathleen watched the object across a field about 700 feet away, as it moved in a southeasterly direction "with a glowing yellow vapor trail." To Harold, the object seemed the same as before, possibly because he was filling in details from his previous experience. The others, in the increasing darkness, could make out the yellow vapor, a greenish glow in the clouds above, and a faint outline of the object. After watching it for about a minute, they reported that it moved off in the direction of Jamestown, disappearing over a hill.

Trooper Haas, accompanied by Trooper Neilson, arrived shortly afterward. Together with the youngsters, they walked toward the spot where Harold had first seen the object, several hundred feet from the barn, and beyond the post in the field where the bull was tethered.

For the first time, Gow reports, a distinct, pungent odor was detected, and later Mrs. Butcher noted that Harold and her younger daughter both complained of upset stomachs. It was fully dark by this time, and the troopers, using flashlights, did not find anything unusual at the site. The cows at the Butcher farm, however, reacted sharply. Instead of their normal two and a half cans of milk, they barely filled one. The following afternoon, Captain James A. Dorsey and five other officials of the Niagara Falls Air Force Base came to the Butcher farm to investigate. Harold had found a purple liquid substance which he said "smelled like 3-in-1 oil." Mr. Butcher dug up a sample of this and put it in a shoe box, giving it to the State Police who in turn gave it to the Air Force for analysis. Although no Air Force report on the substance is available under the regulations, the base did indicate to the Buffalo *Evening News* that the four youths definitely "did see something."

With the Cherry Creek report, NICAP also sent more detailed information on the Texas and Oklahoma sightings during August of 1965, which had pushed their way through the reticence of the editorial staff of *The New York Times*, and which, in fact, had influenced me in doing the column in the *Saturday Review*. In the light of the details, I was a little surprised that the *Times* had apparently not followed up on the story.

Considerable interest was aroused in the darkness of the early morning of July 31, 1965, when a police officer by the name of Louis Sikes, from Wynnewood, Oklahoma, reported a 45-minute UFO sighting and both Tinker and Carswell Air Force bases came up with a fix on their radar. The night of August 1 was jammed with reports throughout the night. Three different Shawnee, Oklahoma, police cars reported diamond-shaped formations of UFOs for 30 to 40 minutes, shortly after 9 P.M. They were said to be moving in a northerly direction and changing colors from red to white to blue-green, and moved from side to side at times. In Chickasha, first news of the sightings came from radio station KWCO, with James Cline, police dispatcher, confirming that he had a report from Patrolman C. V. Barnhill verifying them. In Oklahoma City, police dispatcher Lt. Homer Briscoe said police headquarters received over 35 calls between 8 P.M. and 10 P.M., with most of the estimates indicating that the objects were at an altitude of from 15,000 to 20,000 feet.

"People are upset," Briscoe said. "They want to know what they are, and we can't tell them."

Meanwhile, the Oklahoma Highway Patrol headquarters was trying to keep its teletype clear, and sorting out the reports from all over the state:

SINCE 8 A.M. THE TOWER HAS RECEIVED IN THE NEIGHBORHOOD OF 25 TO 50 VISUAL SIGHTINGS, MANY BY POLICE OFFICERS AND HIGHWAY PATROL TROOPERS, OF VARIOUS UNIDENTIFIED FLYING OBJECTS FROM THE PURCELL AREA NORTH THROUGH THE NORMAN AREA TO CHANDLER AND BACK THROUGH MEEKER AND SHAWNEE.

THREE SHAWNEE OFFICERS HAVE FOUR OF THE OBJECTS IN SIGHT AT THIS TIME, ALSO ANOTHER HAS CROPPED UP FROM THE SOUTH OF TECUMSEH AND IS APPARENTLY GOING TO FLY DIRECTLY OVER SHAWNEE.

THE SIGHTINGS VARY FROM ONE TO FOUR OF THE OBJECTS AT VARIOUS TIMES, STARTING IN A REDDISH COLOR AND VARYING TO A WHITE AND BLUE LUSTER.

SHAWNEE REPORTS THE OBJECTS SEEM TO BE FLYING FOUR TO A FORMATION IN A DIAMOND-TYPE FORMATION. CUSHING HAS REPORTED FOUR OF THE OBJECTS.

OKLAHOMA HIGHWAY PATROL UNITS 30 AND 40 HAVE ALSO MADE VISUAL SIGHTINGS. TINKER AIR FORCE BASE HAS HAD FROM ONE TO FOUR OF THEM ON RADAR AT A TIME AND THEY ADVISE THEY ARE FLYING VERY HIGH AT APPROXIMATELY 22,000 FEET, WHICH SEEMS TO COINCIDE WITH THE VISUAL SIGHTINGS, ALL OF WHICH ARE "VERY HIGH FLYING OBJECTS."

On the following day, Wright-Patterson Air Force Base issued a statement which said: "There has been no confirmation that any of the sightings were tracked on radar." It went on to ascribe the sightings to the planet Jupiter and other stars.

And again the same questions were posed: Were dozens of patrolmen and troopers throughout most of the state of Oklahoma, as well as the entire Oklahoma State Highway Patrol, liars and incompetents? Or was the official Air Force spokesman a liar and an incompetent?

Many people in the Southwest on those fiery evenings in early August took exception to the Air Force proclamations that they were looking at stars or planets. A twenty-three-year-old Sioux City, Iowa, high school English teacher said he tracked one of the objects for a considerable length of time. "Anyone who would say this was a star or planet would be out of his mind," he said. He described the object he saw as he was driving with his wife as "bright, yellowish, and zigzagged slightly. This was replaced with a red light surrounded by three white lights, the red light being the brightest." He got out of his car, turned off the ignition to see if he could hear the sound of an airplane motor. There was none.

An Air Force weather observer in Oklahoma City also took exception to the casual explanation by the Air Force Public Information Office. "I have repeatedly seen unusual objects in the sky," he said, "and they are no mirage. One of them looked like it had a flat top and flat bottom, and it was not a true sphere. There seemed to be two rings around it, and the rings were part of the main body."

Major Hector Quintanilla, chief of the Air Force "Project Blue Book," which analyzes and ostensibly explains sightings as they are reported from over the entire country, actually withdrew his own initial report of a sighting by two Texas sheriffs on the night of September 3, 1965—the same night that Officer Bertrand and Norman Muscarello crouched under the silent object in Exeter, New Hampshire.

Chief Deputy Sheriff Billy E. McCoy and Deputy Sheriff Robert W. Goode were patrolling an area in Texas about forty miles below Houston. In the distance, about five miles away, they noticed a bright purple light, moments later noting a smaller blue light near it. The lights suddenly moved swiftly toward their cruiser.

In a report to the Air Force, the two officers said:

> The object came up to the pasture next to the highway, about 150 feet off the highway and about 100 feet high. The bulk of the object was plainly visible and appeared to be triangular-shaped, with a bright purple light on the left and the smaller, less bright, blue light on the right end. The bulk of the object appeared to be dark gray in color with no other distinguishing features. It appeared to be enormous—about 200 feet wide and 40–50 feet thick in the middle, tapering off toward both ends. There was no noise or any trail.
>
> The bright purple light illuminated the ground directly underneath it and the area in front of it, including the highway and the interior of the patrol car. The tall grass under the object did not appear to be disturbed.
>
> There was a bright moon out [the moon had gone down by the time the Exeter officers made their observation in New Hampshire, over 1,600 miles away] and it cast a shadow of the object on the ground immediately below it in the grass. Deputy Sheriff Goode was in the driver's seat with his left arm laying in the open window. Although he was wearing a long-sleeved shirt and a coat, he later said that he felt the heat apparently emanating from the object.

The two men, shocked by the approach of the craft, drove away at 110 miles an hour. Then, although frankly scared by the sighting, decided to drive back to see if it was still there. It was, and they again drove away to avoid another close encounter.

The report of the local Air Force investigating officer reads:

> After talking with both officers involved in the sighting, there is no doubt in my mind that they definitely saw some

unusual object or phenomenon . . . Both officers appeared to be intelligent, mature, level-headed persons capable of sound judgment and reasoning. Chief Deputy Sheriff McCoy holds a responsible position in the department requiring the supervision of over 42 personnel. Both officers have been subjected to considerable friendly ridicule from their contemporaries and the local townspeople; but have continued to profess the facts of their sighting.

After a phone call to Deputy Sheriff McCoy, Major Quintanilla withdrew his report that the sighting had been a star or a planet, and stamped the sighting UNEXPLAINED.

The press across the country, stirred from its apathy, began to react as the reports increased during August, 1965. In Houghton, Michigan, personnel at the U.S. Air Force Radar Base in the Keweenaw Peninsula slipped for a moment from behind the Air Force UFO curtain to report to the UPI "solid radar contact" with up to ten unidentified flying objects, moving in a V-formation over Lake Superior. The objects were moving out of the southwest and were heading north-northeast at about "9,000 miles per hour," the base reported. They were 5,200 to 17,000 feet high. Seven other objects were spotted over Duluth and jet interceptors gave chase, according to the UPI report, but could not maintain the speed of the UFOs and were easily outdistanced.

Other UPI releases marked the augmented pace of the sightings. UFOs were reported hovering and bobbing over the northern and western Minneapolis suburbs, with Captain Robert Riley of the State Highway Patrol and three patrolmen observing the phenomenon in seven different communities nearby. A total of 50 police and sheriff squad cars radioed in reports between 12:20 A.M. and 2:30 A.M. on August 3, 1965. About 50 miles west of Paris, France, Alexander Ananoff, one of France's leading space experts, reported watching a "flying saucer" at sunset. Ananoff, 1950 winner of the international Astronautics Prize, described the object as "disk- or lens-like in shape." It moved a considerable distance while he watched it and finally disappeared above a cirrus cloud, which, as he stated, "exists only above 21,000 feet." At the Canberra Airport, Australia, Air Traffic Control officers and other expert aircraft observers spotted a mysterious, glowing object which hung suspended at about 5,000 feet for 40 minutes, according to the Associated Press. At Lisbon, Portugal, according to the same source, glowing objects zipped across the sky and interfered with the operation of radios and electromagnetic clocks. These descriptions of the object seemed to tally with those given in an official Chilean Air Force report of sightings a little earlier over the Antarctic.

As the news of such observations increased during the summer of 1965, so did editorial comment. The cautious and accurate *Christian Science Monitor* said:

> Flying saucers sighted early this month over Texas may give scientists something to think about for a long time.
> They were among many reported sightings around the world lately. But they give the clearest evidence of all that something strange was actually in the sky.
> Many Texans definitely saw something that even experienced investigators now admit defies explanation.
> The Texas saucer appeared as a bright light in the sky, with lesser lights clustered around it. It was visible to some for several hours.
> There was no temperature inversion strong enough to produce such an effect.
> It wasn't a scientific balloon, since none had been launched.
> It makes the clearest case yet for a thorough look at the saucer mystery.

The Fort Worth *Star-Telegram* ran these comments on its editorial page:

They can stop kidding us now about there being no such things as "flying saucers."

Too many people of obviously sound mind saw and reported them independently from too many separate localities. Their descriptions of what they saw were too similar to one another, and too unlike any familiar object.

And it's going to take more than a statistical report on how many reported "saucers" have turned out to be jets and weather balloons to convince us otherwise.

The *Times-Star* of Alameda, California, ran a strong editorial. It noted especially the UPI story from Houghton, Michigan, in which the solid radar contact had been admitted by the Air Force:

What distinguishes this story from many others involving Air Force personnel is that it was not accompanied by a paragraph or two explaining that the objects had finally been identified as a flight of ducks, comets, balloons, or something else, equally commonplace.

Why wasn't it?

The most likely reason is that the Air Force spokesmen, whose job it is to explain away the seemingly improbable in terms of the commonplace, have been getting such a workout lately that either they are starting to break down or their superiors are finally coming to the conclusion that they are making the Air Force appear ridiculous.

Of the two, the latter seems more likely. The business of attempting to protect the public from panic—the obvious reason for the Air Force's traditional policy of identifying unidentified flying objects as weather balloons, etc.—is something that cannot be indefinitely sustained, particularly when the source of the presumed potential panic is a mass of peculiar things that persist in flying around where large numbers of persons can see them. To do that is no more possible than it is for panic to be sustained by individuals for more than a few hours at most. It's too exhausting. One can flee a horde of little green men from outer space only so long. Presently one gets tired and decides to do something else, even if it is no more than sitting down.

But whatever the reason may be why the Air Force spokesmen are becoming less vocal, the time is long overdue for the Government to disclose to the public all it knows about the UFOs.

In other words, it would surprise almost no one today to learn that some UFOs are spacecraft from elsewhere in the solar system or beyond. In fact, it would be even more surprising to learn that they were not. Hence, the only way in which the public interest can be served in the matter is for the Government to disclose what it knows about these phenomena.

The recent sightings, the extreme low-level sightings by responsible officials which couldn't possibly be mistaken for planes or stars or balloons, were impressive, as were the 600 older cases documented by NICAP so painstakingly in its book *The UFO Evidence.* Together, the old and new cases covered the entire globe. As a single reporter, I could not possibly track down enough direct interviews over such an area and contribute anything new in clarifying the mystery.

But I could, I felt, take one single microcosmic area where a recent, low-level sighting had been made, and explore it to absolute rock bottom. In a small way, I had done this over the phone with the Exeter experience. With groundwork laid, there would be many advantages in following this up. What's more, although NICAP had done a thorough job in documenting cases throughout the world, they had not completed a crash program in a single area.

To accomplish this, I made plans to go to Exeter to explore in person the incident there, and gather whatever other information might be forthcoming.

CHAPTER V

JUST before I left New York for Exeter, a reader of the *Saturday Review* sent me a clipping and news photograph of the now-famous sighting made near the Santa Ana, California, Marine Corps Air Base. The picture was taken on a Polaroid by Rex Heflin, a county highway department investigator, on August 3, during the height of the summer sightings. Heflin reported that he was working near the air base when he caught a glimpse of a silver object which he estimated to be 30 feet in diameter and 8 feet deep. It made no sound, but a beam of white light seemed to rotate underneath the object. During the time the UFO was near, he had tried to communicate with his supervisor over a two-way radio in his vehicle, but the radio was inoperative. After the object disappeared, the radio worked perfectly.

The picture was amazingly clear: Flat, metallic, looking almost like a squashed German helmet, the UFO was slightly tilted in the air, and barely higher than the telephone poles along the road. Heflin told reporters that he was willing to take a lie-detector test to prove that the picture was not faked. Further, he had used a Polaroid camera, which precludes tampering with a negative.

From NICAP, I also received a reproduction of a dramatically clear picture of a glowing UFO object taken by a youthful amateur astronomer in Beaver County, Pennsylvania, just north of Pittsburgh. James Lucci, seventeen, had been taking a time exposure of the moon when the UFO moved into camera range. Three professional photographers had examined the picture, and declared it to be genuine. It looked like a glowing upside-down dinner plate, dwarfing the full moon in the background and revealing a line of trees on the horizon.

A third picture was a tight close-up of the Wichita Weather Bureau radarscope, showing four unidentified blips which were recorded at the height of the August 1 sightings in the state of Kansas. They were confirmed as unidentified by John Shockley, Wichita weather observer.

Among the summer's reports was one from the Secretary of the Argentina Navy who issued an official public statement:

> On July 3, 1965, a giant, lens-shaped flying object was seen, tracked and photographed at the Argentina scientific base, Deception Island, in the Antarctic. Lt. Danial Perisse, Commanding Officer, confirmed by radio that the large UFO alternately hovered, then accelerated and maneuvered at tremendous speeds. While being tracked by theodolite and watched through binoculars, the unknown object caused strong interference with variometers used to measure the earth's magnetic field, and also registered on magnetograph tapes. Color pictures were taken through a theodolite by a member of a visiting group from the Chilean scientific base.

The Chilean Minister of Defense supplemented this by reporting that a similar UFO had been seen by all personnel at its Antarctic base, and had caused such strong radio interference that it temporarily blocked an attempt to relay news of the sighting to the English and Argentine bases.

A further official Argentine Navy statement indicated that a large UFO had caused severe electromagnetic disturbances on the compasses of its Navy transport ship *Punta Medanos*. The compass needles "suddenly and simultaneously" swung off course, pointing toward the UFO. "The power which caused this electromagnetic interference is indicated by the distance involved," the report said. "The UFO was 2,000 meters (over a mile) away from the ship."

In contrast to this persuasive evidence, I received a letter from Raymond Fowler, the New England subcommittee member of NICAP, indicating that several newspapers around the Boston and Exeter area were ascribing the sighting at Exeter, made by Muscarello and patrolmen Bertrand and Hunt, to a flying billboard owned by the Sky-Lite Aerial Advertising Agency of Boston, and piloted by Daniel Vale, of Londonderry, New Hampshire.

The Amesbury, Massachusetts, *News* began its article with an almost audible breath of relief:

"The unidentified flying object spotted in this area by many residents, has finally been identified!" it began.

Fowler enclosed the clipping with his letter, and went on to say:

> This is a misleading news-story being carried by some newspapers in this area identifying the New Hampshire UFO sightings as an advertising plane. It so happens that our subcommittee makes routine checks with the Sky-Lite Advertising Agency before investigating UFO reports. Many times this plane has been reported as a UFO. However, during the period of the New Hampshire UFO sightings, including the morning of September 3, this aircraft was never flown. I went over the plane's flight paths, and it never left the ground between August 21 and September 10.
>
> Joseph Budina, the owner of the company, also informed me that his aircraft rarely flies into southern New Hampshire and when it does it is usually in the Salem and Manchester area, miles away from the Exeter area. He told me that he told the Amesbury *News* that perhaps some UFOs reported in New Hampshire could have been his aircraft. Unfortunately, this newspaper used his statement to explain the sightings in the Exeter case.
>
> The Sky-Lite aircraft does not carry red flashing lights. It carries a rectangular sign carrying white flashing lights.

It was not airborne during the S. E. New Hampshire UFO flap. I have notified the Amesbury *News* of the true facts and have asked them to set the record straight.

RAYMOND E. FOWLER
Chairman, NICAP MASS SUBCOM

It now seemed logical, however, that some mistaken UFO reports *would* have come in as a result of the use of this advertising plane. But it did *not* seem logical that it could cause an ex-Air Force veteran and now a police officer to file an official report of a low-altitude, silent object hovering just over the treetops, in the company of two other witnesses. Since nothing could be taken for granted, I put in a long-distance call to Joseph Budina in Boston, and arranged to have lunch with him and his pilot there before going up to Exeter. He repeated over the phone that his craft was not airborne at all between August 21 and September 10, and said he was convinced that his craft could only account for a fraction of the many sightings reported in the southern New Hampshire and Massachusetts areas.

One more news item appeared just before I left for Boston, an AP release of October 17th, with the headline:

MEXICANS UP IN THE AIR OVER FLYING SAUCERS

The summer of 1965 could go down in Mexican history as the summer of the flying saucers. Sightings began late in July after reports of similar phenomena from South America. Then, suddenly, all Mexico seemed to be seeing luminous disks, hovering lights and high-velocity balls of light.

Scarcely a day passed without the Mexican press reporting that "unidentified flying objects" had terrorized a peasant family by day or a whole town by night.

Sometimes a string of OVNI [*objects voladores no identificados*] had converged on a cigar-shaped "mother ship."

As the saucer-sighting fever gripped the Mexican capital, staid businessmen could be seen climbing to the roofs of their office buildings clutching field glasses.

However, the stirring of Latin blood has always been assumed to be much easier than to stir that of staid New Englanders with their reputation for laconic taciturnity. If the New Hampshire, Down-East Yankees would talk of their experiences, there would be a better chance of making some kind of journalistic—and realistic—appraisal of the mystery.

I met with Joseph Budina and Daniel Vale, owner and pilot respectively of the Sky-Lite Advertising Company, on October 19, at the new Boston Sheraton Hotel. They had with them a letter which I had asked them to write me, indicating that their plane could not be involved with the incident at Exeter.

"Dear Mr. Fuller," it read. "Regarding the newspaper reports that our airplane was the source of the recent UFO sightings in Exeter, N.H., late at night and early in the morning of September 2nd and 3rd, 1965: Please be advised that our airplanes and equipment were not operating at any time immediately before, during or after the above-mentioned dates." It was signed by Vale, as chief pilot and manager of operations. I had figured, and rightly so as I was to discover later, that many people would be reticent to discuss their sightings if skeptics could accuse them of being unable to tell the difference between an advertising sign and a UFO. NICAP was aware that many people are extremely reluctant to discuss their sightings because of possible ridicule.

Both Budina and Vale were helpful in filling me in on the background of the area and the area UFO stories. It was pilot Vale's theory that newspapers throughout New England had received so many phone calls from people sighting strange objects, that they seized happily on the advertising plane as a quick explanation of the phenomenon. "The reporters that I've talked to," said Vale, "said they received an awful lot of calls, at any time of the day or night. And this thing got to the point where it was never-ending. Of course they really couldn't explain anything. They were left up in the air as to what to say about the things. So as soon as they found out about our airplane, about our equipment, what it did, they immediately got hold of Joe and myself.

"One reporter called me up at home, and was pushing very hard about the story on the Exeter police. Well, when I found out that this took place sometime after midnight, I told him that this couldn't possibly be our plane, because we were never airborne any time after eleven, at the latest. Well, he was all excited about this idea because he thought that he had come up with a real explanation for all the UFO reports. But even though I explained again that the Exeter thing couldn't possibly be our equipment, he said that he thought this would make a good explanation, and he was going to write it up."

Neither Budina nor Vale would relax with a drink at lunch because they were going to be flying that afternoon. But we all ordered cherrystone clams, and went on with the conversation.

"Anyway," Vale continued, "anybody who gets a close look at the sign couldn't possibly be scared, the way a lot of these people who have been reporting UFOs have been. Maybe from a distance, it looks puzzling. But anybody can tell what it is the minute it gets in clear view."

The discussion with Budina and Vale failed to reveal anything new and significant, but did furnish a clear warning: Any testimony about UFOs seen in the neighborhood of Exeter should be checked out carefully against the possibility of people mistaking the advertising aircraft for a UFO. The plane, Joe Budina told me, would of course make conventional aircraft noise. It was a Piper Tri-Pacer, especially equipped to carry the advertising sign.

Budina revealed one other thing of interest: At about 9 P.M. two evenings before he had received a call from the police in a southern Maine town, asking if his craft was in the air. A mysterious object was sighted and tracked on radar nearby and both the police and a Federal Aviation Authority tower wanted to know more about it. Budina's equipment was on the ground at the time, and he never heard more about it.

I planned that day to visit Ray Fowler, the NICAP representative, at his home in Wenham, Massachusetts, and also to check further news items in Boston. The UPI office had little information to offer: They kept no special file on UFOs, although they had of course written up the sightings around Exeter and Portsmouth. The AP also had little new to offer. Both news services were wary of the crackpot element involved in some sightings, as I was, and our conversations underlined the importance of being extremely conservative in reaching any conclusions.

I dropped by the city room of the Boston *Globe*, and talked for awhile with Russell Burbank, a young reporter who had been assigned to several UFO stories, but he was as puzzled as anyone else about the phenomenon. He had done one of the stories on the Sky-Lite Advertising plane, but had not checked out the plane's log against the Exeter sightings. He had been inclined, he said, to close the file on the subject for awhile. In the morgue of the *Globe* were many clippings, some old and some new, but none of them offered more than the usual clues: sightings sworn to by many observers, but no direct and tangible physical evidence available. Dozens of sightings had been reported within a hundred-mile radius of Boston for many years before Joe Budina had launched his Sky-Lite Advertising plane. There was an impressive increase in recent sightings of low-level UFOs—anywhere from 10 to 100 feet from the ground.

Typical of these observations on file in the morgue of the *Globe* was a story from Amesbury, Massachusetts, of a UFO which was seen by at least ten people, not more than 15 to 20 feet above the ground. As Diane Drew and Robert Dore left the home of Dore's grandparents in Amesbury, they noticed that the animals at the house were unusually nervous and restless. They began driving up Hunt Road, when a round, illuminated disk suddenly appeared and began to glide toward them very slowly. They quickly turned and called out Mr. and Mrs. Linwood Dore, the grandparents, and neighbors. The witnesses agreed completely on the behavior of the object: It was shaped like a large dinner plate, close in appearance to an artificial moon. It changed color when it altered direction, moved from side to side as well as up and down. As it changed motion, the colors seemed to change from red to green. When members of the group tried to go near the hovering object, it took off at a tremendous rate of speed, shooting up over the treetops.

Later, the residents all along Hunt Road heard and saw planes flying overhead after the object had left, one of them circling the area for an hour.

With some time to fill before visiting Fowler, I drove to Amesbury, 45 minutes north of Boston, and dropped by the branch office there of the Haverhill, Massachusetts, *Gazette* to talk to Jean Miller, of that paper, and Ken Lord, editor of the Amesbury *News*. It was a typical building of the New England dusty-brick era, when mill towns sprang up at the drop of a waterfall. Sitting in the dingy office, both Lord, a barrel-chested Yankee editor, and Miss Miller, a fragile and intelligent young lady, admitted their puzzlement about the whole UFO situation. They felt, in fact, that they were damned if they did believe in the phenomenon and damned if they didn't. The advertising plane, they admitted, couldn't possibly explain the continuous sightings that kept plaguing them, especially the low-level reports of silent objects which hovered, remained stationary, and then took off at incredible speeds. They each had several stories which they hadn't even bothered to print because of the volume of sightings. The Air Force base at Portsmouth, they reported, was obviously hamstrung for giving any local information, and lamely and continuously referred everybody to the Pentagon, which never made any reports of value in exploring the mystery.

I arrived at Raymond Fowler's house in Wenham that evening, tired and puzzled. It was a modest, cheerful home in which his English wife marshaled his three scrubbed and polished young children at dinner with easy British grace. Fowler, a level-headed, serious college graduate with training as a minister, worked as a reports administrator on Sylvania's Minute Man Project in nearby Waltham. He also works for NICAP, without pay, as all subcommittee members do, taking in enough money from donations at lectures to cover phone calls and investigating expenses.

In his small upstairs office, jammed with books and papers, he revealed his concern about Air Force policy, which he thought was based on the erroneous belief that it would prevent possible panic throughout the country. He felt that since even the Air Force admitted that UFOs seemed to pose no threat to national security, the investigation and dissemination of information about the phenomena should be turned over to scientific agencies.

He was also concerned about far-out and irresponsible UFO groups who publicized anything and everything related by overemotional people, and whose flagrant exaggeration damaged carefully documented cases.

He was impressed by an interview he had with Patrolman Bertrand at Exeter several weeks earlier. "Bertrand told me," Fowler said, "that he didn't want to make any guesses at all. He said, 'I'll tell you exactly what I saw, and no more. I could guess that the object was egg-shaped, because I saw no protrusions, nothing. It seemed to be compressed.' And he said, 'Maybe it wasn't egg-shaped. It could have been another shape. It's only the impression I got.' "

Fowler had several suggestions for my research up in Exeter on the case. "You might check out the major and the lieutenant and the colonel who investigated the case for the Air Force. There's a report that they went up from time to

57

time to the field where Bertrand and Hunt saw the object, and waited for this thing. Another thing is that you might look into some of the other farmhouses in that vicinity. They might have seen something, especially when the dogs were barking; they might have got out of bed and looked out. Maybe they'd be willing to talk. You never can tell in these cases."

Fowler went on to discuss several other cases he had run into, painting a general picture of his extensive activity for NICAP. Oddly enough, in nineteen years of study, he had never seen a UFO himself. But he was impressed by the documentation of the hundreds of cases he had explored, and the apparent validity of the witnesses. "Take a case I investigated in 1963," he said. "The people reported a Saturn-shaped UFO over the power lines in back of their house. It woke the whole neighborhood up. The husband knew nothing about UFOs, and I had a picture from a previous case which he had never seen and knew nothing about. I asked him to sketch what he had seen—and he drew his own picture, which was practically identical to the picture I had. There were the man and his wife, and the neighbors all around who woke up. There were other people in the area who reported it, but I didn't get a chance to check them out."

"What about more recent ones? This year, for instance?"

"Well," Fowler said, "take the case of Dr. Woodruff, Dr. Richard Woodruff. He's the Chief Medical Examiner of the College of Medicine, University of Vermont. Just after the first of the year. I've got signed statements by both Woodruff and a state trooper who was with him. They were both traveling back home after testifying on a case before a grand jury in Brattleboro. Here's the report, as verified by both Dr. Woodruff and the trooper."

Fowler took out the typewritten report, three pages of documentation. The date was the 4th of January, 1965, the time, 5:15 P.M., EST. The place was between Bethel and Randolph, Vermont, on Highway 12. The report began:

Dr. Woodruff, Vermont State Pathologist, a staff member of the University of Vermont College of Medicine and respected scientist, was traveling back to Burlington with Vermont State Trooper ——— [Name withheld on request], after testifying before a grand jury in Brattleboro, Vermont. As they were driving along Highway 12, suddenly, just above distant treetop to their left, a sharply defined object glowing an orangish-red with an intensity somewhat less than an automobile headlight came rapidly in sight and crossed the highway in front of them. Its apparent size was that of a football held at arm's length. It appeared to be round but the exact shape could not be ascertained because of its great speed. Trooper ——— exclaimed, "My God, did you see that?" No sooner had he spoken when a second similar object came into view followed shortly after by a third object. All followed the same flight course climbing slightly and moving west to east to their right and above the valley where they appeared to fade into the distance. Duration of the sighting was 30 seconds. The objects were viewed through the automobile windshield. They appeared to be solid. No sound was heard. Speed was faster than a jet aircraft. Estimated distance of the objects from the observers—½ to 1 mile. The weather was clear, stars were visible and there was no moon. Dr. Woodruff reported the incident to the Burlington *Free Press* and to Mr. Edward Knapp, head of the Vermont State Aeronautics Board. Several Vermont and New Hampshire papers carried a full account of this sighting. In his statement to the press Dr. Woodruff said: "I have hesitated to call. I know everything I say will be open to misinterpretation. But remember, two of us saw the same thing at the same time. I was not seeing things, and I am not too overly imaginative and neither is the trooper."

"Quite a report," I said to Fowler.

"The interesting thing," he said, "is the Air Force evaluation on the second page. They attribute it to 'probable observation of meteors—specifically of Quadrantids.' This is from Major Jacks, the Pentagon Public Information Officer who handles their statements. And here's an excerpt from Dr. Woodruff's comment on the Air Force report."

Fowler pointed to a paragraph on the second page, from Dr. Woodruff's letter of February 9, 1965:

> I am amazed that the major could not come up with a better solution than this. If I had thought that there was a possibility that the three objects we saw were meteors, I never would have mentioned the matter. . . . While I make no speculation as to what the objects we saw might be, I do feel most definitely that they were not meteors.

Following the quote from the doctor's letter were reports of additional witnesses to the sighting: four people in one car in the same area and a statement from Hugh E. Wheatley, Chairman of the Board of Selectmen of Randolph, Vermont. Both descriptions were almost identical to the one filed by Dr. Woodruff and the state trooper.

"Of course," Fowler went on, "you get a variety of shapes and designs reported on UFOs, which leads to the conclusion that there are several types. They all seem to more or less fall into classified patterns, though. We often get reports of the disklike or pancake shapes, with diameters about 10 times their width. And you get various sizes reported—from ten feet or so, up to one hundred feet in diameter. This is probably the most common report. Then the second most common is the cigar, or cylindrical, shape. The third is the brightly defined lights at night. Or lights in formation, which move with purpose. Then you have the Saturn shape, not too many of those, and the round globe and cone shape sightings. But the disk shape is the most common. Sound patterns vary; most are silent; some report a humming or whirring sound. The lighting patterns, of course, change with different speeds, movements and altitudes. That's why you're likely to get variations in descriptions of the objects when they're seen."

We skimmed through some of the dozens of reports on

Fowler's desk. They were detailed and well-documented, with frequent references to possibilities which would rule out the sighting as a valid UFO. There was an airline stewardess in Watertown, Massachusetts, who had been awakened at 4 o'clock in the morning. She had watched a bright, white-silver disk as it moved slowly across the sky over a period of ten minutes before it disappeared. Fowler's report took nothing for granted:

> The moon was 20 days old—the day before the last quarter. It was not visible from the bedroom window that the observer viewed the object from. This agrees with her account. Vega and Altair would be the brightest stars in the western sky. Size, brightness and movement negate stars. These two stars were probably among the few that the witness stated she observed while watching the object. Balloon possibility: Favorable. The sunrise for 7/19/65 was 5:23 EDT. At 4 A.M. EDT the sun would have been approximately 20° below the easterly horizon. Thus any object with an elevation of 20° or more above the western horizon would begin to reflect sunlight. Speed, as balloon possibility: Favorable. The object moved very slowly. Information obtained from the U.S. Weather Bureau shows wind velocity to have been 8 mph (Logan Airport, Boston). Direction, as balloon possibility: Unfavorable. The object moved south to north. Information obtained from the U.S. Weather Bureau shows the wind was west-southwest (Logan Airport, Boston). A balloon would have moved into the northeast, instead of northwest. I telephoned the witness after our interview in regard to the balloon answer. She is familiar with balloons, and was bewildered to think that I suspected she had seen one. The object falls into the class of "Unidentified," and was reported during the beginning of the upsurge of UFO sightings in Massachusetts.

There was no question about it: Fowler was a thorough and painstaking investigator.

One particularly vivid report among the many concerned

61

two sisters in Turner, Maine, in 1959. It was a clear summer's evening, with a bright moon. Emily Deneault, a microelectronics operator, was in her driveway when she heard a humming or whirring sound. She glanced across the road and saw strange lights flying low over a field about 1,000 feet away. At first she thought it was an airplane about to crash, but no motor was heard, and the lights appeared to stop and remain motionless over the field. She sent her son Robert to alert the others in the house. Her stepfather, Alex Blanchard, joined her, while her sister Rita got on the phone just inside the door and told the telephone operator what they were witnessing. The operator contacted the Civil Defense headquarters at nearby Auburn.

The object, after moving back and forth across the field, "floated" down to earth and the lights went out. Then another object crossed the field and hovered over the landed one. They were identical and were described as being like two saucers, one inverted over the other, joined by a dark rim which looked as if it were made of dark glass. Behind this seemingly transparent rim were bright blue lights which revolved around the rim. They were as intense as a welder's torch and made Emily's eyes water as she looked at them through the binoculars. The objects themselves seemed a dull silver-gray in color, definitely solid, and moved about in a strange floating manner. Then the object on the ground floated upward, slightly to the left, and joined the other one. Both took off at a "terrific speed." Later, two jet aircraft flew over an adjoining field. It was not known whether they were attempting to intercept the objects.

The next morning Emily and her father went out to the field where the objects had been. They found a small area of singed grass which smelled as if it had recently been burned.

Fowler checked the characters of all these observers and found them to be unimpeachable. They had withheld the information for several years because of the fear of unwanted publicity.

Fowler's attitude toward the Air Force policies stemmed from his conviction that they were not only withholding information but attempting to block any kind of Congressional inquiry into the UFO mystery, even imposing a form of censorship. He admitted that perhaps 80 percent of the sightings could be explained as relating to airplanes, weather balloons, or birds, stars, or meteors. But 20 percent couldn't possibly be ascribed to these mistakes.

According to the Newark *Ledger,* one group of 50 pilots got together to protest the Air Force policy of pooh-poohing the serious reports dozens of qualified pilots had turned in at the risk of their jobs and reputations. They were later joined in their protest by several hundred other pilots. The cavalier dismissal of such technically qualified personnel was not only irritating, it was damaging.

While the Air Force continues an offhand dismissal of qualified reports, its own "inside" regulations to its personnel are serious and detailed. The official regulation #200-2, as of July 20, 1962, is far from a joking matter. It covers seven full pages of instruction packed into tightly spaced 8-point type.

It describes UFOs as "any aerial phenomena, airborne object or objects which are unknown or appear out of the ordinary to the observer because of performance, aerodynamic characteristics, or unusual features."

It goes on to describe the objectives of the Air Force UFO program: "Air Force interest in UFOs is threefold. First, as a possible threat to the security of the United States and its forces; second, to determine the technical or scientific characteristics of any such UFOs; third, to explain or identify all UFO sightings. . . ."

The official regulation admits that "there is need for further scientific knowledge in such fields as geophysics, astronomy, and physics of the upper atmosphere which the study and analysis of UFOs and similar aerial phenomena may provide."

The responsibilities of reporting incidents, according to

Air Force regulation 200-2, rests on Base commanders, who "will report all information and evidence of UFO sightings received from other services, government agencies, and civilian sources. Investigators are authorized to make telephone calls from the investigation area direct to the Foreign Technology Division (FTD) of the Air Force Systems Command, Wright-Patterson Air Force Base, Ohio. The purpose of the calls is to report high-priority sightings."

The Commander of the Air Force base nearest the location of a UFO sighting is instructed to "conduct all investigative action necessary to submit a complete initial report of a UFO sighting. The initial investigation will include every effort to resolve the sighting."

The job of interpreting the data is left up to the Air Force Systems Command Foreign Technology Division at the Wright-Patterson Base. From here the report goes to the Headquarters of the U.S. Air Force, and no information can be released except from the Office of Information of the Office of the Secretary of the Air Force. Up to the present, this has been a stone wall for any meaningful information.

But further evidence of the seriousness with which the Air Force considers the UFO problem is indicated in Paragraph #5, which states: "Both the Assistant Chief of Staff, Intelligence, Headquarters, USAF, and the Air Defense Command have a direct and immediate interest in the facts pertaining to UFOs reported within the United States."

The releasing of information to the public is definitely a sacred cow. According to Paragraph #7, only the Office of Information, Office of the Secretary of the Air Force, can do this "regardless of the origin and nature" of the UFO.

There is only one exception—and that is significant. The base commander may "release information to the press or the general public *only after positive identification of the sighting as a familiar or known sighting.*" (The italics are mine.) If the sighting is unexplainable, the only statement that the local base can release "is the fact that the sighting is under investigative action and information regarding it will be available at a later date. After completion of investigative action, the commander may release the fact that the Air Force Systems Command (Foreign Technology Division) will review and analyze the results of the investigation. He will then refer any further inquiries to the local Office of Information."

In analyzing regulation 200-2, NICAP has pointed out that several specific paragraphs amount to direct contradictions of official denials of censorship on the part of the Air Force.

In regulation 200-2 is the statement: "Air Force activities must reduce the percentage of unidentifieds to a minimum. . . ." NICAP claims that this shows an obvious intention to explain away UFO reports, not to investigate them scientifically and admit that many cases cannot be explained.

Another statement in the regulation is considered by NICAP as direct censorship: "Air Force personnel . . . will not contact private individuals on UFO cases nor will they discuss their operations and function with unauthorized persons unless so directed, and then only on a 'need to know' basis."

There are other provisions to which NICAP takes exception, and the battle between it and the Air Force continues without letup.

CHAPTER VI

I CHECKED in at the desk of the Exeter Inn on the morning of October 20, 1965, in the somber, paneled lobby, waited over ten minutes for a somnambulistic bellhop to take me to the room. Two tape recorders, a Polaroid camera and a suitcase took up most of the space, but the room was cheerful and I would be spending little enough time in it.

I was there only a few minutes when the phone rang. It was Russell Burbank, the *Globe* reporter who had been helpful to me in assembling the clippings in the paper's morgue. He had just discovered that a United Press International stringer reporter, who lived near Exeter, had herself made a clear sighting of a UFO very recently and he thought I might like to interview her. He gave me her name, a Mrs. Virginia Hale, in nearby Hampton, and I immediately called her.

She told me that she had kept her sighting quiet, had not even reported it on the wire, because she was afraid she might be accused of being "just another nut." She had kept the UFO in view for nearly twenty minutes, ample time for her to study it in considerable detail. I made an appointment to see her at her home the following day, and then went about the job of unpacking.

I met officers Bertrand and Hunt for lunch in the sprawling, tea-roomish dining room of the Inn. Only a few hushed patrons were lunching at the time, and Hunt's bulk as he came through the door of the dining room dominated the room. He looked twice the size of Bertrand in every dimension. He had a quiet, wry New Hampshire accent and a salty sense of humor.

Bertrand was wearing zylonite glasses, was soft-spoken and serious-looking. Although he appeared slight and scholarly, I recalled that his lieutenant had told me over the phone that he was invariably assigned to the tough cases. Over a porterhouse steak I learned more about what had happened and—I was surprised to learn—was *still* happening in Exeter following Muscarello's UFO sighting.

"For quite a stretch there," Hunt said, "three or four phone calls a night would come into the station. Most of them were pretty sensible people, and a lot of them came pretty close to the description of the things we saw."

"I think you'll find," Bertrand said, "that a lot of people are really afraid to report seeing these things. I know I was damn glad when Dave pulled up in his cruiser that night, if nothing else than to check me out. Some people might be making mistakes, but I'm convinced a lot of them aren't. When I was in the Air Force, I used to work right on the ramp with the planes. I could tell what kind of plane might be around, just by the sound of it. Right after this thing went away on September third, an Air Force jet came over. Dave and I both saw it. It was very clear what it was. No comparison at all between it and the object, in either lighting or configuration or sound, or anything else. And of course, the B-47 was high, and the object was low. Right down over the trees. It was impossible to make a mistake in comparing the two. And on the way out to the place with Muscarello, I thought the kid for sure had seen a helicopter. But it wasn't. Not by a long shot."

"He's a pretty cool kid, Muscarello," Hunt said. "It would take a lot to shake him up. And he was shaken up, there's no doubt about that."

Hunt went on to say that Muscarello was now at the Great Lakes Naval Training Station, but suggested I could get some details from his mother.

After lunch, Bertrand and Hunt got in my car, a smallish Volvo sedan which sagged a little under Hunt's weight. We drove out Route 108, then turned left on Route 150 southerly toward Kensington and Amesbury. Hunt pointed toward another road slanting up a hill ahead of us.

"Up this road another kid, Ron Smith, saw the thing too."

"When did that happen?" I asked.

"About three weeks after we saw it. Said it passed over his car twice."

"Anybody with him?"

"Yes, his mother and aunt. They were all scared to death when they pulled into the police station."

"What kind of kid is he?" I asked.

"Pretty decent, from what I know," Hunt said. "Works in the grocery store after school, right across from the police station. You might be able to find him this afternoon."

I made a mental note to interview Smith, just as we approached the Kensington line and Tel. and Tel. Pole #668. We pulled up near it and got out of the car. Stretched across the field was a heavy wire with a metal sign on it, reading KEEP OUT.

"The owner had to put this wire and sign up right after it happened," Hunt said. "Dozens of cars out here every night for weeks afterward. People dropping beer cans and cigarette butts all over the place. Some of 'em used to wait here all night to see if it was coming back."

We looked out over a wide, sweeping field of some ten acres, rimmed by tall evergreens. To the left was the tidy neo-Colonial residence of Clyde Russell. To the right, about a hundred yards away, was the rambling, ancient saltbox farmhouse, its timbers tidily restored by Carl Dining, a gentleman farmer who kept several horses and other livestock. Behind the Dining house was a split-rail fence forming a corral, where the horses were romping. The ground sloped down toward the evergreens, and in the far distance we could see the Atlantic shore at Hampton, a half a dozen miles to the east.

I asked Bertrand to reenact the scene in as much detail as possible.

"Well," he said, "I pulled up in the cruiser right by this pole here. I know it's #668 because I checked it that night. Muscarello was with me. We got out of the car, and looked around. Nothing was in sight. Nothing at all. But the kid insisted that we look around. He was still upset, still tense. I had him describe to me, just as I'm describing to you, exactly what happened. Except that it was dark then, about three in the morning. He told me that he was walking right by the pole here, when the thing came at him from his right—right over the field here. It hovered right over the roof of the Russell house there, he said, and was about twice as big as the house. Then it looked like it was really going to make a dive at him, he said, so he lay down on the ground in the shoulder of the road. Right about there—" And Bertrand pointed toward a gravel gully next to pole #668.

"We got back in the cruiser and waited for about ten minutes. Still nothing showed up. Then I called back the station and told Officer Toland—he was on duty at the desk—I told him, I don't see a thing. But the kid said, Let's go all the way out on the field. Maybe we'll see it then. So I called back on the cruiser radio and said I was going out on the field. Just in case they wanted to reach me for something."

Bertrand pantomimed the motions in detail, reliving the incident.

"Well, we both got out of the cruiser, walked down the field, down the slope, down to over by that fence there."

He pointed to the split rails of the corral, about 75 yards down the slope. "I was shining my light all around to see if I could spot anything. Especially over toward those woods."

He pointed toward the woods several hundred feet away, in the direction of Hampton.

"When he yelled 'I see it! I see it!' I turned fast and looked up. He pointed near the trees over there—the big ones. The leaves are off it now, but they weren't then. It was coming up behind them. It hovered, looked like it banked, came forward toward us. He seemed to freeze, and that's when I grabbed him and ran back to the cruiser. We got in the cruiser and I called in saying I was seeing it. Dave came. Dave came, and it was moving down toward the end of the field, across the tops of the trees."

"Just to the right of the big trees," Hunt said. "That's when I saw that fluttering movement. And the pulsating lights."

"You both were right where we're standing now?" I asked. We were still at the edge of the road looking down the field, next to the KEEP OUT sign.

"We were standing where we are now," Hunt said.

"Dave was right by the car, and I jumped out to join him here. We decided to take off, but we waited a few minutes, and then we saw it go off across the horizon. Toward Hampton."

Bertrand pointed back toward the two big trees. "These trees must have been blocking the light when we first got here," he said. "It was somewhere, but I didn't see it. Then it came up from behind the trees, it's thick there, thick enough to hide it. It came up and it looked like a big red ball when it was still behind the trees."

"Was it rising up slowly?" I asked.

Bertrand moved his hand slowly in an undulating motion, rocking it from side to side. "It was rising like this," he said; "looked like it was waving back and forth. And no noise. That's what got me. No noise. Except for the horses out in the barn and in the corral. I could hear them kicking, kicking hard. Soon as it was gone, they stopped. And before it came up over the trees they were quiet. Same with the dogs. You could hear several dogs howling when it came in sight, then they stopped when it left."

"When the thing was leaving this area," Hunt said, "it moved across the tops of those trees. And it stopped still twice. When it stopped the second time, there's a house barely out there, you can barely see it, I mean. It went from left to right across the horizon, and then dropped out of sight."

I turned back to Bertrand. "Where were you when you grabbed the kid?"

"Right down by the fence. By the corral. There's a little birdbath there. You can see it."

"What was the closest point it got to you?"

Bertrand pointed toward the Russell house. "Right about over that house."

"When you ran back to the cruiser with Muscarello, how did it maneuver?"

"I was yelling on the cruiser radio, and I had my back to it," Bertrand said. "But the kid was watching. And the whole field turned red. That house was red. Everything was red —the inside of the cruiser. Everything was lit up."

"All the way to the trees?"

Hunt said, "Seemed to me to be all the way to the trees."

"And the field?"

"The whole field," Bertrand said. "I was afraid we were going to get burned."

I looked over toward the Russell house. "Is this the house Muscarello ran to?" I asked.

"That one. Yes. The people thought he must have been a drunk. Can't blame 'em."

"When you got back in your cruiser and radioed the station, did Dave come right away?"

"He was already on his way," Bertrand said. "I had just got through calling, and I saw his headlights coming down the road."

Although the story was already familiar to me, through my earlier phone calls, the newspaper accounts, and Ray Fowler's detailed report for NICAP, I wanted to explore every detail fully, even if it was repetitious. What interested me most was the consistency of the stories. Except for very minor variations, the different versions agreed. Occasionally, as I went back over the details, a few new ones would emerge, details half forgotten in the initial excitement.

"About how far above the trees did the thing seem to be?" I asked.

"Well," said Bertrand, "I figure those trees to be about seventy feet high. And it was about thirty feet above them. That's how I figured the altitude of the thing was about one hundred feet."

"A little lower," Hunt said, "and it would have looked like it was skimming the trees. And it was rocking over them. An airplane couldn't do this if it tried."

"And here's another interesting thing," Bertrand said. "Right after the thing disappeared toward Hampton, we waited, and that's when we saw the B-47 going over—a con-

71

ventional jet we see all the time around here. Everybody knows them—and the B-52s and the Coast Guard helicopters. Kids in their knee pants know them here. Grandmothers know them. Anyway, when we got back to the station and Scratch Toland told us about the hysterical man calling from the Hampton phone booth, Dave and I back-timed what happened and figured that the man made this call just about the time the craft had moved from us to Hampton."

"And then I saw it later," Hunt said. "About an hour later, down on the 101 bypass. But it was too far away then, and I didn't make any big fuss about it."

"You couldn't identify it for sure?"

"Not positively," Hunt said. "But I could pretty well say it was the same thing. And it was still over Hampton."

We got back in the car, and Bertrand directed me toward Drinkwater Road, and then over Shaw Hill, where Ron Smith and his mother and aunt had reported their sighting several weeks later.

"They were scared, there's no doubt about that. Shaking. Really white. The second time he saw it, Smith said it backed up over his car. Like it went into reverse gear. Said it was round with bright lights over the top of it. On the bottom, some different colored lights. Said it looked like it was spinning, like a top."

The rolling hills of southern New Hampshire spread out before us from the top of Shaw Hill. The pre-Revolutionary farmhouses, most of them spanking white and freshly painted, sat placidly with their big squat center chimneys, a far cry from the Space Age, and especially an outer-Space Age.

Next to the tiny room housing the police desk is a small courtroom to handle those cases requiring immediate attention. It is spotlessly clean, with shiny brown woodwork out of respect for the serious business of the dispensation of justice.

It was in this solemn room that I interviewed young Ron Smith, a pleasant-looking seventeen-year-old whom I had found in the grocer's across the street, unpacking a carton of chicken soup. His boss at the store, skeptical of the UFO situation, had let him off for a few minutes, on the assurance that I wouldn't let him take a ride in a flying saucer. "He's too good a worker to lose," he said.

Young Smith was used to this gentle ribbing, he said, ever since he and his mother and aunt were driving that night first on Drinkwater Road, then on Shaw Hill, not more than a half a mile from where Bertrand, Hunt and Muscarello encountered their inexplicable craft. "They can kid me all they want," he said. "I know what I saw. They don't. Nobody can tell me I didn't see it. Nobody. That's all there is to it."

Smith, a senior at Exeter High, was planning to go into the Air Force after he graduated. His marks in school were fair to good, averaging around a gentleman's C. His boss at the store, in spite of the ribbings he liked to tender Smith, thought he was a top worker. Mrs. Oliver, at the police desk, knew the boy, described his character as exceptionally good.

Sitting at the attorney's desk in the tiny courtroom, I asked him to describe his experience in as much detail as possible.

"Well," he said, "I was riding around with my mother and aunt. It was a warm night, I guess around eleven-thirty P.M., and this was just about two or three weeks after the officers here saw this object. All of a sudden, my aunt said, 'Look up at the sky!' I thought she was kidding, but I looked up, and then stopped the car. I saw a red light on top and the bottom was white and glowed. It appeared to be spinning. It passed over the car once and when it passed over and got in front, it stopped all of a sudden in midair. Then it went back over the car again."

"Stopped in midair?"

"Stopped in midair, went back over a second time, stopped again. Then it headed over the car a third time and took off. It scared me, it really did. And I started to come back into

73

Exeter to report it to the police. I got partway back—all the way to Front Street—when I came to my senses. I wanted to go back to make *sure* it was there. To take another look to make sure I wasn't seeing things. We did go back. And sure enough, it was in the same spot again. It passed over the car once, and that was the last time I saw it."

"Did it take off fast, or slow?" I asked him.

"Well, it didn't rush. It just sort of eased its way along. Then it took off fast."

"How about sound? What kind of sound did it make?"

"It didn't make any real sound. Just sort of a humming noise, like a cat when it purrs. And incidentally, I got up again that morning, about four A.M., to see if I could see it again. But I didn't see it."

"What did your aunt and mother say at the time you first saw it?" I asked.

"Well," Smith said, "my aunt first thought it was a plane. And then she saw that it was oval, and didn't have any wings on it. We could see that it wasn't a plane and we watched it for the first time about fifteen minutes. When it was passing over the car, I could see it best. It was oval, it didn't seem to be completely round, it was oval. It moved along slowly, sort of a bright light, a glare, like an ordinary light bulb, shiny."

"Any color at all?"

"There was a red light around the edge, but the center was white."

"You say it went right over the car?"

"Yes, it was right over the car. It was a very clear night. . . . It was kind of flat, but it wasn't completely flat. Sort of like an upside-down plate."

"What about its surface? Could you tell anything about that?"

"No, you couldn't distinguish it that well. But it was big."

"You say you're familiar with the Air Force planes, like the B-52s. How did it compare in size to one of them?"

"It was bigger. It was huge. You couldn't get it mixed up with a B-52. Or a B-47. This was down low enough so you could distinguish it pretty clearly. Not more than half a mile up at the most. Not much over two thousand feet or so."

"How about a meteor? Did you stop to think it might be one of those?"

"No, not a chance. This was a machine. I've seen a lot of meteors."

"Or a helicopter?"

"Helicopters make an awful racket. All this did was hum. And you could see it clearly enough to see that it *wasn't* a helicopter. A helicopter wouldn't scare me, or my aunt or my mother. This did, and I mean scared us."

"The weather was good, you say?"

"You could see clear as a bell. And it was right up above us, right over the car. The red light was very bright—like the color of a fire engine light that flashes. It was real bright. And it tilted. It tilted and you couldn't see any wings or anything. That's why I was sure it wasn't an airplane. It didn't move like any aircraft. It seemed to creep along. And when it left, it zoomed right off. It wasn't ten seconds in getting out of sight. And another funny thing happened that night."

"What was that?"

"The field up on Shaw Hill. It seemed to light up, not from the craft in the air, but from something else. You know what a landing strip at an air base looks like? The colored lights that outline the runways and taxi strips on the field? Well, I saw a group of lights on this field that looked a little like that. I thought if I drove around to the other side of the hill, there would be something there. So I did, but by the time I got there, I could see nothing. Just as dark as anything. So then I drove around back to where I was before, and there were the lights again. I couldn't understand it."

After Smith left to go back to the store, I looked over the story he had given the police that night. There were no discrepancies, and Mrs. Oliver noted that from all reports from the night-duty officers, Smith was as scared as he said he was.

I went to a phone booth, though, and called his mother. She confirmed the account in detail, but was a little reluctant to talk about it. This was a pattern I was to find repeated many times. In addition to Yankee reticence and taciturnity, the subject matter here was so strange, so bizarre, that those involved with it had a constant underlying fear of ridicule. Yet when they did summon the courage to speak, they did so with impressive energy and conviction. As the police lieutenant had said in my first inquiry over the phone, "If I had seen this thing, and I was alone, nobody else would have ever heard about it!"

Shortly after the interview with Ron Smith, I learned that Bob Kimball, a newsreel cameraman and stringer in New England for all three of the major television networks, lived in Exeter and had been very interested in the Muscarello-Bertrand-Hunt incident. I had worked with Kimball before on several documentary films I had produced, and knew him to be a hardy and pleasantly cynical man, traits which often characterize the newsreel cameraman in any area. At dinner that night at the Exeter Inn, I welcomed the chance to get his opinion, which I knew would be well-weighed and considered.

Kimball frankly admitted that he was puzzled and baffled. He had a long-standing habit of spending a great deal of time at the Exeter police station, especially late at night when he found it hard to sleep. Used to the irregular hours his profession demanded, Kimball was essentially a night person. His habit was to drop by the police desk about midnight, chat with Officer Scratch Toland at the desk, follow up on any interesting cases which came over the radio. Along about three in the morning, he would join Rusty Davis, owner of the local taxi company and another one of the night people, and the two would drive over to a bakery in Hampton, in the rear of a small restaurant and bakery called "Sugar 'n Spice," for coffee and hot doughnuts, just out of the oven. This was a ritual for both of them.

"Unfortunately, I wasn't around the night of the Muscarello case. I was sleeping, which is something I don't usually do, and don't approve of. I would have given my left arm and an Arriflex camera to have caught a picture of that thing. Gene Bertrand finally did wake me up—about four-thirty A.M., I guess it was—but by the time we got out there, nothing was in sight, and I was still half asleep. And Gene was still shaken, which is very unusual for Gene. He's a tough cookie. So is Hunt. They're not the kind to go around making up any story."

I asked him what he made of it all.

"I just don't know," he said. "I can't figure it out, and I find it hard to even guess at it. Something was there, and something is continuing to happen. That much I'm sure of. Too many people all around the area are reporting this seriously, and a lot of them aren't dummies by a long shot. I kept thinking if I could only get a picture, a good picture, a close-up, then we'd have something to work on. I carry a loaded camera in the car with me all the time, but still no luck."

"If so many people are reporting sightings, why wouldn't the chances be in favor of your catching one?" I asked him.

"Well," Kimball said, "there are a lot of things to consider. In the first place, you can never predict where a report is going to come from. It might come from Manchester, from Portsmouth, from Derry, from Kensington—it's just not predictable. You'd have to have a dozen photographers stationed in as many separate localities as possible, sitting all night long and waiting. This is impractical. And some of them have been reported so high, you'd need a special lens. You can never tell what time a report is going to come in. And then it might be a false alarm. I estimate about thirty to forty percent of these sightings are mistaken identity. But the way these things are described, and the type of people who are describing them, I'd say most were definitely something strange, something unknown. But this is still a guess on my part. Nobody around here has had the time to really check this thing out."

"What's the scuttlebutt around the Portsmouth Air Base?"

"There's a lot. Constant reports of jet fighters being scrambled after the UFOs all the time. They don't regularly base any fighters there—the whole Pease operation is a SAC base, with just B-52s and B-47s and tankers for refueling. The fighters would have to be brought in from Westover or some other base, if there's any truth to the rumor. Then there's all kinds of stories that a couple of UFOs have landed right by the runways of the base. But there's no way of checking these out, because anybody with any real authority isn't going to say anything anyway."

Kimball offered to drive me around after midnight, and invited me to join him and Rusty, the taxi man, in their nightly ritual at the bakery. He also offered to point out several of the many spots from which reports of UFO sightings had been made both before and after the September 3rd event.

"UFO hunting has become a popular sport. All along Route 88, on the way to Hampton, and 101-C. You see cars waiting out there every other night."

"Anybody collected their stories and put them together?"

"None that I know of."

"You still haven't told me what you really make of all this."

"I'm going to wait until I see one myself," Kimball said. "And then I'll tell you."

The streets of Exeter at midnight are ghostly and quiet. The shops on Water Street, which sprawl along the bank of the Squamscott River, are dim and silent. Across from Batchelder's Bookstore, featuring cards, gifts, stationery, the faint blue fluorescent light POLICE flickers and glows uncertainly from the side of the Town Hall building. Inside,

Desk Officer Scratch Toland holds a nightly rein on cruisers #21 and #22, most frequently manned by patrolmen Bertrand and Hunt on the Midnight-to-8 A.M. tour of duty.

Scratch Toland, with a round and impish face, is a veteran officer on the force, with a sharp and dour Yankee tongue and a pleasing wit. With his help, I was able to cull the names of over a dozen witnesses to UFO incidents, many more than I had anticipated, from the police blotter.

"This is interesting," I told Toland. "I didn't know you had so many leads."

"Lot of people were keeping 'em quiet," Toland said. "Afraid people might think they were nuts. Thing that brought so much attention to the September third sighting was that there were two officers on hand to testify directly."

"Do you think there are many more sightings unreported, not on the blotter?"

"I *know* so," said Toland. "Keep running into people who tell me they saw such-and-such quite a few weeks ago, a few nights ago, or whenever it was. It's getting now so that people aren't even bothering to report them."

Although I knew it was going to be repetitious, I asked Toland to go over the night of September 3 with me in detail. Somewhere, I felt, some new clues might emerge.

"When was the first you heard of this?" I asked.

"Well," Toland said, "the Muscarello kid come in. He must have come in around twenty-five minutes past two, I think it was. And he was all shook up. He said he'd been watching this thing, and said it had been hovering over the field out there."

"How shook up was he?" I asked.

"He was *real* shook up," Toland said. "And he ain't the kind of kid that shakes up too easy, either."

"How did he act?"

"He was lighting one cigarette after the other, you know. And the first thing he told me—when he come in the door—he said, You're not going to believe me, but I saw a flying

79

saucer. I kind of smiled, and I could see he was so shook up over this that I called Bertrand in. And that's when that coincidence come up. When I told Bertrand, when I told him, You want to go out with this fellow on Route 150 in Kensington and check out a flying saucer? And Bertrand, that's when he said, Gee that's funny, I just stopped by a woman out on the bypass. I saw the car stopped, I thought it was out of gas. So Bertrand says he went over and asked the woman, What's the trouble? And she told him this big thing had been following her in the air, over her car, all the way from Epping. When he told me about it, that's when I said it might be a good idea to go out with the kid."

"How did you feel about the kid when you first saw him that night? It's a pretty wild story to be hit with cold. Did you doubt him?"

"Well, I did and I didn't," Toland said. "You could tell he meant what he was saying. You don't get all upset like this over nothing. And this kid wasn't faking."

"He was so shook up you were inclined to believe him?"

"Yea," Toland said. "If he wasn't so shook up, I don't think I would've. He told me it was so low that it hovered right over the roof of this guy's house. He said it lit the whole top of the roof up, it was so low it almost hit the chimney. He said then it would sweep down like this"—Toland made a sweeping motion with his hand—"and when it did, he said he hit the road. He said it really scared him. When I figured he'd come that close to an object, sending Bertrand out didn't sound like such a bad idea."

"When was the next you heard from Bertrand?"

"When he got out there on Route 150," Toland said. The low, dim light over the police desk, the small dark room with shadows cast up from the single desk light, made it an ideal place for a ghost story, Space Age or not. "When he got out there with Muscarello, he called in on the radio. He didn't see anything, he even sounded bored. But, he says, we're going to take a walk down the field. Then the radio was silent.

80

It was silent for quite a few minutes. And then the damnedest noise you ever heard. I couldn't even recognize Gene's voice!"

"What was the reaction?"

"Reaction? That's no word for it. He was *hollering*. I never heard him holler that way before or since. 'I see it! I see it!' he was hollering. And I started to laugh then, because I figured he was pretty scared."

"Understand he doesn't scare too easy. Is that right?"

"Bertrand? He doesn't scare at *anything*. I never heard a reaction like that in my life. He's not scared of anything—except something like this, and who wouldn't be? Bertrand will go in anywhere, he's always the first. If there's a fight or a brawl or a prowler in a dark warehouse—you name it, he'll do it. That's why I was so surprised. And I guess that's why I started laughing. I couldn't think of anything else to do."

"What about Hunt?" I asked. "Where was he at this time?"

"Well, Dave, he was hearing all the talk between Gene Bertrand and me over his cruiser radio. Dave was in the other cruiser, number 20. By the time Dave got there, the thing was just taking off over the field toward Hampton. And right after that, I got the call from the telephone operator about the man in the phone booth at Hampton."

"Tell me about that," I said. "I got part of the story from Bertrand and Hunt."

"Well, the night operator at Exeter here called in. She said she had a man in a pay phone booth in Hampton, some man who was calling in all excited. He said this huge object was coming at him from the air, with bright red lights on it. Coming right at him. And then he was cut off or hung up, she didn't know which. I called the Hampton police right away—they said they'd notify the Pease Air Force Base."

"What did Bertrand say when he came back to the station?"

"Well, he was all shook up. He really was. And Hunt? He didn't show it quite as much, but you know Dave. He's like that. And of course, he hadn't seen it quite as close as Gene had. Dave did call me later, though, and said that it gave him an awful weird feeling. Coming from Dave, that's quite a statement."

"Now," I said, "some of these other reports you've had since then—the ones I've taken down the names of—can you tell me about some of them?"

I was working on hearsay now, but I knew I was going to be checking most of the leads directly, and it was possible I could pick up some other helpful details. As long as I could follow it up, I was finding that hearsay could be helpful.

"Of course we've had so many since then, it's hard to remember. Let me take a look at some of the names you've got down. . . ." Toland glanced over the list I had prepared from the blotter. "Well," he said, looking over his semi-lens glasses, "this Lillian Pearce, lives right down on the Hampton-Exeter line. Just off 101-C. She'd be a good one to interview. She said she saw one in July, and was afraid to report it. Then she saw a couple more, and after Bertrand and Hunt admitted it, she reported them. The last one she saw, she said a plane from the air base was out chasing it. And as soon as the plane got near it, the lights on the object went out, and the thing seemed to disappear. Then the plane went away, and the lights came on again. And you know, it's a funny thing, we get a lot of calls like that—about a plane from the air base chasing these things. I got a call from a fellow on Hampton Falls Road, a ham radio operator. This was about a week after this Mrs. Pearce called in. There was a plane from the air base circling around Hampton Falls, and they called the ground on shortwave radio and asked for anyone on the ground that could hear them to come in. And he picked the call up, and they asked him to call in at the Exeter Police Department to see if we'd got any reports of sightings that night. They said they were out chasing a UFO, but couldn't find anything."

"What about some of the other calls you've received?" I asked Toland.

"There was a kid who goes to high school who came in here shaking a few weeks ago. Ron Smith."

"Yes, I talked to him today."

"If you wanted to see a kid shook up, you should have seen him. People don't get excited like that for nothing, you know."

"He impressed me as a pretty level-headed kid."

"He *is*," said Toland. "That's what's so confusing about this whole thing. Most of the people who've been reporting them are level-headed. And I'll tell you something. I've had three different people tell me the same story that night that Bertrand saw the woman on the bypass, and then took Muscarello out. Around eleven-thirty that night, this fellow up in Brentwood. I met him at a restaurant, oh, about a week later. And he was telling me that he woke up that night, and the whole room was lit up. And he figured somebody was coming in the driveway, or down the road with a high beam. So he got up and looked out the window. And there wasn't a car in sight, no sound or nothing. And all of a sudden, the room went dark again. And then the wife of this fellow who runs the machinery over the mill—she woke up and the room was all lit up, and she couldn't remember what day it was, but it was right in the vicinity of the time that they saw it over Kensington. The room was all lit and no cars or planes around, then all of a sudden it went dark again."

The telephone rang, a routine call. Scratch Toland hung up, lit his pipe. "A couple over in Fremont. Their kids came running in one night, said some object out in the field scared the life out of them. And Mrs. Ralph Lindsay, in South Kensington. You've got her name down there. She called in here very early in the morning, just before dawn. She said it was right out her window right at the same time she was calling. It was like a bright orange ball, almost as big as a harvest moon, she said. It just hung there in the sky, but it didn't move. And it wasn't the moon either. She talked to me for about five minutes on the phone. All the time she was talking to me, her kids were at the window watching it. Then she said it took off fast, toward Hampton. Now why would people go to all this trouble—people all over the area—if they weren't seeing something real? People don't call the police station in the middle of the night just for the fun of it."

Toland took a call on the radio from Bertrand in Cruiser #21. A door in a store was unlocked, and he was going in to check. It was now about one in the morning. Kimball and Rusty Davis hadn't come in yet, but they were expected. Outside the station, the street was dark and deserted.

Toland, smoking more matches than tobacco, went on. "The evening after Mrs. Lindsay called, a fellow phoned here after supper, around seven-thirty that night. I wasn't on duty, but Lt. Cottrell told me about it, because he had learned about my call with Mrs. Lindsay. The man said that this big, orange-red object hovered over his house just before dawn the same morning Mrs. Lindsay saw it. He told Cottrell that he never paid any attention to these things before, but that he'd been thinking it over all day long, and thought he ought to call in to the police about it."

"What about the Air Force? Did you run into them when they were investigating the Muscarello sighting?"

"They were in here one night, but they didn't say much. Close-mouthed. They were patrolling around, I understand, in a lot of different places. They got so many complaints about these objects down around Applecrest Farm in Hampton Falls, they sent the officers up to check, in addition to the Muscarello place."

"What's the Air Force's attitude? Do they seem to take it seriously?"

"They're not fooling around, I know that. Now take this sighting of Mrs. Pearce's—the first one. Several weeks before the September third sighting. We got the report that she was driving down Route 88 with her daughter. They saw this big red light in the distance, and they thought it was an accident with police cars or a wrecker, or something like that. The closer they got to it, the bigger it got. And then they began to realize something was funny. Then all of a sudden, this thing took right off up in the air. She told some friends of hers, and they laughed at her. But the Air Force didn't. They investigated, and they found that her description was identical with Gene's. Somewhere, all these pieces have got to add up."

"But what's it all going to add up to?"

"That's what I hope you're going to find out," Toland said. "Like this woman who called up here the other night. It must have been about quarter of eleven. And she asked me all about the thing. And after I got through telling her all I knew about it she said, The reason I'm calling is to find out if I see one, what I should do? And I said, Do what I'm going to do. And she said, What's that? And I said, Run like hell!"

It was nearly two in the morning when Kimball and Rusty Davis showed up at the station. There was a lot of kidding around, and then the nightly pilgrimage for the coffee and doughnuts got under way. We would have a chance to look at some of the favorite places the UFO hunters haunted on the way over to Hampton.

We piled into Kimball's car, a big Chrysler especially equipped for his newsreel and documentary camera work, with a shortwave radio, a mobile telephone, cameras, lights and film stock. It carried a license plate CBS-TV, although he worked for all three networks. "We'll check a couple of these places on the way down," Kimball said as we moved out of the empty streets of Exeter and onto the Hampton road. "But don't expect to see anything. Rusty and I have been looking every night since it happened, and we haven't had any luck. There's one spot on Route 101-C where some reports have come in—and another field on Route 88 where a lot of them have. We'll go by there first."

Rusty, in the back seat, mumbled, "As long as we don't

forget the doughnuts." A shaggy, congenial man with an enormous appetite, he had heard a lot about UFOs as he taxied the citizens of Exeter and environs around the area.

Route 88, from Exeter to Hampton Falls, is dark, winding and lonely, a fit place for a tired UFO to rest, if indeed UFOs did exist. In spite of the evidence, some of it rather startling, it was hard to overcome the resistance of a skeptical outlook, born of the scientific age. And yet one of the prerequisites of science is to keep an open mind.

For the first time the idea began to grow on me that, in spite of official protestations, the Establishment (in the form of official government, Air Force and scientific agencies) was actually in as weak a position as the Protesters or Witnesses, if they could be called that. Regardless of official proclamations, the Air Force offered no definite proof of nonexistence (a paradox, of course, but everything in this case was a paradox, an ambivalence, a dichotomy). But neither did the Witnesses offer proof. They offered only conviction, sincerity, dedication, and resolute resistance to any who would call them false witnesses. What was most distressing to these people was that the Establishment—mainly in the form of the Air Force—was responsible for calling them liars and incompetents with almost unforgivable bluntness. There seemed to be shaping up here a mammoth confrontation between the Air Force and the growing number of reliable observers.

The threat of the UFO was still psychological, however. No instance of any physical harm befalling a human being had been reliably reported in the twenty-year history of the phenomenon's most yeasty occurrences. Even those observers who had had close and frightening encounters experienced no physical harm. Interstellar beings who could conquer the forces of nature to the extent of defying gravity (if thousands of observers were telling the truth), harness electromagnetic forces, and defy G-forces, which the entire NASA space program showed no indication of conquering, should easily be able to do harm at will.

The UFOs had apparently made no attempt to communicate with Earth People, unless, of course, they had communicated directly with the Scientific Elite, who, having reported it to the Government, were promptly restrained from releasing it to the general public.

And then of course the question would come up: Could scientists be squelched like this? Wouldn't some intrepid scientist say to hell with politics and everything else, he was going to bring the Truth to the public because he *believed* that truth was more important than both politics and the Establishment combined?

But if he should be so bold, wouldn't it be possible, as Gordon Evans had suggested at lunch, for the Establishment to neutralize anything he might say by subtly associating him with the lunatic fringe? Alone and disassociated from his sober colleagues, his testimony would be worthless.

On the other side of the fence, if you presupposed a benign and intelligent group of political leaders, or Air Force generals, who were faced with definite evidence and proof of the fact that UFOs of extraterrestrial origin did exist, wouldn't they, out of concern for the entire organized structure of society, feel that they must be most cautious in the manner in which this intelligence should be released to the general populace? The Orson Wells "invasion" in the late thirties, a single dramatized radio program resulted in mass hysteria. Would the same thing—or worse—happen if official government sources announced blandly that we definitely had visitors from another planet? What would a reasonable and prudent man in the position of complete authority—such as the President of the United States—do when confronted with such a decision?

There have been, I learned after I started this research, frequent and continual rumors (and they are *only* rumors) that in a morgue at Wright-Patterson Field, Dayton, Ohio, lie the bodies of a half-dozen or so small humanoid corpses, measuring not more than four-and-a-half feet in height, evidence of one of the few times an extraterrestrial spaceship has allowed itself either to fail or otherwise fall into the clutches of the semicivilized Earth People. What would any of us do if we bore the responsibility of releasing this news to the citizenry? If we were the "reasonable and prudent man" our law courts always use as the measuring stick of judgment, we would probably be very circumspect. We might even delay judgment. It could produce chaos in an overorganized society which has become so dependent on intricate interrelated mechanisms that even a pint-size back-up relay in Ontario, Canada, can plunge 30 million people into inexplicable darkness, with none of the engineering experts in the country knowing exactly why it happened. As Gordon Evans had pointed out, the Brookings report had indicated that the engineers and the scientists would suffer the greatest confusion and who else could the masses turn to, aside from the suggestion that they turn to God? For there would *have* to be an explanation—a sober, logical explanation, from "official sources." And those official sources would have to be the ordinary person, elevated into authority by the mandate of the voters. The President. Or you. Or me.

The whole question of the Space Age ghost story seems to reduce itself to an insoluble ghost story—unless physical evidence of overwhelming validity were suddenly made available; or, unless scientists who *might* have such evidence were willing to share it. The censorship of the political powers in the Air Force seems to be exercising authority far beyond the powers assigned to it by the civilian control under which it is supposed to be operating.

As I drove down the twisting, darkened curves of Route 88 in Bob Kimball's newsreel-equipped Chrysler, thoughts like these were going through my mind.

CHAPTER VII

ROUTE 88, no different from hundreds of other macadam roads in New Hampshire, took on an aura of its own because of the stories which had been reported about it. Rusty, in the back seat, pointed out a darkened field to the right of the car. "This fare I had the other night in my taxi," he said. "His wife saw it right in the field there, right behind that farmhouse, in the daytime. He said she was standing right by the house there, and she seen it go over the field, and then just flutter away. She said it was a great silver object with a dome on it."

"What about the woman in the house by the orchard?" Kimball asked from the driver's seat.

"Well," said Rusty, "she told me she was out in her yard, hanging out the laundry. This thing came right over the house, she described it like the other woman, and then she passed right out. I get all kinds of reports like this from the fares."

Kimball slowed the car down now, pulled into a dark field on the north side of the road. "This is the place where the cars line up to watch for it," he said. "And where a lot of people have made reports from."

The three of us got out of the car. It was a small field, rimmed by the black silhouettes of trees which looked for all the world like a cardboard cutout, against the sky.

"So, this is the place," I said. "It sure is a good place for it, sure as hell out of the way."

Kimball said, "I came down here one night and counted

nine cars. People standing around, looking for it. Another night, I counted fourteen cars. They were camping out here almost."

I said, "How many UFOs did you see?"

"I'll tell you when I get a picture," Kimball said.

We stood there a few moments, looking at the sky, but of course nothing showed up. We climbed back into the car, drove into the silent streets of Hampton, and pulled up behind a low squat building in the village square.

Inside the bakery, the rich smell of freshly ground coffee and hot doughnuts was welcome. Two bakers were expertly chopping circular globs out of the dough, throwing out cheerful insults to the two regular visitors and protesting that it was regrettable I had to be in such unsavory company. The doughnuts were warm and light, the coffee bracing, helping to clear the cobwebs from my head, after a day of accumulating and taping information.

Another ritual assumed by Rusty and Kimball was to deliver a parcel of doughnuts and hot coffee to the police station at Hampton Beach, the resort section of the town, swarming with visitors during the summer, now deserted and boarded up in October. We drove along the ocean, past the shells of the summer hot dog stands and curio shops, and pulled up in front of the police station, the only light visible in the entire seashore community. It was close to 3 in the morning by now, and the only sound was the echo of the breakers on the beach.

Sgt. Joe Farnsworth was on night duty, a gray-haired gentleman who tendered more friendly insults to the regulars for being so late with the coffee.

He recalled the night of the frantic phone call from the man in the unknown phone booth, pulled out the blotter and showed me the record of it.

"There's another story, though," he said, "much more interesting than this one. It's not on the blotter because we turned the whole thing over to the Coast Guard station and they took it from there."

"Tell me about it," I said.

"Well," the sergeant said, "this was about two months ago. That would make it some time in early September or late August. I don't have the names of the two fellows involved, but the Coast Guard does, if they're allowed to give them to you. Anyway, I was cruising up on the boulevard. It was late, about four in the morning, I think. This car was parked along the side, and I eased up to it, to see what was up. There were these two boys in it, I guess they were in their late teens. As soon as they saw me, they came running to the cruiser. And they were scared to death, I mean scared to death. Both of them. And this one boy said, 'You'll never believe what I'm going to tell you!' Right away, the way they were acting, I checked to make sure they were both sober. And they were. No liquor on the breath, nothing like that. They were just plain hysterical. So they told me they were going down the boulevard, and this thing come in from the ocean right over the top of their car, and it stayed still over the car. And they stopped short, they thought it was a plane that was trying to land and they didn't want to get involved underneath it. Then this thing stopped, too, whatever it was. Right in the air. Pretty soon, they got scared and took off—and when they did, this thing did, too. But when they went up the boulevard straight, this thing suddenly came right at them. That's when they pulled over, the thing shot off out of sight, and they were too hysterical to do anything until I pulled up, I guess. So I took them up to the Coast Guard station."

"How far is that?" I asked.

"Couple of miles up the shore from here. Right on the beach. So anyway, the Coast Guard had these guys write out statements about what they saw, and everything. And they had somebody come over from the air base, I don't know who it was, and check on it. And I don't know what they found, but these kids definitely saw something."

"You don't have the names of the kids anywhere?"

"No, I'm afraid I don't. But the Coast Guard does. And the next day, the story was flying around so much I was believing it myself. Especially the way these kids were so hysterical. They couldn't have faked that in a million years."

"Any other cases come your way?" I asked.

"Oh, a couple of weeks ago," the sergeant said. "After the beach closed. About a week or two after Labor Day. We got a report, you might have heard about it, that the thing was over the marsh, back of the police station here. I went out there, but I didn't see anything. Then there's the woman who works at the high school in Exeter. And I took her to school one morning, her car had broken down. She saw it. She was going up the Expressway toward the Exeter line when she saw it, and she said the thing stopped off to one side of her car. She got petrified and stopped the car and couldn't make up her mind what to do. All of a sudden, she said there was a big white flash from the thing, and it was gone." The sergeant paused a minute, and leaned back in his chair. "Now I still don't know what to make about all this," he said. "Do you suppose it's something the Government is working on?"

"That's one possibility. All I can say is that it's anybody's guess."

"It seems to me, and I might be wrong," said the sergeant, "that every night we got a report on this, it's been foggy, hazy."

"Most of the time," Kimball said, "in Exeter, it's been clear. So I don't think that holds up."

"That night the kids went up to the Coast Guard station, it was quite foggy. But you know—on a second thought, I don't think it could belong to the Government, because the Government can't keep its mouth shut that long. They'd be

92

so proud of themselves if they had a vehicle that could do all this, they'd have it on TV the next day."

"Well," said Rusty, "they can't be dangerous. Because they've been around enough that they could have done plenty of damage by now, if they wanted to."

It was almost dawn when I got back to the Exeter Inn. I had an appointment with Chief Irvine the next morning at eight, followed by an interview with Lora Davis, daughter of Rusty, who had reported a UFO on Country Club Hill in Exeter not long after Bertrand and Hunt had seen theirs. Tired as I was, I found it difficult to get to sleep; everything that had happened during the long day of October 20 ran through my mind.

The possibilities seemed to boil down to one of three things: first, a revolutionary government secret weapon, unannounced and unpublicized. Second, it might be a foreign craft, Russia's perhaps, that was so fast, maneuverable and invincible that it could thumb its nose at our own Air Force, and survey the country at will and without fear of being captured or shot down. Third, it could be an interplanetary craft, coming from a civilization far advanced beyond our own.

These were it seemed to me the only speculations possible unless it could be assumed that the sightings were psychic aberrations. From the quality of the official and technical witnesses making low-level observations, such as the one Bertrand and Hunt had reported, mistaken identity could almost surely be ruled out. The Air Force explanations of some of these sightings were actually harder to believe than the sightings themselves. Psychic aberrations? Maybe—but highly unlikely. There was photographic and radar evidence, too. Bertrand had refused point-blank to believe the reports of the lone woman on the 101 bypass, of Muscarello, too, until in the company of both Muscarello and Hunt the thing suddenly loomed above him.

93

Of the three major speculative possibilities, there seemed to be arguments against any one of them being likely, also. If it were an experimental aircraft of our own design and making, it would be required to carry conventional running lights simply for air safety, if nothing else, regardless of its secret nature. And the Federal Aviation Agency would prohibit it, secret or not, from zooming straight at automobiles on the highway, forcing people into nervous shock. It would most certainly not be permitted to hover and maneuver in populated areas at night, skimming over housetops and cars. And if it were *that* secret the Air Force would not want it in populated areas anyway. If it were not secret, as Sergeant Farnsworth had said, it would be all over TV along with the astronauts, whose feats would be overshadowed by the power and maneuvers of the UFOs.

If the craft were of foreign origin, why had it not set off vociferous complaints about violation of air space in our country, or any other of the countries which had reported UFOs so frequently? The single U-2 which had flown over Russia at 60,000 feet had created a major international incident, blasted the hopes of a summit conference, and brought before the United Nations a case which still echoes through its halls. Logic would seem to rule out this possibility, also.

If the UFOs were extraterrestrial, why had they not attempted to communicate with us? Certainly, a civilization advanced enough to create interplanetary or even interstellar craft should be able to make it plain to us that we had visitors from space for the first time in recorded history. Unless, of course, they had already communicated with authorities who had decided to withhold this intelligence on the theory that the public might panic.

The latter possibility is at once the most logical and still most illogical (again the paradox). It is more logical than the other two only because the other two possibilities (advanced U.S. or foreign man-made craft) are so totally illogical under the circumstances. It is, at once, illogical because there seems to be no physical proof whatever.

NICAP has developed a theory about why, if the craft are interplanetary or extraterrestrial, they have not yet made direct contact with people here on the earth. It draws a comparison between what extraterrestrial astronauts might be instructed to do on investigating a populated planet and what already has been suggested for NASA by the RAND (Research and Development Corporation) for our own space exploration, now moving ahead so rapidly with unusually generous Congressional support. If the report, commissioned by NASA, represents a *quid pro quo* situation, any possible extraterrestrial visitors might be following the advice laid down by our own scientific researchers for our own astronauts. The Rand Corporation directive states flatly:

> Any indication that a planet is already inhabited by intelligent creatures would signal the need for proceeding with the utmost caution. . . . Before a manned landing is made, it would be desirable to study the planet thoroughly . . . *for a protacted period of time; to send sampling probes* into its atmosphere and to send surveillance instruments down to the surface.
>
> Contacts with alien intelligence *should be made most circumspectly,* not only as insurance against unknown factors, but *also to avoid any disruptive effects on the local population* produced by encountering a vastly different cultural system. *After prolonged study,* a decision would have to be made whether to make overt contact or to *depart without giving the inhabitants any evidence of the visitation.* [All italics are the author's.]

It is important to remember, but difficult to keep in mind, that these statements are not from science fiction. They are sober, considered proposals made by our own scientists for the benefit of our *own* astronauts in this realistic Space Age. If the recommendations apply to us, they could as easily apply to more advanced explorers. And if the UFO visitations are of extraterrestrial origin, a good part of the recommendations seems to be already in effect. As NICAP points out, though, the UFOs apparently have not followed part of the prescribed routine, in that they have certainly not (assuming for a moment the reports of sightings to be true) made any attempt to conceal their operations. They have seemed, however, to painstakingly avoid leaving any physical evidence of their existence, except for the scattered photographs that have been taken, and some marks or impressions in the ground. They have not shown any evidence of aggressiveness.

The mass hypnosis and psychic illusions recorded all through history kept coming back to my mind as an explanation. What about this possibility? Frankly, I didn't believe it had any bearing on the people I had interviewed so far. It would take a pretty strong hypnotic effect to influence officers as tough as Bertrand and Hunt, with each of them predisposed to be totally skeptical before their own sighting took place. Further, it is impossible to hypnotize a radarscope and equally impossible to hypnotize a camera. There had been enough reports clearly observed on radar throughout the country, and enough pictures found to be valid to indicate that the psychic phenomenon theory was very weak at best. Constant accounts of the effect of UFOs on dogs, cattle, ignition, electromagnetic instruments, radios, and lights were also outside the realm of psychic disturbances.

I finally slept and I barely made my appointment with Chief Irvine at the Exeter police station at eight the next morning. There was not much new I could gather from him because he had been on vacation during the time of the sightings his officers had made. He could only confirm the fact that the Air Force had made several inquiries about the incident, and for some time after it had happened, Air Force officers patrolled the roads at night. He also confirmed that officers Bertrand and Hunt were highly responsible and intelligent members of the force.

I spoke at length with Patrolman Leonard Novak of the Exeter force, a husky and articulate officer whom I had met briefly the day before. As we leaned against the fender of his cruiser, he told me his experience with Mrs. Lillian Pearce, the woman who lived on the Exeter-Hampton line and who claimed several encounters with UFOs in her vicinity.

"I was driving along Route 88 one night, a couple of weeks ago," Patrolman Novak said. "And there was quite a crowd down there, down by the field where they all seem to collect to keep an eye out for these things. I stopped for awhile to listen to what was going on. This Mrs. Pearce was really kicking up a storm, talking to the colonel from the Air Force base and complaining about the fact that the Air Force didn't seem to know as much as the whole neighborhood did about UFOs. There must have been ten or twelve people from the neighborhood there, but Mrs. Pearce was doing most of the talking."

"The colonel had come all the way down from Portsmouth?"

"Not only the colonel, but a major, too. Evidently she had been to Pease Air Base that day, and was claiming to the colonel that she had seen these things four or five times, according to her. She had taken pictures of it, and they were trying to get her to give them the film. Said they'd give her a new film if she gave them the exposed roll. But she'd have none of that. She said, Oh no. I'm going to get these things developed and find out what they are myself."

"Is this what all the fuss was about?"

"Not all, no. The colonel was trying to persuade Mrs. Pearce and the rest of the neighbors that what they had seen were the strobe lights from the air base runway, which is about ten miles away. And apparently the colonel had sent the major back to the air base in his car, to have them turn the runway lights on and off at a regular pattern of intervals so they could see if this was it. He was still trying to impress the people there that what they were seeing was a reflection from these landing lights. Now, the major had just come back. And he asked the colonel if he had noticed what had happened. He said that for fifteen-minute periods he had turned the runway lights *on* for two minutes, and off for three. And the colonel had to admit that, no, he hadn't seen a thing, and everybody else there said no, we didn't either. And they didn't. There was no reflection or nothing. So that kind of blew the colonel's theory."

"What did Mrs. Pearce say to that?"

"She was all upset. She said, See what I told you? See what I mean? It was quite a scene, believe me. She was backing the colonel and the major all over the place."

The incident chiefly serves to indicate that the Air Force was taking this thing very seriously, and that people were aroused enough to demand some kind of explanation. I phoned Mrs. Pearce and made an appointment to see her at home that afternoon.

After breakfast I drove to Rusty's taxi office, run by his daughter Lora while he did the driving. It was a small room in a building behind his house, dominated by an overstuffed sofa and the shortwave radio equipment used for coordinating the taxi calls. Before I began to talk to Lora Davis, a radio call came in from Rusty saying he'd just learned of a woman in Stratham, a community not far from Exeter on the way toward Portsmouth, who had made a very clear sighting of a UFO in daylight and would be willing to talk to me about it. I took down the name and address, and then turned to Miss Davis.

"I can't for the life of me remember the exact date," she said. "But it was a Saturday night, sometime after the fuss about the policemen here in Exeter and the time they saw it. A couple of us decided we'd try to get a look at it—if there was such a thing—and we stayed up very late waiting for it, up on top of Country Club Hill. I guess it must have been about two o'clock in the morning, and I first thought what I saw was a plane, with a little green light on it. And suddenly it went off, and there wasn't any green light. It had turned into a big, huge red light. Just a big red light, blinking on and off. Then it started moving in closer, I guess maybe it came within about three miles of where I was. It was much too big to be a plane, the distance it was."

"You say it had a bright red light?" I asked.

"Very bright. Much brighter than an airplane light. It was coming in from a distance, from the southeast, sort of parallel to Route 101-D, the bypass, and it was headed toward the ocean."

"Was it moving on a steady course?" I was trying to check out whether it could be a plane.

"It was for awhile, and then it stopped suddenly. Right in the air. Then it started off in a different direction."

"Could you make out any shape, or any pattern of lights?"

"Well," she went on, "the shape from where I saw it and from how I can determine it, was like a small cone. The top was round, and then it sort of curved under. Like a top."

"How about the surface? Could you make that out?"

"Not really," she said. "It seemed as though it had a metallic color to it. But I couldn't be sure of that. Because the lights were blurring my eyes and I didn't see it that close to be sure."

"How long were you able to keep it in view?"

"Oh, about five minutes. Maybe a little longer. Between five and eight minutes, I'd say."

"Could you describe the way it moved?"

"Well, when it moved, it moved quite fast. Not like a B-47, though, we see them all the time. Don't forget, this thing stopped right still in midair. Did you ever see a plane do that?"

"You say it had a brilliant red light. Was the object all red? Any other colored lights?"

99

"Just that green one at first, but that changed to red. And then it seemed as though the red light was blinking on and off. It's kind of hard to describe."

The taxi radio came in with an inquiry and I had time to appraise Miss Davis and her testimony. She was calm in her outlook, unemotional in her reaction to the object, and appeared to be of above-average intelligence. While her observation was a little vague, she spoke with authority about what she saw, without decorating her description with unessential detail. If I had been on a jury, I would have graded her as a fully believable witness. What's more, she was aware of her compass directions, a rare attribute for a woman. She also showed some familiarity with the aircraft in the vicinity.

I checked the name and address of the new observer with her—a Mrs. Harlow Spinney, of Portsmouth Avenue, in Stratham. She and her husband were ham radio buffs, and frequently talked to Rusty on his taxi radio.

The Spinney home, with its large shortwave radio antenna, was cheery and sprinkled with good non-fiction books. Mrs. Spinney was blond, attractive, articulate. She was painstaking with details, and kept a well-organized diary.

"When I heard you were coming over," she said, "I looked in my diary to check the date of this. It was September 27, just about ten o'clock in the morning. I was driving from Exeter toward Portsmouth, and when I first saw it, it was in the distance. And it wasn't more than fifty feet from the road at that time, but I was, oh, maybe a mile from it. I thought at first it was a low-flying plane, so I hurried and got around this tractor that happened to be in the road, and got a little closer to it. It appeared to be going toward Portsmouth, not directly along the highway but in that direction. But when I got within two or three hundred feet of it, darned if that thing didn't turn around and come back so I got a *perfect* view of it in broad daylight."

By now, I was beginning to notice some similarities in the accounts these observers were giving. Without knowing each other, and without collusion, they constantly referred to the objects as "the thing" or "that thing." This had a certain convincing ring to it, because by implication it indicated that instinctively they were not confusing the sighting with a plane or ordinary aircraft. I still had no clear or vivid description of the texture of any of these objects, however, and I asked about this one.

"I'd say it was definitely metallic. Yes, it was. That's why it didn't frighten me. I thought at first, What kind of plane is that with no wings? But then I thought it wasn't frightening at all, because it looked just as if it were guided."

"Did it go fast—or did it move slowly?"

"It went slowly when I first saw it," she said. "Then I pulled up and stopped. I wanted to listen, you know, to see if I heard any noise or anything. I didn't. It was silent. It hovered, as I said, and it turned around and came back and I got a *beautiful* look at it. And then it went *furiously* off—I suppose it was toward Manchester."

Mrs. Spinney reacted with none of the eeriness the others had felt, but perhaps this might have been because she had seen it in broad daylight in a populated area. Her account was ingenuous and disarming, as natural as if she were describing a friend's new car.

"You're sure," I asked, "that this craft moved contrary to most airplanes?"

"Believe me, it didn't look or act like anything I had ever seen. Except possibly a helicopter. And a helicopter it was definitely *not*."

"Any glow or light to it?"

"No. And there wasn't a cloud in the sky, incidentally. It was a beautiful, clear day. I could see no openings in it, no numbers."

"It was smooth in texture then?"

"Yes, it was. Just about as smooth as the surface of the fuselage of a B-47 or a B-52, which go right over my house here all the time. We're right in the middle of the landing pattern, sort of. But it was so close I know I could have seen an opening if it happened to have been on the surface."

"About how long did you have it in view?"

"Oh, I don't imagine it was more than a minute or two."

"Do you have a rough idea how high it was?"

"Well, I really can't tell how high it was, but if you saw a plane that low, you'd be frightened. It probably wasn't more than a couple of a hundred feet up. And you know something—"

"What's that?"

"I said to myself: Am I really seeing this thing—or is it because I want to see it? And I told myself, yes. Yes, I'm really seeing it. You really question your own eyesight in a case like this."

"What's the closest you would say it came to you?"

"Oh, I would say less than two or three hundred feet. But it went so quickly, that it was hard for me to tell how big it was."

"That's the next question I was going to ask you."

"Well, it *is* hard to tell," she said. "But if I *had* to estimate it, I'd say it was about thirty feet in diameter."

It was nearly 11:30 that morning of October 21, and I was already late for my next appointment with Mrs. Hale, the UPI stringer in the area, several miles away. I gave a mental B-plus to Mrs. Spinney as a witness, and got in my car. Driving from Stratham toward Hampton, I began to realize that I was setting a pattern for myself in this research problem. I had screened out fanatics or irresponsible observers because I simply did not have the time to waste with them. In the leads that Scratch Toland had helped me cull from the blotter, I had checked beforehand to make sure I wasn't going to get involved with anyone who could obviously be ruled out as an incompetent or fanatic. I had often heard in courtroom cases the phrase "a parade of witnesses," which seemed to signify that such a group could prove or disprove a case. In the UFO case, such a parade seemed to be the only practical way to make even a small dent in the mystery.

To be totally objective in the research, I should also interrogate "negative" witnesses. But what was a negative witness in this case? A person who had never seen a UFO? That represented most of the population including myself. Conversely, that still didn't prove that UFOs were nonexistent. How many people have seen an albatross, a white whale, a plover's egg, a pair of Siamese twins, or a cyclotron? An infinitesimal fragment of the population. Yet no one contests their existence. Why aren't they contested? Because authorities have proclaimed them to exist. But to this date, no Master Authority had proclaimed that UFOs exist, except indirectly. Oddly enough, the UFOs' greatest enemy, the U.S. Air Force, had admitted their existence because they have set up a complete, officially regulated UFO program. You cannot reasonably set up a program to investigate a nonexistent thing. The Air Force has this program, and I had already examined it in detail, in its regulation 200-2.

Nor would the Air Force have taken the trouble to spell out the subject so thoroughly in its public relations booklet *Questions and Answers About the United States Air Force.* In paragraphs numbered 148 and 149, the subject is discussed extensively, if lamely.

In answer to its own posed question *Are there really flying saucers?*, the official booklet of the Air Force says: "The term 'flying saucer' is really a science-fiction term that was coined several years ago [immediate downgrading attack on the subject]. No unidentified flying object has given any indication of threat to the national security [this, again, is tacit recognition of the fact that UFOs do exist]; there has been no evidence submitted to or discovered by the Air Force that unidentified sightings represented technological developments or principles beyond the range of our present scientific

103

knowledge [this, of course, gives tremendous leeway. Our present knowledge includes theories by Dr. Einstein and Professor John Wheeler of Princeton and others that cope with and understand electromagnetic and gravitational forces far beyond the scope of modern engineering and its capacity to put it into practical use. UFOs, under this premise, could be thousands of years ahead of our capacity to produce such a craft, and still come within the confines of this definition]; and finally, there has been nothing in the way of evidence or other data to indicate that these unidentified sightings are extraterrestrial vehicles under intelligent control." In addition to admitting conclusively here that UFOs exist, the Air Force makes a statement which NICAP vociferously contests. We are back again, at this point, to NICAP's contention that the Air Force is, in the most simple and direct terms, lying. By the same token, of course, the Air Force is calling NICAP a liar.

The Air Force booklet goes on, in Paragraph #149 to pose its own question again: *What is a UFO?*

"A UFO," the booklet, printed in 1965, states, "is an *unidentified flying object*. Since the inception of the Nation's program of investigating UFOs, for which program the Air Force is responsible, only 7.7 percent of the reported cases have remained unidentified."

Close examination of this statement indicates that there are hundreds of cases in which the Air Force was forced to throw up its hands and say, "We don't know." Under normal conditions, this would be perfectly acceptable to the general public, because it doesn't know either. But the attitude which the Air Force assumes exaggerates its own shortcomings. What the Air Force further fails to disclose is the percentage of *expert, technical, or pilot* sightings which still remain unidentified, if indeed that is any mark of particular merit. Latest *Project Blue Book* figures on this are not available.

The Public Information booklet concludes: "As the

Service primarily responsible for aerospace defense, the Air Force will continue to apply the services of its highly qualified scientists and technicians to the task of continuous investigation of all reports of unusual aerial objects over the United States."

Here, of course, is the real bone of contention that NICAP has been chewing on for a good many years. The Air Force does, and there is no reason to doubt it, apply the service of its "highly qualified scientists and technicians" to the task of continuous investigation—but what does it give back to the public? The most generous and enthusiastic supporter of the Air Force would have to admit that it gives back absolutely nothing in the way of information. It has, in a very subtle manner, gone out of its way to insult hundreds, and perhaps thousands of respectable citizens.

I finally had to admit, as I drove from Stratham toward Hampton in the shadows of two B-52s which circled low in a landing pattern over my car at that moment, that I had lost my objectivity completely as far as the Air Force was concerned.

It was playing dirty pool in relation to the citizenry, regardless of what the truth concerning UFOs turns out to be.

CHAPTER **VIII**

MRS. Virginia Hale—the UPI stringer and reporter for the Haverhill, Massachusetts, *Gazette*—lived in a generous ranch house on a trim residential street in Hampton, not far from the ocean. Mrs. Hale was an experienced observer. She knew every conventional flight pattern of the nearby Portsmouth Air Base, as well as the commerical air lanes reserved for airliners on their way to Boston.

She took me immediately to her kitchen window, set above her spotless stainless-steel sink, and pointed out the portion of the sky in which she first saw the unknown craft. She had kept it in clear view over a five- to ten-minute period. She pointed to a soapish smear on a pane of her window.

"I put my finger in the dishwater the minute I saw this thing in the sky," she told me, "because I wanted to clearly mark the position where it was when it first came into view. The only thing I had handy to do this was the soapy water, and you can still see it there—faintly of course. But it's there."

It was. Enough of a mark to line up a fix on a certain portion of the sky, above the rooftops of her neighbors' homes, and out over the Atlantic a short distance. It was from this general portion of the sky, I recalled, that Sergeant Farnsworth had described the craft coming in over the two hysterical young men on the Hampton boulevard that early morning when they had whisked to the Coast Guard station to make their report. I was planning to explore that event also.

"I don't know the date I saw this," Mrs. Hale told me, in the kitchen, after she had poured a cup of black coffee. "I'd say two to three weeks ago. I was standing right here by the sink, about twenty-five after six in the evening. It was dusk, it wasn't quite dark, and there was still plenty of light. The reason it caught my eye was because it was bright and because it was going slow, very slow. Not at all like the path of the planes as they come over. So I automatically figured something is wrong. Then—it stopped dead over that house—"

She pointed to the roof of her neighbor's house, just out the kitchen window. "It was about three times the height of that chimney," she continued, "and it hovered there. Now you know four minutes is a long time, and that's why I hesitate to say that. But I'm pretty sure it was that long. Then I

106

marked the window with the smear from the dishwater, so I could remember where I lined up the spot."

We moved outside, as she reenacted what had happened. "At the moment the object stopped I came out here on the terrace. Now, I would estimate that it was out beyond the Coast Guard station which is right on the shore, just over these houses here. After it started up again, it moved much faster. The B-47s go further east and further north before they cut back. And when this thing cut back toward the southwest, coming directly back and losing altitude fast, coming in really fast, and coming, almost, I swear I thought it was coming right at me. Of course, to be frank, I was hoping it would land. And it cut over this house behind us here, and I knew I would lose sight of it. But also, it was going so fast I thought it was going to crash."

"Could you get a clear look at it at this time?"

"Well, at this point I could see from underneath, too. It was dome-shaped, and underneath, it was flat. Its altitude was now about twice the height of that chimney. By the time it was over here, I could see the bottom and the front of it plainly. And here I got a full view of the bottom and the back, and tail, if you want to call it that. It didn't really have a tail, maybe you'd call it a fin. Then I went into the house and looked out the front window."

"You could definitely rule out a plane?"

"Definitely," she said. "If you're around here any time at all, you'll notice the B-47s come by here on their landing pattern, and they go just about directly over this house. Then they head out to sea, to the east, turn slightly west, and come in by Rye and North Hampton. So I am familiar with all that. And, oh, there was one thing I forgot to tell you. Right after I saw this, there was a commercial plane moving on a steady flight pattern and I used that to contrast it with this thing, and to check the altitude and erratic movement of the object. I also checked the time, and called this girl, another correspondent, in Seabrook. I thought she might have seen

107

what I didn't see. Now what exactly did it look like? I'd say maybe it looked like a golf ball, sliced off more than half, and with another slice taken off where this fin was. As close as I can describe, it was very bright, not like any kind of light I can think of. I know I've seen something like the texture of this light, not a regular electric light. Matter of fact, the Puritron was the first thing I thought ot."

"What's a Puritron?"

"It's an ultraviolet light, an air purifier. I have one here, and I'll show you. The light was bluish-green, but more green and white than it was blue. It had very definite outlines, and that was what I wasn't quite sure of at first. It did have a little glow around it, but that could easily have been a reflection of what was coming from within."

"Can you tell me what portion the glow was coming from?"

"Well, more or less from around the rim, that's what I noticed when it was going north along the coastline. And it sort of spread up the top part of the dome."

"Was it a bright light? Anything like neon?"

"You're getting close," she said. "When I described it to my daughter—she's fourteen—she said you mean something that makes heat? But I would say more like one of these modern streetlights that glow so brightly. Except that it seemed more contained. It seemed to have more substance."

"Could you tell if the surface was metallic or not?" Mrs. Hale's description was so articulate, I wanted to get every possible detail.

"I could not say that it was," she said.

"Any portholes?"

"No, nothing like that."

"Jet trail?"

"No."

"Sound?"

"Absolutely none. None at all."

"When it stopped, you say it stopped still?"

"Absolutely."

"Did it wobble at all? Rock?"

"No."

"Absolutely stationary?"

"Yes. That's the thing that struck me. It hovered only in the sense that it remained suspended. I had heard of some of the other reports, and they had said that it rocked or wobbled."

"Did it behave aerodynamically like a plane at all?"

"Well, when it came back toward me, it was going too fast for anything that I know. That's for sure. And in the pattern that it was coming, none of the planes around here would use that pattern. Not even the local ones. When it was out in the east, I thought it might have been a reflection from the chute that the B-47s use just before they touch down on the runway."

This, I noted, showed an inclination to check out her own sighting against other possibilities. It helped support the accuracy of the testimony.

"About the shape again. Could you give me any more detail?"

"Well, if you turn a real deep, very deep saucer upside down, you do come close to it, if you break out a corner on it. If I could think of the right type of light I've seen and the right type of plastic to put it inside of, that's the impression I had."

"A glow from within that left a halo effect?"

"That's about it."

"And the size of it? Could you give any estimate of that?"

"It was big."

"If you saw a B-47, which you know so well, going over in a landing pattern, how would it compare?"

"If it were strictly on its landing pattern, I would say that a B-47 would be half as big."

"What about your own personal reaction? Were you scared at all?"

"No, I was strictly too much of a reporter. But I did have the feeling, oh goodness, don't tell me that thing knows I'm here. That's really how I felt."

Mrs. Hale showed me the Puritron, an air purifier which glowed inside with a bright, greenish-blue ultraviolet light. We also experimented with putting a light bulb inside a semi-opaque plastic pitcher, which, if the light had been brighter, she felt would have approximated the appearance of the strange light of the unknown object.

I had lunch that same day, with Conrad Quimby, editor and publisher of the Derry (N.H.) *News*, Ken Lord of the Amesbury (Mass.) *News*, and June Miller, of the Haverhill *Gazette*. We ate at the Cock & Kettle, a rambling early-American hostelry with an open fire, grog, and steaming New England food. They were as interested as I was in the progress of the research, but unfortunately I was not far enough into it to give them any real pattern of the scene as it unfolded.

Quimby, a penetrating and intelligent young man, had even arranged for the Sky-Lite Advertising plane to fly over Derry so that the townspeople could determine whether this was the source of many of the local UFO reports.

The results had been inconclusive, and Quimby himself believed that there had to be much more to the story. He had run into a very convincing account of a UFO incident in upper New Hampshire, and was extremely impressed by the intelligence and honesty of the person who had reported it. "The thing that gets me," Quimby said, "is that the source of so many of the UFO reports that we get, and continue to get, are *embarrassingly* intelligent. They can't be sloughed off."

He himself had talked personally to two officers at the air base, one of whom personally believed UFOs were interplanetary craft, and the other who simply said that he wasn't sure what the answer was. Neither officer, of course, could speak officially.

Ken Lord and June Miller expressed their puzzlement again. I reviewed briefly the interviews I had had, and none of the reporters at the lunch were familiar with any of the cases except the Exeter police incident. As reporters, they of course had their hands full with many kinds of stories to cover. None of them had had the time or the opportunity to probe really deeply into the mystery, and this again indicated to me that intensive research in a limited area might shed more light on he subject than had been generated before, in spite of the amassing of the worldwide and countrywide evidence. If the reports in a concentrated area turned out to show many similarities, perhaps some conclusions could be drawn about the possible behavior patterns of the objects, not readily evident from widely scattered reports.

There were already some reasonably intelligent speculations I was beginning to pick up. Ken Lord had noted some evidence from his investigations that sightings seemed to concentrate near atomic plants, although they certainly were not so limited. NICAP had previously speculated about this.

Some of the police at Exeter had said that the objects seemed to choose SAC air bases to concentrate on, but there was much evidence that UFOs were seen elsewhere. A half a dozen of the people I had talked to did bring up one point which I had not in any way checked out as yet: the tendency of the UFOs to be reported over and near electrical power lines, the high-tension wires which cut across the country to deliver power to communities. I made a note to follow this idea up further, because I had been told that several of the locations most popular for flurries of reports were at the base of these power transmission lines. And of course, if there were any truth at all to the theory that UFOs were operated on electromagnetic principles, there could be a physical affinity of the objects for the power lines, which set up an electromagnetic field around them.

Conversation at lunch was mostly speculative and theoretical. I mentioned that I was basing my research on two foundations: First, many reports of UFOs had been made in the Exeter area. This, at least, was uncontestable. Second, the problem then became one of trying to find out if they were *valid* reports.

Up to this moment, only the second day of the research, I could say that I believed the reports I had checked so far *seemed* valid. The people I had talked to, the policemen, the high school student, the taxi radio operator, the ham radio housewife, the UPI stringer—all of them had stood up under fairly intensive questioning.

Their competence to distinguish between fact and fiction seemed more than adequate and they could certainly distinguish between various types of known aircraft. A reporter, like a juryman, has to make appraisals and exercise judgment as to whether he can believe and accept the testimony he hears. On sober reflection, I could find far more reason to believe these people than not to believe them.

In general, the other reporters at the lunch table felt the same way about the people they had encountered in communities within a dozen or so miles of the Exeter focal point.

Quimby, who was familiar with my column in the *Saturday Review*, asked me if I would mind coming over to Derry the next morning and saying a few words about the UFO research to the English students in his wife's class at the high school there. The subject was very popular among the students. I told him I'd be glad to, emphasizing that I was a journalist, not a UFO expert. I arranged to see him in Derry the next morning.

Meanwhile, I discovered that I was late again, this time for my appointment with Mrs. Pearce, on the Exeter-Hampton line, and I had to leave the luncheon in ungentlemanly haste.

The Pearce home is in a miniature Levittown-type development on Warner Lane, a split-level house surrounded by well-kept shrubbery with the usual quota of bicycles on the lawn. I rang the bell, and waited a moment, until Lillian Pearce, a large, handsome woman with a shock of blond hair, opened the door and let me in. I was almost stunned by what I found inside. Sitting in a semicircle was a group of a half a dozen or so of the neighbors, waiting for me, and anxious to tell me of their many experiences with UFOs. Also in the room were several teen-agers, mostly of high school age, who were ready to volunteer their personal stories. I had been expecting a single description from Mrs. Pearce and instead, I was faced with a neighborhood meeting. It was helpful, of course, because I could compare several stories with the others I had heard. For the first time in the research, I got the feeling that the UFO incidents were far more widespread, more frequent, and more recent than I had suspected.

The room was so crowded, it was difficult to keep the meeting coherent. Mrs. Pearce dropped the opening bombshell by announcing that she had encountered a low-level UFO only the evening before, as she was driving her children and those of a neighbor home from a dance. I quickly scanned the other faces—both the housewives' and the teenagers'—to see if any disbelief was registered. None was. There were only nods of assent. I was a little numbed by this, but went on with the questioning.

"This was a real odd craft last night, I kid you not," Mrs. Pearce said.

"It was definitely not a plane?" I asked.

"Definitely. It was treetop level and had an enormous span."

"Where was it in relation to your house here?"

"It was up by the next farm," Mrs. Pearce said. "Just as you turn the corner here on Route 101-C."

We were on Warner Lane, just off this road, one of the main highways from Exeter to Hampton.

"About what time?" I asked.

"About ten," Mrs. Pearce said. "These kids here were with me."

I looked around the room, at the teen-agers. If there is any proclivity that can be said to be certain, it is that of teen-agers to debate or neutralize any parent who tries to exaggerate in front of them. I was watching carefully for this reaction. "All of you saw this?" I asked the teen-agers.

They replied, almost in concert, that they had.

"It was real wide," said Mrs. Pearce. "It went right over our car. I'm not kidding you. Mrs. Deyo—Doris here—was with us."

I looked in Mrs. Deyo's direction. She nodded in assent.

"How can you be sure it wasn't a plane?" I asked.

"Do planes make no noise?"

"This was silent?"

"This was absolutely silent. This was not a plane. All of us here know planes, day or night."

Mrs. Deyo spoke. "It looked like it had a lot of little, I call them portholes, except they were square. The light coming through them was solid white."

"There were other lights on it, but they were dim," said Mrs. Pearce. "Several colors, red, green, orange. All over. And the surface seemed to be metal. I don't mean that metal can change shape, I mean the lights all around it, they can change the pattern, and make it seem to change shape. I say the lights can camouflage it in the air, they definitely can. I believe that one hundred percent."

"This thing just dropped down toward the car," Mrs. Deyo said. "It dropped down, and it seemed to take on red lights, and it followed us. My son was in another car near us, and he saw it over our car."

"How close over the car?"

"I mean close," Mrs. Pearce said. "Not more than eight to ten feet above it. The lights seemed to circulate, rotate around it. Airplane lights don't do this. They flash on and off."

The atmosphere in the room was tense and electric. It was still hard to control the group, to keep everybody from speaking at once.

"Let's go back," I said to Mrs. Pearce, "to your first experience. And the objects you saw closest to you."

"The first experience I had was on July 29th, this past summer. This was before anybody had seen anything around here. That I know of, anyway. And I thought I was losing my head. I was with my daughter here, my fourteen-year-old, and we first thought it was an accident down the road. With these bright, flashing red lights. It seemed to be right on the road. When we got near it, I could see this wasn't an accident. It was a huge craft, right on a field beside the road. Then it suddenly took off. My daughter won't go out at night alone anymore, since then. I'm not a brilliant brain, but I'm not stupid, either. I can tell you what I saw. I don't care if anybody believes me or not. These things I saw. And nobody's ever going to try to convince me any way different."

Like the others in the room, Mrs. Pearce was passionate in her testimony. It was a little difficult to keep her on the track, but she was a basically intelligent woman, and I encouraged her to go on.

"It's just like I told the colonel at the air base: You show me the craft, I said. He said he couldn't show me the craft, the Air Force had no such thing. I said, Then what is it? He said, It's a UFO. All right, I was told that over the phone, when I called the base after this July incident. I wasn't even going to call them. I told one of my friends that they'll think I'm nuts. According to the officers, none of them have seen these things. When the major and the colonel came down, we looked at what appeared to be a star, except that it was blinking red, green and white. It didn't appear to be a star to the major, but he didn't know what it was. The colonel did see two very puzzling red things in the sky, and he had some very, very poor excuses for it. Very poor, as far as I'm concerned."

115

"Was this the night when they came down to Route 88?" I asked. "When they experimented with the strobe lights?"

"Oh, the strobe lights. That *is* funny. The colonel sent the major and a lieutenant back to the air base to have the strobe lights turned on. This was after Doris and I had gone up to the air base to talk with them. We were all down on Route 88. While we were waiting to see what would happen, we were talking, and a strange object went across the sky, not low, the way the ones which have scared us, but high. I asked him, What do you call that thing there? He said, Well, that's an airplane. I said, Oh is it, well how come it doesn't make any noise? Well, it's too far away, he said. I said, No it isn't, Colonel, and there were about fifteen or twenty cars there by the field piled up. He asked me why they were there and I told him. Then I said, What kind of plane is it, are you going to tell me it's a jet? He said, No, it isn't. Well, what is it? I said. Then he sort of, you know, couldn't quite name it. Then he came up with a name, I can't even remember it. I said, I'm sorry, I don't agree with you, Colonel. I didn't. So then another object started over the road, right down on Route 88, right across the road. By the Applecrest Orchard. So the other one starts over, and I said, Okay, what's that? Oh —that's a plane. I said, Oh, you think it is. Okay. So one guy there in the crowd had binoculars, I didn't have any at this time, I went out and bought some later. I asked if he'd let me use them, and he did. The colonel looked through them and his face dropped. It did, I could tell. Now what is *that?* I said. Well, he says, you know there are passenger planes that come into Boston along here. I said, Oh, you mean they stop in the orchard to have apples? That's pretty stupid. I said, I'm sorry, I don't agree with you. No, I mean it, I don't care what I say. Nobody's going to tell me I can't see something. So, anyway, one woman was standing in the background, she said, I'll tell you something, I've seen those things and they're *not* airplanes. She said, There's no noise to them.

116

She said, I never saw a plane look like that. I believe that woman down there, she said, meaning me."

I had to admit that I was spellbound by Mrs. Pearce's vivid recollection of the scene. She continued.

"Now he's a colonel in the Air Force, he should have much more intelligence than that. So, anyway, finally he decided he had to leave. I said, Oh, Colonel, what about the strobe lights? You were trying to tell us that we were having hallucinations or seeing reflections from the air base runway. By this time, the major had returned and admitted that the lights had been turned on and off on a regular pattern, and we had seen nothing unusual at all while they were doing this."

Mrs. Pearce took a deep breath. "All I can say is that if they're from another planet, the Air Force being the way it is, I hope they're friendly people."

"All right," I said. "Let's get back to the closest sighting you made."

"This is the one that went right over my car, and I hung out the window trying to get a picture of it. And the Air Force wanted the negative. Unfortunately, it didn't come out. I would say it was as big around as a jet. The front was rounded. And it had sort of fins in the back, flat out, not upright. There was a dome shape to the top and it looked sort of like hammered metal. It had smaller lights all over it, both sides, the bottom and the top. It had larger red lights surrounding the edge of it. They were of different colors on the other parts. As I mentioned, I say it can change shape, not the metal, but the light patterns. The lights go on and off all over it. And it can glow all over. And the underneath part, like the old dirigibles, there was what I call little square windows across, square compartments on the bottom of this thing."

"How did it maneuver?"

"The thing was ahead of me. It would play tag with me,

whatever you want to call it. It went ahead of me, with red, orange and white lights on at that moment. All right, the thing turned, and I stopped my car there, I had the motor running and the lights on dim, but I had stopped. Doris Deyo was on the road, I was hanging out this side of the car, out the window with a camera. That thing turned around and came directly, like this, right over the top of my car. Now there was no noise, no rush of air. I know that sounds foolish, but there wasn't. The first thing I saw then was like flood-lights hitting the street, right into the middle of the street. But I felt no heat."

I encouraged her to go on.

"I think it's pretty odd," Mrs. Pearce continued, "that there's a craft flying around, that no one around the country seems to know what's going on. It's very odd. It's odd the Government seems to know nothing about it, or if they do, they won't tell you. I asked the Air Force men if it's some-thing Russia has got, or Red China's got, or a secret of your own. The only answer I got from the colonel is that they're UFOs. They're there. They're still around, they're not gone."

I turned to another neighbor. "Tell me what you've seen."

"Well," she said, "it was the first time I've seen one. This was last night, as we were driving on the highway, Route 101-C. All of a sudden it came right across the road, it dipped right in front of the car. It had lights, we only saw two lights on this one, the width of a wingspread. They were white, or yellow. There weren't any red lights on it. It dipped, it came over the car, and went up in the sky. We lost it, it just dimin-ished. As it goes up, it diminishes and they go so high up they seem to become stars. But not really stars, because they come down, and then up again. This one went down in the road almost, and then up over the trees. I believe they land."

Another neighbor spoke. "It's fascinating and it's weird. And none of these things have any sound to them at all."

Mrs. Pearce spoke up again. "The real close ones I've seen

have been four or five feet above the ground, if not on the ground. They hover right in the fields. That's what these people up at the air base are so foolish about. I mean it's stupid. I don't know why someone can't catch one of these things or get within distance of it."

A Mrs. Edmund Liscomb, who lived a few houses up Warner Lane from the Pearces' spoke. "The one I saw last night was a big, orange ball. Nothing but orange."

"I've seen an Air Force plane chasing one," a teen-aged girl said. "It was before dark, the sun had just barely gone down, about seven o'clock. And several people saw it, because I was over in North Hampton. It was reported by several others that day. It was light enough so that you could make out the jet plane clearly and it was tearing across the sky. Just ahead of it, and up a little bit from the plane, was this orangish-red ball, like a red ball of fire. And they were both tearing across the sky. And the plane couldn't get anywhere near it."

"They seem to send planes out after these things all the time," Mrs. Pearce added. "On the 17th of September—I made a note of it, because I've now begun to keep track of these things—we were going up to Exeter. This thing with red, green and white lights on it stopped over a house. We watched it for two or three minutes, and then a jet plane came. And when it did, every single light on the object went out. The plane went by, and the lights came on again. The plane came back, and the lights went out. Then the object went off, and the plane remained there circling and recircling the spot. And the air base tells you nothing. That's why I get sick of telling them about it."

The atmosphere in the living room had simmered down a little now, and I was anxious to turn my attention to the younger people. I spoke first with Mrs. Pearce's thirteen-year-old daughter Sharon. She was an attractive youngster, a little nervous under the questioning.

"Can you tell me what you saw, and when?" I asked.

"Well," she said. "This was in July—the one my mother mentioned to you."

"That's all right," I said. "I want to hear what it looked like to you."

"We went over to Mrs. Shaw's house, and we were coming home about eleven-thirty. And we saw these bright lights in the field. And my mother thought it was a wreck, so she started down the side of the road. We didn't know what it was, and as we got close to it, we stopped and we were sitting there for a couple of minutes. And we heard no sound at all. We just didn't know what it was. It was sitting just above the road, and it was hovering."

"How high from the ground was it hovering?"

"It wasn't over the trees."

"And about how big did it appear?"

"About as big around as a car, maybe bigger."

"As big around as a car. And could you make out the shape?"

"The lights were so bright, it was hard. But I think it was kind of oval-shaped."

"What were the lights like?"

"They were steady, they weren't blinking."

"Then what happened?"

"Well, we drove away. My mother told me to keep watching out back."

"How far were you from it when you watched it hover?"

Sharon looked out the window, pointed to a car about thirty feet away. "About from here to that car," she said.

"Could you give me a better idea as to the shape?"

"We couldn't see too well. But the top was molded, like a dome."

"It was just hovering below the treetops, over the road or over the field?"

"Over the field."

"And you and your mother drove away?"

"Yes, 'cause it looked like it was coming toward us. So we took off fast. We were really scared."

I was watching Sharon closely during the interview. There was no question at all that she was telling the truth as she saw it. What impressed me was that the people here in this modern development, with its ordinary streets, its tidy lawns, its typification of suburbia, reported so convincingly a phenomenon which, if it turned out to be true, would signal a whole new era of history. Their spontaneous reactions indicated that there was no hoax here, no collusion, no attempt to fictionalize their stories. Mrs. Pearce, the most verbal, the natural leader of the group, was vociferous and strong. She had, according to both her own and Patrolman Novak's testimony, stood toe to toe with the Air Force colonel and major, demonstrating a firm conviction.

The frequency of the reported sightings was also startling. I had come up to Exeter expecting to explore a single incident. Now it seemed to have developed into a constant, steady flow, not just from the group on Warner Lane, but in scattered places throughout the area. The press and even NICAP had not had a chance to observe and evaluate this type of single-community reaction extensively.

My talk with the Pearce neighbors and the teen-agers continued for over an hour. Reports on Route 88, on 101-C near some high-power transmission lines were the most frequent, but some of them had seen the unknown objects along Drinkwater Road, and in Kingston near the sighting by the Exeter police officers. I kept questioning their capacity to distinguish whatever objects they saw from ordinary planes, military or commercial. They insisted that regular planes continually passed over, day and night, and that the objects they were reporting had nothing to do with them.

"How would you feel," Mrs. Pearce said, "if you had a daughter who wouldn't go out the door at night because of these things?"

I figured that mass hysteria here could not be discounted,

121

that it had to be seriously considered as part of this cluster of sightings. In the meanwhile, I was going to reserve judgment. When Mrs. Pearce and Mrs. Deyo asked me if I wanted to look over the locations they had described, later on in the evening, I said that I would. I had to admit I felt a little odd; this would be the first time I had ever gone UFO hunting, and I made a mental note to check Bob Kimball to see if he would come along. If by the remotest chance we did see anything, I would want to have a solid man like Kimball around, who, in addition to being a newsreel cameraman, was a fully licensed pilot, familiar with all types of running lights on airplanes.

I told Kimball about the interviews I had had that day, and welcomed the chance to analyze them with someone who had a technical and journalistic attitude. As a newsreel man, Kimball had covered every kind of story, and had a healthy show-me attitude. The contrast was welcome after the charged atmosphere of the Pearce meeting.

I played him some of the Pearce interview tapes on the battery tape recorder.

"This thing gets crazier every day," he said. "And just to show you I'm a complete nut, I'm going to bring my Filmo tonight and keep it on hand."

We picked up Mrs. Pearce and Mrs. Deyo at 7:30, and drove to several spots where she had said she sighted the objects. The first was along 101-C, about two or three miles west of Hampton. It was at the bottom of a moderately long hill, at the junction of the Exeter and Hampton Electric Company power lines. They crossed Route 101-C at right angles, cutting a wide swath through the woods on either side of the road.

"We've often seen them come along these lines," said Mrs. Pearce. "And right here by the poles, one of these crafts came right down over my car, dropped down four or five feet off the ground. You could see a metal surface, and the orange, red and white lights on it. Right by that tree there."

We waited for several minutes, but as we expected, nothing happened. I was interested, though, to note the location by the power lines, for it seemed to suggest that one of the theories put forward by the Exeter police might have some substance. But there were so many reports and theories that it was hard even to guess at anything. The variations in description of the UFOs could result not only from the apparent changing light patterns on the objects, but also from the tendency of all people who witness anything to report subjectively on what they see, projecting their own personalities and past experiences into the descriptions. The power-line theory was at least objective: either they were, or weren't, seen frequently in the vicinity of power lines, and this could only be examined in the light of many interviews.

We covered two or three locations on Route 88 that both Mrs. Pearce and Mrs. Deyo described as places where they had seen the objects. When we reached the field where the colonel and the major had been confronted by Mrs. Pearce's wrath, we got out of the car to see if any strobe lights were visible from the runway of the air base, over ten miles away, and to study the landing- and running-light patterns of planes which might be over the area. Both Kimball and I wanted to do this to examine with Mrs. Pearce and Mrs. Deyo the possibility of mistaken identity of planes.

Over a 15-minute period, we saw the running lights of four planes, which Kimball pointed out would be making a landing pattern for the air base. Both Mrs. Pearce and Mrs. Deyo immediately recognized them as running lights on planes, and didn't, as I had half expected, attempt to convert them into UFOs. This was a strong point in their favor, and helpful in making a better assessment of the amazing testimony given me that afternoon.

The night was dark, moonless, with a very high overcast.

No stars were visible, of course, so that the winking running lights of the planes stood out clearly against the gray void above.

Just as we were getting ready to get back in the car, Kimball noticed the running lights of a smaller plane, moving at a considerably faster speed than the lumbering B-47s and B-52s coming up from the northwesterly horizon from the vicinity of the Air Force base.

"That boy is really moving," Kimball said. "If he's anywhere near the landing pattern of the field, he's breaking speed limits at that altitude."

The plane was coming toward us, moving southeast at a rapid clip. Its running lights were plainly visible, in conventional aircraft pattern. It took perhaps 20 seconds for it to get almost abeam of us, and the roar of its jet engine could now be heard. Its altitude seemed to be about 6,000 to 8,000 feet, according to Kimball. We were both watching it rather intently because its pattern was entirely different from the other planes we had observed.

Just before it drew abeam of our position, Kimball nudged me. "What the hell is that?" he said.

I looked and saw a reddish-orange disk, about one-fifth the size of a full moon. It was about three or four plane lengths in front of the jet, which appeared to be a fighter. The plane was moving as if in hot pursuit. The disk was perfectly round, dull orange more than red. It was luminous, glowing, incandescent. The plane was not closing the distance between it and the object. We followed both the plane and the object for 18 or 20 seconds until they disappeared below the southeasterly horizon.

If Mrs. Pearce or Mrs. Deyo were saying anything, I didn't hear them because Kimball and I kept up a running commentary with each other on what we were seeing as the plane moved from abeam of us until it went over the horizon.

"Check me," Kimball was saying. "What exactly do you see?"

"An orange disk," I told him. "Immediately in front of the running lights of an apparent jet fighter."

"A little to the port of it, too, wouldn't you say?" Kimball asked.

"Maybe. Not much to port."

"Do you see any running lights on the disk?" he said.

"No. Nothing but the orange glow."

"Right," said Kimball.

In almost precisely the time in which we carried on this conversation, both the plane and the object had disappeared. The whole thing happened so fast, that I'm not sure how I reacted. I said to Kimball, "Well, that sure as hell is the most interesting thing I've seen."

Mrs. Pearce, however, seemed to shrug it off. "That was nothing," she said. "Wait until you see one close up."

Driving back to Exeter with Kimball, we rehashed what we saw, so that we would neither minimize nor exaggerate it. It had happened so fast that Kimball couldn't have taken a film of it, even if he hadn't left his Filmo on the front seat of the car. Only special lenses and a tripod would have made it possible to get even some kind of a light smear. But we had seen something which was totally without logical explanation, and there was no question that we agreed on what we saw.

"What I'm trying to figure out," Kimball said as we drove back, "is not *what* we saw, because we saw it, there's no mistake about that. What I'm trying to do is to find any possible logical and familiar explanation for it. Let's set up some possible things. They were both going at about the same speed. I've been thinking, if two jet fighters were flying in formation, it could be that. And the running lights on the forward plane might have gone out, and all we could see was the afterburner of the first plane. But that's not logical, either. An afterburner would be a streak, with some blue in it. Not an orange disk. If two jet fighters were flying in formation, and the running lights on the forward plane conked out, it would immediately drop behind the other plane and let it take the lead, cut the speed, and get the hell into the nearest airport. But the jet we saw was moving under a wide-open throttle. Not full power, but it had a lot of power on. The orange disk was really too clearly defined, too round, to be the glow of an afterburner. Frankly, I don't know what the hell the answer is. I'm just trying to consider everything possible."

"You're the pilot," I said. "I'm leaving it up to you to come up with the answer."

"Well," said Kimball, "I don't have one."

Knowing that we would get no information from the Air Force, we saw no reason to report it.

Patrolman Eugene Bertrand's modest home on Pickpocket Lane is kept cheerful and sprightly by his wife, Dorothy, and I arrived there that night of October 21 shortly after 9:30. I was still a little shaken by the experience with Kimball, still perplexed, and a little annoyed that as long as we were going to have the privilege of seeing a UFO, why couldn't we have seen one close and clear?

I told Bertrand and his wife about the incident, and then turned to Mrs. Bertrand to fill in more details about what had taken place on the morning of September 3.

"When did you first see Gene after this happened?" I asked.

"The next morning when he came home from work."

"About what time was that?"

"Oh, I guess about 8:30," she said.

"What did you think about it?"

She smiled. "I didn't believe it. Not until after the reports came in."

"Can you recall anything more?" I asked Gene. "Anything you haven't told me already?"

"Well," said Bertrand, "I keep going over this in my mind

126

all the time. You don't get over an experience like this very quickly. I'm trying to describe the lighting on the thing, because that was what made it so eerie. Like a neon sign, maybe, but a neon sign won't light up everything around it the way this did. A headlight will give off light, like a beam. But this is not the way it was. This was a glow, a brilliant glow. The trees turned red, the field turned red, everything turned red. Gave off a real spooky feeling. All the way over from the police station—it's a four-mile ride—Muscarello kept telling me and telling me what a thing this was. And of course, I was just telling myself this is fantastic, he was just imagining this. That's when I was sure he had seen a helicopter."

"How about what happened earlier that evening? Could you reconstruct it?"

"Well, I drove my car down to the station that night, it's a 1961 Chevrolet, and I went into the station and read the blotter to see what had to be done, to catch up on the news. See what cars to look for, what was stolen, general information. The lieutenant was on duty that night—Lieutenant Cottrell. I was with this fellow Dickinson from twelve-thirty A.M. until two A.M. He was a new man, and I was helping him get used to the routine. We were cruising out along the bypass, and I see this red and white station wagon parked on the side. Dickinson was driving, and I'm sitting in the passenger seat. So I told him to hold it a minute, you always check cars parked on the bypass, it's sort of like Route 95. It goes from Manchester to the beach at Hampton, or rather it hooks right up with the superhighway going to the beach. And I realize that a woman could be stranded out there quite awhile, so I had Dickinson pull over, right alongside of her, and she had her window rolled down, so I rolled my window down and said, Can I help you, madam? That's when she told me that she had been driving all the way from Epping with this flying object playing tricks over her car. So I turned to Dickinson and he turned to me, like she's a kook or something. We pulled over and waited for awhile, but we didn't see anything, and she was okay. So we left, and I didn't think any more about it until Scratch Toland called me into the station about the Muscarello kid. Then the two things sort of made sense, together."

Back at the police station, Lieutenant Cottrell was just getting ready to turn over the desk to Scratch Toland. It was nearly midnight, and it had been another exhausting day. I had not yet talked with Cottrell except over the phone at the time I was writing the column, and still wanted to hear whatever additional facts and background he could contribute. Like everyone else on the force, he was puzzled and curious about the wave of sightings, hoping that some light might be shed on the mystery.

"I was working for three weeks while the chief was on vacation," he said. "And of course this came right during this period. I frankly wish it had been some other time, myself. I won't say how many reports I had come in, but it seemed three or four times a day, I'd be getting calls from the girl in the office to come in because somebody wanted to see me. Just about every case it was reporters, newscasters, and so forth. And we had calls from people, of course, reporting what they saw. The only thing we could tell anybody was that the office did report seeing this UFO, and we had forwarded the information to the officials at the Pease Air Base."

"What happened the day of the big incident?"

"The first thing I heard about it was when I came on duty here in the morning, and read the report on it. I got in touch right away with the officials at the air base, because that's what we're expected to do. And they didn't take long to come over. They were here shortly after noon. They went with both Bertrand and Hunt to the location."

"What was their attitude? Did they take it seriously?"

"They were very serious. They went out right away on it, but they never gave us any further report. And the problem is this: If no one knows what it is, what can they do about it? I really believe something exists, now. Two police officers, together, leave written report of it. Nobody has ever been hurt by it. It hasn't attempted to do that. I wouldn't think it was coming from a nation that was out to get you. And where does it go in the daytime?"

"Well," I said, "I've got two reports of people seeing it in the daytime. One of them, at dusk."

"I've often wondered about that. But what strikes me funny in talking to Gene and Dave is the maneuverability of the thing. It defies all the aerodynamic laws. It floats, soars, goes off in any direction, turns at right angles. As I told you over the phone, if I didn't believe these guys, I'd put them in a room with some blocks to play with. And I think it would be a help if the Air Force did tell us more about this. Simply tell you enough so that people wouldn't be scared to death of it. I suppose there are people who might go along the high-way, and be exposed to something of this nature, and have a heart seizure. If the Air Force would just simply *tell* some-body, it is nothing that is going to hurt them, just something we're experimenting with. That would quiet the whole thing down. I think that is all that would be necessary, we wouldn't be giving away any secrets. I really and truly wish someone would come out and say this will not hurt anybody, we *do* know what it is, but at this time, we can't say. Take the offi-cers that night on Route 150. Both of them, we know, are in top physical shape. But how do you know for sure? I think some day the whole story will be told. I'm a firm believer there's a reasonable explanation for everything. I'm a firm believer in that. Now if there is something that the Almighty knows about that we don't know about yet, then we can all have our own ideas. But I think there will be a reasonable explanation for it."

The night shift was coming on duty, squeezing by the desk to go into the locker room for their revolvers, billy jacks, and other paraphernalia. Another night was beginning, with the quiet patrolling and routine checks going on while the town slept.

Back at the Exeter Inn, I got ready for bed and turned on a few portions of the tapes from the day. The voices were sharp, strong and convincing.

I listened until I got sleepy, then snapped off the tape recorder. I wished that I could be as confident as the lieutenant that there was a reasonable explanation for everything concerned with the case.

CHAPTER IX

JUST before leaving for Derry on the morning of Friday, October 22, to see Conrad Quimby, the editor and publisher, I discovered that another friend lived in Exeter. I had not seen George Carr in years, and he had recently moved to Exeter from Massachusetts. A methodical man, with an engineering mind, I welcomed the chance to talk with him about the strange and bizarre UFO mystery, and arranged to drop by his house just outside Exeter that evening. The necessity of checkpoints like this became more apparent as the research progressed. The passion which the observers of UFOs brought into their accounts had a tendency to be overpersuasive. With Kimball and now Carr I felt I had two important controls on the situation, people in whom I had confidence, whom I had known before, and neither of whom was being buffeted by the astonishing collection of stories I was gathering.

Quimby, in his newspaper office in Derry, was another

good foil against drawing conclusions too quickly from the fast-accumulating tapes I was collecting. He was a sharp and penetrating man, clinical but open-minded. He was carrying on a strong campaign for tolerance and liberalism in opposition to a competing arch-conservative paper.

News in Derry is usually gentle, as in any country area. A Kiwanis apple sale, a Harvest Ball, a PTA New England boiled dinner affair, a Cub pack meeting, or a golfer's banquet. On the editorial page, however, editor Quimby was lashing out strongly against the John Birch society and other threatening extremist groups.

Interest in UFOs was running so high in the town, he explained, that his wife's English class at the high school would probably be profoundly attentive. I again emphasized that I was anything but an expert, but that I'd probably use the talk as a device for getting the kids interested in how to dig for a story to make their themes and reports more interesting. He and Mrs. Quimby both agreed this would be a good idea.

It was the first time I had ever spoken to a high school class, and I must admit that it made me nervous. Youngsters of this age are alert these days; they refuse to take anything for granted, and they are highly sensitive to anything phony. When I started sliding off the UFO story, and into ways and means to make theme-writing fun, I think they detected my plan right away, for their interest seemed to lag. However, I stuck doggedly to it, partly because I believe the agony of theme-writing results from the failure of students to play reporter; and partly because I simply had no conclusion to state concerning the UFO story, and hated to admit it.

I was, however, struck by their interest in the subject. Why were they so intense about it? Was it something in the air, something which foreshadowed the whole trend of the Space Age? For this group had been growing up at a time when it was no longer absurd to think of astronauts, when spacemen were not ridiculous comic-strip characters in Buck

Rogers suits. They were real; they were here. And if the Earth People could do it, they seemed to reason, why shouldn't some other cosmic inhabitants do the same?

Some weeks later, Mrs. Quimby sent me some of the themes which her students had written about the UFO mystery. I was interested in what the papers revealed, in view of the unproven theory that the Government was paternalistically shielding the population from the idea that UFOs were interplanetary, and likely to create panic.

"If ever a UFO pilot were to make himself known," wrote one young lady in the class, "I don't think I'd be scared of him. Of all the UFO sightings that have been made, none of them has tried to harm us. They are probably too intelligent for war.

"We have been making our way into outer space, so it is very possible that they come from another planet, and want to explore earth. . . . Fear of war is very great, and it wouldn't take much to scare the people into thinking that men from outer space were going to invade our world, but yet there has been so much talk about it and there have been so many sightings that people have been gradually getting used to the idea. I feel as if I wouldn't be scared."

Other students in the class echoed her thoughts. "I think if I saw a UFO land, I would be surprised but I don't think it would scare me at all," wrote a boy in the class.

"If I saw a UFO," wrote another boy, "I would observe it as long as possible. If it landed, I would hurry as fast as I could to the spot where it came down. I don't think I would be afraid. . . . If I had a chance to be taken away by a spaceship, I think I would go."

Others indicated that they would "like the idea," or be both "scared and curious"; only a few admitted they would be frightened. The other interesting attitude emerging was that the group, in general, seemed to take the existence of UFOs as a foregone conclusion. The younger generation, it seemed, was moving in this direction faster than the adult population.

It was nearly noon when I returned to the center of Derry, stopping at the village drugstore for a bite of lunch. I had several leads that I could follow that afternoon, but had not yet decided which to try. The thought did occur to me that it might be interesting to try random sampling, without specific police leads. If there were anything to the reports that the area was so rife with UFO sightings, a random check might substantiate this theory. If it failed to uncover many leads, then the theory might be refuted. I asked the girl behind the counter if she knew of anyone who had seen an Unidentified Flying Object, and she looked at me rather oddly, saying she would talk to me in a few moments. Meanwhile, she served me an egg-salad sandwich and a chocolate *frapp*, as they called milk shakes there in Derry, and I waited for her to come back to my part of the counter.

She returned in several minutes, apologetic. "My boss was right near me when you asked that question. And he must think I'm nuts. I've seen one myself, I have lots of friends who have seen them, and none of them look anything like this crazy advertising sign they flew over here. My boss can laugh all he wants, but I know what I saw and so do my friends."

She went on to what was now becoming a common description: a dome-shaped saucer which glowed red, with brilliant white rounded sides. She suggested that I explore thoroughly in Fremont, about halfway between Derry and Exeter, because she had heard many reports from that neighborhood. "I get so *mad*," she said, "when people laugh at me. Don't they think we have enough brains to know the difference between a weird thing like these objects are, and an airplane of any kind, whether it's got a sign on it or not?"

I thanked her for her information, left a generous tip, and

made my way toward Fremont. On the way over, I tried to decide just how much weight should be given to the *intensity* of the testimony I was picking up. It is hard to fake sincerity and intensity, and so far, none of the people I had interviewed had shown any sign of doing this. Their marks for the "Intensity-Sincerity Quotient" would be A-plus. A certain number, on the other hand, might be said to be lacking in the capacity to document clearly what they saw. I was again vacillating about what to believe, or how much to believe.

I came into Fremont sooner than I had expected. It was a fresh and unspoiled New Hampshire town, its houses suggesting that it had changed little since the Revolution. There was a post office, a white-steepled church, a town hall, with the clean lines of pure Early-Americana. I was told that I could find Chief of Police Bolduc at the lumber mill, where he worked during the day.

I pulled up beside a long shed where logs were being rolled in and prepared for milling. A worker disappeared into the shed and returned with the Chief, a glowing, hearty New Hampshirite with a broad smile, carrying a lethal-looking pike designed to roll and handle the logs at the mill. He came at me pointing the instrument like a bayonet, then winked and asked me what I wanted.

"Well," he said, "perhaps you could find out a lot around here—and perhaps you can't. You never can tell, can you?" He winked again, and waited for me to do the pumping. I was interested, I told him, in recent sightings, and low-level ones, not fleeting glimpses.

"That's a pretty tough assignment, wouldn't you agree?" he said. I agreed that it was. In spite of the fact that it was difficult to get information out of him, he was at once infectiously humorous and likable. "I'd suggest you take a run down the road a piece here and talk to the folks at Heselton's Garage. They'll keep your feet on the ground because they don't seem to go along with the idea at all. You're going to need that kind of outlook to kind of keep your sanity after you hear what some of the other folks in town might have to say. Then after you talk to the garage, you'd better go see my wife. She might have some interesting information for you."

I thanked him and drove down to the garage, where Mr. Heselton, a beefy and direct gentleman, was sitting in the small, overheated office eating a sandwich.

"You want to know what I feel?" he said. "I don't believe it. I just don't believe it. Oh, I know you're going to hear a lot of talk, and you're going to get all sorts of stories. Now take this Exeter police case. This UFO was spotted on a Thursday night or early Friday morning, September third, just prior to Labor Day. This woman claims she was followed from Epping to the Exeter line, along Route 101. This object followed her, I mean. Now I went out the following Tuesday night, on 101, just parked there, around midnight. And at no one time was there a greater span of time than three minutes that a car did not pass. Tell me, why didn't another car observe this thing if she was followed all the way to Exeter? This, mind you, is just before a holiday weekend, and I checked the highway on a Tuesday night after the holiday."

"At what time?" I asked him. I was making it a point to ask repetitive questions through all these interviews, as accuracy checks.

"The same time she did, about," he said.

"About one-thirty in the morning?"

"Whatever time she saw it. I forget, exactly. I think I checked it from something like quarter past twelve to quarter past one, something like that. And I observed absolutely nothing. There was no span of time, more than three minutes, that a car did not pass."

Mr. Heselton, I could see, was a vehement Devil's Advocate. "What have you heard around this area?" I asked.

"A lot of talk, a lot of talk," he said.

"Anybody special reported anything?"

"Well," he said with the greatest reluctance. "Bessie. Bessie's Lunch down the road here. All these stories seem to center around there. It's close to the place that everybody seems to see these things. Down by the power line, where it crosses Route 107. There're a lot of people who drop into the diner who say they have seen these things. *I* haven't, you understand. I know of several occasions, in fact I was there, when someone said 'There it is, there it is!' And it was a jet or a tower. On Route 121, there's a relay station for some outfit in Boston with a red blinker and they would see this."

The mention of the power lines again drew me up sharply. Fremont was a good 15 miles away from Exeter, and I felt there was probably little communication between the communities in the way of comparing notes about the electric power-line theory. Perhaps I was reaching one common denominator in connection with the erratic behavior of this puzzling phenomenon. It was still too early to tell, however.

"Any reliable people reporting them?"

"What these people say, who's to say what's reliable? There's a fellow, a friend of mine, called me the other night, his car was over here being repaired. He told me about this sighting that he had made, and he became fairly indignant when I sort of doubted him. He firmly believed that he saw something. Claimed he very definitely saw something."

"What did he describe?"

"I'm not going to describe what he saw, because I didn't see it myself. And I don't think it's rightly good to give you his name without his permission. I will say that he said he never would have seen anything if his electric power saw hadn't stalled. But the damn power saw stalled, and he looked up and there it was. So he watched it for quite awhile. Apparently, right about that time, a neighbor called to tell him to look. He was seeing the same thing."

"What about some of the other stories you've heard around Bessie's Lunch?"

"Well, as I said, there's a power line down there, see. Few hundred yards below it. and maybe some nights, there might be fifty cars there. And out of the fifty, there might have been fifteen to twenty people who see it. This is because some of 'em get sick of waiting, and might not stay long enough to see it. But there was a man and woman down there, in their forties, I'd say, and they come in here and told me. They can't describe it. He said it was an object flying along in this fashion with a bright light on it, you couldn't hear a sound from it. And still it was there quite close to him." Like many others, Mr. Heselton was not quite so skeptical as he appeared to be at first.

"Just the other night, some other people saw it along another section of the power lines. And it sounded like the same thing, with a bright light, and then an orange and a red one. And it was seen again, near the same place, only a couple of nights ago. It moved over near the trees, they said, and it goes down low behind the trees and goes up again. And when they see it, they say that you see it for a few seconds, and it's gone. Someone I know stayed there for weeks, down by the power lines, just to catch a glimpse of it. But how can you describe it if you don't see it yourself?"

Although Mr. Heselton had warmed up considerably, I was anxious to see what I could find out directly from Bessie's Lunch. Mr. Heselton warned me that if I "passed the power lines, I had gone too far."

The power lines again. I drove through the village, which looked as if it were out of a Currier & Ives print, and discovered Bessie's Lunch in a lonely wooded clearing not far out of the village. It was a rustic diner, catering apparently to passing truck drivers, tourists, and local residents as well. It was homespun and friendly in atmosphere, with barely enough room behind the long row of stools to stand. A tall,

137

angular Yankee behind the counter turned out to be Mr. Healey, husband of Bessie, in whose honor the diner was named.

Mr. Healey was friendly, but reserved. I ordered a cup of black coffee, and finally confessed that I was on the track of UFO reports, and perhaps he could help me.

"Understand you got several reports down here about them. Is that right?" I asked.

"Where'd you learn that nonsense?" he said.

"Couple of people up in the village," I said.

"You hear all kinds of stories these days, you know," he said, and continued cutting some pie and cleaning up the counter. A couple of truck drivers came in, ordering apple pie and coffee.

Finally, I tried again. "Had any recent reports near here?"

"All depends," he said, "what you mean by reports."

"Well," I said, "people who seem to be sane enough, who might have seen some of these unidentified flying objects and might have talked to you about them."

I noticed that he was eyeing my tape recorder, slung over my shoulder in a tan leather case. "Watch'ya got there, a camera?" he said.

"No, it's a tape recorder. I'm trying to get all the information I can on these things. Good and bad."

"You from Boston?" he asked.

"Nope. New York."

"How do you get people to talk for one of those things? Don't they freeze up?"

"Not really," I said. "I'm taping our conversation right now." I figured the only thing for me to do was to put my cards on the table. Another man came in, sat two stools down from me, ordered coffee.

I seemed to be getting nowhere with Mr. Healey, so I turned to the customer, apparently a resident judging by his friendly greeting to Mr. Healey.

138

"I was just asking Mr. Healey about any reports of Unidentified Flying Objects," I said to him.

"What'd he tell you?" asked the newcomer.

"Nothing, yet," I said.

The newcomer smiled at Healey. "For gosh sakes, why don't you tell him about what Bessie saw?" he said.

Mr. Healey shrugged. "I don't want to put words into Bessie's mouth."

"Is she here?" I asked.

"Nope. But she will be soon."

"I better have another cup of coffee, then," I said.

Mr. Healey drew another. "We get so many of these reports," he said, "that I don't know what to make of them. That's why I'd rather have Bessie tell you herself."

Mr. Healey liked to warm up to a subject slowly. The newcomer, a Jim Burleigh, had also heard a good many reports.

"Ran into one couple here," said Mr. Healey, "who saw it pretty close. Right along the power lines down here. They all seem to describe it pretty much the same, that's what gets me. No matter what place they see them in. If the people were making it up, I don't think they'd come in with the same descriptions. This couple who come in from South Hampton or Hampton, I don't know which one it was. I've known the father ever since I was a kid, and I know he wouldn't lie about it. And his was the same description as all the others has given—dozens of 'em. And we have so many that come from different parts dropping by here. We had a woman in here who come all the way from Epping. She claims she saw it, and she described it the same way: a round flying object with bright lights, and then it's got this orange and red light. And she said it flies along that way—no noise, not one of them. They all say close to the same thing, that's what gets me."

"About how many people have talked to you about them? Besides your wife?"

"One time a woman come in here," he continued, "a woman pretty high-strung, you know. Nervous. And she was, ooooohhh, all excited. You wonder. And then somebody comes in afterwards and tells you the same thing. I saw it! I know I saw it! It was so quick I couldn't tell! I can't describe it! There was another fellow. And his wife. I don't know their names. He was driving along and all at once he sees this thing come out from behind the treetops. And his wife yells, 'My God!' and she sees it too. You know it's a funny thing, it's hard to be called malarky. It really is. And this man's at least four times come down here to try to see it again. To see if he could make out more, to see again what it was like. Out around the power line. Whether it's due to some atomic energy stuff that would be liable to be attracted that way, or what, I don't know."

We were interrupted when Bessie, a plain and honest-looking woman, came in with her daughter, a smiling girl in her twenties. I lost no time in questioning her daughter, who mentioned her own sighting first. It had happened as she was standing in her backyard in Fremont.

"It was just a round thing, you know," she said. "And it was all red. But underneath you could see silver things hanging down from it."

"What did it do? How did it act?"

"Well," she said, "first it was staying stationary, and then it would go up and then it would go back down amongst the trees."

"It was that low?"

"Oh, yes," she said.

"About how far from you was it?"

"Oh, dear," she said. "I'm not good at miles. But it was so that you could see it real plain."

Bessie herself first saw the object with her other daughter.

"The first one I saw," Bessie said, "went right down in back of the trees. It was white, and then it turned red. Dark red. But first it looked greenish-like. And then there was a plane that seemed to be trying to circle it. And I was with my other daughter, we both saw that. She has seen it more times than that, too. We saw it two nights in a row, the same time of night. Early evening. I went out Tuesday night—just last Tuesday, out at the clothesline, and I said, Gee, am I seeing things? It was really close. That night it was round, just as big, and you could see these silver things coming down from it. So I went in and called my neighbor, and I said, Come out on the field, quick. But her husband yells, We can see it better from the attic, and he called down he could see it real good. Then it went down behind the trees, and came up again. It's just like the one we saw the other night. It went right down the power line. That's what it always seems to do—hover over the power lines."

Bessie could not be called an expert witness, but there was no question that she recalled the incident vividly and genuinely. And here again the power lines were indicated, miles away from Exeter.

"It changes lights, you know," Bessie said, echoing Mrs. Pearce's contention. "When my husband came out in the yard with me, it was bright red, with orange around it. And gee, then it moved away as fast as it could go. But it hovered before that, like they say. And this plane was flying around, looking like it was trying to get it."

"Could you make out any more detail?" I asked.

"No," said Bessie. "When I first saw it, it was white, sort of round-like, and then it kind of glittered like a gleam, and then all of a sudden, it was red. Not a real red, but more like an orange."

I thought back to the sighting Kimball and I had made. I didn't mention this to her, but her description jibed closely with what we had seen.

"Three years ago," Bessie said, "before there was such a fuss about these things. This friend of mind, her kiddos were playing in this field with the neighbor kids. And one little boy, he stutters, and he came in, you know, and all the kids

141

yelled at once—Oh, Mommy, a spaceship landed up in the field. And the mother says, What are you talking about? And the little boy said, Yes, he said, yes! And she said, Oh, you kiddos go out and play. And then when all of this started up, she said, I wonder if those kids did see something?"

I asked Bessie about the date of her most recent sighting. It was the previous Tuesday, October the 19th, about 6:15 in the evening. At first the thing was high, and then it came down directly over the power lines.

Jim Burleigh spoke now, recalling a recent evening when his sister phoned him to come down to her house quickly. She lived, he said, right at the base of the power lines. There was a beacon there, which flashed, but everybody knew about that. "When I got down there," he said, "this object was up higher than the beacon, and traveling along at a good clip. Right straight along the power line. It was far away when I got there, so it only looked about the size of a baseball, and then it started going along the tops of the trees. I watched it closely to see what it was, and at that time, it looked like a big orange flare. Like a globe. And at times the light seemed to change. Pulsate."

"Sure it wasn't a plane?"

"Nossir," he said emphatically, "it wasn't a plane. There was no sound from it, and a plane couldn't travel that slow, then all of a sudden speed up. A helicopter could, but a helicopter would make a lot of noise. This here thing would go along, and then stop."

"What about the other people around here who have seen it? How do they react?"

"Well, I'll tell you this much. Some of them get excited, some of them say they get a little scared. Me, I'd like to see one close up."

Jim Burleigh finished his coffee and agreed to take me to the Jalbert family, a few hundred yards down the road. It was a small house by the side of the road, not more than forty or fifty feet from the poles of the high-tension power lines which crossed the road at that point. The lines, part of the now-famous Northeast Grid, interlock communities with electrical power, and permit different utility companies to exchange power when a peak demand requires "borrowing" electricity from another community. Some transmission lines are mounted on huge, gaunt steel towers; others use oversize lighting poles, as was the case here. When they are constructed, a wide ribbon of clearing is made extending dozens of feet on each side of the lines, in order to keep the wires free of any entanglements with foliage or tree branches. This creates, in effect, wide highways or swaths of clearing which sweep across the country.

Before we went into the Jalbert house, I examined the power lines carefully. The swath must have been over a hundred feet wide, and you could look down it in either direction for several miles. Overhead, some ten or twelve heavy wires were suspended, sweeping along the open swath until they disappeared in the distance.

Mrs. Jerline Jalbert, a pleasant and unassuming widow, had made a modest home for her boys, Joseph, Jr., sixteen; Jerle, fourteen; Kent, twelve; and a smiling four-year-old. They were bright kids, standing high in their classes at school, innately friendly and curious. The entire family often stood watching by the power lines at dusk. Mrs. Jalbert told me what she had seen the previous week.

"It was a funny-looking shape," she said. "Very hard to describe. This was Tuesday night. About quarter of seven when I saw it. We had just been outdoors and we happened to look and we saw this bright red thing in the sky there. It was really close, because you could see something hanging down from it that night. I don't know what it was. When I had gone in the house to call a neighbor, it had moved across the field by then. Then it slowly disappeared out of sight."

"Can you recall the shape a little more clearly?"

"Well, it was big and it was round. Like a glowing light.

You'd think it was just like the moon rising out of the sky, but of course it wasn't that. It was the size of the moon, or bigger, though, when I first saw it."

"What was your reaction?"

"It doesn't scare me any. I'd just like to know what it is."

"How about the way it moves?"

"Well, it does both. First it goes fast, and then it goes slow. Slows right down. Then it seems to go up and down. It's the darndest thing."

"Now this thing that was hanging down. What was it like?"

"It was silverish. Several things. And you could see them, because it was glowing in that part of it."

"How long were you able to watch it?"

"A good half hour," Mrs. Jalbert said. "And you see, this is only one time. We see it regularly along here. Always seems to be somewhere near the power lines. It often comes around seven o'clock, and by quarter of eight it's gone. Monday night we saw it—" She turned to Jim Burleigh. "Was it Sunday I called you up about it? Anyway, it goes way up in the sky finally, and it gets smaller and smaller as it goes up, and gets more orange. And a lot of times, this airplane comes out and chases it."

I turned my attention to Joseph Jalbert, the sixteen-year-old.

"When we saw it the first time," he said, "it was even with the power line. Right beside it."

"That low?" I asked. I was fascinated because for the second time in as many days I had run into a cluster of people who reported seeing the objects regularly, people who had no connection with Mrs. Pearce's group, who were not even aware of the others' existence.

"All of a sudden," Mrs. Jalbert added, "it'll disappear. Then, just as sudden, it'll come back. Then little red lights will sometimes come on top of it, and one on the bottom. Off and on."

144

"Now you say it seems to stay pretty close to these power lines?"

"Yup," said Mrs. Jalbert. "It seems to stay over these lines most of the time it's been down through here. It's always over those wires."

"We were looking at one with field glasses one night, a guy in a car down here had some," said Joseph. "We were watching it go up and down. You'd see a red light and when you'd be looking, it would turn white."

"Now you're sure this wasn't a plane? Running lights?"

"No," said Mrs. Jalbert, "we all know planes around here. The boys can name every part of a plane. And a plane wouldn't be orange. This is orange, just like Halloween orange. And no noise. We never hear any noise."

Young Joseph spoke up, the sixteen-year-old: "Remember the time Mr. and Mrs. Bunker were down here?" he asked the others. "It was what? Three or four weeks ago? Me and Kent were down at the power line. There was seven or eight people down there with us watching for this thing. And it come around about quarter of eleven that night. It come from way down over that end of the power line, it was going right along the trees. And there's a big oak tree out there that's dead. When it got to that tree, it went right up and over—no noise at all, just a red light and two white lights, like a house window when it's lit. We didn't see it anymore, but Jerle, my brother, he was in the house, he saw it out the back window, and he saw a blue thing come out of it, and that was it. That right, Jerle?"

Jerle nodded.

"When you see it, it's sort of a round shape, and when you had a chance to see the bottom part, where these windows were, there was a big red light sitting there. And you'd see it and one time you'd see a red light, the next time you'd see a white light, then a red light, then a white light."

"And oh, so white," Mrs. Jalbert added. "There's no airplane with a light that color."

"You know that one time we saw it so close," Kent said, "it was so quiet you could have heard a pin drop. It showed up light enough so that you could have read a book."

I turned to Joseph. "What kind of feeling do you get when you see it?"

"A shivery feeling," he said.

"How about you, Kent?"

"I don't know. When it's going over you like that, and you don't know what it is, you just don't know what to think."

"It does give you a funny feeling," Mrs. Jalbert said. "I have the feeling if it should land, I don't know what I'd do, whether I'd run, or what."

"How about the size of this thing? Any estimates?"

Joseph said, "I'd say it was as big around as a car."

"You're sure there's no sound?"

"No sound at all."

"You know the running lights on a plane, Joseph?"

"I sure do," he said. "Nothing like that at all. Nothing."

"How about the surface of this thing, Kent?" I asked.

"You really can't tell. The lights are too bright. And when it's orange, it just glows. Like a light bulb."

Jim Burleigh, who had been listening in the background quietly, spoke again. "You asked how fast it travels," he said. "I was up to my mother-in-law's, about three miles from here, and they called up and said they had spotted this thing over the power line. I didn't have the time to go down, but it was moving so slowly then that it was in sight for about half an hour."

Joseph raised his hand politely, as if he were in school. "I have a theory about it," he said.

"All right," I said. "Let's have it."

"I think it's going over those power lines to recharge its batteries, or something like that. Taking all the electricity from the wires."

"That's a very interesting theory," I said.

"I also think they have a kind of radar, like bats, because they never bump into anything. They give you a real spooky feeling. And one time, when one came by close, my radio went out for a few seconds on me."

I turned off my tape recorder and chatted informally for awhile, trying to appraise all this testimony. The descriptions of the objects at a distance fitted Kimball's and mine. The plane chasing or looking for the object also fitted in with what we had seen. The youngsters were bright, exceptionally intelligent, as was Mrs. Jalbert in her quiet and unassuming way. I was forced to conclude that there was a great deal of truth in what they were saying, allowing for the exaggerations of enthusiasm. Their response to questions was totally spontaneous. But were they mistaken?

Still, what they said jibed with information from many other people I had interviewed, without any possible collusion. And the boys were keen and up on airplanes. Youngsters of this age are often far more familiar with aircraft than their parents. Their eyesight is better. And they checked each other out regularly in what they were saying, not in any conspiratorial way, but to verify their own recollections.

I jotted down the names of a Mr. and Mrs. Bunker, whom the Jalberts thought lived fairly near, and they also felt that it was worth while for Kimball and me to come back that evening at 7 o'clock to see if by any chance we could see another UFO. I doubted it, of course, but we had doubted we were going to see anything when we went to Route 88 with Mrs. Pearce and Mrs. Deyo.

I called Kimball from the Jalberts' house, and we arranged to have a quick early dinner in Exeter, in time to return at 7 that evening.

When we reached the Jalbert house after a hurried snack in Exeter, the weather was miserable. There was a low overcast and it was extremely hazy. The power lines stretching

147

across the road were swallowed up in mist within a few hundred feet. The tall, oversize poles, four abreast, stood at quiet attention like a halted company of infantrymen.

Joseph, the oldest Jalbert boy, was gloomy and pessimistic. "We almost never see them on nights like this," he said. "I know just how you feel. You can't believe it until you see it. And this is a bad night for it." He was apologetic.

"You didn't believe them until you saw them?" I asked.

"Nossir," said Jospeh. "Not at all. When people came down here in their cars and told me about them, I thought they were off their rocker or something."

"When did you change your mind?"

"Well, I said to myself, gee, they're making all of this up. They had to be. Because here we were, living right here, and why hadn't *we* seen any?"

"You say a lot of cars suddenly started coming down here?" There were no cars except ours tonight. In addition to the mist, it was raw and cold, and I was glad I had brought my parka.

"Yeah," said Kent. "They all started coming down here, a whole mess of cars. And just sat here, waiting and watching. They kept telling us about it."

"How long did this go on?" Kimball asked. He had put his Filmo back in the car now, the mist was so thick.

"Well, they must have been collecting down here a week," said Joseph. "Until I decided to come down here and see for myself."

"How long ago did the cars first start coming down?" I asked. Joseph was an intelligent kid, and I was interested in the fact that he had been a full-fledged skeptic before all this started.

"Four or five weeks ago, I guess," he said. That would have made it in the latter part of September. "The cars would come down here, and then the next day at school, everybody was telling me, Hey, we were down there with my father, and we saw this and we saw that. And you know what I said? I told them they were crazy. So finally after about a week of everybody telling me in school about all this, me and Kent decided to come out of the house and see what was going on. So we came out here, and we said we're not going to leave till we see such a thing. And finally I was getting so I knew it wasn't true. And then when I saw it—right then I changed my mind. Right then and there 'cause I knew it wasn't a plane when I looked at it, because of the light structure. And how it looked when it spun around. Ever since then, I've believed them."

"What do people tell you when you tell them about it?"

Joseph thought a moment, standing there in the cold, dim glow of the parking lights of Kimball's car. Then he said, "They tell me I'm nuts. That is, until one of them comes down and sees it. Then other people call *him* nuts. You got to see it to believe it. That's all there is to it."

After nearly twenty minutes of fruitless waiting, Mrs. Jalbert came out of the house to join us. "I don't think you'll have much luck on a night like this," she said. "I'm sorry."

Kimball and I couldn't help smiling. Everybody who had reported "The Thing" seemed to feel such a personal responsibility for it.

I had not yet talked to Chief Bolduc's wife, as he had suggested, because of the unexpected activity resulting from dropping by Bessie's Lunch. Kimball agreed it would be a good idea to stop by at the Bolduc house to see what we might uncover. We were not really disappointed that we saw nothing at the power lines, and we were already batting .500 in the two times we had somewhat sheepishly looked for the objects.

Chief Bolduc and his numerous family lived in a rambling old farmhouse not more than a few hundred feet from Heselton's Garage. Kimball and I were admitted by the Chief, congenial as ever, into the sprawling country kitchen, where an assortment of children and adults were in varied stages of finishing up dinner. Mrs. Phyllis Bolduc, plump and cheerful in spite of the confusion, was as cordial as her husband.

At the head of the large kitchen table was Meredith Bolduc, the twenty-two-year-old daughter-in-law of the Chief, who was sitting in the corner in an easy chair. Jesse Bolduc, married to Meredith, leaned back against the wall in a wooden chair underneath a rack packed with hunting guns, while children and grandchildren of assorted ages made occasional excursions in and out of the room off the kitchen which housed the television set. The scene created the impression of a Yankee version of a Bruegel painting of friendly family confusion.

I told the group that the Chief had suggested earlier in the day that they might be able to give me some information on Unidentified Flying Objects.

Meredith, an attractive young housewife with short black hair, spoke first. "Go no further," she said. "I tell you that the experience I had is enough to make your hair curl."

"Tell me about it," I said, slinging the battery recorder off my shoulder and turning it on.

"Oh, dear," she said. "Am I going down in history?"

"Doesn't make you nervous, does it?"

"Not really. Maybe a little."

"Just relax and forget about it."

"It's these men of mine here who really make me nervous," she said, referring to her father-in-law and husband. "But anyway, I know exactly what I saw and I'm going to tell you about it, no matter how much they kid me. Actually, they know better."

"You're darn right they do," said Mrs. Bolduc. "They know this is no joke."

"Anyway," Meredith Bolduc continued, "this thing was coming up the power lines toward the road, this was going from Fremont toward Kingston, at the power lines right down near the town line. It was coming, and it didn't stop. I just kept on going on to Kingston, to my folks. And when you see one of these things, you don't forget them. This was last week, just a few days ago. But I saw it much closer two weeks ago Wednesday, that would make it—that would make it October sixth. This is the closest it ever came to me."

"Where were you at the time?" I asked.

"On the Raymond road. Driving."

"Did you stop?"

"No. I didn't know whether to goose the car, or turn around and go home."

"It was close?"

"Yes. Came right down toward the car."

"What was your reaction?"

"Scared! Scared to *death*. In fact, a couple of minutes after that, I saw a light shining over my shoulder and I turned around and jumped a foot—but it was only the moon!

"This was the only night I was really afraid of it," she continued. "The other nights it was fascinating, it was way off in the distance. What good is it going to do to reach for a gun or to goose your car and make it go faster?"

"How about how high up was it when you saw it that close?"

"I'd say a couple of treetops high. You just had to look up a little, right in front of the windshield, and there it was."

"Could you make out any detail?"

"Well, it was bright, and white, with sort of fluorescent red around the rim. Like a big light bulb, the way the white part of it shone. It might have been more whitish-yellow, the main part of the thing was."

"What about the shape?"

"It wasn't flat, but it wasn't round either. Not oval like an egg, but it was oval—not quite as oval as an egg. You could tell it wasn't round, but it wasn't square and it wasn't flat. It was a funny shape."

"Where was the red?" I asked. I was continuing to ask the same question more than once, as a double check on accuracy.

151

"On the outside of it. Around the rim. And I'll tell you this much—I don't particularly care about seeing it that close anymore."

The men chuckled. Meredith reacted quickly.

"By God, you guys laugh!" she said. "But wait until you see it up close! And I'll also say this: I absolutely refuse to drive alone at night anymore."

"Now both our older boys saw it," said Mrs. Bolduc. "One of them told me it hovered right over our house here."

"That's right," said Meredith, "the night it put the lights out."

Kimball sat forward on that statement. "It put the lights out here?" he asked.

"Well," said the Chief, and now he was serious, "we have one of those automatic lights out by the barn—outside light, lights up the whole area. It's got one of those photoelectric cells on it, so's it goes off when the sun comes up. This one night, Mrs. Bolduc saw the whole bedroom light up with this bright red light. And the next thing you know, the barn light went out, and then went on again when the thing went away."

"Damn interesting," said Kimball.

"Yeah," said Mrs. Bolduc. "I saw it right by the house. Looking out my bedroom window. I said, there's that saucer again. Seems so that it's getting that every time I look out my window, I seem to see it. And I've seen planes circling around after it twice. That was the time we watched it with binoculars, Joe, remember?"

"What did it look like through the binoculars?"

"I put the binoculars on it, and it looked like the shape of a football, with lights around the middle."

My mind went back to the report from Cherry Creek, New York, hundreds of miles away from Fremont, New Hampshire. The description was almost identical with the one given by young Harold Butcher, as the bull twisted the metal pipe out of shape with his nose ring, and the radio interference blocked out the program. Here in Fremont, the light in the barnyard had gone out. I had to conclude that these similarities couldn't possibly be collusion or coincidence.

"And you know Carol McFarland—that's Mrs. Herbert McFarland—she lives just up the line there, she says that it followed her home on the Red Brook road, and that road is just down below the power line. She said this thing followed her all the way home. And you know something—there were so many people down there by that power line one night, it looked like a beach party down there, it really did. A beach party. One woman was there with a nightgown on, with a baby in her arms."

"I'll tell you this much," said the Chief from his easy chair. "It's gotta be something. It's just gotta be something!"

Kimball and I were silent on the first part of the drive back to Exeter. Finally I spoke.

"*Now* what do you think?" I asked.

Kimball just shook his head.

"I certainly never expected to run into so many reports, two days in a row," I said.

"I never expected to run into so many reports two years in a row," said Kimball.

"All these things that keep repeating themselves," I said. "Like where do the cars always seem to congregate?"

"By the power lines," said Kimball. "Both Fremont and Exeter."

"How many people have had the damn things come right at their cars?"

"Let's see," said Kimball. He was driving slowly because the fog was still rather thick. "There's the woman that Bertrand reported on the 101 bypass. There's Mrs. Pearce, down on the Exeter-Hampton line. There's the two young fellows the Hampton police took to the Coast Guard station. Muscarello, he wasn't in a car, but he had to dive down on the road to get away from it. Actually, it came right at Bertrand, too, wouldn't you say? When he was out on the field with the kid."

"Well," I said, "he started to pull his gun on it."

"That's close enough," said Kimball. "And then there's that electric light bit. In the barnyard."

"Could you call that physical evidence?"

"In a way, I guess you could," said Kimball.

"I think I have to say that I'm convinced that these people believe what they saw. Now I guess the question is: Did they see what they believe?"

"I think we have to admit that they did. I wouldn't have said this two days ago, except for Bertrand and Hunt. I know them well enough to know that they wouldn't report it if they didn't mean it."

"Then if all this is true, and if it could be deduced that these objects are interplanetary, why aren't we able to break the story? I know the answer to that, it's just a rhetorical question. There is overwhelming evidence, but still no proof. It's still a ghost story."

Kimball was silent a moment, then: "I'm trying to be impartial and completely objective about it. I'm trying to give it, on purpose, as much of a negative viewpoint as I can give it. In other words, I say to myself: It must be something else. But I *can't* prove it's something else, any more than I can prove it *is* what they say it is. I've got to look at it from the wrong side of the street, from the wrong side of the tracks, to make it seem as if they were seeing a star, or a plane, or something normal. But let's face it, it's *not* something normal, and there's no use in kidding ourselves. People just don't get wrought up like this over an illusion."

"It sure as hell seems unearthly," I said.

"I try to do that—I get myself in the complete negative— like let's go against it. You've got to avoid conning yourself into believing things you shouldn't believe. But it turns out you sit and talk to all these people and you're the one who's crazy, not them. Because all the damn stories fit together."

"One thing that makes it difficult," I said, "is that not one element, or one interview, is enough to make a story. But a consensus, an *accumulation* of the stories is. It's the collection of these damn tapes that's making it hard *not* to believe this thing. Not just one tape, but dozens."

"And then you've got to add to that, the thing we saw."

"I know. I think we can both agree that we weren't seeing things."

"Definitely no," said Kimball. "We were not seeing things."

"We could see the running lights on the plane very clearly, right?

"Very clearly."

"So there was absolutely no danger of misinterpreting what we saw as a plane. And yet the object was moving the same or faster speed than the plane right behind it. And it was overcast. We couldn't have confused it with a star or planet or anything else. To me it looked like a miniature sun on a foggy evening, very dull red orange, and moving like hell. I guess we have to agree we saw it, that we can't rule it out."

"The thing that makes me mad is that it would have been impossible to get a picture of that. It was too high, too dim. If we could just find one down closer, I'd be happier."

A close, low picture would help. But it would be a matter of extreme luck and infinite patience. After Kimball dropped me off at the Inn, I decided to stop by the home of George Carr, play him some of the tapes, and get an entirely fresh viewpoint. Carr, who had worked with and developed many new techniques in high-vacuum processes, possessed a very shrewd analytical mind.

In his living room with a glowing fire to take the chill off the evening, I went over the story with him, played him portions of several different tapes.

He was impressed. "But you still have to get that physical evidence," he said.

I agreed. I told him of the many NICAP reports of impressions on the ground, singed grass, melted ice impressions, and the photographs. He felt that the impressions could be too easily faked or mistakenly identified, and I was inclined to go along with him on this. The pictures, though, were most interesting if the background of the photographer, the circumstances under which they were taken, and the examination of the negatives were fully explored. I told him about the picture NICAP had sent me from the amateur astronomer near Pittsburgh, in which the shape of the object was clearly defined, with the moon in the background as a checkpoint, and the tree line also easily discernible as a further checkpoint. Carr felt that a study of that photography would be a major step in establishing some kind of physical evidence to go along with the hours of testimony recorded on the tapes.

I decided that I would clean up whatever loose ends I could the next morning, see my agent and editors in New York, and then leave for Beaver Falls, Pennsylvania, where the rather startling picture had been taken. I knew that NICAP had already investigated the circumstances very thoroughly, along with the negatives involved. On the other hand, I could not include a major point in the book unless I explored it first hand. At the same time, I made plans to go to Washington to talk again with NICAP, and perhaps get some basic information from the Federal Aviation Agency regarding the regulations for experimental aircraft. It was hard to understand why, if the theory that these objects were experimental aircraft of the Air Force were valid, they were permitted to so upset citizens in populated areas. And why was the Air Force apparently sending fighters after them? And again, why were they permitted to fly in conventional flight lanes without rigidly prescribed running lights? Regardless of military secrecy, there are some safety precautions which cannot be violated, and the consideration of these questions made the secret-aircraft theory seem extremely flimsy.

CHAPTER X

SATURDAY, October 23, was my fourth day in and around Exeter. There were many details I had not had the chance to follow up, but some of them would have to wait until after I had returned from Pennsylvania and Washington. What about the two men who had been taken to the Coast Guard station at Hampton, almost in shock? What about the dozens of other names from the Exeter police blotter, which I had been unable to follow up individually? What about a thorough random-sample questioning, a cold-turkey probe to get a clearer idea of the probable incidence of these sightings? What about the power-line theory? What information could I get from the local power companies? What about a personal call at the Pease Air Force Base in Portsmouth, even if the results were to be negative? What about Muscarello, the eighteen-year-old boy who had started all this? He was a boot trainee at the Great Lakes Naval Training Station in Illinois, and impossible to reach by phone.

I followed several leads that morning by phone, with the stories jibing closely with the accounts I had already recorded from the others. Again, there were several independent mentions of the power lines. In spite of different wording, the description followed the same pattern and the sincerity and conviction were there on the phone, as in person.

Stopping for a second cup of coffee on my way up to the Muscarello home to talk to his mother before I left, I glanced through the pages of the Manchester *Union-Leader*, and came across a headline which by now had become almost commonplace: INDEPENDENT OBSERVATIONS: TWO MEN IN SUNCOOK WATCH FLYING SAUCER. The article stated:

> A vivid report of actually observing a "flying saucer" through binoculars was made yesterday by Oscar J. Augur of Cemetery Road yesterday, as he recounted the details of the rare experience.
>
> What gave added credence to Augur's story was the uncovering of another person who had sighted a "flying object" at about the same time and about 15 minutes later.
>
> Augur said he was driving south on Pleasant Street, Hooksett, at about 6:50 P.M., and when he neared the intersection with Merrimac Street he noticed a bright object over the Merrimac River on his right.
>
> "I hurriedly got out of my car and with a pair of binoculars, I unmistakably saw the saucer as clear as day," Augur excitedly recalled. "There was no mistaking the vehicle as I observed it for several minutes as it maneuvered erratically in the valley. The top of the saucer was domed shaped and glowed red while the rounded sides were bright white.
>
> "It was still light enough at the time for me to see it plainly as it maneuvered about," Augur related.

The article went on to relate the story of another resident who observed it at an altitude of 300 to 400 feet, and about 300 yards away. "The object remained stationary for about a minute," he told the reporter, "and then it began to sway slightly from one side to the other and suddenly moved quite rapidly in a southerly direction. The only sound I heard was a hissing sound like we hear coming out of a steam radiator valve."

I was tempted for a moment to drive to Suncook, some 30 miles west of Exeter, but then thought better of it. The stories matched so closely to the dozens I had already recorded that nothing new would be added. Descriptions from any reliable source could almost be predicted, it seemed.

Mrs. Dolores Gazda, Muscarello's mother from a previous marriage, lived in a modest but spotless apartment on Front Street in Exeter, about a mile out from the center of town. An outdoor wooden stairway with a small landing on the top led to the door, and she sat me at the kitchen table for a cup of coffee. She was young-looking and trim, barely old enough, I thought, to have an eighteen-year-old son.

"Do you want me to tell you something interesting?" she said as she poured the coffee. "When this whole thing started, I told my son I really couldn't believe him. He had been out all night, and he came walking into the house at about four in the morning. I was really concerned, and very upset. You see, he'd sold his car because he was going into the Navy in a few weeks, so he hitchhiked all the way to Amesbury to see this friend, and that's how the whole thing started. Well, of course, I could hardly believe this fantastic story, but when the two police officers told me what they went through, I knew that all *three* of them couldn't be pulling my leg. Well, he told me that this photographer from the Manchester paper had been over in the police station and took his picture, and the story was going to go into the paper. And I went all to pieces. Because I knew that dozens of people would be coming up here, trooping into the house, and I hate any kind of publicity and that sort of thing.

"I had no sooner said that, later that morning, when all these people started coming to the door. And then the people from the air base started coming, and then the Navy, and it just doesn't look right, plus half the time my son wasn't here and I was stuck talking to them. So finally he saw all the people—there were ten in the living room alone one afternoon, they all came at once. He began to see what I was talking about, and he understood it. He said, If you want, I'll talk to them somewhere else. I told him, I don't mind if you're here, but I don't want this a continuous thing.

"Well, things started calming down a bit, and then his curiosity began to get under his skin. He was just as determined as he could be to see that thing again. He knew that some people doubted the story—although why they should I don't know, with two policemen seeing it at the same time with him—but he got some of his friends together, and they'd go up to Route 150, near where he first saw it, practically every night. And one time he said he sat there until the sun came up, and they saw one in the daylight. He said it was definitely a saucer shape, and it had a bluish hue to it. He said it must have been some kind of metal to give off that color. And while he wanted to see that thing again, he did get a little sick of telling the same thing over and over again to people. The newspaper reporters would keep him talking for hours. He said, You know, Mom, I want to cooperate, but I am so tired of telling the same story over and over.

"And of course, I got interested in all this myself, and I used to go up there with him with some friends. We didn't have much luck at first, but two of my friends told me they were coming out of the Exeter Hospital one evening, and there it was right over the hospital. Right over the hospital! Somebody in the hospital called the police that night, and they said it was bothering all the electricity in the hospital— lights and equipment.

"Now my son says it was as big as a house, and that's about the description of it when it was over the hospital. And then one night I went down with these friends on Route 88. I still hadn't had any luck, all those nights I went with Norman. But this night, we weren't there more than ten minutes, when all of a sudden, this thing, you couldn't see what it was shaped like, came out from behind some trees, like if it was just parked and rose. Now I describe it as being beautiful. It went right along the top of the trees, oh, several hundred yards away. It was hard to tell the distance. It was huge, it looked awful big even from that far away. What it looked like to me, there were lights on the bottom going around it like pinwheels. Red ones. And it was very bright and it was beautiful. Since then, I've seen it right over the house here. And the other night, the whole neighborhood was shook up. I could see it right here from the landing. And I went and told all the neighbors, and they all saw it with me. It was very low, and spinning like always, with these red lights. So a few minutes later, an airplane came over, and made a circle around it. And darned if that thing didn't just turn around and take off like a bullet."

I arranged to meet two of Mrs. Gazda's neighbors, and they confirmed her story. Meanwhile, I asked Mrs. Gazda about the Air Force investigation.

"Well," she said, "at that time, I could only tell them what my son had told me. When he came in, they took him to a restaurant to talk. But they were very interested. Very. When I started asking questions, though, they just started asking back. Now why do you suppose they're so interested? If the things were their own, I don't think they'd be wasting their time talking to Norman and me, do you? I frankly think they don't know any more than I do. I think they feel that everybody would be scared to death if they turned out to be interplanetary, that's what I think. But I've seen them and I'm not afraid. The only time I might be afraid, if one of them should ever land near me, would be radiation. That I might worry about."

Mrs. Gazda got up from the kitchen table, poured another cup of coffee.

"One thing that interests me is the way they seem to change color. From white to this special kind of orange, and the red, too. And maybe you can tell me about this: Has anybody ever mentioned to you about these things following power lines?"

I told her I was investigating that.

"And also water. I've heard some people say they look for water, but of course that's all just guessing."

It was nearly two in the afternoon when I checked out of the Inn and began driving toward my home in Connecticut. I had to admit my head was spinning.

I had talked with and interviewed, either singly or in groups, nearly 60 people. I had nearly 20 hours of tape recordings.

Driving along the broad, straight superhighway toward Boston, I tried to summarize in my own mind just what specific conclusions could be drawn from these long and involved days in and around Exeter. What had I been able to gather that was irrefutable evidence?

First, it was uncontestably true that Unidentified Flying Objects had been reported and verified in many cases by more than one reputable person at regular intervals over a wide area of southern New Hampshire.

Second, it was uncontestably true that the reports were coming in very frequently.

Third, it was uncontestably true that many reports indicated the objects sighted over, near and along high-power electrical transmission lines, although sightings were not confined to such locations.

Fourth, it was uncontestably true—to Kimball and me, at least—that we had seen an object that could not be identified as any known aircraft in existence.

Fifth, it was uncontestably true that some people were in actual shock or hysteria as a result of extremely low-level encounters with these objects.

The tape recorder was beside me in the front seat of the car, as I circumvented Boston on Route 128, and continued along the Massachusetts Turnpike. I picked up the microphone and began dictating a memo to my agent and editors in an attempt to give them a brief picture of the progress of the research to date. I indicated that I could not understand why some kind of major newsbreak should not be forthcoming on this subject in the light of the material I had gathered.

"I say this after several days of intensive research in Exeter, in which I interviewed nearly sixty people and tape-recorded hours of testimony," the memo began. Then it continued:

The people who have given this testimony have been checked out as far as character and reliability are concerned. For the most part I would say that their judgment and capabilities range from average to better than average.

The testimony adds up to this:

There is overwhelming evidence that UFOs or "Flying Saucers" do exist.

They seem to exist in uncountable numbers.

They move at incredible speeds and in aerodynamically impossible patterns.

They are reported, checked and verified almost continuously.

They hover for considerable time, often at less than tree-top level.

They have been reported to have landed.

At low altitude, they sometimes assume a domelike shape with an inner red or white glow. A pattern of red pulsating lights is frequently observed in some cases; in others a red whirling pattern is reported around the edge.

They are usually absolutely silent, although in some cases, a high-frequency hum is heard.

They move almost directly overhead of cars and people, at times causing fright and panic.

At least four women, living in widely separate areas, are afraid to go out alone at night, and they refuse to do so.

At least four people report extremely large objects—60 to 80 feet in diameter, rising up silently from behind trees.

The low altitude movement has been reported to consist of a yawing, kitelike motion, wobbling in the air and moving slowly back and forth, sometimes with a fluttering pattern, like a leaf.

At times, it is reported to throw a brilliant red light glow, which paints the side of white houses a brilliant red. It can light up a wide area on the ground around it.

At high altitudes, in some cases, it seems to assume a shape of a small disk, in the relationship of a pinhead (star) to a tennis ball (UFO).

Reliable, but off-the-record information from the Pease Air Force Base in Portsmouth indicates frequent radar blips and fighters are *constantly* scrambled to pursue these objects. This information is not official, but it comes from a reliable source.

The objects are often reported in the vicinity of high-power transmission lines: Some of these locations have been crowded with cars many nights, with group sightings some-times reported.

No one has ever been harmed physically by any of these objects, although psychological trauma has been evident.

The area covered by the research extends from Hampton, N.H., on the coast some 20 miles west to Derry, N.H., near Manchester.

In most interviews, I was able to determine the reasonable capacity of the respondent to differentiate between a heli-copter, balloon, jet, prop plane, planets or stars. Some sight-ings have been described in daylight.

I tried to take it easy over the weekend, but wasn't very successful. It was frustrating and annoying to have so much evidence, without a shred of proof. I reviewed the tapes again, trying to discover false notes in the voices of the peo-ple I had interviewed. This quality was simply not present. The observers were not fictionalizing, they were not lying. In dealing with many people over so wide an area, it seemed impossible to create a hoax. For the most part they were sober and reliable people, and their voices and convictions were loud and clear. Then there was the sighting that Kimball and I had made. Not so close and near and traumatic as some of the others but it *had* happened, we had checked each other out, and it was clearly a craft or object which neither of us had ever seen before. Kimball, as a pilot, was more technically qualified than I but we both were rational (we hoped) and accurate observers who had made every effort to rule out mistaken identity and illusion.

On Monday, October 25, I went to New York with the tapes to play them for my agent and editor. This was helpful, because I had become so involved with the project that I was beginning to lose some of my objectivity. They were impressed with the tapes, as I had been. They agreed that it would have been impossible for the people I interviewed to have faked such similar descriptions even if they had tried. They were puzzled, as I was, by the unanswered questions, the loose ends, the seeming paradoxes. If the trip to Pennsylvania and the full investigation of the photograph added even the slightest clue, we all agreed it would be worthwhile. Most important were a) the character and reliability of the photographer, and b) expert analysis of the negatives.

Two days later, October 27, I drove from Pittsburgh north some 30 miles to Beaver, Pennsylvania, in a rented car. The *Beaver County Times,* an extremely able newspaper covering a large population in the Pittsburgh area, had covered the picture and story in depth, I had learned, and I planned to talk to their reporter first before interviewing the youthful photographer directly. NICAP had informed me that the newspaper story and the investigation by their own representative had tallied completely.

Autumn was in full swing. I drove through the narrow twisting roads, typical of the western part of Pennsylvania, laid out in curves by the Alleghenies, which rimmed both sides of the road. I was so conscious now of high-tension power lines that I scanned the tops of the hills on each side, noticing a string of the power-line towers parading across the tops of the hills. Later I learned they carried power from the Shippingport Atomic Electric plant near Pittsburgh, the first atomic power plant in the country. Naturally, I speculated on whether this might have anything to do with the appearance of the UFO which had been so clearly photographed.

One especially interesting thing had shown up in the picture: under the upside-down luminous dinner plate shape was a whirling halo, a misty cloud extending beneath it like a ghostly tail of a kite, which had not been visible to the naked eye but which had shown up on the photographic negative clearly. Since film will pick up some invisible infrared and ultraviolet light, this might provide a clue to the power source of the objects.

I found Tom Schley, reporter for the *Beaver County Times* who had covered the story, at his desk in the large, modern building of the paper.

He had plunged into the subject cold, and was as mystified as I. He was convinced that the seventeen-year-old James Lucci, who had taken the picture, was sound and able, an amateur photographer who often took pictures of the stars and moon as part of his hobby. His father was a professional photographer for the Air National Guard, and both the family and the boy were highly regarded in the community. At the time of the observation and the taking of the picture, James Lucci was with his brother, and a third witness, Michael Grove, saw the UFO from his home across the road.

NICAP had discovered in its investigation that James was making time exposures of the moon in the driveway of his home in Brighton Township, Beaver County, at about 11:30 P.M. A round, thick object, glowing brighter than the moon, came into the field of the camera from over a high, steep hill behind his house. Realizing the camera must have caught it, James closed the shutter quickly, wound the film down for another shot. Before he could get a third shot, the object climbed rapidly out of sight.

The entire Lucci family was afraid, as many other people were, of ridicule and publicity, but friends persuaded James to bring the picture to the *Beaver County Times,* where three photographers superimposed negatives and made other tests which showed the UFO had slowly moved closer, left to right, as described by the witnesses. After a full evaluation, they labeled the photograph genuine. The boy's character was vouched for by the Chief of Police, Brighton Township, the high school principal, and Beaver County police.

Lucci took the picture with a Yashika 635 camera, with Altipan 120 film (ASA 100). The lens opening was f 3.5, set at infinity, exposed 6 seconds. The film was developed 12 minutes, with fresh D 76, 70 degrees, with agitation.

At lunch, the reporter filled me in on the background of the story as he covered it.

"The pictures were taken," Schley told me, "on a Sunday night—August the eighth. And young Lucci was finally persuaded to come in to the paper a day or two later. He showed them to some photographers here, and they studied them carefully. They became very interested, and they took one negative and laid it over the other one and matched them up. And when they did this, the edges, the tree line of the hill, all matched. The moon matched, too. And in one picture, the object was farther away on the left. In the other, it was closer and to the right of the moon, which indicated some movement between the two pictures.

"We all got interested in it here on the editorial staff, and they had the boy come back and talk to me. And I sat and talked to this boy and a friend of his, I can't remember his name. And after I talked to them, and since I was a little skeptical myself, I contacted the Air Force because I never had had any experience with these things."

"How far's the Air Force base?" I asked him.

"Pittsburgh."

"Any Strategic Air Command base around?" I was probing for any correlation between this incident and the one at Exeter, which of course had been so near the Pease Air Force S.A.C. base.

"No," said Schley. "It's not an S.A.C. base."

"How about high-tension lines?"

"Lots of high-tension wires around here. They go all across the mountains. I'm not sure about the place where the picture was taken, I really didn't check for that. Anyway, in spite of the fact that the boy was obviously sincere and intelligent, I was naturally a little skeptical. I had never, as I said, handled any of these reports."

"That's when you contacted the Air Force?"

"Right," Schley continued. "So I contacted the Air Force and I got a little bit of what I now call a runaround. My city editor was pushing for the story, he didn't want to wait till the next morning, so I called the Air Force back and put a little pressure on them. I wanted to talk to someone right away, not wait all night. So I finally got hold of a lieutenant at the Pittsburgh air base. And I asked him my questions. And he said he would have to call back. And he did. My questions were: Were there any UFOs reported recently, a matter of a couple of weeks? He said, Yes, there had been several. Then I got more specific. How about that particular night? Especially around 11:30? His answer was yes. There was one reported at that time. And I asked where was it. His answer was: Nearer to Pittsburgh."

"You're lucky you got that much from him," I said.

Schley smiled. "That's what I found out later. Then I said to the lieutenant: Could you tell me if this was a naked-eye sighting? Or a radar sighting? What type was it? Well, he said, I can't say any more on that. Of course, here again, I didn't know the Air Force position on this. So my immediate suspicion was that they got something on radar because why would they hesitate to tell me if somebody said they saw it? So then, a few days later, I went ahead and wrote my initial story about what the boy said he saw, and we ran both pictures. Apparently someone sent a copy to NICAP in Washington, and someone sent one to Bill Weitzel, the subcommittee chairman down in Pittsburgh. He came down and began investigating, and he struck me as a pretty thorough and accurate man. I had never heard of this outfit before."

"They impress me as being very careful," I said. "From what I've seen, they try to knock a story down before they'll accept it."

"This is my impression," said Schley. "As far as my experience goes, I've met two of their people, and both of them impressed me very much in their serious attitude. They were very thorough in their examination of the material. They almost seemed to try to *disprove*, as you said. And I was very impressed with this. They spent five or six days here. And I got more interested in the story myself. We had a few other reports that came in, too."

"Any below treetop level?" I asked.

"No, nothing below that level," Schley said. "But I picked up a very interesting story from a couple who had sighted one of these things. This is really weird. At the time they saw this thing, their dog started acting very strangely. The wife said it was always a very friendly dog, and it began to try to hide, and it was cowering in the cellar. Its hearing seemed to be affected. As though it was hearing some sort of high-pitched noise they couldn't hear."

My mind immediately went back to Exeter, to Gene Bertrand's vivid description of the animals on the Dining farm. More bits and pieces of the puzzle seemed to be coming together—but we were still far from any kind of convincing proof.

"You see," said Schley, "the thing is this: As a newspaperman, I don't like to be taken in, and this is immediately the suspicion that you get with a story like this. So that's why I was particularly concerned about the whole thing. I did everything I could to discredit the story before I wrote it, but I couldn't. If I had, I would have backed off from the story fast."

"That's just about the way I feel," I said. "If I could explain this thing either way, I'd be happy."

*　　*　　*

With reporter Schley's help, I was able to catch two of the photographers on the newspaper who had made the examination of the Lucci negatives, Harry Frye and Birdie Shunk. We joined them in the cafeteria.

"How do you go about checking out the negatives?" I asked.

"The only way," said Frye, "is to make completely sure that there's no double exposure involved, or anything like that. If the negative is faked by a double exposure you have overlapping images. Now I studied the negatives for considerable time and I don't think they could possibly have been double-exposed. Everybody else in the department agreed on this."

"It wasn't a lens-reflection freak in the development, either," Shunk added. "We examined the negatives thoroughly for that possibility."

"After we all had studied them, we couldn't help but come to the conclusion that the image was a definite picture. There was no other way it could have been done."

"How did you go about matching up the two negatives?" I asked.

"Well," said Frye, "we put the two negatives, two separate exposures, we put them together and lined up the trees, the horizon line, the moon, and other things that were in both negatives. And you could see where the object had moved across the film. From my judgment, the object had moved from a position closer to the camera to a position a little farther away and across."

"And that would have been difficult to fake?"

"It would be, yes," said Shunk. "It would be difficult to fake it in another way—to put something up there and photograph it, and still get the things that are seen in the background. Just about impossible, I'd say. You also noticed that tail of mist coming down from the object."

"That wasn't seen by the naked eye," I said. "What sort of

170

thing does a film pick up that the eye doesn't? Infrared? Ultraviolet?"

"Ultraviolet will appear on a film and not to the eye," said Frye. "It would tend to produce a white image."

"Then is there a possibility that these rays coming down from the object could be ultraviolet?"

"Well," said Frye, "this is something I couldn't answer. It could be, and it could be also something else. There is a lot of light outside of the visible spectrum that you can photograph."

"How about infrared?" I asked.

"That will also photograph on a plate to a certain extent, especially with certain film."

"We discussed ways that the picture could have been faked," said Shunk, "and we couldn't come up with a logical way you could do it."

"In other words," said Frye, "if somebody asked us to go out and duplicate this picture, we would find it impossible."

I thanked Schley and the photographers for their information, and then left to see James Lucci and his brother, John, to reenact the way the photograph was taken, and to see what other information I could pick up in their neighborhood.

James Lucci was quiet, soft-spoken, shy. His brother John was twenty, three years older. He was a student at Geneva College nearby. Both were articulate and friendly. The Lucci house nestled at the bottom of a steep hill, so typical of western Pennsylvania. I got both boys to take me to the exact spot where their camera had been set. It was in the gravel driveway, directly beside the house, and we stood there, looking up at an angle toward the hill. The trees stood out sharply in silhouette against the sky, the same tree line which had showed up in the pictures.

I asked James Lucci to point out the exact spot where the object was when the picture was taken.

171

He pointed to the high ridge, at about a 45-degree angle from where we were standing.

I looked up, following the direction of his finger, and caught my breath.

For immediately below the part of the sky he indicated were the sweeping wires of a high-power transmission line, extending from a tower on top of the ridge and stringing across the valley to the next hill. It was Exeter all over again, this time with a striking photograph to go with it.

I found it a little difficult to remain calm, but I asked the Lucci boys to give me the details of their story.

"I had set the camera up that night," John said. "My brother and I both work together on this. Last winter, I had taken a picture of the moon through an icicle, that turned out to be beautiful. This time, we thought we might get an interesting effect by shooting the moon through the very faint haze, or thin overcast, that was around that night. It was just sort of nice and misty, but you could still see the moon through it. I let my brother handle the camera that night, because we take turns doing it. It was about eleven-thirty. And all of a sudden, the bright, round object came up over the trees. And it shocked us, it really did. We didn't have a shutter cable, but he took the time exposure, and then wound it down to the next picture. And he got a second picture, as it hovered in different positions. But before he got a chance to get a third picture, it shot straight up in the air and it was gone."

"Fast?" I said.

"Just like that," said John. "Boom. Gone."

"Which of you saw it first—you or James?"

"I don't know who exactly saw it first. We saw it at the same time, I guess."

I turned to James, who had been at the camera at the time, and who had actually taken the picture. "You were the one who took the picture. Did you see it through the viewfinder?"

"I was looking through the camera when I saw it."

172

"What did you do?" I asked. "How did it work technically?"

"I had my hand over the shutter to make a time exposure of the moon, and the object came right into the frame," James answered. "I waited for a couple of seconds and it stopped. I wound the camera down, and took the next picture. I was going to take another one, but it went up. It took right off."

Now I turned back to John. "You saw it with your naked eye, rather than through the camera. It was coming over those trees, you say?" I pointed up to the top of the hill.

"It was a big white light," he said. "I couldn't make out a very clear outline. But it was brighter than the moon. We were just standing here and it just crept up over the trees. It didn't just pop up, but it didn't just creep up. It came over the trees like an airplane would go. Then it stopped dead in the air."

"Any sound?" I asked.

"No," said John. "Absolutely no sound at all. It's dead quiet out here in the middle of the night, and I was standing right here, and I didn't hear a thing."

"Any other lights, other than the white light?"

"No."

"Any pulsating lights?"

"No."

"What shape?"

"Disk shape. Just like the picture."

"In its motion, did it seem to—what? How did it move?"

"It would stop," said John, "and it would just move around in different areas. Hover here, hover there. It would hover for a brief moment, then move to a different spot. It didn't seem to wobble too much."

"The light was all uniformly white?"

"Yes," said John.

"Did it look as if it were luminous—lit from the inside?"

"I couldn't tell," John said. "It wasn't a reflection, it was

173

its own light. But I couldn't tell whether it was outside or inside."

"Did it have a clear surface?"

"We still couldn't tell. It was misty that night. You couldn't tell the surface actually. It was just like a big, disk-shaped light."

I spoke to James. "What did it look like to you? You saw it just through the viewfinder? Or with the naked eye, too?"

"I just saw it through the camera."

"What did it look like to you through the camera? Beyond the details you see in the picture?"

"It was hard to tell," said James. "I was trying to focus at the same time I was taking the pictures."

"What about that haze underneath the object in the picture?" I asked. "I understand you couldn't see that with the naked eye?"

"That's right," John said. "You couldn't see that."

"Tell me about your own reaction to the thing," I said to John.

"I didn't know what to do. I was scared to death. I was standing right here when the thing first came up. I didn't realize what was happening at first. And then it started to hit me. And I didn't stand around here long, I'll tell you that much."

"Can you remember what you said to James when you saw it?"

"I can't actually remember my exact words, but I didn't want to stick around. I wanted to get back in the house."

"How did you feel, James?" I asked.

"I just picked up my camera and ran into the house and developed my film."

"How did the experience affect you?"

"I guess I felt more happy than scared."

"I was more shocked than that," his older brother confessed.

"Now," I asked. "Can you tell me again as to where the object was in relation to those high-tension power lines?"

John studied the area a moment. "I'd say it was right up there, directly over the wires. Not more than fifty or sixty feet."

We went into the house, and I again studied some prints of the pictures. The object was bigger than the moon in the background. The disk shape was clear and unmistakable. They were the clearest photographs I had seen of the objects, and the shape was very close to many of the descriptions given in Exeter. The light in this case was uniformly white, as reported by the brothers, but there had been so much testimony to the effect that the lighting patterns changed frequently that this didn't seem significant.

I asked the boys about other sightings and they told me there had been several that they had heard about.

"There's a fellow and his wife who live right up over the hill from here," said John. "He said he and his wife were watching television one night, and the dog started acting up. Then the TV picture got all scrambled. He went outside, and he told us he watched one of these things—he described it very much like the picture—for a long time."

"Where does this fellow live?" I asked. Again, the disturbed animal behavior, I noted.

"Right up over the hill behind the house here," John said. "I know that during August and September, there were a lot of reports around this neighborhood. People were calling in to the police and the newspaper every other week, practically."

"Do you know these people—the ones whose dog was scared?"

"We know them slightly," said John.

I asked the boys to take me up there, and they agreed.

Mr. and Mrs. Donald de Turca lived in a spanking new development on the top of a hill about five miles away from the Lucci home. Mrs. de Turca was at home, preparing dinner for her husband who was due back any minute from his job as an officer for the Pennsylvania Turnpike Commission. Mrs. de Turca, an attractive young woman, was a case investigator for the Department of Welfare.

"It's been so long since we talked about it," she said. "The date was August 11, on a Wednesday. Both my husband and I made a big note about the date, because it was such an amazing thing, so hard to believe. Of course, I had gone to work that day, and we had gone to my aunt's house to visit. When we came back, it was around midnight. And it was beautifully clear that night. As we were driving along, my husband said, Look how clear it is. And he turned off the headlights for a moment. The moon was so brilliant you could see everything. We stopped at the house, and we have a dog, and my husband said, I think I'll take the dog for a walk. And he did."

Donald de Turca arrived at this moment and told a graphic story of how he had stepped outside the door with the dog just as a huge, disklike object hove into view not more than 200 or 300 feet above his neighbor's house. It appeared to be 60 to 70 feet in diameter, and he showed me a sketch which he had done before the NICAP investigator had shown him the photograph taken by the Luccis. It was almost identical. The object he reported differed in description from the photograph in only one way. At the time he saw it— it hovered for nearly half an hour—there appeared to be brilliant red lights whirring around the rim. In addition, the object gave off a clearly discernible high-frequency hum. And down the street from the de Turcas' was a section of the high-voltage transmission lines. Mr. de Turca, a former paratrooper, knew the configuration of nearly every aircraft.

"I had such a long time to study this thing," he said, "and it was so low, that there couldn't be any remote possibility of mistaking this for a plane or helicopter or balloon. Then there was the dog. He ran around in circles. You can't fool a dog, can you? He almost went crazy."

Standing on his lawn, he pointed to a neighbor's house. "It came in from the west, directly overhead, right overhead here," he said. "Then it zigzagged a few yards, hovered a little, and came back. But it remained nearly all the time in the same area, right over that house there, three or four rooftops high. When it took off, it didn't make any sound. Took off real quick. Faster than a jet. And this was the first time I observed it moving in a straight line."

With this and other accounts covered by reporter Schley, it was apparent that events in Exeter were being repeated in western Pennsylvania. The parallels were startling not only in description, but in other ways: the behavior of animals, the changing of light patterns, the hovering, the fast and slow movements, the quick change of course, the blinding speeds, and the attitude of the local Air Force.

But most startling to me was the appearance of the objects over or near the power lines. Whatever clue this might be, the observation had been repeated too many times to be treated as incidental.

CHAPTER XI

ON Thursday, October 28, I had been invited by Dean Rusk, along with other journalists, to a National Foreign Policy Conference for Editors and Broadcasters at the State Department in Washington. It was a conference I wanted to attend, and I planned to cover it, as well as visiting with NICAP to try to get any up-to-the-minute material they might have. Because of a late arrival from Pittsburgh, I had to choose between the two. Somewhat reluctantly, I decided that the UFO story was developing so fast that it transcended even the precarious international situation in impact. I could not help feeling that something was bound to break soon in the story, and any interruption of the research would be unwise.

I met Richard Hall, the assistant director of NICAP, for lunch. A young, soft-spoken and intelligent man in his thirties, he filled me in on the overall activity of the organization, that Major Donald Keyhoe had founded in the face of an antagonistic national press.

"Is there any pattern of sighting throughout the country you've been able to discover? Any special areas where they concentrate?" I asked him.

"About the only thing we've been able to discern," he said, "is that the sightings seem to concentrate in small geographic areas during any wave. But that concentration area will shift around. In 1960 there was a concentration in northern California. Other times, it's been over the Midwest. In 1952, there was the famous cluster of sightings over Washington, involving radar at the control towers of the airports in the area. But there are always outlying reports, too. We don't have any idea what they're up to."

We were talking about a map of the United States in his office, with markings—by pins of different colors—of recent reports on it. "What do the yellow pins represent?" I asked.

"The yellow ones are reported landings or near landings. We've found a lot of people are reluctant to report these because of ridicule. When you've talked to as many witnesses as we have here, from all walks of life, you begin to notice people like the small-town school principal who came in here. He had sighted an object, very close to landing, several years ago. He didn't want to be ridiculed, didn't want his position to be jeopardized. He came in and unburdened himself to us because he knew he would have a sympathetic hearing, and he described, unknown to him, things that had been seen by many other people across the country."

"I've been wondering about that myself," I said. "I've been tape-recording a lot of testimony. These people are sensible, reliable. In a courtroom, their testimony would have to stand up against any judge or jury. This is what puzzles me."

Hall smiled. "On the basis of legal-type evidence, this case would have been proven a long time ago. Of course, what most people are waiting for, and what most scientists are looking for, is hardware. They want a piece of one or something they can analyze before they will commit themselves. But I don't think this is very becoming to the scientific fraternity, to want something in hand before they at least study it."

"NICAP, I understand, has reached the hypothesis that UFOs are probably extraterrestrial. Have you any further speculation?"

"Except for our published statements, which we think are a reasonable hypothesis that these could be spaceships, that's about all we could say."

"Is there any scientific agency that is willing to investigate on this?" I asked.

"Not as an agency, no," Hall said. "We have a great many individuals all over the country in government, agencies, Cape Kennedy, Huntsville, and so forth, on an individual basis."

"What seems to be the main resistance to studying the subject?"

"The lack of governmental recognition to the phenomenon, and the fact that it is debunked officially."

"The Air Force remains absolutely inflexible?"

"Since 1952, yes. At that time they were much more open about it."

"What's the most interesting confirmation they ever gave the subject?"

"The famous *Life* article in 1952 was reported to be encouraged and sponsored by some high-placed generals in the Pentagon. They presented some of the better cases in their files to back it up. And they're similar in character to the reports we're getting today. But again they suffered from lack of concrete evidence. It was a very strong suggestion that we had interplanetary visitors."

"What about the Federal Aviation Agency?" I asked. "Certainly these things are violating safety regulations for any craft—experimental or not. Have you learned anything from the FAA?"

"We tried to get a Congressional investigation to look into this, particularly in one case. An American Airlines captain in 1956 took his plane off course to pursue a UFO, which is all against C.A.B. regulations. The Senatorial committee found the case very interesting, and listened attentively to our tape-recorded interview with the pilot, stating that he had done this. He denied this later publicly. But the committee said that they would be accused of digging skeletons out of the closet if they used it. So nothing came of it. The FAA, again on an *individual* basis, is very interested. We get very good cooperation out of the FAA when we make inquiries about radar trackings. As far as we know, there is no organized attempt to gather the information. We've had people who call the airport when they've sighted something. And often they would be put on to an FAA man who is interested in gathering the information. We suspect it is just a matter of individual curiosity."

"Are you able to speculate on government lack of interest, or apparent inactivity?"

"Frankly," Hall said, "I think they have a tiger by the tail at this moment. They started out with immediate secrecy when they started getting these reports, and they've gone on for so many years denying that there is anything to it, that it would be very awkward and embarrassing to admit that there was something to it, all of a sudden. And if they did, they would appear awfully stupid in the past. Now the way we feel today—we have the choice of two views. One, they are *not* aware of what's going on. This seems highly unlikely. Number two, they are *well* aware of what's going on. And for various reasons, they are suppressing it. The third alternative is that there is nothing at all to it. That would be the hardest of all to accept."

I recalled the sighting Kimball and I had made. "What about the reports of Air Force fighters scrambling after the objects?"

"The business of people observing aircraft, usually military aircraft, chasing after UFOs is a quite common report. And very often, all authorities will deny that they have any planes up chasing anything. They profess complete ignorance."

I sketched for him the sighting Kimball and I had made, mentioning the fighter plane and a description of the object.

"This happened over Washington last January, when we were having a flurry of sightings in nearby Maryland and Virginia. A group of Signal Corps engineers downtown on Constitution Avenue saw a group of shiny oval objects in the direction of the Capitol building in the late afternoon. Not directly above it; you couldn't tell the exact distance. And chasing these objects was a sweptwing jet. It was apparently in hot pursuit. All the Washington papers inquired about it, and it was completely denied that any military craft were up chasing anything. We got indirect confirmation, verbal confirmation, that something was tracked on radar at the National Airport, but we were not able to document the military part of the story. I think what has misled most of the general American public are the crackpot reports, which are extremely wild. We keep away from these completely."

"From some of the material you sent me," I said, "I understand you have some landing reports that aren't completely wild. Like the one in Buffalo, where they found a blue dye."

"Yes," said Hall, "we got there before the Air Force and interviewed the witnesses. But the sample wasn't found until the Air Force was there, and they got to the sample first. There was some left which we got, and we had it analyzed. The report is all in obscure chemistry jargon, but they state there is nothing particularly unusual about it. Titanium was one of the major constituents, which was a little surprising to us. But it didn't prove anything."

"What other landing reports has NICAP investigated in full?" I asked.

"The landing in New Mexico, where a police officer by the name of Zamora saw it, was interesting. He had a particularly high standing in the community, which made his story quite believable. He was the one who saw the egg-shaped object on the ground. We got soil samples, we got a shiny material that was on a rock right adjacent to one of the imprints that was left."

"What kind of imprints were they?"

"They were rectangular, four of them. And it looked as if, assuming this was some kind of craft with a landing gear, it looked as if the landing gear had scraped down along this rock and left some metal on it. We had that analyzed at a Washington government laboratory, very well equipped, on an off-the-record basis. And they identified this substance as silica, which is very surprising because we were not aware that silica could give this shiny metallic appearance. But they say it can under certain weather conditions. So again it was inconclusive. If it proved to be a metal, even if it wasn't a particularly unusual metal, it could have been interesting."

"Tell me a little about some of the scientists who have been working with NICAP," I said.

"Well," said Hall, "the most prominent scientists who are associated with the UFO subject, or stick their necks out to some extent, are in general the type who have a little more daring and imagination. Dr. Carl Jung, the famous psychoanalyst, before he died, was a member of NICAP. In his final letter, he said that he had read Major Donald Keyhoe's last book, and he had pretty much concluded that we were dealing with real objective phenomena in the sky, in contrast to some erroneous quotes about his own book that he believed that they were only psychological manifestations. But this impression about Jung's book was incorrect. Because if anyone had read it carefully they would have noted that all he said was that he had to deal with the psychological aspects of it, because that was his field. But he left open the possibility of the reality of the thing. A very prominent scientist on our Board of Governors is Dr. Charles P. Olivier, President of the American Meteor Society, and Professor Emeritus of Astronomy at the University of Pennsylvania. He doesn't take any position as to the nature and reality of UFOs. He stated that he believes there should be a much more thorough and careful investigation of the subject. And as such, he's one of the few astronomers willing to endorse the basic scientific principle to investigate and study before passing judgment. We have numerous members who are also members of the American Association for the Advancement of Science, including my brother, Dr. Robert L. Hall, who is program director for the National Science Foundation for sociology and social psychology. He's one of NICAP's special advisers. Then there's Dr. Leslie Kaeburn, a biophysicist on the faculty of the University of California, and a member of our panel of special advisers. There are many others—competent professional scientists who are willing to take a position and at least willing to encourage further investigation of the subject, and not entirely satisfied with government findings."

"Have you found your job frustrating?" I asked.

"It has been frustrating in past years, but recently there has been a swing in the other direction. If this keeps up, I don't see how Congressional hearings can be avoided."

"Where does the resistance to the subject come from about a Congressional hearing?"

"Well," Hall said, "Congressmen in general are likely to take the Air Force as the best authority on the subject. They may be, of course, but they're not letting anyone else know what they know. Also in 1961, there was a three-man group set up in the House science committee to explore the possibility of hearings. And the information we had at that time was that they feared they would be laughed at and ridiculed if they brought the subject out into the open. But I don't follow the reasoning on that. They investigated V-girls in Baltimore, and the Ku Klux Klan. Of course the Air Force has a terrific advantage over us. They can parade an impressive bunch of colonels who will state that the situation is well in hand. It's hard to oppose this, and the only thing on our side is when we can win support of academic people and the public. We would welcome anybody checking our sources, because we are very careful about documentation."

"What about reports from Communist countries?" I asked.

"It's very hard to get information from them, of course. But back in 1952 when Major Keyhoe was working very closely with the people in the Air Force project, they were feeding information to him which he used in his early books. He was shown Air Force intelligence reports of sightings in Russia. And occasionally since then, I recall one case a few years ago, where CBS reported from Moscow that there were sightings around there. You occasionally get reports from eastern European countries. In fact, a year or two ago there was a Yugoslavian reporter who went around all over his country interviewing people. He was astonished, because everywhere he went, he found people who had seen them."

"Do you think the official position stems from the fear that people might panic?"

"This was very strongly suggested to people in 1952, and it commonly occurs in all writings on the subject. The idea keeps popping up that people would panic if the truth were known. I don't think people would be that panicky. They've learned to live with the H-bomb, and I think the

184

Government constantly underrates the public about what they can take. We've had over the years, as you can imagine, thousands of letters. In fact, we have a file problem. Far and away the largest percentage of people express intense curiosity. Very few, very rarely, does anyone express fear. The only fear we have encountered is shown by people who did not take the subject seriously enough, were uninformed about it, and were suddenly confronted with it."

"Any reports in the last few days, for instance?" This would be the last week in October, 1965.

"Yes, but they're fragmentary. It takes time for them to get in. I was talking to our subcommittee member in Indianapolis yesterday, and he said that in the last two days there was a case where the State Police were following a UFO around in their car till the wee hours of the morning, trying to catch up with it. And another case, in Marion, Indiana, where a UFO moved over radio station WMRI, and at that moment, nobody could hear the station. Another case of an electromagnetic effect, of which we get many. We got similar reports from Los Angeles by telephone that in the past week there have been many sightings, including one that we call a 'satellite object.' This is a large, reddish, elongated object, often cigar shaped, flying across the sky, and then smaller points of light coming out of it, and moving along independently."

"I've heard a couple of reports up in Connecticut recently —quite recently. Do you have any detail on those?"

"Unfortunately," Hall said, "both of them, after preliminary investigation, appeared to be very shaky cases. One was a photograph taken by a staff photographer of a newspaper. We got the pictures for analysis, and the 35-mm sprockets and the identification of the film was cut off, and until we get an explanation for that, we can't take them too seriously. And the other one was a report of a UFO descending toward a hillside. Some reporters climbed up the mountain, and they found a burned spot there on top of the hill. But our Connecticut subcommittee members report that that was nothing but the remains of a campfire. So again, there's no real evidence. We can't be too careful of how we check these things out. Nothing will weaken our case more than an irresponsible report. There are enough responsible ones without fooling around with the weak cases. Connecticut has had its share, though, of responsible cases. One I recall in '62 or '63, where a state representative saw a UFO around Hartford. This was a triangular-shaped object, it sped by in broad daylight, quite shiny and metallic."

"Could that have been a delta-wing jet?" I asked.

"No, it was shaped more like a Mercury capsule. And a conical object has been observed quite a bit recently, particularly over Virginia, and occasionally other states for the past year. And this is something pretty new in the history of UFO reports."

"What about the apparent capacity to change shape? That seems to come up once in awhile," I asked.

"This," said Hall, "we don't accept as established. I think it's simply a shifting of lighting pattern. At least this seems to be more reasonable. These things often have glows around them, and haze or vapor, and these would very easily alter the appearance of one. And also a disk-shaped object viewed from different angles would tend to create the illusion of different shapes, or changing shapes."

"Now what about that vapor trail that was evident in the picture I investigated up near Pittsburgh?"

"Yes. That wasn't vapor really, that was something detected by the film that was not seen by the eye. We don't know, but if the pictures are authentic, as they appear to be —and we checked them out very thoroughly—we checked them out especially because of the age of the person who took them, a young boy. We're always cautious in such cases, but this one checked out so well, we got such good, strong character statements about him that there seems to be no doubt about him. Granted that the picture is authentic, this would seem to be some kind of a clue to the propulsion which we have some of our technical people looking into right now."

"What about the comparison of some of the sightings with sound, and those with no sound?" I asked.

"Sound appears to be heard only at very close range. And our experience with reports is that seldom has there been a very noisy UFO, one that attracted attention to itself by its noise. Although I believe there are a few exceptions to that. Usually, when sound is reported, it's a very faint hum or buzz. Or whining sound. In fact, it's often been compared to the sound of a generator."

"How about animals? The effect on animals. I've run into several reports of this."

"Yes. Ever since the very early sightings in the United States—I recall back in July, 1947, soon after the first one reported in the postwar period in this country, in Portland, Oregon. There was a policeman walking along near a flock of pigeons on the ground. And the pigeons became very alarmed and agitated, and started flapping around, and he looked up and saw this disk-shaped object passing overhead. Ever since then, there have been sporadic reports of this. But again, in this past year, which I think is really a reflection of our ability to get more information, there have been numerous reports of dogs and livestock and cats and birds reacting in the presence of UFOs. This is reported in all parts of the country. As you know, in the Exeter, New Hampshire, case, this was reported very clearly. We've been getting so much more support lately, that the reports are more expert and technical and more detailed. All these people joining in to support us in places like Cape Kennedy and in the universities. Fact, we received a letter from a City Manager in a Los Angeles suburb which has a population of 90-some thousand, and he wants to form an affiliate for us out there. He strongly endorsed the need for more public information we had mentioned in one of our recent bulletins. But this is very interesting when a city official is willing to stick his neck out and form an affiliate."

"I've noticed," I said, "that your general attitude and that of Ray Fowler, up in New England, and the Pittsburgh NICAP group, seem to be an effort to try to *dis*prove a case first, rather than trying to prove it. What about this?"

"This is very important," Hall said. "There's no question at all that the large majority of things that are reported as UFOs are *not*. They are stars or planets or planes, or something of this nature. But the Air Force carries it on from there, and claims that therefore *nobody* has seen anything out of the ordinary. But—the more people do contribute false reports for the record, the harder it makes our job to prove that there are good observers seeing something unusual."

"Have there been any slip-ups by the Air Force which indicate that they are holding back information?"

"I think there have been, in various regulations and statements on the subject. They put out annually, I guess, or at certain intervals, a thing called *The Inspector General's Brief*. It goes to all base commanders. And in one issue, they had a little headline: 'UFOs are serious business.' And the story was that all air base UFO officers should be equipped with all sorts of equipment, including Geiger counters and cameras and sample-collecting kit, and all this sort of thing. This would seem to imply that they were taking UFOs very seriously. This was not a classified document. Somebody happened to come across it and got a copy for us. Similarly, their own regulations spill the beans about their real attitude about the subject. The regulation is now labeled 'for official use only,' and they're trying not to give it out any more than they have to. This regulation states quite clearly that the only cases that will be publicly given out will be those which will have a conventional explanation. Anything unexplained is simply not to be released to the public. And a little interesting sidelight on that is that we cited this regulation in our bulletin, referring to Paragraph Number 9. Since then, they shifted that to another paragraph number—juggling the paragraphs around a little bit. I don't know whether that was deliberate or not, but it looks funny. I see no reason why they suddenly juggled the paragraphs."

"Has there been any direct pressure put on NICAP by the Air Force or Government?"

"None whatsoever," said Hall. "I think that since we've kicked up the biggest storm about this subject, if anybody were to be approached by the Government, certainly it would be us. And nobody has ever suggested that we have been doing anything wrong or harmful. And on the contrary, we've had trickled-down reports from government authorities that they approved of what we were doing. I've noticed that the Air Force often assigns people to the UFO subject who know little about it or its history. And they often make very seriously embarrassing statements to the public—gross errors which certainly weaken the Air Force position."

"You feel the close-range sightings are increasing?"

"The reports at very close range have been building up, especially in the past year. It is my firm conviction that if presently existing scientific equipment were brought to bear on these things, we'd have all the proof anyone would need. But it's not being done."

I knew personally a responsible official in the Federal Aviation Agency, and I dropped by his office in Washington late that afternoon. I felt that if I could get an informal picture of the FAA's attitude, it might help in making further appraisal, even though I was certain there was not much I could learn officially. A consultation with several men at the Agency, who preferred not to be named, produced very little. From the descriptions of the objects and their flight patterns, the people at the FAA admitted that the UFOs were grossly violating safety and identification regulations for any kind of craft whatever, if the descriptions from the witnesses were believable. Some of the men there granted that they were puzzled and baffled by the whole situation. One, a former Air Force pilot, said that he had heard many reports from his fellow pilots about UFOs, and that they had been just as baffled as anyone else. A secretary in the office said that she had just received a letter from Gettysburg, Pennsylvania, where people were reporting sightings several times a week. And as in Exeter, dozens of cars brought people nightly to try to see the objects. Officially, all the FAA people could say was that the subject was an Air Force responsibility, and that all information was supposed to be turned over to them for appraisal. No new light was shed on the subject.

Two new developments were shaping up, however, which were important because they would enable me to extend the time I could devote to researching the project. Both *Look* Magazine and Irving Gitlin, former producer of the carefully documented NBC-TV *White Papers* and *The Dupont Show of the Week* documentaries had read the original *Saturday Review* column I had done, and both *Look* and Gitlin were interested in the possibility of both a longer article and a documentary film. Since I had written and directed several films for Gitlin and NBC-TV, we were no strangers. We arranged to get together in Connecticut on the next evening, Friday, October 29, so that he could listen to the tapes and appraise the story for a possible film.

We both listened to portions of the tapes for over three hours. Gitlin agreed that so much testimony could not be faked or invented, and made a decision to begin the initial planning for a one-hour special documentary on the UFO mystery.

Meanwhile, several people called from Exeter to report that an unusual case had broken in the Boston and New Hampshire papers involving a highly respected couple who had encountered a UFO at close quarters back in 1961, and who had been so traumatically shattered by the experience that they had had to undergo hypnoanalysis by one of the highest-ranking medical psychiatrists in Boston in order to repair the damage they had suffered. I had heard of this case from the Exeter police but had not followed it up because I was confining my research strictly to recent cases. Although I was resolved to keep to this plan, I felt it was necessary to explore a development resulting from this case, which was that the couple had decided to speak at a meeting at the Pearce Memorial Unitarian-Universalist Church in Dover, New Hampshire, on November 7, breaking a four-year silence they had observed because they did not want publicity or ridicule that might accrue from the exposure of their story. However, since the New England press had broken it, they wanted to correct any misconceptions arising from the sensationalized newspaper accounts, and agreed to speak on invitation from the church.

But I was to learn later of an interesting angle of that invitation. Lt. Alan Brandt, a public information officer at the Pease Air Force Base, was a member of the church, and had helped arrange the meeting. Perhaps this was significant. I learned by phone that it was just possible that the Air Force was unofficially permitting a story to leak out as a test reaction on the part of a public meeting. But this was pure speculation. I was interested in the meeting for another reason: With the interest in UFOs as high as it was in the area, what kind of turnout could such a meeting expect? Dover was about 15 miles north of Exeter, but there had been many reports of sightings from there also and nearby Portsmouth had its share. A large turnout would be some evidence of how much regional interest there was in the phenomenon.

These two factors prompted me to cover the meeting: possible Air Force connection with it, and an indirect Gallup-type poll as to general public interest. Further, Mr. and Mrs. Barney Hill, the couple who were speaking, had evidently experienced a severe reaction from their sighting, even though it had occurred four years earlier. The case involved

191

hypnoanalytic therapy and could not be explored fully without far more research time than I had available at the moment, but the results of that therapy had brought out some amazing speculations. Under separate hypnosis, I learned, both husband and wife penetrated a period of amnesia which had lasted for two hours following the UFO landing next to their car. Under hypnosis, they related that they had been taken aboard the strange craft, assured that they would not be harmed, given a physical examination by a group of humanoid creatures, and released with the assurance that they would have no conscious memory whatever of the experience. The sessions were taped by the psychiatrist, then funneled slowly back to the conscious minds of the couple as the therapy progressed. The technique was successful in eliminating the dreams and nightmares both husband and wife had suffered following the experience. But neither Mr. nor Mrs. Hill made any claim as to the validity of what they had related to the psychiatrist under hypnosis. They had told close friends only that this was what had come out on the tapes, accounting for two hours which had mysteriously disappeared from an evening in their lives.

The story had broken in the papers, four years after the event, through a meeting of the Hills with technical people interested in the UFO portion of the story. The Hills had spoken at this session at the request of Walter Webb, a member of the staff of the Hayden Planetarium in Boston. It was the first time the couple had mentioned the episode to any but their closest friends. They were acutely sensitive to adverse publicity because Barney Hill, a leader in the New Hampshire NAACP, was a Negro; his wife Betty, a social worker for the state of New Hampshire, was white. Representing a mixed marriage, they knew that involvement with a sensational story like this could have damaging results because of the prejudices of some sections of the population. Both Hills were extremely intelligent, and highly regarded. Barney Hill had received citations and awards for his community work from both the Governor of New Hampshire and Sargeant Shriver. Betty Hill was a dedicated social worker, whom the Exeter police said was unflagging in her work to help the poor. The psychiatrist involved was an outstanding medical man, known throughout the world for his accomplishments in the neuropsychiatric field.

It was a complex, bizarre story. However, because it was four years old, I resolved to confine myself to the church meeting and to the exploring of any possible Air Force interest in it, official or unofficial.

CHAPTER **XII**

I ARRIVED back in New Hampshire on Sunday, October 31, late in the afternoon. In order to be based in a slightly different location, I registered at Lamie's Motor Inn, an attractive motel in Hampton, just a few miles from Exeter. Prior to the Hill meeting at the church in Dover, a week away, I planned to tie up the loose ends left from my previous research.

The Exeter police reported some minor sightings in my absence, but none very interesting. In a follow-up call to Mrs. Gazda, Muscarello's mother, I learned that she and some friends had seen more of the objects, hovering over a field along Route 101-C. There seemed to be three of them, at low altitude, with varicolored lights, the general overall color being orange. I tried hard to persuade her that she might have seen ordinary aircraft, but she refused to be budged from her story because she insisted that the things remained stationary over the field, and that no sound whatever came from them. I showed her the print of the picture from Pennsylvania, but she could not say positively that the shape was the same as the ones she had seen. "Perhaps I might have looked at them from a different angle," she said, referring to earlier sightings. "And the ones I saw when you were away were cigar-shaped, which would rule out the disk shape you have in the picture. However, I will say that the sketch my son drew after the sighting he made with the two police officers *did* look like this. Almost *exactly*."

Mrs. Lillian Pearce, on Warner Lane, however, agreed that the Pennsylvania picture did look like some of the objects she and her neighbors had seen, although she had seen other shapes, too. "Unless, of course, the changing lights make the difference," she said.

While I was talking with Mrs. Pearce about the picture, a group of youngsters from the neighborhood—there must have been five or six of them—came bursting in in great excitement saying that they had just seen a huge red object glide slowly across the trees at the end of the road, and disappear below them. They were excited, and I felt that this was no prank. On the other hand, they were all talking so excitedly at once, that I had trouble getting a clear description. They urged me to come out on the chance that it would reappear again, and taking my tape recorder, I walked down to the end of the road.

There was nothing in sight, but I made them go through what had happened a few minutes before, carefully listening to their inflections and tone of voice. They were still talking all at once, but the substance of what they were saying was that a couple of dogs had started howling, they looked up and the object, almost as big as the moon, moved slowly from left to right above them. It was mostly orange, but there were red lights around the rim, flashing off and on. They had it in view for almost five minutes, they said.

I was ready to charge this off to mass hysteria and imagination when I overheard one youngster, about twelve, say to her friend, "You know something, I really wish we could move away from here. It's just too scary with these things around all the time." She was not saying it for my benefit, and was so sincere and almost plaintive that I could not rule the incident out entirely. When a neighboring housewife, standing in her front door down at the end of the street, confirmed the youngsters' story, I was inclined to consider it at least a possibility.

On the following morning, November 1, I followed up half a dozen leads by phone; they were interesting mainly because they indicated the high frequency of sightings in the area.

At noon, I stopped by the power plant on Drinkwater Road in Exeter, and spoke to a couple of the engineers for the Exeter and Hampton Electric Company. They had heard many stories about UFOs but had not been aware that so many people were reporting them above or near power lines. They were intrigued with the idea, though, and planned to investigate it. They said that high-voltage power lines do create an electromagnetic field, and that if the objects had any kind of affinity for electromagnetic fields, the power lines would be an obvious attraction. There had been no unusual voltage losses reported on the meters, but, they added, it would be possible for an object to enter an electromagnetic field without affecting the voltage.

The question as to whether the power lines could create the image of a UFO was brought up, but since the phenomena had frequently appeared far from the lines, and since most descriptions indicated the UFOs as a structured craft, this theory was highly unlikely. Most descriptions also were contrary to St. Elmo's fire, sun dogs or other known phenomena.

I made a mental note to check more thoroughly with the electric power companies later. At the moment, I planned to begin what I had wanted to find the time to do since I started the research: make a random check, with mostly cold-turkey interviews, in a circle around Exeter. This would, I felt, preclude any rehearsal of descriptions. I had done this, in a sense, when I dropped by Bessie's Lunch in Fremont, but I had learned ahead of time that there had been a concentration of sighting near the place, and consequently it could not be considered a purely random check.

Before going out on this new survey, I went to see Bob Kimball, who was with his brother George in their living room on Grove Street. George Kimball had been an Air Force pilot. One key to the whole mystery, to me at least, was the sighting Kimball and I had made. Although it was so brief and at such a high altitude, our own sighting made more believable what others were reporting. The tendency for Kimball and me was to alternately believe and disbelieve what we heard about UFOs. To believe that hovering machines stopped in midair, came directly at cars and people, hurtled off into space at lightning speeds, was difficult even though you didn't doubt the character of the people involved. But *not* to believe such overwhelming, continuous, and repetitive testimony was equally hard.

Bob Kimball, his brother and I rehashed the sighting again in detail.

"I had the binoculars," said Bob, "and I looked at it with the glasses. It was still an orange ball, or a disk on end. I couldn't tell which. By the time I could hand them to you, both the plane and the object were gone."

I said, "The plane was too small to be a B-47 or -52, but it was a jet, so it had to be a fighter. No private plane could move at that speed."

"We can assume that," said Kimball. "There's no question it was a jet fighter."

"And the fighter looked as if he were in hot pursuit, trying to close in on the object. But he was making no headway."

George Kimball spoke. "Assume the plane was going six hundred miles an hour, and they're in sight to you for one hundred miles—horizon to horizon, say, at an altitude of five thousand to eight thousand feet, which would give you a wider horizon than normal. That's fifty miles to your left, and fifty miles to your right. You would have fourteen seconds of visibility."

"The speed was probably less than that," Bob Kimball said. "The B-47s and B-52s fly over here at about one hundred twenty knots. This plane was going much faster than that. He was moving. He was low. I was surprised to see a jet fighter that low at night. Much faster than a jet usually moves at that altitude in that area. He was moving out."

We continued discussing it at length, checking George Kimball for details which his Air Force experience might clarify. At the end of the talk, the situation remained the same. We had seen something unexplainable in ordinary terms.

The first stop in the partially random survey was a grocery store called Puggio's, on Front Street, a mile or so out from the center of Exeter. The proprietor had not seen any UFOs himself, but he told me that three or four weeks before, the entire neighborhood was up in arms about a strange object which crossed the sky. He did not leave the store to go out and look himself, but he said, "The people from across the street were out gazing up there. Some people came out with field glasses, and they were all excited about it. Two or three funny things moving up and down in the sky, they said. They all said it wasn't Echo or a satellite."

I walked across the street, knocked on the door of a house, and a woman told me: "I was out several nights looking. The one I saw was not quite the size of a full moon. It was bright and round, between a yellow and a natural color. Before that it was high, and I thought it was a star. Then it moved down fast and got bigger. Then it moved sideways, stopped, moved again. I don't know what it was."

I drove out toward Kensington, spotted an elementary

school, and went inside to find a teacher. At least the report—positive or negative—would be articulate. I found one in Mrs. Esther Prescott, who taught the 5th and 6th grades. She was gracious enough to let me interrupt her class because she thought it was important that this subject be explored thoroughly.

"Our daughter," she said, "is a junior at the University of New Hampshire, and her experience was so frightening that somebody has got to find out what these things are. She came home one night almost hysterical. This was two or three weeks before anyone around here had reported anything like this. She told us, and there were some other young people in the house, and they laughed at her. So my husband and I, just to calm her down, told her that we'd go out with her and look ourselves. She was so upset, I can't describe it to you. But by the time we drove to where she had seen it, nothing was there. Then later, when the police officers from Exeter reported a description of almost exactly what she had seen, she was so relieved, I can't tell you how relieved she was. And she is a very lucid, calm person. Her father and I didn't doubt her in the least, because we know what kind of a girl she is. She said she had never seen anything like it before, that it was literally as big as a house, and it had a red glow. And not a bit of noise. Not a bit. This took place directly over what we call Round Hill. It was a genuinely frightening experience."

She mentioned several other people, including the two librarians who had sighted the objects later.

So far, the random survey was bringing amazing results. I had no reason to doubt either the store owner, the woman or the schoolteacher, each of whom had been called on without warning or preparation. I drove farther south from Kensington, spotted a large farm machinery sales and repair agency, and went in to talk to several of the men there. Each of four men knew people who had seen the objects, but had not seen any themselves.

I drove eastward toward the ocean and stopped at a small motel called Johnson's Motel. One of the men in the farm machinery agency had heard that there had been sightings over there. Although this would not strictly be part of a random sample, I wanted to find out if the lead was valid. In a sense, it was. Mrs. Johnson, a motherly woman who ran the homespun motel, had not seen a UFO herself, but some three weeks before, her three grandchildren had run in screaming to tell her that a huge object had come down low in the field right outside the motel. "They screamed that it was an airplane, but it wasn't making any noise. I told them I'd be out later, but like a darn fool, I waited too long. By that time it was gone. They said, Nanny, it's way down low, and it's got all funny lights on it. Well, I still wouldn't have thought too much of it, except another person and his wife saw the same thing right near here, and were nearly scared out of their wits. My daughter lives in Amesbury, and a fellow who works with her husband also saw the same thing that night."

I got the name of this man—an Albert Doughty in Amesbury—and called him on the phone. Mr. Doughty told me with considerable emphasis that he had had quite an experience. He was driving from Seabrook toward Prescott Farms about three weeks previously, at 9 or 9:30 P.M., with his wife at the wheel. "When I first saw it, it was all lit up, and it was high. I told my wife, that's not a plane, stop the car. It was all lit up all over, and there were red and green lights going around it. And it was stopped still in the sky. We went on for awhile, then stopped again. We watched it for quite a time, and then it started to move. Then right near the shopping center, the darn thing just started to zoom right toward our car. Right directly at us. Very, very fast. Right toward us. And it scared the holy hell out of my wife. She said, For God's sakes, Albert, get home as fast as you can. It seemed to come right down straight, and it was so big. And my wife actually almost went into a panic. All she was interested in was getting home."

199

"What did it look like when it got closer?" I asked.

"Well," Mr. Doughty said, "I was so darned scared and so was my wife, that to tell you the truth, I don't really know. In fact I don't know how close it really got. Then when I learned that some other people had seen these things, I said to my wife, Thank God we're not going out of our minds. You know, you really wouldn't believe these things unless you saw them yourself. I'm convinced now that everybody can't be wrong, can they?"

I thanked Mr. Doughty for his information, drove to Route 1, and stopped at a grocery store. For the first time, no one I spoke with there had seen any sort of object, nor did they know of any leads. Statistically, though, the survey was ahead of the game, and it continued that way in the evening when, at the lounge in Lamie's Motor Inn, I conducted a more comfortable survey. I spoke with eleven guests and employees. Of the eleven, three had seen and described with reasonable accuracy a sighting following the general pattern. Eight others knew personally people who had encountered the phenomenon in some form or other.

On the morning of November 2, I finally got around to the Hampton Coast Guard station to see about the incident involving the two young men who had been brought to the station in a state of shock by the police. Francis Bajowski, chief of the installation, could not release the names of the men involved, however, because of regulations. But he agreed that if the Air Force base in Portsmouth would allow it, he would do so, and also have the man who had been on duty that night tell me informally what had happened when the two youths had come into the station. All other statements, the Chief said, would have to come from the Coast Guard information office in Boston. Throughout our talk, the Chief was cordial, but somewhat evasive. I tried to reach Lieutenant Brandt to get permission for the Chief to release the names, but he was off duty that day. Meanwhile, I stopped at seven stores, gas stations, and restaurants in the Hampton-Exeter area. Five out of the seven gave me direct leads to friends who had seen the objects.

In midafternoon, I went to Officer Bertrand's house to get his reaction to a story the Pentagon had released to the local papers about his and Officer Hunt's sighting. It was such a garbled distortion of facts that I could not understand how the Pentagon could release it. Later, an officer at the Pease Air Force Base told me he was "shocked at the Pentagon's stupidity."

With a Washington, D.C., dateline of October 27, 1965, the news story read:

> The Pentagon believes that, after intensive investigation, it has come up with a natural explanation of the UFO sightings in Exeter, New Hampshire, on September 3.
>
> A spokesman said the several reports stemmed from "multiple objects in the area," by which they mean a high-altitude Strategic Air Command exercise out of Westover, Mass., was going on at the time in the area.
>
> A second important factor was what is called a "weather inversion" wherein a layer of cold air is trapped between warm layers.
>
> The Pentagon spokesman said this natural phenomena causes stars and planets to dance and twinkle.
>
> The spokesman said "We believe what the people saw that night was stars and planets in unusual formations."

I was confident that no one, including the Air Force, had investigated this sighting in greater detail than I had. What's more, the release was a direct slam at both Bertrand and Hunt and their capacity to distinguish between "stars and planets" and an enormous, silent craft which had brought Bertrand almost to the point of pulling his gun. I had spent part of two nights patrolling with Bertrand and Hunt, and

201

had come to respect them and their jobs. For the Pentagon to ascribe their sighting to either "high-altitude exercises" or "stars and planets in unusual formations" was patently absurd. If anything, it could only lead eventually to the embarrassment of the Pentagon.

Bertrand was very calm about it. "If they want to turn out ridiculous statements like that," he said, "that's their business. I know what I saw. They don't. And of course I can't accept what they say there. I know for sure it had nothing to do with the weather. I know for sure this was a *craft*, and it was not any plane in existence. I know for sure it was not more than a hundred feet off the ground. I'm not saying it's something from outer space. I'm saying I don't know what it was, and from this newspaper story they've released, I know damn well they don't either. I know it didn't have any wings, and I know it wasn't a helicopter. Or no balloon, or anything of that sort. It's absolutely stupid of them to release something like that."

For the first time since I had met Bertrand, I saw him grow irritated. "I'm not getting paid for all this, and I'm not trying to make up a big thing. And I saw an unknown craft of some sort. It was no helicopter. I was near enough to hear the choppers, if it had been one. It had brilliant lights on it, that you just don't see on aircraft, plus it had no wings whatever. You couldn't see any tail section. In fact, the first reaction I got was that it was a huge, red fireball. But then I could immediately see that it wasn't. It was a huge, compact round thing with lights going back and forth. When Dave got there, it was a little farther away, but we sure as hell both checked each other out. Maybe if I stood in the field and watched it, I could have made out the image better. But all I could think of was getting the hell out of that field with the kid, because of being afraid of being burned. Do they think I would run from a star or a planet? Or a chopper or a balloon or an airplane? As I told you, an aircraft did go by later, far away and overhead. It was miles away—but I could still make out the

202

wings and the running lights plainly. And there was no fog, no heavy air. Some nights there's a fog, and being near the seacoast, you get a heavy atmosphere. This was a crystal clear night. No humidity. Real dry. I just know that what the Pentagon says in that news story is not true. I don't care. They can believe what they want. I know it's a craft of some kind. If the Air Force wants to come and tell me they have an aircraft with no wings on it, and brilliant red lights, that can stop, hover, turn on a dime, and move without a damn bit of sound at one hundred-foot altitude, I'm willing to believe it. And I'll go along with it, because that is what Dave and I did see. I'm not saying it's anything from outer space, but they don't seem to be able to. They make it look worse by printing things like this. They make it look like they're trying to cover the thing up. Now all of a sudden they seem to discover that they had these 'high-altitude exercises' from Westover Field. But it was a month, nearly two months, before they came up with this explanation. Of course, they must be doing this for the general public. They must know that they can't fool Dave and me. But I've heard people say: 'Well, it's all solved now. We can relax.' But *you* know from the people you've talked to, *I* know from what I saw, that they really *can't* relax."

From this moment on, Bertrand, Dave Hunt and I would have trouble believing anything the Pentagon released on the UFO subject. I had to admire Bertrand for not blowing his top completely.

Bertrand asked me if I had made any more headway in connection with the power-transmission line theory. I told him of the coincidences I had found near Pittsburgh, showed him the Lucci picture, and told him how this object had been hovering directly over the wires out there in Pennsylvania. In turn, he was reminded of a case he had been called out on several weeks after his own experience, which he had forgotten to pass along. The police desk had received a call from a woman named Sloane, on the Epping Road, who reported a bright red object which had lit up her home, her bedroom, and the surrounding fields. It was so bright that it had awakened her. Bertrand and Hunt had been dispatched to investigate, but by the time they got to the house the object had disappeared. They noticed, however, that Mrs. Sloane's house was right next to the high-power wires where they crossed the road near the Brentwood line. The thing had been hovering directly over the lines.

I drove out to the Sloane house, but no one was at home. The transmission lines, I noted, were not more than 50 feet from the house. The neighbors across the street, Mrs. Ruth Williams and her son Galen, were at home, however. Galen had spotted a glowing red object on Route 88 several weeks before, but had not seen any near his home. The object near the legendary Route 88 had moved up, down, back and forth over a group of trees about 100 yards away. He and a friend completely ruled out an airplane, and when they arrived in Hampton, they immediately phoned the Pease Air Force Base in Portsmouth. The officer in charge, in a rare expansive moment, told him that someone had sighted a similar thing in Dover, just about the same time.

Mrs. Williams, although she had not seen any object herself, had a full report on Mrs. Sloane's sighting. She had told Mrs. Williams about it the next morning: a huge red disk which had illuminated Mrs. Williams' house as well as her own. Mrs. Sloane had said that she was going to phone at the time, but decided to call the police instead because of the lateness of the hour.

I continued with the random survey, getting some hearsay, some direct accounts, from people who cannot be named, most of whom are military personnel.

—A coastguardsman from New Hampshire told me that although his station would never release any official information, he was on watch one night when an enormous reddish-orange disk moved slowly up the beach, not more than 15 feet above it. He confessed that he was so shocked by the sight that he went into the radio shack and closed the door.

—From an Air Force pilot I learned that pilots had been ordered to shoot at any UFO they came across in an effort to bring it down. But he said that they were apparently invulnerable, and that they were capable of outmaneuvering any aircraft the Air Force had. He said that he simply ignored the orders to fire on such objects, since he felt personally it would be better not to alienate them.

—A military radar operator reported that a UFO came directly toward the base, was clocked both visually and on the radarscope. It seemed as if it were brazenly going to land at the base. But instead of landing, it hovered over the base. The officer-of-the-day was notified, and he put a telescope on the object. As he watched, it suddenly accelerated to a speed of over 800 miles an hour, as clocked on the radarscope. It disappeared within a minute.

—A brilliant orange object landed directly off the edge of one of the runways at the Pease Air Force Base, illuminating a wide area where many of the Air Force officers and their families lived, according to a member of a high-ranking officer's family. Some wives reported that the light was so bright that they thought it was morning; one actually started to get dressed until she realized it was still the middle of the night. Phone calls swamped the switchboard at the air base, and eventually the base was cut off by the commander from outside communication. The fire unit of the base was dispatched to the end of the runway as the object took off and disappeared at an unclocked speed.

—I was given several more reports about the constant scrambling of jet fighters after the strange objects; when radar sightings had been made in concert with visual sightings.

—Constant radar reports were being made at the Portsmouth Navy Base. In one instance, an object hovered over a water tower at the base before taking off at incredibly fast speed. It was checked both visually and by radar.

—One highly qualified officer at the Pease Air Force Base told me that he had been skeptical about UFOs before he had been assigned to the command at Portsmouth. He was no longer skeptical at all. At least 15 pilots at the base felt the same way.

—An Air Force refueling officer told me that a refueling operation was broken off abruptly when an enormous UFO appeared directly off the wing of a KC-97 tanker, confirmed visually by the crew and by instrument by a radar tower.

—An Air Force pilot claimed that the most sophisticated jets and weaponry were no match at all to the speed and maneuverability of the objects.

—Two additional officers of the air base told me that they were shocked and dismayed by the Pentagon report issued about the Bertrand and Hunt case in Exeter. They said it was so unbelievable in the light of what local authorities knew, that it could make the Pentagon a laughingstock. They said in no uncertain terms that the report was severely damaging to the Air Force.

Although none of the personnel supplying this information can be identified, for their own protection, these reports are no less real than any of the other information I put directly on the tapes. In fact, in view of the position of these people, the stories reinforced the thesis that UFOs not only existed, but were beyond the capacity of the military to deal with them. This impotence, of course, might be the underlying reason why the Government was carrying out its ostrichlike program of nonrecognition. The public has a naïve and childlike faith in the military, and anything admittedly beyond its control might shatter this faith forever.

CHAPTER **XIII**

BY Wednesday, November 3, I realized that I was coming to a full impasse in the research. The scuttlebutt, the rumors, and the off-the-record remarks of the military had convinced me of the impact of the mystery, but the evidence was repetitive and did not indicate a conclusion.

Several new frustrations developed that day. One was that I learned I would not be able to see young Muscarello for several weeks, when he would return to Exeter on leave from his boot training at the Great Lakes Naval Training Center. The other was that although the Air Force had granted permission for the Coast Guard at Hampton to release the names of the two young men who had had such a harrowing experience, it was impossible to find out immediately their whereabouts, because they were summer workers at an ocean-front restaurant which had closed for the season. I was able to get at least some of the details from the Coast Guard station regarding the case, which was most interesting because of the low altitude of the object, and the total shock the principals had experienced.

The Coast Guard log, of course, was laconic and in the customary officialese language:

At 0400 on 2 August, 1965, Walter Shipman and Chris J. Kalogeropoulos, both working at Connie's Cozy Kitchen, Salisbury Beach, Massachusetts, reported an Unidentified Flying Object to the Hampton Beach Police, who brought them to the Coast Guard Station, where a UFO report was made.

(Anthony Warren, the coastguardsman on duty at that time, told me they were cold sober, something he established immediately, because he would have recommended their arrest otherwise.)

Police Sgt. Farnsworth, according to Warren, came by with the two men, but both were so shaken that they refused to get out of their car. They were finally persuaded to come into the station, where they reported that the object moved in from the ocean, directly toward their car. They thought at first it was a helicopter or a jet in trouble, but eliminated that explanation because there was no sound, and it moved up, down and sideways as it followed their car. They increased their speed, but still it followed them. Finally, they made a U-turn, and the object did likewise.

Warren had them fill out a form in detail, went over the road where the sighting took place, but was unable to see anything. "When I opened the door of their car," said Warren, "the first thing I checked was whether they were drunk or not. They definitely were not. I didn't want to get involved in reporting any story from crackpots. I asked them how big it was, but they were so upset they couldn't say exactly. All they could say was that it was *big!* After that, I wrote down what they saw, and sent it on to Pease."

With all the investigation I had done, I suddenly realized that I had never studied the original location of Bertrand's and Hunt's sighting on Route 150, to see if there had been any high-tension power lines nearby. While it would not prove anything if there were, it might add another piece of evidence to the theory that the objects at least seemed to utilize some kind of electromagnetic force from or be attracted to the power which surges through this network of wires which makes up the Northeast Grid.

On the way, I noticed an appliance store on Route 1 near Hampton, and since a cable was loose on my tape recorder, I decided to see if it could be repaired. At the Downer Appliance Company, I ran into a Phillip McKnight, who went to work on the ailing cable. At the same time, I asked him if he had run into any reports of UFOs and he said he knew of several. As a Boy Scoutmaster, he knew families of his troop members who had clearly observed the objects, some at close range. He told me that Mrs. Parker Blodgett, of Shaw Hill, had encountered a particularly vivid sighting near her home. He was impressed with this, because Mrs. Blodgett was an able and prominent citizen, and president of the New Hampshire PTA. This interested me, because Shaw Hill was the area where young Ron Smith, his mother, and aunt had encountered UFOs twice at close range.

I talked with Mrs. Blodgett in the living room of her restored pre-Revolutionary farmhouse that commanded a sweeping view of the countryside.

"It was September 21, and it was after midnight," she said. This was approximately the date Ron Smith had indicated he had seen an object in this same area, although he could not remember the exact date. "I was going to bed, between one-thirty and two A.M. And I turned off the lights in the living room here—they face on the southeast. And I suddenly saw this very bright, blinding ball of light up over the trees there, about one hundred yards away. It was deeper red, almost, on the top, in sort of a semicircle. At the bottom was an extremely bright glowing light. It was just sort of hovering there over the trees."

"How big did it look?" I asked.

"It covered an area from the chimney of that house there, to the tree here in the yard," she said. This, I noticed, would make it enormous. The area spanned almost a hundred feet, as far as I could estimate.

"It was above the trees when I first saw it," she said.

"How far above them?"

"Not very far. Just above them. I would say it was above the pine trees you see in the distance, rather than over my house here. It was a little farther off. It was just hovering, and I was thinking I should call somebody and get them up and let them see this. Because they're going to think I'm crazy in the morning. Then—it started to spin real fast, and went zoom. And it was out of sight."

"It spun?" I had had other reports of this, and wanted to get a clearer description.

"It spun," Mrs. Blodgett said, "just a circular motion, then it went zoom. And it was gone within a second."

"How did it spin?"

"It just gave a spinning motion."

"Can you tell me a little more about the color?" I asked.

"It was a reddish color. Reddish to an orange, a red glow. But it did have a lighter, a light glow underneath it. Which I thought might be due to the fact that it was slightly hazy that night."

"Hear any sound?"

"No sound *at all*."

"Did the lights make any pattern?"

"I saw no pattern of lights, as it's been reported. There was a twinkling around the edge, but no pattern."

"You're familiar with running lights on airplanes?"

"Oh, yes. Of course. They go over here every night. It wasn't like that at all."

"Was this the only one you've sighted?"

"This is the only one I have sighted. A friend of mine claims he saw it. And there was an Air Force plane following close behind the thing. So they must be well aware of it. Some officers have stopped by here inquiring, as a matter of fact. But they give us nothing to go on. The thing that bothers me is that these things should not look like they're out of science fiction—but they actually do. It's all so fantastic. Really, it is."

"Are there any high-tension power lines near here?" I asked.

"What are they, exactly?" she said.

"They're the high poles or steel towers that carry electrical power. Not the ordinary poles that go along the road. These usually go across country, with a wide path cut through the trees around them."

"Now that you mention it," she said, "I think there are. Right down the road here."

I went out and looked and about a quarter of a mile away, I saw familiar multiple poles and heavy strands of wire.

From Shaw Hill it is only a short drive to Route 150, and to the spot where Muscarello, Bertrand and Hunt watched the object hover above them in the field. I parked my car but I could not see any high-tension wires from that point. I decided to go to the house directly across from the spot, and was greeted by Jeanne Fiset, a student at the University of New Hampshire, who commuted to classes from her home. Miss Fiset learned the next day about the incident that had taken place only a few yards from her house, having slept through all the confusion and excitement.

"You were sleeping when the police cars came out here?" I asked.

"Yes."

"Did you hear anything at all?"

"No, I did not. Not that night. The following night I did, though."

"What happened then?"

"The following night we began seeing all these cars across the road, and we thought maybe the flying object was going to come back, because so many people were gathered out there looking for it. I guess it was about nine o'clock when all the cars started coming. And we had heard that this boy, Muscarello, was planning to come back. But neither my father, mother, nor I saw anything. And I don't think anyone else did, either. The following week, the boy talked to us and told us what he had seen. And how it scared him."

"Was he convincing?" I asked.

"Yes, he was very convincing. He said he was not going to leave the area until he had seen another one. He wanted to prove to everyone that he had seen something. He was coming out here every night, he said, with either his friends or his mother. And he did. He asked us if it was all right to come and knock on our door, no matter what time it was, if he saw it again. He wanted us to see it, too. We said that would be all right. And a couple of weeks after that first night, it was about one-thirty in the morning, I heard this knock on the door. It sounded as if someone was trying to tear the house down. My mother and I went to the door, and the boy was there and said he had seen it again. He had a friend with him, and the friend had seen it, too. My mother and I looked in the sky, and at first, we didn't see anything. Then, all of a sudden, coming across the sky, we saw this red object, it was about the size of a ball. It was smaller than the moon, but not as small as a star. The boy said, That's it, I know it is, because just a few minutes before, he had seen it flying low. A plane was apparently chasing it."

"Did you see the plane?"

"Yes. And we could hear it, too."

"You could see the running lights?"

"Yes. They were flashing."

"The object was ahead of the plane?"

"Yes."

"About how far ahead was it?"

"It's hard to tell. Say the object was way down the field across the road, and the plane was up by the house here. This object, the first object, not the plane, went down by the trees across the road, behind the house, came out from behind it, and just plain stopped in the air. Then it came back from the same direction. Now, a plane just doesn't do that. Also, did they tell you about the animals in the neighborhood? Everybody told us that the dogs in the neighborhood really kicked up that first night, and especially the horses across the road began making all kinds of noises."

"I heard about that," I said.

At this point, Miss Fiset's father arrived home, and I talked with him about the night of the original sighting.

"I heard a lot," he said, "but I didn't check it out at that time."

"What did you hear?" I asked.

"My dog was whining. And he seemed very scared. So I got up to see what was the trouble. Then I heard the horses, all the way across the road. And they were whinnying away, they were *really* acting up. I got up and I spotted the police cars sitting outside there in the darkness. I couldn't figure out what it was. I could see the lights flashing on and off, the dome light of the cars. And my wife got up, and she looked out too. I thought it must be just a minor accident or something, so I went back to bed."

I was not able to talk to Norman Muscarello until several weeks later, when he came back to Exeter on leave from the Navy. But the interview with him was strangely anticlimactic. The recorded tapes of Officer Bertrand, Officer Hunt, his mother, Officer Toland, Miss Fiset, so surrounded the incident in detail that Muscarello's story was simply a total but necessary confirmation of everything which had happened on that predawn morning of September 3. It coincided almost exactly with the description given by officers Bertrand and Hunt. He demonstrated how he had dropped down on the shoulder of the road to keep away from the object when it came toward him. When the Look *photographer, Jim Kareles, asked him, "Why did you do that?" he replied: "Wouldn't you?" The interview with him completed the cycle of the original incident at Exeter, which had set into motion such a long and arduous period of research. Most*

213

interesting was the lack of any basic distortion in the many accounts of that incident.

After leaving the Fiset house, I walked once more across the Carl Dining field, and down the slope, as Bertrand and Muscarello had done. I reached the far end of the field and looked toward Hampton. I was almost shocked to see what I had been looking for: a long line of high poles and wires of the high-power transmission lines of the Exeter and Hamptom Electric Company. They had been hidden by the trees when I first looked for them. They added another piece of evidence to the power-line theory.

Before the scheduled meeting at the church in Dover on Sunday, November 7, I had time to return to New York and arrange for the start of the documentary film with Irving Gitlin, and also to see *Look* Magazine about arranging for their photographer and senior editor to make plans for the picture story to accompany the article.

At home in Connecticut I found a letter bearing the return address of A. Reid Bunker, Sr., of Plaistow, New Hampshire. I immediately recognized the name of one of the people recommended as a witness by Mr. Healey, of Bessie's Lunch. I had called him during the latter part of October, but far from getting any kind of clear report of an observation, he would scarcely admit that he had seen anything. I was disappointed at the time, mainly because he had been recommended so highly as a witness. I opened the letter and read it:

DEAR MR. FULLER,

When you called the other night (October 24) I thought that it might be one of my fellow workers—I get a lot of ribbing about seeing flying saucers, etc.—I hope you understand. I will try to put down on paper what my wife and I saw—hoping it might help you in your investigation.

We were *under the high-power lines* [the italics are mine] at Fremont, N.H. (Route 107). And we were there about an hour or so, when at 10:45 P.M. we saw an object approach from the northwest going to the southeast. It had red lights mostly, and sort of green and white lights. The lights *did not* flash on and off. It was completely silent, and was within a quarter of a mile of us. It was at treetop level, and gave the impression of a long graceful bounce instead of a straight flight like a plane. Now, if this was a saucer-type object, and was revolving or tipping back and forth, we might have seen the lights on the other side of the object, thus giving the impression that it was bouncing very slightly in flight. We watched it for about half a minute, then it went behind the trees toward the southeast.

About five minutes later, two men on another road came over to where we were, and asked us what we saw—they had seen the same thing and were quite excited about it. Hope this helps.

Sincerely,

A. REID BUNKER, SR.

The letter was interesting as a reflection of the reluctance of many witnesses to discuss the subject at the risk of being ridiculed by their friends, plus the mention of the ubiquitous high-tension power lines.

Also in the mail was an editorial Conrad Quimby had written for the Derry *News*, which demonstrated the impatience many people in New Hampshire were feeling about the attitude of the Government and the Air Force. Its headline was: UFO PHENOMENON: TIME TO HEAR FROM THE WHITE HOUSE. It had appeared in the issue of October 28. The editorial began:

> Several weeks ago, we became interested in the story of several people in and around Exeter who said they had been approached at night by a huge object which was glowing red, and tilted as it moved toward and away from them. The source of this UFO sighting was so close

to Derry that we decided to send a reporter over to see what he could find out. . . .

It's been speculated by some, such as the National Investigations Committee on Aerial Phenomena, that the President and the Pentagon are fearful of public reaction to official reports that might reveal a whole new concept of interplanetary life. . . .

If the White House is holding information about UFOs because it fears that the public might go haywire, we find the observation about as wild as some of the more lunatic UFO stories. We believe that the public can take just about any kind of explanation, even one which might tend to make the White House look like a teller of Halloween tales. . . . It seems to this paper that the White House is acting like a fretful old spinster in not parting with its version of what lies behind the UFO phenomenon.

I could only agree with Quimby's thesis. Regardless of the initial shock, the public had shown its capacity in many disasters to react and recover with resiliency. The people who had encountered low-level UFO sightings unquestionably registered initial shock, but most recovered quickly and spent hours trying to see them again. In other words, hysteria shifted quickly to interest and fascination. The truth cannot be kept under cover indefinitely, and the situation could be worse if the public were unprepared for a sudden announcement. What in the history of human beings could possibly be worse than the hydrogen bomb and the threat of nuclear war? What evidence had UFOs shown that they were hostile, assuming of course that they were in such plentiful existence as the reports all over the world seemed to indicate?

In the same mail was more news, sent along by Gordon Evans, which was most illuminating. It was a reprint of the Proceedings of the First Annual Rocky Mountain Bioengineering Symposium, *held at the United States Air Force Academy* in May of 1964. The symposium was sponsored by the USAF Academy itself, along with the Committee on Electrical Techniques in Medicine and Biology of the Institute of Electrical and Electronic Engineers. It included a paper presented by a highly respected scientist, Frank B. Salisbury, of the Department of Botany and Plant Pathology, Colorado State University. His subject was "Exobiology"—in plainer terms, the study of life beyond the earth. His opening remarks, and other comments, struck me as being extremely apt in the light of the research which had been completed in and around Exeter:

> The existence of this symposium testifies to the possibility that man shall in the relatively near future discover or fail to discover some form of extraterrestrial life in the solar system. The purpose of my discussion is to present briefly some of the current arguments for and against the existence of extraterrestrial life in the solar system.
>
> It is quite amazing how rapidly this topic has expanded in recent years, and how it has moved from the realm of science fiction into a field of thought dignified by the impressive title "exobiology"!

The paper went on to discuss the possibilities of this form of life, citing in detail some unanswered questions about Mars, meteorites, and other solar system phenomena. The material was carefully documented. And in one section, the scientist turned his attention to UFOs:

> To complete our list of evidences in favor of extraterrestrial life, we should cite the testimony of various witnesses who claim to have experienced or seen a visitation by an extraterrestrial intelligent being. Many of these accounts fall into the realm of religion, and because of their nature, they cannot be objectively studied by the methods of science. A number of others, however, involve non-religious accounts of sightings of unidentified aerial phenomena, including flying objects which might conceivably be interpreted as extra-

terrestrial spaceships. Since 1947, a few thousand of these sightings have been carefully recorded and placed in the files of various organizations, and thousands and perhaps hundreds of thousands more have occurred but have not been reported. Many of these are easy to shrug off as misinterpreted natural phenomena (meteorites, ball lightning, the planet Venus, etc.) . . .

The ones which are not so easy to dismiss as natural phenomena or as unreliable witnesses might some day prove to be psychological phenomena. This is the faith of many investigators. At this point, however, we have no proof of this, since most of the phenomena are certainly not explained by our present concepts of psychology. In many cases, the most parsimonious explanation remains that of the extraterrestrial spaceship.

It is my conviction that the accounts should be eagerly studied by the exobiologist. As evidence for exobiology, the unidentified aerial phenomena are probably no more borderline than some of the other evidence already mentioned above.

The paper states that the number and quality of the sightings are much higher than is imagined by most people who have not made a special study of the question. It points out that many of the witnesses are scientists, engineers, and other highly competent observers, and mentions the numerous simultaneous sightings on radar, from aircraft, and visually from the ground.

Salisbury also pointed out that a number of photographs have been obtained, accompanied by the witnessing of the object simultaneously by a large number of reliable people, essential to corroborating the taking of the picture. The Salisbury paper continues:

At present, we seem either to be afraid of the topic or to feel that it is unworthy of scientific comment. . . . Certainly fear has no place in the search for truth, and if the

218

unknowns relating to the topic are someday solved, then we will have made considerable scientific progress.

I couldn't help noting that while the Air Force was busy pretending to the public that UFOs were nonexistent, the Air Force Academy was sponsoring a symposium that was deadly and scientifically serious about UFOs and their possible effect on "exobiology."

In another statement made by Salisbury, he says:

> I must admit that any favorable mention of the flying saucers by a scientist amounts to extreme heresy and places the one making the statement in danger of excommunication by the scientific theocrasy. Nevertheless, in recent years I have investigated the story of the unidentified flying object (UFO), and I am no longer able to dismiss the idea lightly.

I had to agree that this thought was fast becoming my firm position.

CHAPTER XIV

THE Pearce Memorial Unitarian-Universalist Church in Dover is a gaunt and Gothic structure, struggling against the erosion of years, weather, and parishioner indifference. A new, younger group has given the parish fresh life lately, and its regular Sunday evening series of provocative discussions and lectures was beginning to build new interest in the church. Attendance at these meetings had averaged slightly above 50 people on Sunday evenings, and although the hall was able to hold some 400, this small attendance was a respectable figure for a new program in the developmental stage.

I felt that the size of the audience on the night of November 7 would reflect local interest in the UFO subject. Mr. and Mrs. Hill, who were to talk about their traumatic experience with a UFO some four years previously, were anxious to counteract some of the sensationalism of the New England press. If the church hall were nearly filled, it would indicate that the recent frequency of the sightings had impressed a considerable portion of the population. If there were a small attendance, it might mean that the sightings I had recorded were more limited in the area than I thought.

The weather was miserable. The raw, cold rain and a cutting New Hampshire wind might encourage people to stay by their firesides instead of beating their way to a drafty auditorium. But although the meeting was scheduled for 7:30, the audience began arriving over an hour in advance. By 7 o'clock the auditorium was filled, and by 15 minutes after the hour, literally hundreds of people were being turned away. A loudspeaker was hastily improvised for the basement, where part of the overflow gathered. People were standing against the back wall up to the limit of fire regulations. It was a totally unprecedented crowd, far beyond the expectations of the church committee who had planned the event. Some people had driven from towns 40 miles distant, only to be turned away. Church members found they were unable to gain entrance to their own church. My earlier guess had been that there would be a large crowd, but I had changed this estimate when the heavy rain began in the early afternoon and continued without letup.

I was also surprised to see that Lt. Alan Brandt, the Public Information Officer at Pease AFB, was on the speaker's platform in his Air Force uniform. It indicated that there was at least tacit Air Force approval of his being a speaker at the meeting, but whether or not it suggested that the Air

Force was ready to leak out UFO news at a meeting like this, or test public reaction, no one could tell. Lieutenant Brandt's introductory speech was certainly vague and unilluminating. He merely reviewed the Air Force policy on UFOs as expressed in its own handbook, without any further elaboration. He did indicate that the Air Force took UFO sightings seriously and that anyone sighting them should report them to the Pease Air Force Base immediately.

The Hills spoke very circumspectly of their experience. They pointed out emphatically that although their hypnotic therapy had revealed to them on tape recordings that they were taken aboard the strange craft and given a physical examination by intelligent humanoid beings, they could not testify that this was the truth. They *could* testify to their conscious sighting of the UFO as it came down near their car, but beyond that neither the Hills nor the psychiatrist could fully explain the mystery of the two hours of amnesia which followed, aside from the astonishing information revealed under regressive hypnosis.

The crowd packed into the church sat spellbound as the Hills related their experience. The couple had left Canada, driving south toward Portsmouth, and stopped at a restaurant in Colebrook, New Hampshire, on the Canadain border. "When Betty and I left Colebrook," Mr. Hill said, "we never remembered the exact time until we were regressed back under hypnosis. Here, I had looked at a clock on the wall, and the time was five minutes after ten at night. We drove down Route 3, and when we arrived at Groveton, Betty called my attention to a light that was moving in the sky. And I looked at it, and actually to me it was nothing unusual except that we were fortunate enough to see a satellite. It had no doubt gone off its course, and you could see that it was going along the curvature of the earth. It was quite a distance out, meaning that it looked like a star.

"So, this is exciting in itself, and we had 7 x 50 binoculars with us, which we always take with us on vacation. And I stopped the car, so that we could both get a look at the object. Suddenly, Betty said, Barney, if you call that a star or a satellite, you are being ridiculous. Just look at it. So with the naked eye, without taking the binoculars, I could see that it was not a distant thing far out there, but now more like a plane. I said, Betty, we obviously made a mistake. That's a commercial plane on its way to Canada. It was traveling from the south, going north. And I was facing west, meaning I was facing toward Vermont. So I took the binoculars and started looking, and then I was completely amazed. Because instead of continuing on the northerly pattern, it turned toward the west, toward the direction of Vermont, completing the turn and then coming in toward us. Then I noticed a winking sort of light pattern, not at all like a conventional aircraft. And although I was amazed, I told Betty that it was probably a Piper Cub or some other light plane, and that it wasn't anything to be concerned about.

"We got into the car, and started driving south on Route 3. Betty continued to look out and she said, Well, Barney, if it is whatever you're calling it, I don't know why. Because it's still out there, and still following us. I would slow down occasionally, and would look out and see that it was still there. And I felt a little uncomfortable about the whole thing. I thought that probably some hunters or fishermen had a light plane, and could see us on the highway, and were following us.

"So when we reached Cannon Mountain, if you're facing south, Route 3 goes to the left of it. And this object went around the western side of the mountain. So that when we passed Cannon Mountain, there's a figurehead, referred to as the Old Man of the Mountain. The object now hovered around and was now facing us on the highway, still some distance away. I was completely baffled by this, and I was hoping a car would pass us one way or another, because there was some comfort thinking I could stop someone and ask if they saw the same thing."

Mr. Hill then described the actual encounter. The object settled down, about 200 feet in the air. He began walking toward it, peering through the binoculars. It looked to both him and his wife like a huge pancake. Around the base was a band of light, and through the binoculars he saw a row of structural windows. What's more, he could actually discern figures inside the craft, and he ran back to the car, jumped in, and started to drive off.

Then the craft rose up, circled the car, and went out of sight over the roof. Both the Hills heard a strange, electronic beeping sound and began to feel a strange tingling sensation. It was at this point that their memory was blocked completely for a two-hour period of total amnesia.

The Hills refused to discuss the details of their experience as recalled on the tapes under hypnosis. They did not regain consciousness until they had driven some 30 miles to the south. The professional help they sought was instrumental in relieving them of the traumatic neuroses resulting from the experience, but they both insisted that they were making no claims beyond the conscious recollection of the incident.

"We just don't know the answer," Mr. Hill concluded. "We sought the best professional psychiatric help possible, and this is the answer we got."

So intense was the interest of the audience, that the question-and-answer period following the talk lasted for over an hour. Several in the audience revealed their own experiences with UFOs.

After the session, I joined the Hills and Walter Webb, of the astronomy staff of the Hayden Planetarium in Boston, for a cup of coffee. Webb had been instrumental in arranging professional help for the Hills, and was extremely interested in the UFO aspect of the case because of the stature and reliability of the couple. Webb pointed out that in spite of the strangeness of the information revealed under hypnosis, he and several other scientists were taking the case very seriously. The Hills, he said, had shown great restraint in keeping the incident away from the glare of publicity for over four years, and both husband and wife ranked far above average in intelligence. Although the case remained a mystery, it was still under serious study.

Monday, November 8, was spent mainly with Gereon Zimmermann, a senior editor of *Look*, and Jim Kareles, staff photographer of the magazine, as we made the rounds of several of the key witnesses to review their stories and photograph them for the picture story to accompany the article. I was relieved to have others spot-check the interviews. We covered Mrs. Hale, Mrs. Gazda, the entire community in the area of the Pearce home, the police, Ron Smith, Bessie's Lunch, the Jalbert place by the power lines in Fremont, and Chief Bolduc and his family in the same neighborhood. In reviewing their sightings with them, it was interesting to note that the descriptions remained basically the same as when they had given them to me a few weeks previously.

At the Bolduc house, Jesse Bolduc had joined the ranks of the observers since the time I had first talked to him. He confessed that he no longer laughed at his wife, and admitted that he had to eat his own words.

At the Jalbert home, the entire family reported continued sightings, and both Joseph Jalbert and his mother recounted a most interesting observation which had happened since I had first met them.

Joseph had recently noticed a reddish, cigar-shaped object in the sky, high over the power lines. It hovered there motionless for several minutes—exactly how many he did not know because he was so absorbed with watching it. After a considerable length of time, a reddish-orange disk emerged apparently from inside the object, and began a slow, erratic descent down toward the power lines. As it reached a point within a quarter mile of them, it leveled off, then moved over the wires until it reached a point several hundred feet away.

It then descended slowly until it was only a few feet above the lines. Then a silvery, pipelike object came down from the base of the disk and actually touched the lines, remaining there for a minute or so.

The protrusion then slowly retracted into the body of the object, and it took off at considerable speed—exactly how fast, Joseph could not estimate—then rejoined the reddish-cigar-shaped object and disappeared inside it.

Joseph's mother had not seen this but had observed a similar occurrence some 20 miles away, near Manchester. The only difference in their descriptions was that the protrusion extending down from the object she observed was reddish rather than silver colored. Joseph was very reluctant to bring this sighting up. His younger brother had prodded him into telling about it, and when Zimmermann, Kareles and I asked him why he was so hesitant, he told us that the whole thing looked too scary and he didn't like to talk about it. "It's the first time I've ever seen one of these things touch anything," he said, "and it happened so near to me that I really tried to put it out of my mind."

By Tuesday, November 9, I was ready to close out the research and begin the long job of trying to correlate all the tapes and notes. Several more reports of sightings were brought to our attention that morning, but most proved to be repetitive, and I could see no reason for extensive interviews. One, however, I looked into thoroughly because it involved an alleged landing outside a house in Exeter in a heavily populated area.

Mr. and Mrs. Joseph Mazalewski lived at 2 McKinley Street in Exeter, in one of a group of modest houses separated, in some cases, by vacant lots. They occupied the first floor of the house, and both of them worked during the day, coming home at noontime for lunch.

I caught them at noon on November 9. They were each in their sixties; both pleasant and cordial. At approximately

2:30 in the morning, sometime in September of 1965—neither could recall the exact date—Mrs. Mazalewski was awakened by a brilliant light illuminating her first-floor bedroom. At the same time, she heard a loud humming noise which startled her. Her husband, asleep in another room, was not aware of it at this time. She sat up and was able to see out the window from her bed. A large cluster of different-colored lights approximately 20 feet away from her bedroom window were blinking in an indefinite pattern.

"I watched for fifteen minutes," she said. "I sat on my bed and kept watching it. I said to myself, what the heck is that? And it kind of scared me, you know. I kept hearing this noise. It scared me."

"Could you imitate this noise?" I asked her.

"I really don't know if I could," she said. She tried, making a sound similar to the humming of an electric generator. "It was right flat on the ground," she went on. "In back of that tree."

She pointed to a small tree, now leafless, about 15 feet from her window.

"Flat on the ground?"

"Yes, right on the ground, as far as I could see. And those lights kept blinking and blinking."

"Could you make out any shape?" I asked.

"No, the lights were too bright," she said. "They looked almost like Christmas tree lights, you know?"

"What was your reaction to it? How did you feel?"

"I was wondering what it was. It really scared me. I sat here, just watching and watching. I didn't even think to wake my husband up in the next room at first. Then when I finally did get so scared I couldn't stand it anymore, I called in to him. I said, Gee, Joey, there's something out there in that field. There's all bright lights out there."

Joseph Mazalewski spoke up. "I was already putting my pants and my shirt and my slippers on. I wanted to go out in the field, to see it close. She said to me, No you ain't going out there!"

I turned to Mrs. Mazalewski. "Why wouldn't you let him go out?"

" 'Cause I didn't have any idea what it was out there. And I was scared. I didn't want something out there pulling him into something."

"Did she really stop you?" I said to her husband.

"She sure did," he said. "She wouldn't give me my slippers. I started toward the door, and she stood in front of it. She said, You're not going out there!"

"I had the funniest feeling through me," said Mrs. Mazalewski. "It gives you the funniest feeling. It was an *awful* noise."

"The lights kept blinking all the time?"

"Yes. And that noise kept going all the time."

"Flat on the ground? Not vertical?" Mrs. Mazalewski was so intense and upset about recalling the incident that she had trouble articulating.

"This was flat on the ground," she insisted.

"You sure you couldn't make out the shape of the object behind the bright lights?"

"No, I really couldn't make out what was behind them."

"Did the sound stop suddenly?"

"Yes, it did. And when I looked out again, it was completely gone."

"I went out the next morning," Mr. Mazalewski said, "and I couldn't notice anything unusual in the field. It must have just been floating right above the grass."

"Anybody else in the neighborhood see it?" I asked.

"Nobody that I know of," said Mrs. Mazalewski. "A lot of people around here keep talking about seeing these things, but I don't know if anybody saw anything this exact time."

Mrs. Mazalewski had obviously undergone a traumatic

experience. Unfortunately, her description was too vague to be of much help, but the low-altitude report was of interest because it represented the second one in two days.

I met the *Look* Magazine men back at the motor inn in Hampton for dinner. It was a cold, sparkling clear night, with a brilliant hunter's moon, and the huge fireplace in the dining room was a welcome sight. We met at about 5:30, and as I was leaving my room, I noticed that the electric lights flickered, faltered for a few seconds, and then came on brightly again. I thought nothing of it, went on into the dining room where Zimmermann and Kareles were waiting for me in a booth. We ordered martinis and prepared to relax.

As the waitress brought the drinks, she had a broad smile on her face. She had been helpful in the past in supplying the names of people she had heard about who had sighted objects, and was interested in the story as it developed.

"I suppose this is all your fault," she said, putting the martinis down on the table.

"What is all our fault?" I asked.

"You mean you haven't heard about it?" she said.

"Heard about what?" Zimmermann asked.

"The blackout. The power failure. All over the east."

"You're kidding," I said. The lights in Hampton were blazing brightly. I did recall, though, the flicker as I had left my room.

"It just came in over the radio in the kitchen," she said. "New York, Albany, Boston, Providence, all of Massachusetts, are absolutely black. Not a light burning. This is no joke, I mean it."

This seemed so incredible that we hardly took it seriously. I got up, went back to the room, and turned on the television set.

I was startled to see the news staff of NBC-TV broadcasting in faint candlelight. The picture was fuzzy and barely discernible. The commentary, of course, confirmed all that the waitress had told us, and more. I still found it hard to believe. And, of course, the first thing which crossed my mind was the long series of UFO sightings involving the power lines, such as Joseph Jalbert's report the evening before. I forgot completely about dinner.

When Jim Kareles came back into the room, I was already pouring through the 203 pages of transcript of the tape recordings. The words "power lines" or "transmission lines" appeared on an alarming number of pages. I began making a notation in the margin of the transcripts wherever a reference like this was made. Jim Kareles helped me correlate the information. There were 73 mentions in various locations by various people. These included either the actual use of the words, or references to locations near where the power lines ran.

I sat glued to the television set, waiting for some word as to the cause of the unprecedented failure. The news commentators were as confused as everybody else. No one seemed to have any idea of the cause, and never in history had there been a power blackout of such extent. I tried to phone my home in Connecticut, but was told by the operator that the only calls she could put through were those that were a matter of life or death.

The Portsmouth-Exeter area, we learned, was one of the few pockets of light in the entire Northeast. I found small comfort in that, because I thought of the millions of people in the large cities who must certainly be trapped in cold, dark subways or jammed, stuffy elevators.

I waited in vain throughout the evening and early morning hours for more news but no announcement came which gave even a clue to the mystery. I ran through the transcripts again, still noting the phrases and descriptions referring to the power lines. Suddenly, the major emphasis of the entire UFO research—the power lines—was now becoming the focal point of a new mystery—no less mysterious than the UFO phenomenon I had been dealing with for weeks.

The country was moving, it seemed, from one Space Age ghost story into another.

Or were they both the same?

CHAPTER XV

THE blackout caused by the failure of the Northeast Power Grid created one of the biggest mysteries in the history of modern civilization. Eighty thousand squares miles and 36,000,000 people—one-fifth of the nation's population—were suddenly plunged into inexplicable darkness.

Massachusetts, New Hampshire, Rhode Island, Connecticut, Vermont, New York, New Jersey, Pennsylvania and parts of Canada were totally or partially affected by the failure. The President ordered a sweeping investigation. Nearly 800,000 persons—equal to the entire population of Washington, D.C.—were trapped for hours in elevator shafts, subway cars, or commuter trains. Airline pilots circled vainly to find a way to land at darkened airports.

The miracle was that panic and darkness failed to leave a massive death toll. Only a few accidents were reported, and these might have happened with or without a blackout.

By November 11, *The New York Times* was reporting that the Northeast was slowly struggling back toward normal, but that the cause of the blackout was still unknown. Authorities frankly admitted that there was no assurance whatever that the incredible blackout could not occur again, without warning.

There was a curious lack of physical damage: The utility companies looked for something to repair, but there was nothing. Only a few generators were out of action as a result of the power failure, not a cause. What's more, the utilities were able to restore service with the exact same equipment that was in use at the time of the blackout. What happened that night was not only far from normal; it was mystifying.

If there had been a mechanical flaw, a fire, a breakdown, a short circuit, a toppling transmission tower, the cause would have been quickly and easily detected. Mechanically, however, the system as a whole was in perfect repair before and after the failure.

William W. Kobelt, of Walkill, New York, is one of the thousands of line patrol observers who, according to *The New York Times,* went into action to try to discover the trouble. He is typical of all the others. He flew over the lines of the Central Hudson Gas and Electric Corporation at daybreak after the blackout. Cruising close to treetop level, he checked wires, insulators, cross arms and structures of the high-power transmission lines. He looked for trees, branches which might have fallen over the wires. "We looked for trouble—but couldn't find any at all," he said.

Robert Ginna, Chairman of the Rochester Gas and Electric Corporation, said that his utility had been receiving 200,-000 kilowatts under an agreement with the New York State Power authority, which operates the hydroelectric plants at Niagara Falls. "Suddenly, we didn't have it," he said. "We don't know what happened to the 200,000 kilowatts. It just wasn't there."

Edward L. Hoffman, assistant to the chief system electrical engineer of Niagara Mohawk, told *The New York Times* that it was true that some generators dropped out of phase, but that this was "secondary to the main cause of the failure."

Early in the blackout, it was announced that a line break

near Niagara Falls had caused the trouble. A fast check immediately ruled that theory out.

At 10 P.M., it was announced that the crux of the difficulty lay at a remote-controlled substation on the Power Authority's transmission lines at Clay, New York, a town 10 miles north of Syracuse. The high-tension 345,000-volt power lines stretching over Clay are part of the authority's "superhighway" of power distribution, running into Niagara Falls, east to Utica and south to New York City.

Niagara Mohawk repairmen who drove out to Clay found the substation in apparently perfect order. There were no signs of mechanical failure, fire or destruction. Another report sent FBI investigators and State Police to the desolate Montezuma Marshes outside of Syracuse, but they found nothing out of order there, according to *The Times*.

Something else happened outside Syracuse, however, which was noted briefly in the press, and then immediately dropped without follow-up comment. Weldon Ross, a private pilot and instructor, was approaching Hancock Field at Syracuse for a landing. It was at almost the exact moment of the blackout. As he looked below him, just over the power lines near the Clay substation, a huge red ball of brilliant intensity appeared. It was about 100 feet in diameter, Ross told the New York *Journal-American*. He calculated that the fireball was at the point where the New York Power Authority's two 345,000-volt power lines at the Clay substation pass over the New York Central's tracks between Lake Oneida and Hancock Field. With Ross was a student pilot who verified the statement. At precisely the same moment, Robert C. Walsh, Deputy Commissioner for the Federal Aviation Agency in the Syracuse area, reported that he saw the same phenomenon just a few miles south of Hancock Field. A total of five persons reported the sighting. Although the Federal Power Commission immediately said they would investigate, no further word has been given publicly since.

Pilot Ross's sighting took place at 5:15 P.M., at the moment when the blackout occurred in the Syracuse area. At 5:25 P.M., a schoolteacher in Holliston, Massachusetts, watched through binoculars with her husband an intense white object in the sky moving slowly toward the horizon. At the same time, David Hague, a seventeen-year-old from Holliston reported an identical object, moving toward the southwest.

In New York City, simultaneously with the blackout, two women declared in two separate statements that they sighted unusual objects in the sky.

In the statement of Mrs. Gerry Falk, she says: "Between five and five-five P.M., November ninth, I was driving along Mt. Prospect Avenue, West Orange, New Jersey. As I reached the corner of Mt. Prospect Avenue and Eagle Rock Avenue, I noticed a red streak in the sky. I stopped for a light and saw it again. I tried to get the attention of the driver in the next car, but was unable to do so. It is a heavily wooded area and hilly, and as I reached the crest of a hill, I saw it again.

"It was shaped rather like a half-moon, with two tips facing up. It was pale red, not like a flame, and there appeared to be something at the tip. It was very high in the air. At first I thought it was a sky-writer, but then I saw it was different from anything I had ever seen. The sun was going down to the right. This was on the left. It continued going up."

Mrs. Sol Kaplan, of Central Park West, New York City, was watching television in her bedroom, which faces the Hudson River to the west. Her TV set went off and the lights went out. "I looked out the window," she states, "and there were a number of planes in the sky, more than usual. As I kept looking, I saw a big circular dome—it was not flying, but going up and down and sideways. It was silvery-looking, no lights like an airplane. I was looking through binoculars."

Life photographer Arthur Rickerby took a strikingly dramatic picture of the New York skyline just after the blackout.

In the western sky, a brilliant, silvery object appears that has not in any satisfactory way been explained, after it appeared in the November 19, 1965 issue of *Time*. Although some claim it is Venus, photographer Rickerby is inclined to disagree.

In Philadelphia, several witnesses in many parts of the city reported seeing a "curious cloud, shaped like an up-ended coin with a handle" in an otherwise cloudless sky, according to Ruth Montgomery, Hearst columnist. They later discovered it was seen at almost the exact moment that the power failure occurred. Philadelphia itself was unaffected by the blackout.

Walter Voelker, a research engineer, told Miss Montgomery: "The most curious aspect was that by the time my wife and I saw the 'cloud' and could stop the car in traffic for a better look, it had shifted to the other side of the sky. We saw it in three different locations. Later, we learned of others who had had similar experiences in sighting it." Several sightings of a similar description were made in and around Bloomfield, Connecticut, at approximately the same time that the blackout struck.

According to NICAP, at 4:30 P.M. on the day of the blackout, pilot Jerry Whittaker and passenger George Croniger saw two shiny objects above them, chased by two jet planes. One UFO put on a "burst of speed" to outdistance them. Other UFO reports at the time of the blackout came from Holyoke and Amherst, Massachusetts, Woonsocket, Rhode Island, and Newark, New Jersey.

In spite of the lengthy report issued by the FPC, the Great Blackout has still not been adequately explained. Ostensibly, backup Relay #Q-29 at the Sir Adam Beck generating station, Queenston, Ontario, was eventually pinpointed as the source of the massive failure. But further investigation, hardly noted in the press, showed that nothing in the relay was broken when it was removed for inspection. In fact, it went back into operation normally when power was restored. The line it was protecting was totally undamaged. "Why did everything go berserk?" *Life* Magazine asks in an article about the blackout. "Tests on the wayward sensing device have thus far been to no avail." A later statement by Arthur J. Harris, a supervising engineer of the Ontario Hydroelectric Commission, indicated that the cause was still a mystery. "Although the blackout has been traced to the tripping of a ciruit breaker at the Sir Adam Beck No. 2 plant, it is practically impossible to pinpoint the initial cause." As late as January 4, 1966, *The New York Times* in a follow-up story indicated a series of questions regarding the prevention of future blackouts. The news item says: "These questions more or less are related to the cause, *still not fully understood,* of last November's blackout." The italics are ours.

The Great Northeast Blackout was a mystery, but not any more puzzling than what followed on its heels. On November 16, a series of power blackouts hit many parts of Britain. Dozens of sections of London were darkened, and telephone operators in Folkestone, on the south coast, worked by candlelight.

On November 26, NICAP was advised that power failures in St. Paul, Minnesota, were reported by the Northern States Power Company simultaneous with the appearance of objects overhead giving off blue and white flashes just off Highway 61. Fifteen minutes later, just north of the original sighting, a resident on Hogt Avenue reported a "blue-glowing" UFO as all house lights and appliances in the area went dead. A motorist also reported that his car lights and radio went out.

The power company announced that it was unable to determine the cause of that blackout.

By December 2, sections of two states and Mexico were plunged into darkness after a widespread power failure in the Southwest. Juarez, Mexico, was hit, as well as El Paso,

Texas, and Las Cruces and Alamogordo, New Mexico. Authorities were unable to explain the cause of the trouble.

A few days later, on December 4, portions of east Texas were knocked out electrically, with 40,000 houses losing power. It was the third major blackout since the Northeast Grid failed.

By December 26, the mystery was growing deeper. The entire city of Buenos Aires, and towns as far as 50 miles away, were plunged into darkness by a power failure, with hundreds trapped in subways beneath Buenos Aires' streets. The cause was thought to be a single generator.

On the same date, four major cities of south and central Finland were hit by a loss of electrical power attributed to a single insulator.

Going back to 1962, an interesting fact was revealed by Eileen Shanahan of *The New York Times*. "Still not widely known in the eastern United States," she wrote under a November 21, 1965, dateline, "is that the Northeast power blackout was not the first wide-area power failure experienced in recent years. *There was one covering an area four times as large* [our italics] as the New York-New England blackout, and a less extensive one last January. Both were in the Midwest and involved such major cities as Omaha and Des Moines.

"Although the 1962 wide-area failure in the Midwest was well known to power experts before the Commission's survey was completed last year, the National Power Survey [published about a year before by the Federal Power Commission] made no significant mention of it, while recommending an enlargement of the kind of interdependence that made Tuesday's blackout so extensive. The Commission has offered no explanation for the omission."

Further evidence tabulated by NICAP on electrical interference of UFOs in the past enhances the possibility that there may be some relationship between the phenomenon and the wide-area power blackouts:

—On September 3, 1965, a glowing disk-shaped object hovered at low altitude over Cuernavaca, Mexico, as the lights of the town went out. It was witnessed by many, including Governor Emilie Riva Palacie, Mayor Valentin Lopez Gonzalez, and a military zone chief, General Rafael Enrique Vega.

—On August 17, 1959, the automatic keys at a power station turned off as a round-shaped UFO passed overhead, following a trunk power line. As the object disappeared, the keys went on again automatically, and service returned to normal.

—On August 3, 1958, parts of Rome, Italy, were darkened as a luminous UFO passed overhead.

—In 1957, lights went out at Nogi Mirim, Brazil, as three UFOs passed overhead. Also in 1957, a UFO hovered over Tamaroa, Illinois, as the electrical power failed.

One news story on January 13, 1966, is particularly interesting because it received little attention in the press aside from the Portsmouth, New Hampshire, *Herald* of that date, even though it was an AP release, with an Andover, Maine, dateline:

> The Telstar communications satellite tracking station was blacked out by a power failure which hit a 75-mile area in western Franklin County.
>
> Electrical power failed at 4:30 P.M. Wednesday and was restored at 11:20 P.M.
>
> A spokesman for the Central Maine Power Co. blamed the failure on "an apparent equipment failure which somehow corrected itself."

Noteworthy are two things: 1) The power failure involved a space satellite, and 2) in this age of science and engineering, the equipment "somehow corrected itself." Coupled with the stories of the numerous other blackouts, this is strange indeed that the engineers could not figure out how it went out—and how the failure was remedied.

On the following day, an AP story datelined Augusta, Maine, stated that Chairman Frederick N. Allen of the Public Utility Commission indicated that there was no negligence by the two power companies involved. The Central Maine Power Company said that the blackout was caused by the failure of a big transformer in its Rumford substation.

CMP Vice-President Harold F. Schnurle went on to say that it had not been determined why the transformer failed or why it restored itself to service nearly seven hours later.

The relationship of the Unidentified Flying Objects to the power failures is entirely circumstantial, of course. Both UFOs and the Great Blackout still remain unsolved. But stranger yet is the incapacity of modern science to come up with any kind of real answer to either question. More baffling still is the attitude of the large bulk of the scientific fraternity in presumably laughing off a phenomenon testified to by hundreds of technicians, other scientists, airline pilots, military personnel, local and state police and articulate and reliable citizens.

In addition to NICAP, another organization is probing hard into the phenomenon, maintaining strict objectivity, and committed to the premise that the UFO phenomenon, whether it consists of physical fact or rumor, is important enough to warrant objective investigation. Under the direction of Mr. and Mrs. L. J. Lorenzen, the Aerial Phenomena Research Organization (known as APRO), Tucson, Arizona, includes in its membership Dr. James A. Harder, Associate Professor of the College of Engineering, University of California; Professor Charles A. Maney, Emeritus Professor of Physics and Mathematics, Defiance College; Dr. Robert Mellor, Assistant Professor of Botany at the University of

Arizona; Dr. R. Leo Sprinkle, Assistant Professor of Psychology, University of Wyoming; Dr. Frank B. Salisbury, Professor of Plant Physiology, Colorado State University; and many others of high standing in the academic community. Research Director of APRO is Alvin E. Brown, Staff Scientist and member of the Research Laboratory, Lockheed Missiles and Space Company.

When more scientists become able and willing to investigate the subject without prejudice, some progress might be expected that has been lacking to date.

I started on this story as a friendly skeptic. I ended the research with a conviction that it is no longer a laughing matter, and that it is vital and important for the mystery to be solved one way or the other.

In the hands of the Air Force and the Secretary of the Air Force office in the Pentagon, the investigation can almost be considered a farce. The statements made by the Office of Information of the Secretary of the Air Force are often inaccurate, unfounded, and demonstrate a lack of objective investigation that even a reporter would hesitate to utilize in assembling a hasty news story. The embarrassment of the officers at the Pease Air Force Base regarding the Pentagon explanation of the Bertrand-Hunt-Muscarello incident on September 3, 1965, was genuine. Any well-informed officer at the base knew that "stars and planets in unusual formations" or "high-altitude exercises" could not possibly explain a huge, silent craft hovering at rooftop level, lighting up the entire area, especially when one of the witnesses was both a police officer and an Air Force veteran, and the other a police officer of excellent reputation on the Exeter force.

The Pentagon explanation was released to the local press on October 27. To the general public in the vicinity of Exeter, a final evaluation had been made, and the case was closed. Officers Bertrand and Hunt were, in the eyes of the local community, grossly incompetent, incredibly poor observers, or simply unadorned liars.

239

But in the third week in November, a month after the Pentagon explanation, officers Bertrand and Hunt jointly received an undated letter from Wright-Patterson Air Force Base, and signed by Major Hector Quintanilla, Chief of the Project Blue Book. It read:

MR. EUGENE BERTRAND, JR.
MR. DAVID R. HUNT
Exeter Police Department
Exeter, New Hampshire

GENTLEMEN,

The sighting of various unidentified objects by you and Mr. Norman Muscarello was investigated by officials from Pease Air Force Base, New Hampshire, and their report has been forwarded to our office at Wright-Patterson Air Force Base. This sighting at Exeter, New Hampshire, on the night of 2 September has been given considerable publicity through various news releases and in magazine articles similar to that from the "Saturday Review" of 2 October, 1965. A portion of this article is attached for your information. This information was released by the National Investigations Committee on Aerial Phenomena, a private organization which has no connection with the government. As a result of these articles, the Air Force has received inquiry as to the cause of this report.

Our investigation and evaluation of the sighting indicates a possible association with an 8th Air Force Operation, "Big Blast." In addition to aircraft from this operation, there were five B-47 type aircraft flying in the area during this period. Before a final evaluation of your sighting can be made, it is essential for us to know if either of you witnessed any aircraft in the area during this time period either independently or in connection with the objects observed. Since there were many aircraft in the area, at that time, and there were no reports of unidentified objects from personnel engaged in this air operation, we might then assume that the

objects observed between midnight and 2 A.M. might be associated with this military air operation. If, however, these
aircraft were noted by either of you, then this would tend
to eliminate this air operation as a plausible explanation for
the objects observed.

Sincerely,
HECTOR QUINTANILLA, JR., *Major, USAF*
Chief, Project Blue Book
1 atch.
Article "Saturday Review"

Curiously, the letter was not only undated, but the large
brown envelope in which it was mailed bore no postmark
whatever. The Air Force labels bear the legend POSTAGE
AND FEES PAID—DEPARTMENT OF AIR FORCE, so
that cancellation is unnecessary.

The letter referred to the sighting as September 2, when
of course it took place on September 3. It also indicated that
the high-altitude exercises were conducted from midnight
until 2 A.M., while the police officers encountered the close-
range object at approximately 3 A.M. But most ironical was
the indication that the case was still in process of "final evaluation," while the Pentagon had already released its own
"final evaluation" over a month before the letter arrived.

Officers Bertrand and Hunt replied to the Air Force with
this letter on December 2, 1965:

HECTOR QUINTANILLA, JR., *Major, USAF*
Chief, Project Blue Book
Wright Patterson AFB
Dayton, Ohio

DEAR SIR:

We were very glad to get your letter during the third
week in November, because as you might imagine we have
been the subject of considerable ridicule since the Pentagon
released its "final evaluation" of our sighting of September 3,

241

1965. In other words, both Ptl. Hunt and myself saw this object at close range, checked it out with each other, confirmed and reconfirmed the fact that this was not any kind of conventional aircraft, that it was at an altitude of not more than a couple of hundred feet, and went to considerable trouble to confirm that the weather was clear, there was no wind, no chance of weather inversion, and that what we were seeing was no illusion or military or civilian craft. We entered this in a complete official police report as a supplement to the blotter of the morning of September 3 (not September 2, as your letter indicates). Since our job depends on accuracy and an ability to tell the difference between fact and fiction, we were naturally disturbed by the Pentagon report which attributed the sighting to "multiple high altitude objects" in the area and "weather inversion." What is a little difficult to understand is the fact that your letter (undated) arrived considerably after the Pentagon release. Since your letter says that you are still in the process of making a final evaluation, it seems that there is an inconsistency here. Ordinarily, this wouldn't be too important except for the fact that in a situation like this we are naturally very reluctant to be considered irresponsible in our official report to the police station.

Since one of us (Ptl. Bertrand) was in the Air Force for four years engaged in refueling operations with all kinds of military aircraft, it was impossible to mistake what we saw for any kind of military operation, regardless of altitude. It was also definitely not a helicopter or balloon. Immediately after the object disappeared, we did see what probably was a B-47 at high altitude, but it bore no relation at all to the object we saw.

Another fact is that the time of our observation was nearly an hour after 2 A.M., which would eliminate the 8th Air Force operation Big Blast, since as you say this took place between midnight and 2 A.M. Norman Muscarello, who first reported this object before we went to the site, saw it somewhere in the vicinity of 2 A.M., but nearly an hour had passed before he got into the police station, and we went out to the location with him.

242

We would both appreciate it very much if you would help us eliminate the possible conclusion that some people have made in that we might have a) made up the story, or b) were incompetent observers. Anything you could do along this line would be very much appreciated, and I'm sure you can understand the position we're in.

We appreciate the problems the Air Force must have with a lot of irresponsible reports on this subject, and don't want to cause you any unnecessary trouble. On the other hand, we think you probably understand our position.

Thanks very much for your interest.

Sincerely,

PTL. EUGENE BERTRAND
PTL. DAVID HUNT

Nearly a full month went by, but the officers received no reply whatever from Wright-Patterson. Finally, on December 28, the officers wrote again:

HECTOR QUINTANILLA, JR., *Major, USAF*
Wright Patterson AFB
Dayton, Ohio

DEAR SIR:

Since we have not heard from you since our letter to you of December 2, we are writing this to request some kind of answer, since we are still upset about what happened after the Pentagon released its news saying that we have just seen stars or planets, or high altitude air exercises.

As we mentioned in our letter to you, it could not have been the operation "Big Blast" you mention, since the time of our sighting was nearly an hour after that exercise, and it may not even have been the same date, since you refer to our sighting as September 2. Our sighting was on September 3. In addition, as we mentioned, we are both familiar with all the B-47s and B-52s and helicopters and jet fighters which are going over this place all the time. On top of that Ptl. Bertrand had four years of refueling experience in the Air Force, and knows regular aircraft of all kinds. It is important to remember that this craft we saw was not more than 100 feet in the air, and it was absolutely silent, with no rush of air from jets or chopper blades whatever. And it did not have any wings or tail. It lit up the entire field, and two nearby houses turned completely red. It stopped, hovered, and turned on a dime.

What bothers us most is that many people are thinking that we were either lying or not intelligent enough to tell the difference between what we saw and something ordinary. Three other people saw this same thing on September 3, and two of them appeared to be in shock from it. This was absolutely not a case of mistaken identity.

We both feel that it's very important for our jobs and our reputations to get some kind of letter from you to say that the story put out by the Pentagon was not true; it could not possibly be, because we were the people who saw this; not the Pentagon.

Can you please let us hear from you as soon as possible.

Sincerely,

PTL. EUGENE BERTRAND

PTL. DAVID HUNT

By mid-January, the patrolmen had received no reply. On January 19, 1966, I went to the Pentagon to call on Lt. Col. Maston Jacks, press information officer in the Department of the Air Force, to see if there was some further information available about the case and to try to learn first hand the general attitude of the Air Force beyond its statements of policy.

Colonel Jacks was congenial but not very communicative. He restated the Air Force policy routinely, tapping a pack of Belair cigarettes on his desk and looking nonmilitary in a brown civilian suit.

"We don't attack people who say they saw these things," he said. "We don't really question what a person thinks he saw. We don't quarrel with it. We issue our reports resulting from our investigations, and our conclusions are that UFOs are no threat to national security, and that they are nothing ad-

244

vanced beyond known phenomena. If there's anything to it beyond that, I'd like to be among the first to know."

I asked him if he would like to review the tape recordings of the people I had interviewed in the Exeter area, but he wasn't interested. "I told a neighbor of mine, someone who is supposed to have seen one of these things," he said. "And I said: 'If you want to believe in UFOs, have fun. Enjoy it. God bless you.'"

For statistical information, the colonel brought to his desk Mrs. Sarah Hunt, who handles this in the Community Relations Division of the Office of Information. She would, the colonel explained, have more exact information on the Exeter police case.

When she arrived, I asked her the exact status of the case. "That is one of the few which have been classified as being unidentified," she said. She explained the apparent discrepancy between the Wright-Patterson inquiry, the early, incorrect Pentagon release, the wrong date and time in Major Quintanilla's letter, and the lack of a date on the same letter as a combination of inexperienced secretarial help and the setting up of a new filing system. "You very seldom find these reports jibe as to date and time," the colonel added. When I pointed out that the police officers in Exeter seemed to be rather upset about this, both the colonel and Mrs. Hunt expressed their regrets.

I went to the Community Relations Division on another floor with Mrs. Hunt to arrange for getting more details on the Exeter case. On the way, I indicated to her that the Pentagon's stories and releases simply didn't add up, and that I had trouble believing them. Lt. Col. John F. Spaulding, in charge of the division, told me that he was sure the Exeter case was a case of mistaken identity, but admitted that he had not investigated it personally. I asked him if he were keeping an open mind about the case.

"Are you saying that I'm lying about this?" he asked, with a sudden archness.

"Not at all," I said. "I'm just wondering how you are able to be so certain on the basis of secondhand reports."

The colonel didn't take to this too cheerfully. He drew himself up and said, "Sir, you are talking to an officer in the United States Air Force!"

Then he melodramatically walked off and out of sight. Later, when I said to Mrs. Hunt that it looked as if I had upset the colonel, she told me that he had had a lot of problems on his mind during the day, and wasn't feeling in too good a mood.

In spite of his mood, Colonel Spaulding later sent along copies of many of the records the Air Force had on hand of the Exeter case. Among the points which provided new information were:

—In his signed statement to the Air Force investigators, Patrolman Bertrand said: "At one time [the lights] came so close, I fell on the ground and started to draw my gun." He also noted that the lights were always in line at about a 60-degree angle, and when the object moved, the lower lights were always forward of the others.

—In the official Air Force report of the investigation by the Administrative Services Officer of the Pease Air Force Base to Wright-Patterson, dated September 15, 1965, the following information was included: *Identifying Information on Observer:* (1) Civilian. Norman Muscarello. Age, 18. 205½ Front Street, Exeter, N. H. Unemployed (will join Navy on 18 Sept '65) Appears to be reliable. (2) Civilian. Eugene F. Bertrand, Jr. Age, 30. Exeter Police Department. Patrolman. Reliable. (3) Civilian. David R. Hunt. Age, 28. Exeter Police Department. Patrolman. Reliable.

—In the same official report, a statement by Major

David H. Griffin,* Base Disaster Control Officer, Command pilot. *"At this time have been unable to arrive at a probable cause of this sighting. The three observers seem to be stable, reliable persons, especially the two patrolmen.* I viewed the area of the sighting and found nothing in the area that could be the probable cause. Pease AFB had 5 B-47 aircraft flying in the area during this period *but do not believe they had any connection with the sighting."* (Our italics)

The difference between this report of the actual investigating officer at Pease AFB, and the one officially released by the Pentagon to the local press on October 27 is marked and startling.

When I left Exeter, the sightings were still continuing, seemingly without letup. In the early months of 1966, as many as two or three reports a week were being received by police in the vicinity of the town, one of which induced a dyed-in-the-wool skeptic to run to the police station with a full account of a UFO viewed by at least seven people on February 15, 1966.

The publication of the *Look* article, under the title "Outer Space Ghost Story" brought a wave of reaction from all over the country. Letters poured in from obviously intelligent and reliable people who had never before been willing to reveal sightings of UFOs of their own. I was invited to appear on many major network television and radio shows, that had previously steered away from the subject. Even the Voice of America recorded a 40-minute interview with me on the Exeter incident. In all these interviews, I pointed out that Exeter was only one location of many, that the story was growing more intense daily everywhere in the world. On

* The Exeter police recalled the name of the investigating officer as Major Thomas Griffin. Both men are at the base.

247

Christmas Eve, before the *Look* piece had appeared, I was interviewed by U Thant's Chef de Cabinet on the research I had completed for the article. Since then, the UN has expressed serious interest in the phenomenon.

On the discussion program *The Open Mind,* moderated by Dr. Eric Goldman, on leave from Princeton University to act as academic adviser to President Johnson, I met with Dr. Menzel, head of the Harvard University observatory, Dr. Hynek of Northwestern, Dr. Sprinkle of the University of Wyoming and Dr. Salisbury of Colorado State University. Only Dr. Menzel precluded the possibility that UFOs could be a reality, but his reasoning was so resistant to new evidence that had developed that we engaged in a rather sharp exchange of words on the air. His answer to the Exeter case was that the policemen involved were "hysterical subjects," but he could not even recall their names on the air, had never met them, had not investigated the case personally at all. His answer to the Beaver Falls, Pennsylvania, photograph was that it "appeared to be a double exposure"—yet he did not know the name of the photographer, knew nothing about the circumstances under which the picture was taken, had not examined the negatives, nor talked with any of the photographers who had done so. I was surprised and startled that a man of Dr. Menzel's standing could make such flat, unsubstantiated statements publicly. It seemed to symbolize the resistance of part of the scientific fraternity to approach the subject with an open mind.

* * *

On February 9, 1966, the day after the *Look* article appeared on the newstands, the Pentagon finally wrote a letter of apology to Patrolmen Bertrand and Hunt:

DEPARTMENT OF THE AIR FORCE
Washington

OFFICE OF THE SECRETARY   *February 9, 1966*

Based on additional information you submitted to our UFO investigation office at Wright-Patterson Air Force Base, Ohio, we have been unable to identify the object you observed on September 3, 1965. In 19 years of investigating over 10,000 reports of unidentified flying objects, the evidence has proved almost conclusively that reported aerial phenomena have been objects either created or set aloft by man, generated by atmospheric conditions, or caused by celestial bodies or the residue of meteoric activity.

Thank you for reporting your observation to the Air Force and for your subsequent cooperation regarding the report. I regret any inconvenience you may have suffered as a result.

> Sincerely,
> [s] John P. Spaulding
> Lt. Col, USAF
> *Chief, Civil Branch*
> *Community Relations Division*
> *Office of Information.*

Mr. Eugene Bertrand, Jr.
Mr. David R. Hunt
Exeter Police Department
Exeter, New Hampshire

In thinking back over the research, the highlights that stand out on those points detailed in this book that are almost irrefutable:

—Dozens of intelligent, reliable people reported UFO sightings, many reluctantly because of the fear of ridicule.

—Most of these reports were widely separated, and the people concerned were not involved in any collusion.

—Most of the sightings were similar in description, in spite of minor variations which can be expected, and should be expected, from varied viewpoints.

—Police and military were reporting the same type of phenomenon as the ordinary layman.

—The constant relationship of UFOs to the high-tension power lines of the Northeast Grid was inescapable.

—The constant reports of the effect of UFOs on animals pointed up the possibility that human error was unlikely in these cases.

—The reports of electromagnetic effects on lights, ignition, radios and television indicated a similar conclusion.

—Photographs checked by experts, with full character investigation of the photographer, added further evidence that psychic aberrations, mass hypnosis or hysteria or mistaken identity could be ruled out.

—The verified cases of genuine shock and hysteria indicated further that the low-level, near-landing reports were valid.

—Radar reports and scrambling jets chasing the objects indicated that the Air Force was not only cognizant of the objects, but appeared to be impotent to do anything about them.

—Federal Aviation Agency regulations minimized the possibility that the craft were developmental weapons of the United States, since such craft would not be permitted to operate at such low altitudes in populated areas, causing shock and hysteria to the population.

—Secret foreign craft would be unlikely because such actions in the violation of air space would have long since brought about an international incident, just as the single case of the U-2 over Russia had done.

The most logical, but still unprovable explanation is that the Unidentified Flying Objects are interplanetary spaceships under intelligent control. NICAP and others have been supporting this hypothesis for years. Its credibility, however, has suffered by the support of the crackpot fringe. In spite of this, the hypothesis remains stronger than any other theory advanced.

The biggest remaining question is the apparent attitude of government and scientific authorities who have shown no indication of setting up a full-scale project either to prove or disprove the existence of UFOs. Or if they have, the ostensible paternalistic protection of the public is not consistent with democratic principles. The reaction of those who have experienced close encounters with UFOs in the Exeter area has been one of shock, followed by intense curiosity rather than sustained panic. An unprepared public is far more likely to panic than an informed one. Truth isn't likely to remain hidden forever.

In the light of recent developments, the situation has reached a point where it appears to be the duty and responsibility of the Government either to reveal what it knows, or to order a scientific investigation on a major scale and report the findings immediately to the public at large.

THE
INTERRUPTED
JOURNEY

INTRODUCTION

On December 14, 1963, Mr. Barney Hill presented himself at my office to keep his appointment for a consultation. It was like any other day. The appointment had been made in advance, and Mr. Hill had been referred for the consultation by another psychiatrist. At the time I knew nothing of Mr. Hill's problems, but when he introduced his wife, who is white, I wondered, fleetingly, if their interracial marriage might be involved in Mr. Hill's disturbance. At his request I saw the couple together and soon realized that both needed help.

A month after the "sighting" the Hills had been interviewed by Walter Webb, a lecturer at Boston's Hayden Planetarium and a scientific advisor to the National Investigations Committee on Aerial Phenomena. With a copy of Mr. Webb's report to NICAP as a basis, Mr. and Mrs. Hill unfolded the story which follows in Mr. Fuller's book.

At the time there was no indication that either the interracial marriage or the UFO experience bore more than a tangential relationship to the central problems which Mr. and Mrs. Hill presented—crippling anxiety, manifested by him in fairly open fashion and by Mrs. Hill more in the form of repetitive nightmarish dreams. Aside from its topical interest, the UFO experience was important because it presented for both Mr. and Mrs. Hill the focal point of the anxiety which had apparently impeded the psychiatric treatment Mr. Hill had been undergoing for some time. This point appeared to be a period of time in the course of their trip home from Canada in September, 1961. They were constantly haunted by a nagging anxiety centering around this period of several hours—a feeling that something had occurred, but what?

A treatment program was outlined for the Hills, and it was decided first to try to unlock the door to the hidden room (the amnesia), and that for this aspect of therapy, hypnosis would be used. Plans were made to begin treatment after the coming Christmas holidays, the first treatment session being set for January 4, 1964.

Apart from the unique quality engendered by the UFO story, treatment proceeded apace as might be expected with two very anxious and cooperative patients, and continued regularly until terminated at the end of June, 1964. During this time there was no portent of the unfolding drama which began on December 14, 1963, which was to extend back in time for two years and to extend forward to this moment exactly two and a half years later when I would be writing an introduction to the book which was to revive the whole drama—the unfolding of events of which I had had no hint during the whole period of treatment. It was a drama which culminated in Mr. Fuller's book and my introduction, which is rather unique in being an apologia for my presence on stage as a reluctant member of the dramatis personae.

The formal treatment program was terminated on June 27, 1964, and from then until late summer of 1965 the Hills and I maintained contact through reports of their progress by visits and telephone calls. I had no indication of the developing storm until the late summer of 1965 when I received a telephone call from a newspaper reporter who appeared to be aware of the Hill story, their treatment, and my part in it—including the use of hypnosis; he requested an interview with me—which I refused, informing him that I would not discuss the Hills' case without their written consent and that even with their written permission any discussion would have to depend on my judgment of its potential effect on their emotional health. A month or two later Mr. Hill, in considerable distress, called to say that the reporter had approached them for an interview—which they had refused. He (the reporter) claimed to have data on the case which he would publish without an interview with them if they refused to comply. It appeared to me that there was nothing that could be done on this basis. The question of giving an interview would be a matter for themselves to decide, perhaps with legal advice.

While I was attending professional meetings in Washington during the week of October 25, 1965, my office called that "All hell had broken loose." There were calls from Mr. Hill and calls from a great many strangers. All seemed to be connected with the appearance of a series of articles in a Boston newspaper. These were written by the reporter to whom I had refused the interview and, apparently, without permission from Mr. and Mrs. Hill. My associates and our office staff did the best they could with the calls pending my return. On my return Mr. Hill telephoned and expressed their great distress over this series of articles—which I had not yet seen. He felt that they distorted the truth and considered them a violation of his right of privacy. He wanted my advice, and I suggested that he seek legal advice. From Mr. Hill I also learned that I had been named in the articles, which explained the large number of calls coming to my office.

The nature of these calls gave me a fairly good clue to the way the articles were being interpreted by the general public. The callers could be classified into four major groups:

1. *The Despairing:* These were people who were apparently emotionally or mentally ill and who saw in hypnosis, as it was presented by the reporter, the magical solution to their problems.

2. *The Mystics:* People who were interested in clairvoyance, extrasensory perception, astrology and other related phenomena. Many of this group saw in the experience and the hypnosis support of their own ideas and beliefs.

3. *The "Fellow Travelers":* These were the self-appointed interviewers who knew the answers to the mysteries of life and saw in the Hills' experience and the hypnosis confirmation of their beliefs. Most of them seemed to be motivated by the wish to bring themselves to my attention as mutual supporters—perhaps for their gain.

4. *The Sympathizers:* A number of callers expressed sympathy for my "persecution" by the writer, who mentioned me either as a Boston or Back Bay psychiatrist, or by name, in all but one of the articles. The use of my name was quite subtle, and I was regularly credited with refusing to violate the doctor-patient relationship by discussing the case. Quite subtly, however, the total impression created in the articles was that some of the fantastic statements which were made came from revelations made under hypnosis, and in some way from me; hence my many phone calls and letters from the public.

After consultation with friends and their counsel, the Hills decided that the best way to handle the newspaper articles and any further forays into this field would be to publish the truth. At the time Mr. John Fuller had been investigating UFO phenomena in the New Hampshire area and was working on a book about incidents in the Exeter area. The Hills discussed the matter with me and asked me to make available to Mr. Fuller my records, chiefly the tape recordings of their treatment, so that they could present an authentic version of the true story as they had experienced it. Public interest, rather than abating, had been increasing, and there was danger that other stories might be published which would increase their distress.

For therapeutic purposes, all of the treatment under hypnosis had been recorded verbatim on a tape recorder. It was inevitable, I suppose, that Mr. Fuller would want to have this verbatim and incontestable material, and the Hills' request was understandable.

The physician's records are his property, but the contents of these records should be available in the interest of his patients. In this sense they are also property of the patients. I decided ultimately that the paramount issue, the emotional health of Mr. and Mrs. Hill, would best be served by releasing the recordings if I could be assured that they would be used honestly, and not detrimentally to them. It appeared that both Mr. Fuller and I had had the same idea and had checked each other's biographies in *Who's Who in the East* to our mutual satisfaction. Conferences with Mr. Fuller and the Hills ensued, and it was agreed that I would have the right to pass on all medical data in the book to prevent, as much as possible, the creation of false impressions and conclusions. It was also agreed that no information of a personal and intimate nature would be revealed if it was not relevant to the UFO experience and the period of amnesia. Mr. Fuller hoped to revivify the experiences and the emotional reactions which were so well expressed in the tape recordings—a difficult task indeed.

The decision to release the recordings created a corollary problem for me—the matter of my professional anonymity, one of the canons of our profession. In this I was already the victim of the newspaper articles in which I was mentioned without my consent. By now this was no longer a local matter involving only the city of Boston. I received calls and letters from other cities, and when I received a request for information from as far west as Wisconsin, it was obvious I no longer possessed any anonymity, and the disclosure of my participation could cause me to be identified with certain statements and conclusions by the reporter about the Hills' experiences, with which I strongly disagree. The mystique of hypnosis and my position as the mystical "Master" by the simple act of association with the statements in the story seemed to give them the quality of an authenticity quite at variance with the facts.

Though I have confined my active participation in this book to editorial supervision of medical statements, I feel that I should make clear the status of hypnosis because of public misconceptions which often envelop hypnosis with an arcane charisma, and the practitioner with the robe of Merlin. Hypnosis is a useful procedure in psychiatry to direct concentrated attention on some particular point in the course of the whole therapeutic procedure. In cases like the Hills', it can be the key to the locked room, the amnesic period. Under hypnosis, experiences buried in amnesia may be recalled in a much shorter time than in the normal course of the psychotherapeutic process. Nevertheless, there is little produced under or by hypnosis that is not possible without. The charisma of hypnosis has tended to foster the belief that hypnosis is the magical and royal road to TRUTH. In one sense this is so, but it must be understood that hypnosis is a pathway to the truth as it is felt and understood by the patient. The truth is what he believes to be the truth, and this may or may not be consonant with the ultimate nonpersonal truth. Most frequently it is.

In the exercise of my editorial rights over Mr. Fuller's book I have confined myself as strictly as possible to the medical data—my observations and records. I have tried to avoid loose speculation insofar as my own data is concerned without inhibiting Mr. Fuller's free expression of his own reasoning and conclusions as long as my data was not distorted. To me the story is the partial documentation of fascinating human experience in an unusual setting connected with what are popularly called "Unidentified Flying Objects." Their existence (the UFO's) as concrete objects is of less concern to me than the experience of these two people showing the cumulative impact of past experiences and fantasies on their present experiences and responses. To Mr. Fuller the former is understandably of greater concern. It follows that his reasoning and speculations are his own, based on his evaluation of my data, the Hills' statements, his past experience and his present convictions.

I have no doubt given him sleepless nights and many moments of despair. I am sure there have been times when he felt I was taking the life of his child; but he has always taken my criticism with good grace and has managed to remove the objectionable or restore the missing in a manner which would be acceptable to me, so that even I, who have lived through much of it, find the book good reading indeed.

Benjamin Simon, M.D.

June 14, 1966

FOREWORD

I stumbled on the story of Barney and Betty (she rarely uses *Eunice,* her formal name) Hill entirely by accident, or rather by a series of accidents.

I knew little or nothing about the subject of Unidentified Flying Objects until I explored a rather startling case involving the police department of Exeter, New Hampshire, and wrote a short piece about it in the Trade Winds column in the *Saturday Review.* As a result of this piece, I went on to write a more extensive article on the case for *Look,* which later became the book *Incident at Exeter.*

In the process of doing the research in southern New Hampshire for all this, I spoke to Conrad Quimby, editor and publisher of the Derry, New Hampshire, *News* who mentioned the fact than an extremely intelligent and reliable couple he knew had encountered a UFO in the White Mountains back in 1961. The incident had caused them considerable emotional strain. He further said that they had been very reluctant to discuss their case except with a few close friends because they did not want to be considered eccentric, and the subject was so controversial that they thought it might interfere with their dedicated work in the Civil Rights movement.

At the time Mr. Quimby mentioned this to me, I was concentrating only on the rash of sightings made in the summer of 1965, still continuing as this is written. Since I found over sixty persons in the area who had seen UFO's at tree-top level within the current year, some of these people experiencing the objects coming directly over their cars not more than twenty or thirty feet in altitude, I felt that it would be difficult to document the current cases. I made a brief note about Barney and Betty

Hill, realizing that I would probably not need to interview them. If they were reluctant to discuss their case publicly, I did not want to persuade them against their judgment in a matter of personal choice.

My research in the Exeter area extended for several weeks. I had at first suspected that the UFO story could be explained by careful, painstaking research in a single area, and that a rational answer should turn up. It didn't. The more the evidence accumulated, the more it became impossible to maintain my skepticism. Police, air force pilots and radar men, navy personnel and coast guardsmen all confirmed the incredible reports that dozens of reliable and competent citizens in the area were giving me in grueling cross examinations.

I took advantage of the Exeter police station as a base from which to conduct the research, since current reports of the phenomenon gravitated there. Toward the end of my research period, a message was left at the police station that Mr. and Mrs. Hill would appreciate it if I'd call them in nearby Portsmouth. As a social worker for the state of New Hampshire, Mrs. Hill made regular visits to the police station to check on various welfare cases in which the police might be involved. The Hills had indicated to the desk officer that they might be able to supply me with some helpful information on the UFO research.

Later that day I talked with Mrs. Hill, who felt that the subject was becoming important and needed exploration by responsible research. She gave me the names of some people in the area who had come to her with reports of seeing the objects—she felt they were of unimpeachable character and were, in her estimation, accurate observers.

But she said nothing whatever about her own case. It was obvious to me that she was reluctant to discuss it, and knowing her attitude from Conrad Quimby, I did not press the subject.

Several weeks later, a series of articles broke in a Boston newspaper, telling without the full background material the story of Barney and Betty Hill and how, while under hypnosis by a Boston psychiatrist, they had told of being abducted aboard a UFO, given a physical examination, and released with the assurance that they would not be harmed. The Hills said the story had been written without their permission, or without their being interviewed by the reporter involved, and they were extremely upset about it. They had known nothing about the forthcoming story when I had talked with Mrs. Hill on the phone.

The possibility of privacy was destroyed by the articles, and the Hills felt that as long as the story had been released, the facts of the case should be carefully presented. The Hills had sat on this story for nearly five years; they were not seeking publicity.

The Hills asked me if I were interested in documenting the story with their cooperation. I agreed that it would be a project of overwhelming public interest. Instead of writing one book, I have ended up by doing two.

The feelings of the Hills themselves can best be explained by the letter Betty Hill wrote to her mother regarding the release of this book:

Dear Mother:

Barney and I are writing to you to let you know that we have finally reached a decision in regards to our UFO experience. As you know, from the very beginning of our experience, we questioned our position and responsibility.

In the beginning we felt that this was our own personal experience, and believed that there really was not any great public interest. A few people who had witnessed UFO's were interested in the subject, but we believed that the overall picture was one of boredom, disbelief, and apathy. We personally became interested in obtaining more information in our seeking of answers to so many questions. And we still are seeking.

In the last few weeks we have been questioning this attitude of our personal right to privacy. I really think our feelings began to change following the publication in the article you read in the newspaper about us. When the reporter contacted us for an interview, prior to the release of his story, we refused to meet him or discuss our experience with him. We asked him *not* to release the story. We were fearful for we believed that we would face scorn, ridicule, and disbelief. The reporter said that we had no right to ask that publication be stopped, for he felt that our experience was of great public interest.

To our amazement, public reaction was not what we expected. Fortunately for us numerous sightings occurred in our local area—well documented reports which were well publicized. In the midst of these, the newspaper story was released. Public reaction was instantaneous—everyone wanted to know about our experience. We received telephone calls from Europe, Canada, and all over the United States; we were contacted by TV and radio stations; newspaper reporters visited; and letters—from everywhere, from people of all kinds of backgrounds; from all age groups of the printed letters of small children to the spidery writing of an elderly person.

Students wrote wanting to know more, asking advice on books to read, thinking about space travel and life on other planets. One boy wrote a thank-you note to us saying that he had read the books we suggested and used the information in a Science Fair Project, winning a prize.

When we visited a school in connection with our work, teachers asked us to speak briefly to the class. High school teachers asked us to discuss UFO's in their assemblies.

People came to us and told us of their own experiences with UFO's. They asked advice. One woman called to say a UFO was flying around the back field and her husband wanted to go out to it. Did we think he should do this?

Then the rumors started. Fantastic fantasies that people wanted so desperately to believe. How was the trip? Did we go to Venus and Mars? Did they try to give us a miraculous cure for cancer, or heart disease, etc. Were they going to save us from ourselves and solve our unanswerable problems for us? Did we believe that this signified the second coming of Christ? As well as the question—were we sober?

We feel that first of all, we must clarify what actually happened and set the record straight. This would necessarily include the information obtained while under treatment by Dr. Simon. We have made arrangements with the author, John G. Fuller, to write the book for us. Since Mr. Fuller felt that the material on the tape recordings was necessary for an adequate presentation, we asked Dr. Simon to make his records available to him.

We hope the publication of this book will enable the reader to judge for himself and to decide if this is illusion, hallucination, dream, or reality.

Love,
Betty and Barney

I can only add that working with the Hills and Dr. Simon has been a rewarding and educational experience. All three have a passion for accuracy and a profound respect for understatement and documentation. If this comes through in the book, I will have accomplished my objective. One final note: Most of the dialogue taking place between the Hills during the incident is taken directly from the recordings of their hypnosis sessions with Dr. Simon.

John G. Fuller

July, 1966
Westport, Conn.

THE INTERRUPTED JOURNEY:
Two Lost Hours "Aboard a Flying Saucer"

CHAPTER ONE

September in the White Mountains is the cruelist month. The gaunt hotels, vestiges of Victorian tradition, are shuttered, or getting ready to be; motels and overnight cabins flash their neon vacancy signs for only a few fitful hours before their owners give up and retire early. The New Hampshire ski slopes are barren of snow and skiers, the trails appearing as great, brownish gashes beside the silent tramways and chair-lifts. The Labor Day exodus has swept most of the roads clear of traffic; very few vacation trailers and roof-laden station wagons straggle toward Boston or the New York throughways. Winter is already here on the chilled and ominous slopes of Mount Washington, its summit weather station clocking the highest wind velocities ever recorded on any mountain top in the world. Bears and red foxes roam freely. In a few weeks hunters in scarlet or luminous orange jackets will be on the trails, intent on deer or ruffed grouse, or anything legal in sight. The skiers follow later, their minds on powder snow and hot buttered rum, as they bring back the gay holiday mood of summer. Once again the White Mountains will take on a new life.

It was in the doleful mid-September period of 1961—September 19, to be exact—that Barney Hill and his wife Betty began their drive from the Canadian border down U.S. 3, through the White Mountains, on their way home to Portsmouth. It was to be a night drive, brought on by a sense of urgency. The radio of their 1957 Chevrolet Bel Air hard-top made it clear that a hurricane coming up the coast might cut in toward New Hampshire, an event that in previous years had uprooted

3

trees and spilled high-tension wires across the roads. They had failed to bring along enough cash to cover all the extras of their holiday trip, and their funds had dwindled sharply as they had driven leisurely up to Niagara Falls, then circled back through Montreal toward home.

They had cleared through the U.S.-Canadian custom house at about nine that evening, winding along the lonely ceiling of Vermont's Northeast Kingdom, a section of the state that is said to have threatened to secede not only from Vermont, but from the United States as well. The traffic was sparse; few other cars appeared on the road before the Hills approached the welcome lights of Colebrook a half an hour later, an ancient New Hampshire settlement founded in 1770, lying in the shadow of Mt. Monadnock, just across the river from Vermont. The lights of the village, though a relief from the endless turns of the narrow two-way road they had been traveling, were few. A forlorn glow came from the windows of a single restaurant, and realizing that this might be the last chance for any bracing refreshment for the rest of the trip, they decided to turn back even though they had driven past it.

The restaurant was nearly deserted. A few teen-agers gathered in a far corner. Only one woman, the waitress, in the quiet restaurant seemed to show any reaction at all to the fact that Betty and Barney Hill's was a mixed marriage: Barney, a strikingly handsome descendant of a proud Ethiopian freeman whose great-grandmother was born during slavery, but raised in the house of the plantation owner because she was his own daughter; Betty, whose family bought three tracts of land in York, Maine, in 1637, only to have one member cut down by Indians. Regardless of what attention their mixed marriage drew in public places, they were no longer self-conscious about it. Their first attraction to each other, one that still remained, was of intellect and mutual interests. Together, they stumped the state of New Hampshire speaking for the cause of Civil Rights. Barney, former political action and now legal redress chairman of the Portsmouth NAACP, was also a member of the State Advisory Board of the United States Civil Rights Commission and the Board of Directors of the Rockingham County Poverty Program. Both he and his wife are proud to display the award he received from Sargent Shriver for his work. Betty, a social worker for the state of New Hampshire, continues after hours with her job as assistant secretary and community coordinator for the NAACP, and as United Nations envoy for the Unitarian-Universalist Church to which they belong in Portsmouth.

But what was to happen to them this night of September 19, 1961,

4

had nothing whatever to do with their successful mixed marriage, or their dedication to social progress. Nor was there any hint of what was to happen as they sat at the paneled restaurant counter in Colebrook, Barney unceremoniously eating a hamburger, Betty a piece of chocolate layer cake. They didn't linger too long at the counter, just long enough for a cigarette and a cup of black coffee before they continued down U.S. 3 toward home.

The distance from Colebrook to Portsmouth is a hundred and seventy miles, with U.S. 3 remarkably smooth and navigable in the face of the deep mountain gorges it must negotiate. Further south, below Plymouth, nearly thirty miles of four-lane highway—more than that now—invite safe speeds up to sixty-five miles an hour. For the other roads, Barney Hill liked to drive between fifty and fifty-five, even if this should be a shade above the limit.

The clock over the restroom in the Colebrook restaurant read 10:05 when they left that night. "It looks," Barney had said to Betty as they got in their car, "like we should be home by 2:30 in the morning—or 3:00 at the latest." Betty agreed. She had confidence in Barney's driving, even though she sometimes goaded him for pushing too fast. It was a bright, clear night with an almost full moon. The stars were brilliant, as they always are in the New Hampshire mountains on a cloudless night, when starshine seems to illuminate the tops of the peaks with a strange incandescence.

The car was running smoothly through the night air, the road winding effortlessly along the flat ground of the uppermost Connecticut River valley, an ancient Indian and lumbering country, rich in history and legend. The thirty miles south to Northumberland, where Rogers' Rangers made their rendezvous after the sack of St. Francis, passed quickly. Betty, an inveterate sight-seer, enjoyed the brilliance of the moon reflecting on the valley and the mountains in the distance, both in New Hampshire to the east and over the river to Vermont in the west. Delsey, the Hills' scrappy little dachshund, was at peace on the floor by the front seat at Betty's feet. Through Lancaster, a village with a wide main street and fine old pre-Revolutionary houses all dark now on this September night—U.S. 3 continues south as the Connecticut River swings westward to widen New Hampshire's territory and narrow Vermont's. Here the smooth, wide valley changes to a more uncertain path through the mountains, with the serrated peaks of the Pilot Range, described lushly by one writer as "a great rolling rampart which plays fantastic tricks with the sunshine and shadow, and towards sunset assumes the tenderest tints of deep amethyst."

There was no sunshine or amethyst now, only the luminous moon, very bright and large, and a black tarvia two-lane road which seemed totally deserted. To the left of the moon, and slightly below it, was a particularly bright star, perhaps a planet, Betty Hill thought, because of its steady glow. Just south of Lancaster, the exact time she cannot remember, Betty was a little startled to notice that another star or planet, a bigger one, had appeared above the other. It had not been there, she was sure, when she looked before. But more curious was that the new celestial visitor clearly appeared to be getting bigger and brighter. For several moments she watched it, said nothing to her husband as he negotiated the driving through the mountains. Finally, when the strange light persisted, she nudged Barney, who slowed the car somewhat and looked out the right-hand side of the windshield to see it. "When I looked at it first," Barney Hill later said, "it didn't seem anything particularly unusual, except that we were fortunate enough to see a satellite. It had no doubt gone off its course, and it seemed to be going along the curvature of the earth. It was quite a distance out, meaning it looked like a star, in motion."

They drove on, glancing at the bright object frequently, finding it difficult to tell if the light itself were moving, or if the movement of the car were making it *seem* to move. The object would disappear behind trees, or a mountain top, then reappear again as the obstruction was cleared. Delsey, the dog, was beginning to get slightly restless, and Betty mentioned that perhaps they should let her out and take advantage of the road stop to get a better look. Barney, an avid plane watcher who sometimes liked to take his two sons (from a former marriage) to watch Piper Cub seaplanes land and take off on Lake Winnipesaukee, agreed, and pulled the car over to the side of the road where there was reasonably unobstructed visibility.

There were woods nearby, and Barney, a worrier at times, mentioned they might keep an eye out for bears, a distinct possibility in this part of the country. Betty, who seldom lets herself get concerned or emotional about anything, laughed his suggestion off, snapped the chain lead on Delsey's collar, and walked her along the side of the road. At this moment, she noted that the star, or the light, or whatever it was in the September sky, was definitely moving. As Barney joined her on the road, she handed

Delsey's leash to him and went back to the car. She took from the front seat a pair of 7 x 50 Crescent binoculars they had brought along for their holiday scenery, especially Niagara Falls, which Betty Hill had never seen before. Barney, noting that the light in the sky *was* moving, was now fully convinced that it was a straying satellite.

Betty put the binoculars up to her eyes and focused carefully. What they both were about to see was to change their lives forever, and as some observers claim, change the course of the history of the world.

*   *   *

The holiday trip had been a spontaneous idea, originating with Barney. For some time now, he had been assigned to the night shift at the Boston post office, where he worked as an assistant dispatcher. He liked the job, if not the hours and the long commuting drive from Portsmouth to Boston each night—60 miles each way. The commuting was especially exhausting, with no train or bus available at the late-night hour he began work. The rigors of the daily 120-mile round trip had, Barney felt, been instrumental in causing his ulcer to kick up, a condition for which he was under medical treatment.

He began thinking about the idea for the trip while he was driving into work on the evening of September 14, 1961. Betty had a week's vacation coming up, a badly-needed one from her job as a child welfare worker for the state, handling a rather overwhelming case-load of 120 assignments at one time. With luck, Barney would be able to take some of his vacation leave and relieve some of the pressure while waiting for the results of some recent X-rays of his ulcer his doctor had taken. All during that night at work, the idea appealed to him more. It grew on him as he went through his usual routine, standing in front of some 40 clerks sorting mail, calling out numbers of towns or sections of the city of Boston. The clerks in turn would put the mail from designated slots onto a conveyor belt, where the mail handlers would carry the process on as the hampers moved to the elevators to be dispatched. Barney, with an IQ of nearly 140, could handle more complex jobs than this, but like so many post-office workers he found the frustration of routine work compensated for by the civil service advantages. Further, the steadiness of the job gave him ample time for his community service work which, he felt, was both demanding and rewarding.

He punched out of the Boston post office at 7:30 the following morning and drove toward Portsmouth in anticipation of surprising Betty. Just the idea of getting away relaxed him. Though the harsh realities of the New Hampshire winter would soon be on them, the roads would be free and clear now, and the traffic would be light—ideal for leisurely motoring.

They planned their trip that morning over a cup of hot coffee, Betty accepting the idea at once. But trip money was not in the budget. Barney's main regret was that his two sons couldn't join them, for they both had made a pleasing adjustment to the second marriage, with mutual affection springing up spontaneously between boys and Betty, a condition that Barney whimsically attributed to Betty's expert cookery.

The total adjustment to their mixed marriage had been remarkably smooth. Betty was as proud of her liberalism as she was of her long New England lineage. "In my family," she once wrote in a theme, "it seems to be a belief that the purpose of one's life is to bridge the gap between the past and the future; over this bridge flows all the past, good or bad, to influence the future, and the future of the world depends upon the individuality and strength of the bridge."

All through her family history, Betty points out, various members have fought for unpopular causes. The Dow branch of the family were Quakers in 1662, were attacked, beaten and driven out of Salisbury, Massachusetts, their property stolen and their homes burned. Just before the Civil War, they were active abolitionists, and were with John Greenleaf Whittier when his printing presses were burned by the townspeople of Amesbury, in the same state.

"The greatest day of my life," Betty once said, "was when I learned to read. My days of boredom were over."

She was a bright student in the one-room school that she attended in Kingston, New Hampshire. With one teacher for six grades, she was able to move ahead at her own rate. She can remember explaining long division to the fourth grade when she was in third, and won all of the contests, spelling bees, dramatic roles and prizes there were to be had. An energetic child, sometimes troublesome, she worked on constant projects to earn money—picking cowslips, wild strawberries, raspberries and blueberries, and selling them at a handsome profit. She was so voracious in her reading that her mother used to limit her to one book a day. When Betty was eleven, at the height of the depression, her mother threw away family tradition to work in a factory. At first, it was to be a temporary measure, part-time. Betty's father, the breadwinner, had become ill, savings had dwindled, and her mother's inheritance had been embezzled. But labor union organizers were moving into the New England mill towns, and her mother, a lady of rigid New England gentility, became enthralled. She helped to organize, led strikes, and became a member of the union's Executive Board. Betty was proud of her mother, watching her on the picket lines, worried about the possibility of attack by hecklers or arrest by police. During this time, the family table groaned not with food, but with arguments between an uncle who was helping to organize the CIO in Lynn, a family friend who was carrying out the same chore in Lawrence, and Betty's mother who was strictly A. F. of L. These were exciting scenes to young Betty, with the strikes, the elections and the celebrations. Her father, working for another uncle who owned a shoe factory, remained stoically neutral.

Betty's experience with colored people was limited. Not too many lived in New Hampshire, but at an early age she lived across the street from an interracial couple and absorbed the snide remarks of her classmates against the colored wife. Later, Betty's mother impressed her by saying that although some people did not like colored people, this was wrong because they were people just like everyone else. If Betty heard anyone talking against them, she should speak up without hesitation.

She did. As a sophomore at the University of New Hampshire, which Betty entered in 1937, a girl who was a Negro from Wilmington, Delaware, enrolled at the college—to the consternation of both the administration and the students. In the late 30's, integration was a problem even in the northern state universities. Betty would find Ann, alone in the corner of the smoking room, ignored by the other students. Betty would say nothing at the time, but seethed underneath. When Ann would leave, the other girls would suggest caustically that Ann should go back where she came from, and Betty would react strongly. On one such occasion, as Ann was leaving the smoking room, Betty went to her, and in front of the others, asked to see her room.

It was the beginning of acceptance for Ann, but not until after a long struggle. At times, Betty would almost physically restrain her from leaving the university. She fought with Ann to stop her from packing her luggage. Eventually, Ann graduated Phi Beta Kappa, went on to Harvard and now teaches on the faculty of a southern college.

Although the roots of Betty Hill's marriage to Barney may lie in the attitude expressed by this incident, their problems as an interracial couple are minimal. Barney, at times, shows concern about rejection in public places: hotels, restaurants or meetings. But in their private social life they are popular, accepted, and almost overactive. Their initial self-consciousness dissolved quickly. "It doesn't have any more meaning to me," Betty once told a friend, "than a person having blue eyes or brown eyes. Everyone wants to meet us; everybody wants to invite us places. We've even had to set up some kind of limits, or we would be going here, there, everywhere, constantly."

* * *

The planning of the trip that was to have such a profound impact on their lives was brief and relaxed. The shortage of immediate funds was partially compensated for by Betty's idea of borrowing a car-refrigerator from a friend. In this way, the expense of too many meals in restaurants would be reduced. Barney, momentarily ignoring the diet for his ulcers, drank a glass of orange juice, ate six strips of bacon and two soft-boiled eggs, as he plotted the course of the trip on a few Gulf road maps. They would drive leisurely, avoiding the throughways, pay a brief visit to Niagara Falls, then circle through Montreal, and back to Portsmouth. While Betty shopped for food, Barney took a nap to recover from his all-night work at the Boston post office.

They finished most of their packing that afternoon, filled the car-refrigerator with food and put it in the deep freeze. By eight o'clock that evening they were in bed with the alarm set for four the next morning.

Barney, an inveterate early-riser, was up first, but in moments Betty had coffee percolating, and the last-minute packing process began. As he loaded the trunk, Barney shoved a bag of bone-meal fertilizer to one side, and packed the luggage around it. Betty had bought the fertilizer to work on the garden during the vacation; it was just as easy to let it stay in the trunk as to take it out. Later, they were to find this comfortably homey material creating an unusual inquiry and speculation.

It was a clear, crisp New Hampshire morning as they drove off, noting the mileage on the speedometer only to lose the slip of paper later—an ingrained habit of Barney's. They drove out Route 4, toward Concord, in a festive mood. Barney, at the wheel, burst into a hoarse version of "Oh, What A Beautiful Morning." Betty, who liked to hear Barney sing, smiled. Barney, who liked to please Betty, smiled back. There was no hint at all of what was about to happen later; nor could there be. No such event would be so thoroughly documented.

* * *

The object they saw in the sky near Route 3 four nights later, south of Lancaster, New Hampshire, continued its unpredictable movement as they passed through Whitfield and the village of Twin Mountain. They stopped briefly several times, and by now Barney was frankly puzzled. His only alternate theory, aside from that of a satellite, was that the object was a star, a theory he immediately discounted because they had proved that it was in movement, changing its course in an erratic manner. At one of the stops, a few miles north of Cannon Mountain, Betty had said, "Barney, if you think that's a satellite, or a star, you're being absolutely ridiculous."

With his naked eye, Barney could tell that she was right. It was obviously not a celestial object now, he was sure. "We've made a mistake, Betty," he said. "It's a commercial plane. Probably on its way to Canada." He got back in the car, and they continued driving on.

Betty, in the passenger seat, kept it in view as they moved down Route 3. It seemed to her that it was getting bigger and brighter, and she kept getting more puzzled and more curious. Barney would note it through the windshield on occasion, but was more worried about a car coming around the now frequent curves of the road. His theory that it was a commercial airliner headed for Canada soothed his annoyance at the fact that he might be confronted with some unexplainable phenomenon. The road was completely deserted; they hadn't seen a car or truck in either direction for miles now, which left them alone in the deep gorges late at night. Some natives of northern New Hampshire prefer never to drive through these roads at night, through long-standing custom and superstition. In winter, an informal group known as the Blue Angels patrols the roads for cars frozen or broken down. It is too easy to freeze to death in these lonely streches, and the State Troopers cannot possibly cover the wide territory frequently enough. Barney, his concern growing in spite of his comforting theories, hoped that he would soon see a trooper or at least another car driving by which he could flag and compare notes with.

Around eleven o'clock they approached the enormous and somber silhouette of Cannon Mountain, looming to the west on their right. Barney slowed the car down near a picnic turnout that commanded a wide view to the west and looked again at the strange moving light. In amazement, he noted that it swung suddenly from its northern flight pattern, turning to the west, then completing its turn and heading back

11

directly toward them. Barney braked the car sharply, turning off into the picnic area.

"Whatever you're calling it, Barney," Betty said, "I don't know why, because it's still up there, and it's still following us, and if anything it's coming right toward us."

"It's got to be a plane," Barney said. They were standing in the picnic area now, looking up at the light which was growing bigger still. "A commercial liner."

"With a crazy course like that?" Betty said.

"Well, then it's a Piper Cub. That's what it is. With some hunters, who might be lost."

"It's not the hunting season," Betty said, as Barney took the binoculars from her. "And I don't hear a sound."

Neither did Barney, although he desperately wanted to.

"It might be a helicopter," he said as he looked through the binoculars. He was sure that it wasn't, but was reaching for any kind of explanation which would make sense. "The wind might be carrying the sound the other direction."

"There *is* no wind, Barney. Not tonight. You know that."

Through the binoculars, Barney now made out a shape, like the fuselage of a plane, although he could see no wings. There also seemed to be a blinking series of lights along the fuselage, or whatever it was, in an alternating pattern. When Betty took the glasses, the object passed in front of the moon, in silhouette. It appeared to be flashing thin pencils of different colored lights, rotating around an object which at that time appeared cigar shaped. Just a moment before it had changed its speed from slow to fast, then slowed down again as it crossed the face of the moon. The lights were flashing persistently, red, amber, green and blue. She turned to Barney, asking him to take another look.

"It's *got* to be a plane," Barney said. "Maybe a military plane. A search plane. Maybe it's a plane that's lost."

He was getting irritated at Betty now, or taking out his irritation on her because she was refusing to accept a natural explanation. At one time, several years before, in 1957, Betty's sister and family had described seeing clearly an unidentified flying object in Kingston, New Hampshire, where they lived. Betty, who had confidence in her sister's reliability and capacity for observation, believed the story of her sighting. Barney neither believed nor disbelieved; he was indifferent to the subject as a whole, had little interest in it. If anything, he was more skeptical of flying objects after hearing her story. He felt that Betty, for the first time in five years, was about to bring this subject up again. But she didn't mention it.

Beside them, the dachshund was whining and cowering. Betty gave the binoculars to Barney, took Delsey to the car and got in and shut the door. Barney put the glasses on the object again, again wishing that he could find some comfort from comparing notes with a passing motorist. He wanted above all to hear a sound: the throb of a propeller-driven plane or the whir of a jet. None came. For the first time, he felt he was being observed, that the object was actually coming closer and attempting to circle them. If it's a military craft, he was thinking, it should not do this, and his mind went back to a time a few years before when a jet had buzzed close by him, shattered the sound barrier, and cracked the air with an explosion.

Getting back in the car, Barney mentioned to Betty that he thought the craft had seen them and was playing games with them. He tried not to let Betty know that he was afraid, something he didn't like to admit to himself.

They drove on toward Cannon Mountain at not much more than five miles an hour, catching glimpses of the object as it moved erratically in the sky. At the top of the mountain, the only light they had seen for miles glowed like a beacon, appearing to be on top of the closed and silent aerial tramway, or perhaps on the restaurant there. They stopped again near the base of the mountain, momentarily, as the object suddenly swung behind the dark silhouette and disappeared. At the same moment, the light on the top of the mountain went out, inexplicably. Betty looked at her watch as it did so, wondering if the restaurant were closed. She could not read the dial very plainly in the dashboard light, and never did get an accurate reading. If there were people up there, she thought, they must be getting an exceptional view of the object.

As the car moved by the darkened silhouette of the Old Man of the Mountain, the object appeared again, gliding silently, leisurely, parallel to the car to the west of them, on the Vermont side of the car. It was more wooded here, more difficult to keep the object in sight as it glided behind the trees. But it was there, moving with them. Near the turnoff for The Flume, a tourist attraction, they stopped again, almost got a sharp, clear look at it, but again the trees intervened.

Just beyond The Flume they passed a small motel, the first sign of life they had seen for many miles. The tidy hostelry looked comforting, although

Barney, his eyes alternately moving between the curves of the road and the object in the sky, barely noticed it. Betty noted a sign, beaming with AAA approval, and the light in a single, lonely window. A man was standing in the doorway of one of the cottages, and Betty thought how easy it would be to end the whole situation right now by simply pulling into the motel. She was thinking this—but she didn't say anything to Barney. Her curiosity about the object had now become overwhelming, and she was determined to see more of it. By now, Barney was beginning to irritate her by trying to deny the existence of the object. In fact, he was. He was still concerned about another car coming around a blind curve while he tried to keep one eye on the object as it moved around almost directly ahead of them on the road.

It was now apparently only a few hundred feet high, and it was huge. Further off, it had seemed to Betty that it was spinning; now it had stopped and the light pattern had changed from blinking, multi-colored lights to a steady, white glow. In spite of the vibrations of the car, she put the binoculars to her eyes and looked again.

She drew a quick, involuntary breath because she could clearly see a double row of windows. Without the glasses, it had appeared only as a streak of light. Now it was clear that this was a structured craft of enormous dimension, just how large she couldn't tell because both distance and altitude were hard to judge exactly. Then, slowly, a red light came out on the left side of the object, followed by a similar one on the right.

"Barney," she said, " I don't know *why* you're trying not to look at this. Stop the car and look at it!"

"It'll go away by the time I do that," Barney said. He was not at all convinced that it would.

"Barney, you've got to *stop*. You've never seen anything like this in your life."

He looked through the windshield and could see it plainly now, not more than two hundred feet in the air, he thought, and coming closer. A curve to the left in the road now shifted the object to the right of the car, but the distance remained the same. To the right, not far south of Indian Head, where another historic stone face surveys the mountains and valleys, he saw two imitation commercial wigwams on the site of a closed-down enterprise known as Natureland. Here, hundreds of youngsters swarm with their parents during summer visits. At this moment, it was silent and tomb-like.

14

Barney stopped the car almost in the center of the road, forgetting in the excitement any problem with other traffic. "All right, give me the binoculars," he said. Betty resented his tone. It sounded as if he were trying to humor her.

Barney got out, the motor still running, and leaned his arm on the door of the car. By now the object had swung toward them and hovered silently in the air not more than a short city block away, not more than two treetops high. It was raked on an angle, and its full shape was apparent for the first time: that of a large glowing pancake. But the vibrations from the motor jostled his arm, blurring his vision. He stepped to one side of the car to get a better look.

"Do you see it? Do you see it?" Betty said. For the first time her voice was rising in emotion. Barney, he admitted frankly later, was scared, perhaps as much because Betty rarely became excited as because of the nearness of this strange and utterly silent object defying almost any law of aerodynamics.

"It's just a plane or something," he snapped at her.

"Okay," Betty said. "It's a plane. But did you ever see a plane with *two* red lights? I always thought planes had one red and one green light."

"Well, I can't get a good look at it," he said. "The car was shaking the binoculars." Then he stepped a few feet away and looked again.

As he did so, the huge object—as wide in diameter as the distance between three telephone poles along the road, Barney later described it—swung in a silent arc directly across the road, not more than a hundred feet from him. The double row of windows was now clear and obvious.

Barney was fully gripped with fear now, but for a reason that he cannot yet explain, he found himself moving across the road on the driver's side of the car, on to the field, and across the field, directly toward it. Now the enormous disc was raked on an angle toward him. Two fin-like projections on either side were now sliding out further, each with a red light on it. The windows curved around the craft, around the perimeter of the thick, pancake-like disc, glowing with brilliant white light. There was still no sound. Shaken, but still finding an irresistible impulse to move closer to the craft, he continued on across the field, coming within fifty feet of it, as it dropped down to the height of a single tall tree. He did not estimate its size in feet, except that he knew it was as big or bigger in diameter than the length of a jet airliner.

Back in the car, Betty was not at first aware that Barney was walking away from her. She was thinking that this wasn't a very smart place to park the car, in the middle of the highway, even though there were no curves nearby. The car was neither on the right nor the left—it was splitting the white dotted line down the middle of the road. She would watch, she thought, to see if any headlights appeared either in front of or to the rear of the car, and at least pull the car quickly out of the way if another should appear on the road. She busied herself doing this for several moments, and then suddenly became aware that Barney had disappeared into the blackness of the field. Instinctively, she called for him.

"Barney," she screamed. "Barney, you damn fool, come back here." If he didn't reappear in a moment, she resolved to go out after him. "Barney! What's wrong with you? Do you hear me?"

There was no answer, and she started to slide across the front seat, toward the open door on the driver's side of the car.

Out on the field, near a shuttered vegetable stand and a single, gnarled apple tree, Barney put the binoculars up to his eyes. Then he stopped very still.

Behind the clearly structured windows he could see the figures, at least half a dozen living beings. They seemed to be bracing themselves against the transparent windows, as the craft tilted down toward his direction. They were, as a group, staring directly at him. He became vaguely aware that they were wearing uniforms. Betty, now nearly two hundred feet away, was screaming at him from the car, but Barney has no recollection of hearing this.

The binoculars seemed glued to his eyes. Then, on some invisible, inaudible signal, every member of the crew stepped back from the window toward a large panel a few feet behind the window line.

Only one remained there looking at him, apparently a leader. In the binoculars, Barney could see appendages in action among the apparent crew at what seemed to be a control board behind the windows of the craft. Slowly the craft descended lower, a few feet at a time. As the fins bearing the two red lights spread out further on the sides of the craft, an extension lowered from the underside, perhaps a ladder, he could not be sure.

He sharpened the focus of the binoculars on the one face remaining at the window. His memory at this point is blurred. For a reason he cannot explain, he was certain he was about to be captured. He tried to pull the glasses away from his eyes, to turn away, but he couldn't. As the focus became sharp, he remembers the eyes of the one crew member who stared down at him. Barney had never seen eyes like that before. With all his energy he ripped the binoculars from his eyes and ran screaming back across the field to Betty and the car. He tossed the binoculars on the seat, barely missing Betty, who had just straightened up from getting ready to slide out of his side of the car, as she heard him running across the hard surface of the road.

Barney was near hysteria. He jammed the car into first gear, spurted off down the road, shouting that he was sure they were going to be captured. He ordered Betty to look out the window to see where the craft was. She rolled down the window on the passenger side, looked out. The object was nowhere in sight. Craning her neck, she looked directly above the car. She could see nothing whatever. The strange craft did not appear in sight. But neither were the stars which had seconds ago been so brilliant in the sky. Barney kept yelling that he was sure it had swung above them.

Betty checked again, but all she could see was total darkness. She looked out the rear window, saw nothing—except the stars, then visible through the window.

Then suddenly a strange electronic-sounding beeping was heard. The car seemed to vibrate with it. It was in irregular rhythm—beep, beep—beep, beep, beep—seeming to come from behind the car, in the direction of the trunk.

Barney said, "What's that noise?"

Betty said, "I don't know."

They each began to feel an odd tingling drowsiness come over them. From that moment, a sort of haze came over them.

* * *

Some time later, how long they were not sure, the beeping sound repeated itself. They were conscious only that there were two sets of these beeps, separated by a time span they had no idea about—as well as what had happened or how long it had taken.

As the second set of beeps grew louder, the Hills' awareness slowly returned. They were still in the car—and the car was moving, with Barney at the wheel. They were silent, numb, and somnambulistic. At first, they rode silently, glancing out at the road to see just where they might be. A sign told them they were somewhere in the vicinity of Ashland, thirty-five miles south of Indian Head, where the inexplicable beeping had first sounded. In those first few moments of consciousness, Betty remembers faintly saying to her husband: *"Now* do you believe in flying saucers?" And he recalls answering: "Don't be ridiculous. Of course not."

But neither can remember much detail, other than this, until they had driven on to the new throughway, U.S. 93. Not long after entering this highway, Betty suddenly snapped out of her semi-wakefulness and pointed to a sign reading: CONCORD—17 MILES.

"That's where we are, Barney," she said. "Now we know."

Barney, too, remembers his mind clearing at this point. He does not even recall being disturbed or concerned about the thirty-five miles between Indian Head and Ashland, about which he seemed to remember nothing.

They drove on toward Concord, saying little. They did decide, though, that the experience at Indian Head was so strange, so unbelievable that they would tell no one about it. "No one would believe it, anyway," Barney said. "I find it hard to believe, myself."

Betty agreed. Near Concord, they looked for a place to have a cup of coffee, but nothing was open, anywhere. Still groggy and uncommunicative, they ploughed on, now turning east on Route 4, swinging across the state toward the ocean and Portsmouth.

Just outside of Portsmouth, they noticed dawn streaking the sky in the east. As they drove through the streets of the slumbering city, no one was stirring. The birds were already chattering, though, and it was nearly full daylight when they reached home. Barney looked at his watch, but it had stopped running, and shortly afterward Betty looked at hers, which had also stopped. Inside, the kitchen clock read shortly after five in the morning. "It looks," said Barney, "like we've arrived home a little later than expected."

Betty took Delsey out on her chain for a morning airing, while Barney unloaded the car. The birds were in full chorus now, a background for Betty's thoughts of the night before, which still haunted her. Barney, too, was thoughtful. They said little. For a reason she couldn't pinpoint, Betty asked him to put the luggage in the back hall, instead of having it in the house. He complied, then went to clear out the rest of the car. Picking up the binoculars, he noticed for the first time an unusual thing: the leather strap that had been around his neck the night before was freshly and cleanly broken in half.

From Concord on down, during the silent drive, both Betty and Barney had looked to the sky at regular intervals, wondering if the strange object would appear again. Even after they went into the house, a red frame structure on a small plot in Portsmouth, they found themselves occasionally going to the windows to look up at the morning sky.

Both had a strange, clammy feeling. They sat down at the kitchen table over a cup of coffee, but not before Barney went into the bathroom to examine his lower abdomen, which for a reason he could not explain, was bothering him. After two years, he still could not recall what made him do this.

After he came out of the bathroom, they reviewed what had happened, and again resolved not to discuss it with anyone. The latter part of the trip was extremely vague; they couldn't recall much of anything about the drive from Indian Head to Ashland. They had some fragmentary recollections of going through Plymouth, just north of the second series of beeps. Barney was baffled and confused by the absence of sound in the craft. He tried to classify it as a known aircraft in spite of the completely foreign appearance, the other-worldly feeling it had created in them.

They remembered two distinct series of beeps. But the sandwich in between was puzzling to them. Betty, with the aid of a strong cup of coffee, could recall very faintly some of the things which had happened right after Indian Head. She could recall seeing a road marker that divided the towns of Lincoln and North Woodstock, but it was a flashing, fragmentary impression. She could remember passing a store in the town of North Woodstock, again an isolated impression. Both recalled very faintly a large, luminous moon-shape, which seemed to be touching the road, sitting on end under some pines. Betty, straining to remember, thought that Barney had made a sharp left turn from Route 3, but could not in any way identify where this might have been. When they had seen the moon-shaped object, Barney faintly recalled saying to Betty, "Oh, no, not again." Betty recalls her reaction to Barney's denial that it could have been an Unidentified Flying Object. She thought: That's the way Barney is. If something frightens him, or he doesn't like it, he just says to himself that it never happened. Barney, to a degree, will confess to this.

Both agree they regained full consciousnesses at the sign on U.S. 93 which indicated that it was seventeen miles to Concord. Before that, one other recollection came to their minds: a fragmentary image of the darkened streets of Plymouth, a half a dozen miles north of Ashland, where the second series of beeps took place.

"When we arrived at our house," Barney said later, "and Betty got out and took the dog on her leash to walk her around the yard, I got out of the car and began taking things out. Betty said she wanted me to throw the food from the refrigerator out, and to keep the rest of the things from the car out of the house. I could hardly wait until I was able to get everything from the car to the back porch so that I could go into the bathroom, where I took a mirror and began looking over my body. And I don't know, I didn't know why at the time, but I felt unclean. With a grime different from what usually accumulates on a trip. Somewhat clammy. Betty and I both went to the window, and then I opened the back door, and we both looked skyward. And I went into the bedroom and looked around. I can't describe it—it was a presence. Not that the presence was there with us, but something very puzzling had happened."

They collapsed into bed immediately after a breakfast snack and their sleep was undisturbed. They were hoping that the incident would fade quickly from their minds and remain only an interesting anecdote that someday they might tell someone about. They were unaware that it would affect their lives profoundly for many years to come.

CHAPTER TWO

It was nearly three that afternoon when they woke up. Their sleep had been dreamless, their relief considerable at being home again, bathed and well rested. Barney, lying in bed with his eyes opened, again began recalling the strange experience of the night before. Most of all, he was baffled and confused by the total lack of sound of the object all during the extended encounter, further puzzled by the absence of any characteristics that could be related to ordinary aircraft. He regretted deeply that neither a state trooper nor a truck had passed to share the experience with them. He still had the feeling that there was a presence around somewhere, a vague and totally indefinable presence. Somewhere, very faintly, it seemed that he had encountered a roadblock during the night. But this impression was blurred and indistinct.

The return of awareness after he had heard the strange electronic sound came back to him very slowly. Before his mind had fully cleared, he had another flash of insight—that he had turned from Route 3 on to Route 104 to approach the expressway to Concord. But the sign CON-CORD—17 MILES remained both his and Betty's symbol of the return to normality. He felt, as he lay in bed awake on this afternoon, that the reason he and Betty said so little all during the latter part of the drive was because he, at least, had been in a mild state of shock. The figures he had seen aboard the craft he shunted quickly out of his mind. He did not want to think about them.

As Betty awakened, the thoughts of what had happened the night before crowded everything else out of her mind. She could not think beyond that trip home and the experience they had had. She was to go around the rest of the day, shaking her head in disbelief. One of her first acts that afternoon, on arising (why, she never fully knew), was to take the dress and shoes she had worn during the night before and pack them in the back of her closet. She has never worn them since.

Barney, on arising, went over to the clothes he had worn the night before and was a little startled to discover that his best shoes were severely scuffed along their shiny tops. Momentarily, he was puzzled by the numerous burrs around the cuffs of his pants and on his socks, until another flood of memory came to him of walking onto and across the lonely field at Indian Head. Barney, who pays special attention to good grooming, could not understand why it was the *tops* of his shoes that were so badly scuffed. He finally assumed that somewhere in that field he had dragged the top of his feet along some rocks, how he did not exactly know, and shrugged it off. Later he was to discover the possible cause.

The sudden recollection of the incident at the field near Indian Head prompted him to go to the back door and look at the sky again. He was expecting something—but he didn't know what it was. He strained to recollect what happened after he put the binoculars to his eyes and rushed back to the car, but was unsuccessful. He simply could not get beyond that point.

At their second breakfast of the day, he discussed it with Betty, who pressed him on why he had rushed to the car in such excitement and why he felt they were going to be captured. Also, why hadn't he heard her screaming for him to return to the car? Later, on one of the many trips they made back to the area, they discovered that it was difficult to hear anyone calling at the distance Barney estimated he had walked into the field. Beyond all this, Barney became aware of an unexplained soreness on the back of his neck.

Their resolution to keep the experience absolutely quiet began to waver during their afternoon breakfast session that day. Barney was trying to hold out completely, but Betty, in the light of her sister's experience with a UFO several years before, wanted to share it with her, at least. Barney grudgingly went along with the idea, although he felt strongly that the best thing to do was to try to forget about the entire incident.

Betty went to the phone and called her sister, feeling a measure of relief in getting the story off her chest to a sympathetic listener. Her sister, Janet Miller, lived in nearby Kingston with her husband and children, the husband being the local scoutmaster and an amateur astronomy buff.

Trying to keep calm, Betty recounted the story of the night before. Janet, who had no reservations about the possibility of a UFO sighting because of her own experience, grew very excited and confirmed Betty's growing feeling that the car or their clothes might have in some way been exposed to radiation if the object had hovered directly over the car. Up to this point, Betty's floating anxiety about some kind of contamination had been instinctive; now she wondered if there were not some kind of basis in reality for the feeling she had. Janet reminded Betty that a neighbor of theirs in Kingston was a physicist, and that she would check him about what kind of evidence might possibly be extant if, indeed, the object had come in close proximity to the car. In a few moments Janet was back on the phone to tell Betty that the physicist said any ordinary compass might show certain evidence of radiation if the needle became seriously disturbed on contact with the car's surface.

Barney's skepticism, on overhearing Betty's part of the phone conversation, stiffened. As she rushed around looking for the inexpensive compass they had used on the trip, Barney was determined to be uncooperative.

"Where *is* it?" she asked Barney, in her impatience to find it and get out to the car.

"I put it in the drawer," he said.

"What drawer?" Betty asked.

None of this was helping Barney put the incident out of his mind forever. "I don't know. You'll have to find it," he said.

Betty was getting extremely aggravated. "Thanks," she said. "You're a big help."

"What do you need the compass for, anyway?" he said. "You don't really need it."

"That's your viewpoint," Betty replied. "Keep your viewpoint, but give me the compass."

Barney finally relented and got the compass for her. She rushed outside and found it raining. She ran the compass along the wet sides of the car. The needle did not react to any appreciable extent, but as she drew it near the trunk of the car, her attention was drawn to an unusual sight: a dozen or more shiny circles scattered on the surface of the trunk, each perfectly circular and about the size of a silver dollar. They were highly polished in contrast to the dimmer surface of the rest of the trunk and the car, as if the paint had been buffed through a circular stencil. She recalled at this point that the strange beeping sounds they had heard the night before came from the direction of the trunk, and in the emotional state she was in after talking to her sister, she was startled by the sight of the round, shiny spots in this vicinity.

Carefully she placed the compass on one of the spots. The needle immediately began wavering. She almost panicked, but got control of herself and placed the compass on the side of the car, where none of the shiny spots appeared. The needle reacted normally, remaining pointed in one direction. Quickly, she shifted the compass back to the shiny spot. Again, the needle went out of control. She ran quickly back to the house.

"Barney," she said, "you've *got* to come outside and look at this with me. There're these bright, shiny spots all over the trunk of the car, and the compass spins every time I put it anywhere near them."

Barney insisted that it was her imagination and didn't want to go out in the rain.

In the meanwhile, a couple renting an apartment from the Hills in the second floor of their house dropped down, and noting that Betty was getting quite upset by something, asked what the matter was. Betty, in her state of excitement, spilled out the story of the UFO sighting to them and told them that she wanted Barney to go out and look at the strange spots and the reaction of the compass. Barney then reluctantly went out with the other couple, while Betty called her sister to report the findings. Janet, in the meanwhile, had talked to the former Chief of Police of Newton, New Hampshire, who happened to be visiting that day, and he had immediately suggested that the Hills notify the Pease Air Force Base in Portsmouth, a Strategic Air Force Command installation that had been the recipient of a steady number of UFO reports in New Hampshire in recent months. The Police Chief had received instructions on this procedure in line with the rash of UFO sightings in New Hampshire.

Barney came back into the living room within a few minutes, just before Betty hung up from the second call to her sister.

"How did the compass act for you?" Betty asked.

"Just like any compass," he said. "Oh, it might have jumped around a little when it got near the tire in the trunk. Things like that."

Betty eyed him coldly. "Well—why did it jump around when you touched it to the trunk?"

"I don't know," Barney said.

"I can see why it might jump around if it were near the battery. But the spare tire? Really, Barney."

24

"Oh, I don't know," Barney said. "Maybe it has something to do with the metal. It acted perfectly all right to me."

"What about the shiny spots?" Betty said. "Did you see those?"

"Yes," said Barney.

"Well—what about them?"

"Oh, probably something dropped on the trunk."

Betty was convinced that he was simply denying all this experience to himself, and she didn't know why. (Later, Barney explained that the experience had been such a nightmare to him, so unbelievable, that he wanted desperately to put the whole thing behind him and forget it. At the moment he was getting very irritated with Betty for persisting in her exploration.)

He again refused to give in when she asked him to go out with her and recheck the compass and the shiny spots. And he urged her to forget it when she insisted on following Janet's advice to call the Pease Air Force Base.

"All right," he finally agreed. "But if you do call the Air Force Base, leave me out of it."

Betty was haunted by the thought that they might have been exposed to radioactivity, but at the same time she realized that this might sound ridiculous to the officers at the Air Force Base. However, she called the Air Police at the base, and after several transfers by the switchboard she finally found one officer who asked her for the details.

She gave him the facts in bare outline, because the officer's attitude was cynical and uncommunicative. Out of embarrassment or shyness, she skipped the details of seeing the double row of windows, feeling that this might make her the target for further cynicism. She did, however, report the fins apparently separating at the sides of the craft, with the two red lights on either side. The officer grew more interested in this, and when Betty explained that her husband had a better look at this part of the craft than she did, the officer asked to speak with Barney.

Barney was extremely reluctant to come to the phone, but he had simmered down a little by now, and finally agreed. He cooperated in giving out as many details as he could remember, but he sheepishly avoided mentioning the figures he had clearly observed on the craft. At one moment, the officer told Barney that he was cutting him in with another extension at the base, and that the call was being monitored. Neither Barney nor Betty was anxious to be involved in a bizarre situation. While Betty felt that the attitude of the officers was one of indifference, Barney disagreed, saying that they *were* intensely interested, that they were at no time impatient, and that they were intrigued by the fins with red lights. To the Air Force officers this was a new slant in the many UFO reports they had screened.

The conversation on the phone made a slight change in Barney's attitude. From his discussion with the officer, Barney learned of other reports, some similar to his, so that he no longer felt as self-conscious about the possibility of being considered irrational in reporting something that he couldn't explain. Both refrained, however, from telling about the shiny spots on the car, and Barney still held back on revealing the figures aboard the craft behind the curved window. This, he felt, might put him in the position of being doubted, and he had enough of his own doubts to contend with at this point. His main concern was not to appear foolish.

On the next day, some of his concern in this respect was reduced when the Pease Air Force Base called back for further information. This gave Barney more confidence in himself and his own experience, but he still did not give out all the details.

It was Major Paul W. Henderson, of the 100th Bomb Wing at the Pease Base who called back the next day, and he told the Hills that he had stayed up all night working on the report and wanted a few more details. He also indicated that he might be calling back later, although after the second conversation the Hills did not hear from him again. His official report to Project Blue Book, the name of the Air Force unit at Wright-Patterson Field, Ohio, which handles the thousands of UFO sightings from over the entire country, indicates that the Hills need not have had the concern about being laughed at when they made their faltering call to the Base after their experience.

Information Report No. 100–1–61

On the night of 19–20 Sept between 20/001 and 20/0100 Mr. and Mrs. Hill were traveling south on Route 3 near Lincoln, N.H. when they observed, through the windshield of their car, a strange object in the sky. They noticed it because of its shape and the intensity of its lighting as compared to the stars in the sky. The weather and sky were clear at the time.

A. Description of Object

1. Continuous band of lights—cigar shaped at all times, despite changes in direction. [Neither of the Hills recalls whether they mentioned the disc shape of the craft at close range.]

26

2. Size: When first observed it appeared to be about the size of a nickel at arm's length. Later when it seemed to be a matter of hundreds of feet above the automobile it would be about the size of a dinner plate held at arm's length.

3. Color: Only color evident was that of the band of lights when comparable to the intensity and color of a filament of an incandescent lamp. (See reference to "wing tip" lights.) [Barney, who felt impelled at this time to understate everything, shied away from giving his full impression of the size of the craft.]

4. Number: One.

5. Formation: None.

6. Features or details: See 1 above. During period of observation wings seemed to appear from the main body described as V-shaped with red lights on tips. Later, wings appeared to extend further.

7. Tail, trail or exhaust: None observed.

8. Sound: None except as described in item D.

B. Description of Course of Object

1. First observed through windshield of car. Size and brightness of object compared to visible stars attracted observers' attention.

2. Angle of elevation, first observed: About forty-five degrees.

3. Angle of elevation, at disappearance: Not determinable because of inability to observe its departure from auto.

4. Flight path and maneuvers: See item D.

5. How object disappeared: See item D.

6. Length of observation: Approx thirty minutes.

C. Manner of Observation

1. Ground—visual.

2. Binoculars used at times.

3. Sighting made from inside auto while moving and stopped. Observed from inside and outside auto.

D. Location and Details

(Here the report recounts the general details of the sighting, including the strange sound of the beepings, which the Hills described to the Air Force interrogator as "sounding like someone had dropped a tuning fork." Under the pressures of the formal phone call, many details were omitted, among them being the varicolored lights seen by Betty, and of course the figures Barney had observed but did not want to talk about.)

The report concludes: "During a later conversation with Mr. Hill, he volunteered the observation that he did not originally intend to report this incident, but inasmuch as he and his wife did in fact see this occurrence he decided to report it. He says that on looking back he feels that the whole thing is incredible, and he feels somewhat foolish—he just cannot believe that such a thing could or did happen. He says, on the other hand, that they both saw what they reported, and this fact gives it some degree of reality.

Information contained herein was collected by means of a telephone conversation between the observers and the preparing individual. The reliability of the observer cannot be judged, and while his apparent honesty and seriousness appears to be valid it cannot be judged at this time.

Struggling to find some correlation between fantasy and fact, Barney suggested to Betty that they each draw a sketch of their impressions of the object. Betty agreed. Sitting in separate rooms, they roughed out two sketches, which when compared were remarkably similar.

Even though Barney's lengthy conversation with the Air Force Major reinforced his confidence in his own sighting, he still wasn't a full believer in unidentified flying objects. He worried about his inability to justify what he actually saw with his conviction that such a thing could not be. Betty, too, was cautious in spite of her belief in her sister's sighting, and in the inexplicable actions of the object that had stayed so long in sight on Route 3. Barney told a friend that his reaction was one of a person who saw something he doesn't want to remember. Later, this dichotomy was to bother him, to reflect itself in the worsening of his ulcer condition that up to this point had been improving considerably.

Where Barney recoiled from the situation, Betty's curiosity was ignited. Two days later, she went to the library to find any possible information on Unidentified Flying Objects, which had, to her knowledge, been receiving rather cavalier treatment in the press. Like most intelligent people, she was of two minds about the subject. She had felt, prior to their own startling experience, that there had to be something to the phenomenon, but of any extensive facts about the subject she knew nothing. At the library, she discovered that background material was sparse. However, a book by Major Donald Keyhoe, *The Flying Saucer Conspiracy,* commanded her attention. She took it home to read it at a single sitting. Barney, although his viewpoint had softened since he talked with the Air Force Base, declined to read it. The lingering resistance he ascribed to his continued desire to avoid the painfulness of the shock he had encountered. He was not, he insists, trying to be arbitrary or stubborn.

Major Keyhoe's thesis in the book, Betty discovered, indicated that the Air Force was making a serious effort to discredit all UFO sightings, at the expense of open scientific inquiry. A former Annapolis graduate and Marine Corps Major, Keyhoe was instrumental in establishing an organization known as the National Investigations Committee on Aerial Phenomena in Washington to correlate and analyze every available UFO sighting in an attempt to find a solution to the mystery, and to prepare the public, if necessary, for the possibility that the objects may be extraterrestrial spacecraft of unknown origin. NICAP, as Major Keyhoe's organization has come to be known, arrived at the conclusion that there are basically only two explanations for the consistent, world-wide reporting of UFO's every year: (1) Widespread and presently unaccountable delusion on a scale so vast that it should be, in itself, a matter of urgent scientific study; (2) people *are* seeing maneuvering, apparently controlled objects in the atmosphere. Members of NICAP, many of whom are reputable scientists, professors, technicians, pilots and former high-ranking military officers argue that the second hypothesis is the more reasonable, and that it is grounded on empirical observations. In its carefully documented study *The UFO Evidence,* the organization analyzes 575 technical and other reliable reports from 46 states, Puerto Rico, Mexico, Canada, and other countries throughout the world. NICAP investigators, serving on a voluntary basis, are instructed to document each case in painstaking detail and to contest wherever possible any wild and irresponsible reports of sightings from the lunatic fringe that has so frequently seized on the subject for either self-aggrandizement or profit. Among the members of NICAP's Board of Governors are Dr. Charles P. Olivier, Professor Emeritus of Astronomy, University of Pennsylvania and President of the American Meteor Society; J. B. Hartranft, Jr., President of the Aircraft Owners and Pilot Association and former Lt. Colonel in the Army Air Corps; Dewey Fournet, former Major, U.S. Air Force in charge of the UFO investigation known as Project Blue Book; Professor Charles A. Maney, head of the Department of Physics, Defiance College, Ohio, and others.

On reading Major Keyhoe's book, Betty gained more confidence in her own experience. She lost little time in sitting down to write him a letter:

Portsmouth, N.H.
September 26, 1961

Dear Major Keyhoe:

The purpose of this letter is twofold. We wish to inquire if you have written any more books about unidentified flying objects since *The Flying Saucer Conspiracy* was published. If so, it would certainly be appreciated if you would send us the name of the publisher, as we have been unsuccessful in finding any information more up-to-date than this book. A stamped, self-addressed envelope is being included for your convenience.

My husband and I have become immensely interested in this topic, as we recently had quite a frightening experience, which does seem to differ from others of which we are aware. About midnight on September 20th [the choice of midnight could be either the 19th or the 20th; Betty Hill chose the latter], we were driving in a National Forest Area in the White Mountains, in N.H. This is a desolate, uninhabited area. At first we noticed a bright object in the sky which seemed to be moving rapidly. We stopped our car and got out to observe it more closely with our binoculars. Suddenly it reversed its flight from the north to the southwest and appeared to be flying in a very erratic pattern. As we continued driving and then stopping to watch it, we observed the following flight pattern: the object was spinning and appeared to be lighted only on one side which gave it a twinkling effect.

As it approached our car, we stopped again. As it hovered in the air in front of us, it appeared to be pancake in shape, ringed with windows in the front through which we could see bright blue-white lights. Suddenly, two red lights appeared on each side. By this time my husband was standing in the road, watching closely. He saw wings protrude on each side and the red lights were on the wing tips.

As it glided closer he was able to see inside this object, but not too closely. He did see several figures scurrying about as though they were making some hurried type of preparation. One figure was observing us from the windows. From the distance, this was seen, the figures appeared to be about the size of a pencil [held at arm's length], and seemed to be dressed in some type of shiny black uniform.

At this point, my husband became shocked and got back in the car, in a hysterical condition, laughing and repeating that they were going to capture us. He started driving the car—the motor had been left running. As we started to move, we heard several buzzing or beeping sounds which seemed to be striking the trunk of our car.

We did not observe this object leaving, but we did not see it again, although about thirty miles further south we were again bombarded by those same beeping sounds.

The next day we did make a report to an Air Force officer, who seemed to be very interested in the wings and red lights. We did not report my husband's observation of the interior as it seems too fantastic to be true.

At this time we are searching for any clue that might be helpful to my husband, in recalling whatever it was he saw that caused him to panic. His mind has completely blacked out at this point. Every attempt to recall leaves him very frightened. This flying object was at least as large as a four-motor plane, its flight was noiseless and the lighting of the interior did not reflect on the ground. There does not appear to be any damage to our car from the beeping sounds.

We both have been quite frightened by this experience, but fascinated. We feel a compelling urge to return to the spot where this occurred in the hope that we may again come in contact with this object. We realize this possibility is slight and we should, however, have more recent information regarding developments in the last six years.

Any suggested reading would be greatly appreciated. Your book has been of great help to us and a reassurance that we are not the only ones to have undergone an interesting and informative experience.

Very truly yours,

/s/ Mrs. Barney Hill
(Mrs.) Barney Hill

As Betty Hill's confidence increased through her study of the NICAP material, so did her willingness to reveal more of the details. For the first time in this letter she was willing to talk about Barney's description of the figures within the craft, although she did so with Barney's extremely reluctant approval. Betty's capacity for ventilating her feelings about the incident was helpful; Barney found himself envying her ability to do so, aware that suppressing the facts in his mind could be damaging.

Some ten days after the sighting, Betty began having a series of vivid dreams. They continued for five successive nights. Never in her memory had she recalled dreams of such detail and intensity. They dominated her waking life during that week and continued to plague her afterward. But they stopped abruptly after five days, and never returned again. In a sense, they assumed the proportion of nightmares. They were so awesome and of such magnitude that she hesitated to mention them to Barney, who was working those five nights and not with her when the dreams took place. When she eventually did mention rather casually that she was having a series of nightmares, Barney was sympathetic but not too concerned, and the matter was dropped. Betty did not press the matter further.

A few weeks later, another puzzling incident occurred that neither Barney nor Betty could explain. They were driving in the car through the countryside near Portsmouth, on a road in a sparsely populated area. Up ahead of them a parked car was partially blocking the road. A group of people were standing outside the car, and Barney began to slow down gradually to avoid an accident.

Suddenly Betty was overcome by fear. She could not explain it, even to herself. "Barney," she said. "Barney—keep going. Please don't slow down. Keep going, keep going!" And she found herself starting to open the car door on the passenger side, with an almost uncontrollable impulse to jump out of the car and run.

Barney was startled and tried to find out what was wrong. Betty was nearing a state of panic. Without asking any more questions, Barney speeded up as fast as was practicable with people partially blocking the road, and Betty recovered her equilibrium. What disturbed her most was that she was not at all inclined to be this emotional; she had never before or since experienced such a sensation. The impact of the unexplainable incident stayed with them for many days afterward, as well as the effect of the nightmares on Betty, that still persisted.

Realizing that Barney was attempting to put the UFO event out of his mind, Betty refrained from discussing the nightmares with him. But she began telling a few close friends, one of whom was a fellow social worker, who urged her to write down her dreams. Feeling that this might relieve her conscious preoccupation with them, she sat down at her typewriter and wrote.

Her dreams were unusual in subject matter and detail. They revealed that she encountered a strange road block on a lonely New Hampshire road as a group of men approached the car. The men were dressed alike. As soon as they reached the car, she slipped into unconsciousness. She awoke to find herself and Barney being taken aboard a wholly strange craft, where she was given a complete physical examination by intelligent, humanoid beings. Barney was taken off down a corridor, curving to the contour of the ship, for apparently the same reason. They were assured, in the dream, that no harm would come to them and that they would be released without any conscious memory of the strange happening.

Betty's written paper on the dreams was in complete detail, with full descriptions of the craft, the examination, and the humanoid beings.

It was to play a large part in what happened two years later, a part she could not anticipate now, in her bewilderment over the incident she and Barney had so recently experienced.

CHAPTER THREE

On October 19, 1961, Walter Webb, lecturer on the staff of the Hayden Planetarium in Boston, opened his mail to read a letter from Richard Hall, then secretary and now Assistant Director of the National Investigations Committee on Aerial Phenomena in Washington. As a Scientific Adviser to NICAP, Walter Webb occasionally investigated the more serious and puzzling UFO reports in the New England area, drafting a detailed document for Washington when the merits of the case warranted it. Hall's letter included a copy of the letter Betty Hill had written to Major Keyhoe and suggested to Webb that it might be worthwhile to drive the eighty miles north of Boston to Portsmouth to investigate the case.

Webb, who had joined the Smithsonian Astrophysical Observatory in Cambridge, Massachusetts, shortly after his graduation from college in 1956, had been interested in Unidentified Flying Objects since 1951, when, as a counselor at a boys' camp in Michigan, he had made a sighting while training campers in the use of a telescope. Although his work with the Smithsonian Satellite Tracking Program required months of photographing satellites against a star background from a volcanic mountain in Hawaii during the International Geophysical year, he had not personally observed any further UFO's since his experience at the boy's camp. His own sighting was totally convincing to him that such objects did exist, but his intense interest in the subject did not bloom fully until the summer of 1952, when a now famous group of sightings was made over Washington, recorded on several radar screens, and confirmed by competent visual observers both in the air and on the ground. Many details on this event were quickly hushed by the Air Force, and further intelligent study of the phenomenon was rendered impossible. The sighting Webb had made with his nature study students at camp followed a pattern reported many times to NICAP. It was a clear summer night, and the three members of the group spotted a red-orange object traveling from east to west over the southern hills beyond Big Silver Lake in Michigan. At first they suspected that it might have been an ordinary aircraft, but its movements shattered all conventional aerodynamic patterns. The object moved in a strange, undulating manner, creating a perfect sine-wave course over the hills in the distance, a course in which the up-and-down dips described a smooth, bell-shaped pattern along the tops of the hills.

Webb's first reaction to Richard Hall's letter was reluctance. It was plain that this case involved a report of the movement of beings on the craft, and Webb was skeptical of this type of sighting. There had been in the past a rash of this sort of thing from highly irresponsible people, none of whom had provided any kind of rational documentation, and who insisted on talking about such incidents in the most exaggerated terms. Webb was determined not to become associated with any such irresponsible case.

He drove up to Portsmouth on October 21, 1961, with his skeptical attitude unchanged. In his mind were thoughts of the sensational nature of the claim, the possibility that the Hills might be seeking publicity, perpetrating a hoax, or suffering from a mental aberration. On the other hand, he felt that Betty Hill's letter was extremely literate, an honest and straightforward account of a frightening experience which had happened to two people. He would reserve judgment until after his interview, which, he resolved, would be thorough and painstaking with special attention to finding flaws in the story. As an interviewer with a scientific background, he was certain he could create a slip-up somewhere if the Hill's story was spurious, and he would not hesitate to crack the story if he could.

He arrived at the Hills' house at about noon. Barney was relieved to find an intelligent man, who would not ridicule or pooh-pooh the experience, showing a demonstrable interest in the event. Barney was at the point where he detested the term "flying saucer," although Webb's reference to UFO's was palatable to him. Further, he hoped that he could learn more about the subject from Webb, to give some kind of answer to the mystery which still burned in him underneath the surface.

To Betty, Webb appeared to be extremely professional, and obviously was skilled and experienced in interviewing people.

The interview began shortly after noon, and continued with little interruption until eight that evening. "I was so amazed, impressed by both the Hills and their account," Walter Webb later said, "that we skipped lunch and went right through the afternoon and early evening. During that time, I cross-examined them together, separately, together, requestioned them again and again. I tried to make them slip up somewhere, and I couldn't; I simply couldn't. Theirs was an iron-clad story. They seemed to me to be a sincere, honest couple driving home from vacation, late at night on a lonely road, when suddenly something completely unknown and undefinable descended on them. Something entirely foreign or alien to their existence."

During the interview, the Hills gave Webb their sketches, drawn independently, yet comparing so identically. As the interview drew toward a close, Barney found himself almost reliving the incident. He could see himself standing in the road confronted by the enormous object. "It was a long grilling," Barney describes the Webb interview. "He began asking us questions, going over in detail all the experiences. First, we had to recite the story. Then he would have us go back and regress to different periods of the experience, so that all the details would come out. Then I would come to this curtain—the moment I put the field glasses on the vehicle and saw this figure close up. And here—as with every other time I've tried to think it through—I could never get past this curtain in my memory. I could go no further, but I had the most eerie, chilling feeling, like watching a late show by myself at night. I get chills as the ghost walks around the old haunted house. And I continually got chills when I got to that point of thought, whether it was during the Webb interview or at other times. I would get chills, I would shudder and I would look briefly around in the room, though I was safely in the comfort of my own home."

Walter Webb had a map with him, and he carefully used it to fill in a complete timetable of the Hills' journey. For some reason, although the Hills explained in detail about the shiny spots on the car, they forgot to show them to him, and Webb forgot to ask to examine them. None of the three can explain this oversight, although Webb said: "I have tried to recall whether I saw those silvery spots they claim to have seen on the car immediately following the sighting. To this day, I can't. I am sure I did not go out and look at the car. I knew of the spots. This is just poor reporting on my part. Poor investigation. Maybe I just didn't think there was anything to these spots. In fact, in my initial report on the case, I reduced the spots and the beeping noises to a very low value. I mentioned them in an embarrassed way—well, here it is, but what is it? And I went on from there. I don't recall ever checking."

"If I recall it," Barney said, "there was so much detail we got into— the position of the moon when we saw it, identification of the stars and weather conditions, things like that, that it slipped our minds to get Webb to check the spots."

At the close of the session, Webb suggested to the Hills that they drive back over the trip, trying to pin down the exact spots where varied events happened: the first notice of the object, the frequent short stops between Lancaster and Indian Head and the exact spot near The Flume and Indian Head where the closest encounter took place. The Hills agreed and Barney gave up most of his reluctance to review the case, as a result of Walter Webb's intensive cross-examination.

*   *   *

Driving back to Boston, Webb mentally reviewed the case. He was extremely impressed by it. His doubts about a hoax, about the Hills' competence, about an aberration, were dispelled. "I had read of such cases before," Webb said later, "but this is the first time I had come in contact with apparently reliable witnesses who claimed to have seen UFO occupants. Of course, we have to be very careful about such cases. Very careful. I was impressed that the Hills *underplayed* the dramatic aspects of the case. They were not trying to sensationalize. They did not seek publicity. They wanted me to keep this just to myself, confidential with NICAP. Barney's complete resistance to the idea of UFO's was most convincing. There were two different personalities here, in a way: Barney—the more careful, scientific, accurate person—and Betty, the talker. But at the same time, she didn't overdo it, either."

Five days later, Webb prepared his report for NICAP in Washington, reviewing the incident in the minutest detail, including compass directions, position of the moon and planets, weather, and detailed description of the object, including the sketches the Hills had given him.

He concluded his lengthy report: "It is the opinion of this investigator, after questioning these people for over six hours and studying their reactions and personalities during that time, that they were telling the truth, and the incident occurred exactly as reported except for some minor uncertainties and technicalities that must be tolerated in any such observation where human judgment is involved (that is, exact time and length of visibility, apparent sizes of object and occupants, distance and height of object, etc.). Although their occupations do not especially qualify the witnesses as trained scientific observers, I was impressed by their intelligence, apparent honesty, and obvious desire to get at the facts and to underplay the more sensational aspects of the sighting. Mr. Hill had been a complete UFO skeptic before the sighting. In fact, the experience so jolted his reason and sensibilities that his mind evidently could not make the adjustment. In his conversation with me (and with his wife since the sighting) a mental block occurred when he mentioned the "leader" peering out the window at him. Mr. Hill believes he saw something he doesn't want to remember. He claimed he was not close enough to see any facial characteristics on the figures, although at another time he referred to one of them looking over his shoulder and grinning and to the leader's expressionless face. However, it is my view that the observer's blackout is not of any great significance [later this was to be seriously challenged]. I think the whole experience was so improbable and fantastic to witness —along with the very real fear of being captured adding to imagined fears—that his mind finally refused to believe what his eyes were perceiving and a mental block resulted.

"Needless to say, neither Mr. Hill nor his wife are UFO doubters any longer. Both are now quite interested in the UFO subject and wish to know more about it and read as much as they can. Near the conclusion of the interview, I was asked many questions concerning the possible nature and origin of such objects. . . .

"It will be noted that there were no electromagnetic disturbances, such as engine and headlight failure [mentioned in other close-range UFO observations]. However, the code-like beeping sounds on the rear of the car (a 1957 two-door hardtop) are an unexplained feature of the case. Neither did the witnesses notice any physiological effects— warmth, burns, shock, or paralysis. The dog did not appear to be alarmed at any time during the whole sighting [the Hills at this point had forgotten to tell Webb about several instances of Delsey's odd behavior]. There were no other aircraft in the sky. Just for the record— not that there is any connection at all—the Hills' sighting took place a day before Hurricane Esther's rains and winds hit New England.

"The Hills live in Portsmouth, N.H. Barney, thirty-nine, is a clerk at a

Boston, Mass., post office (South Station) and Betty, forty-one, is a child welfare worker employed at Portsmouth by the New Hampshire Department of Public Welfare.

"New Hampshire has furnished quite a number of UFO reports in recent years. For example, in 1960 NICAP recorded seven sightings, six of them in the White Mountains area, especially around Plymouth. Of particular interest were the red cigar-shaped objects seen during April—twice from Plymouth (on the 15th and 25th) and once from West Thornton (on the 28th). See NICAP Special Bulletin, May 1960, p. 4. Another "cigar" was observed in the same area, near Rumney, on August 24. See NICAP report form on case. . . .

"About eight years ago, Mrs. Hill's sister, Janet, was driving from Kingston, N.H., to Haverhill, Mass., on Route 125 and saw near Plaistow, N.H., a large glowing object in the sky with smaller objects flying around it. She ran to a house and got others to look at the strange apparition. They all saw the smaller objects fly into the larger one which then took off."

/s/ W. N. Webb
10/26/61

* * *

As a Scientific Adviser to NICAP, Webb had an extensive knowledge of the files of the organization and, of course, immediate access to them. Under the direction of Major Keyhoe, a graduate of the U.S. Naval Academy and former Marine Corps pilot, the organization constantly emphasizes that it avoids any preposterous claims regarding UFO's and instructs its area representatives to disprove cases before accepting the sighting as related. Wherever possible, NICAP concentrates only on those sightings by pilots, radarmen, police, engineers, technicians, and responsible and competent citizens. Major Keyhoe's battle with the Air Force has been going on for over a decade. In the course of its investigations, NICAP receives over forty thousand letters a year, many of which are fresh reports of new sightings that are constantly cropping up in this country and throughout the world.

Beginning in the spring of 1965, four years after the Hills' encounter, reports of low-level and near-landing UFO sightings increased so that the organization was overwhelmed with documentation on the phenomenon. The Oklahoma, Texas and New Mexico sightings during August of

1965 involved nearly forty members of the Oklahoma State Highway Patrol, with its teletypes clogged for three nights with UFO reports made by its officers and hundreds of reliable laymen—sightings corroborated by radar fixes from the Carswell and Tinker Air Force Bases. In Exeter, New Hampshire, two seasoned policemen encountered an enormous UFO at low-level, so low that one of the officers dropped to the ground and drew his gun. During the fall and winter of 1965–66, hundreds of other people in the area reported similar experiences documented by taped interviews and cross-examinations resulting in overwhelming evidence for the existence of the objects.

The Michigan sightings in March of 1966, involving policemen and hundreds of reliable witnesses, brought the subject to a head, including a demand by Republican House Leader Gerald Ford for a full-scale Congressional investigation. In announcing his findings as special consultant to the Air Force, Dr. J. Allen Hynek, Chairman of the Department of Astronomy at Northwestern University and director of the Dearborn Observatory was widely misquoted by the press regarding his statement that the sightings might be attributed to a spontaneous combustion of methane or marsh gas. What Dr. Hynek did say was that two of the sightings might be attributed to this phenomenon, but that these two cases by no means explained the hundreds of unidentified sightings by reliable people that were continuing to be reported throughout the world. In his press release he urged that a scientific panel be set up to study the subject in depth, a statement that was largely ignored by the press.

Back in 1961, when Walter Webb was trying to fit the pieces of the Hill case together, none of this recent and startling evidence was available. But there were thousands of other cases in the files, not as well known to the general public because of the reluctance of the press to cover them and because the challenge to Air Force secrecy had not become as strong.

Webb also was familiar with the findings and research of the Aerial Phenomena Research Organization in Tucson, Arizona, another conservative non-profit group, inclined to take more seriously the reports of intelligent beings associated with UFO sightings, where the craft hovered or landed. APRO, as the organization is known, is under the direction of L. J. Lorenzen, an engineer in the Kitt Peak National Observatory at Tucson. Among its advisers are Dr. Frank Salisbury, Professor of Plant Physiology at Colorado State University; Dr. R. Leo

Sprinkle, Assistant Professor of Psychology at the University of Wyoming; H. C. Dudley, Chairman and Professor of Physics, University of Southern Mississippi; Dr. James A. Harder, Associate Professor in the College of Engineering, University of California, Berkeley, and others.

Dr. Dudley once said, "I recommend we use a bit of scientific curiosity to see whatever is the physics of the phenomena so many people are describing as UFO's. Ascribing the phenomena as due to psychological aberration is nonsense. There is a series of physical phenomena that needs explaining; let's get on with it in an open-minded, scientifically oriented manner. Then let the data provide the answer."

Dr. Harder, of the University of California, added: "I think the evidence for the reality of Unidentified Flying Objects is beyond a reasonable doubt, and that the phenomena is deserving of scientific attention in spite of the existence of organizations on the lunatic fringe that have tended to discredit such attention."

Among the organizations to which members of APRO's advisory staff are associated are: The American Physical Society, the American Psychological Association, the National Science Foundation, the National Institute of Health and NASA.

Among the APRO reports (documented in the book by Coral Lorenzen, *The Great Flying Saucer Hoax,* William-Frederick Press, 1962) Walter Webb found an unusual series of sightings investigated by Dr. Olavo Fontes, in Brazil. Dr. Fontes, the APRO representative in that country, is a medical doctor, and First Vice President of the Brazilian Society of Gastroenterology and Nutrition. Webb discovered in Dr. Fontes' reports that the village of Ponta Poran, Brazil, had been the scene of a strange series of UFO experiences over a period of two and a half months, from December 1957 to March 1958. They interested Webb in relation to the Hill case because of the persistent tendency of the objects to trail and follow individuals and vehicles, much in the same nature as the object in New Hampshire had followed the Hills. For the most part, the objects in Brazil were Saturn shaped, a shape often described in UFO sightings, along with the saucer and cigar shapes more commonly noted. During this extended time period, the objects buzzed jeeps and cars, mostly along the lonely roads near Ponta Poran. The actions of the objects were interpreted as a probe to discover human reactions to their presence.

The incident near Ponta Poran, on the southwestern frontier of

Brazil, a landscape consisting of a forest-covered plateau known as Mato Grosso, was the first one recorded. It was approximately 6:30 in the evening of December 21, 1957, when a farm woman, her driver and servant, and three young sons were driving toward the town in a jeep. Two glowing objects, flying side by side, approached them and glided along the side of the road, oscillating in a strange wobbling motion. They were described as metallic spheres, about fifteen feet in diameter, encircled by a rotating ring. The upper half of the objects was fiery red, the lower, silvery white. Each gave off a blinding glare, with variable intensity.

For two full hours the objects followed the jeep, darting ahead of it and around it in circles. In the two times the driver stopped the jeep, one of the objects came down to just above the ground, while the other hovered high in the air. When the jeep entered Ponta Poran, both objects climbed into the sky and disappeared.

On February 19, two sightings were made near the town, one of them at 4:00 A.M., the other at 10:30 P.M. The early-morning sighting involved the same family, this time with the object dropping down over the road and hovering in front of the jeep, its red glow dimming and turning to a silvery color. The people in the jeep were afraid—as Barney Hill had been in the field near Indian Head—that they were in imminent danger of being captured. The driver turned around and sped back to the village, where the object climbed to a high altitude and hovered over the town for half an hour longer. Six other witnesses were rounded up, and the group loaded into two jeeps to drive out to the lonely section of the road where the UFO had first been spotted. The object followed them, but remained at a distance, again climbing to a high altitude. It was not until 6:00 A.M. that it shot upward at tremendous speed and disappeared.

That night, four highly respected citizens of the town, including a professor, a law student, a notary and a tax clerk went to the location on the road where the object had first hovered so low. At 10:30 the brilliant reddish object approached them from the sky, oscillating from side to side. When another object appeared to join it, the group panicked and drove back to town.

On March 3 a similar incident took place, with the object finally hovering a few feet above the road in front of the jeep. When the driver tried to ram it, it shot straight up and disappeared. (Interestingly, over a dozen strikingly similar accounts to these were recorded in Exeter, New Hampshire, and many other locations in the United States in 1965–66.)

What interested Webb was that these stories, and many others like them in both NICAP and APRO records, were close parallels to the Hill case, yet they had occurred in different parts of the world, and none knew of the others' experiences.

On November 2, 1961, Webb wrote the Hills to thank them for their cooperation, indicating that he had submitted his extensive report to NICAP. None of the three knew at that time that there was to be another even more extensive report by Webb that would far exceed his first in interest and impact.

*　　　*　　　*

About a month before Webb filed his NICAP report, Robert Hohman, a staff scientific writer on both engineering and science for one of the world's most notable corporations in the electronic industry, and C. D. Jackson, a senior engineer for the same company, went to Washington to attend the XII International Astronautical Congress as part of their regular routine. Both had been deeply involved in work on the space program and were preparing a paper on three experimental scientists of previous years: Nikola Tesla, David Todd, and Marconi, the acknowledged father of radio. Their paper was to examine the original data of these scientists in response to a rhetorical inquiry by the Office of the Director of Defense Research and Engineering: "What research is being done to keep abreast of the scientific advances of the past . . . to see that there is not needless duplication of effort?"

The paper presented evidence and deductive scientific reasoning to indicate that Tesla, Todd and Marconi observed laboratory data and related phenomena that suggested the possibility that they were monitoring interplanetary communications during the period of 1899 to 1924. They also noted that during the same period exactly, the Russian theorist Konstantin Tsiokovsky deduced a model of an intelligence existing independently of terrestrial influence. The paper examined the possibility of identical radio signals in this time span, emanating from Tau Ceti, a celestial body some 11.8 light years away.

As technicians working in advanced fields of science, both Hohman and Jackson were interested in the data being accumulated on the UFO subject by NICAP and arranged to have lunch with Major Keyhoe during the Astronautical Congress. Hohman happened to mention to the Major that he had not heard of many recent UFO reports and wondered if the entire phenomenon were dropping in frequency. Major Keyhoe brought up the letter NICAP had just received from the Hills, one of the organization's most interesting cases in many months. Hohman and Jackson were at once interested, but the story seemed so incredible that they were cautious in accepting it. On the other hand, if there were any truth to the story, they wanted to investigate it with an open mind.

They debated the idea for several weeks and finally got in touch with Walter Webb, who had just completed his report. He sent them a copy, and they studied it carefully. Knowing of Webb's reputation for accuracy, they were considerably impressed. His appraisal of the character and competence of the Hills led them to take immediate action. On November 3, 1961, they wrote the Hills:

Dear Mr. and Mrs. Hill:

This letter will introduce Mr. C. D. Jackson and myself. Our interest in writing you at this time concerns your recent experience of September 19–20, 1961. . . .

Your participation in this event was brought to our attention by Major Donald Keyhoe with whom we had luncheon during the recent XII International Astronautical Congress, Washington, D.C., on October 4–5, 1961, and more specifically, through Mr. Webb, NICAP representative in the Boston area.

Whereas our principal interest in this subject is concerned with the attempt to verify the origin of these vehicles according to existing scientific theory maintained by Professor Hermann Oberth, of Germany, there is, naturally, a similar interest in trying to determine as well, the meaning of the whole phenomenon. Your own recent experience might offer some help in this latter regard.

Mr. Jackson and I would like to visit with you at a time and place convenient to you. We are mature people associated with a major electronics and engineering corporation. Our discussion would be entirely objective. Having a close familiarity with most of the unclassified (military) literature dealing with this subject, and dating back to 1947, we would like to be of assistance in answering your questions, as well as continuing our own investigation on this subject.

For the purpose of scheduling, we would be able to visit in Portsmouth, New Hampshire, during the week of November 13, 1961, preferably the 18–19th of that week.

Sincerely yours,
/s/ Robert E. Hohman

Hohman and Jackson were not able to get together with the Hills at their home in Portsmouth until a week beyond their suggested date. But on November 25, they arrived to review the story of the strange experience. Visiting the Hills at the time was Major James McDonald, an Air Force intelligence officer who had just recently retired from active duty, and a close friend of the Hills. Later, in 1962, Barney and Betty Hill were to stand up for the Major when he was married to one of Betty's close friends and associates in her welfare work. Further, when NICAP made additional inquiry about the character and reliability of the Hills, Major McDonald was to give them an unqualified recommendation.

The group—Betty and Barney Hill, Robert Hohman, C. D. Jackson and Major MacDonald—conferred for another long session, beginning at noon and running almost until midnight.

The Hills were impressed by the businesslike and professional attitude of Hohman and Jackson, with Barney again reflecting surprise that so much attention was being directed toward a subject he still had lingering doubts about, in spite of his own traumatic experience.

Hohman and Jackson inquired about many facets in the case that puzzled Barney, particularly an inquiry as to whether there were any nitrates or nitrate derivatives in the Hills' car. "The only thing I could think of that possibly had some connection with nitrates," Barney later said, "was gunpowder. I did have about a dozen shotgun shells in the car, left over from a trip to the South when I had practiced shooting at tin cans on my uncle's farm, but aside from that, I couldn't think of anything. The reason they were asking, they said, was that in several close UFO encounters, the people had been in rural areas where they were exposed to nitrates or nitrate fertilizer. Then it hit us: Betty had left the bone-meal fertilizer in the trunk of the car before the trip, and I hadn't bothered to take it out. Now who knows? Maybe it does have significance, maybe it doesn't. It was interesting that they should bring it up, when we had forgotten all about it. And they asked a lot of questions that started me thinking—questions like did we have anything new in the car, any new object, and had it disappeared? There had been reports, apparently, of people having close sightings, and something they had recently purchased, had disappeared. They asked if anything had disappeared out of our car, but this was two months later, and we had a lot of junk in there. I couldn't remember.

"One of the questions they did ask was: Why did we take the trip? This might seem to an unrealistic question. But in thinking on it, it's not too far-fetched. Number one, there was no preparation for the trip. I had gone to Boston that night and had worked and was returning to Portsmouth that day. I decided during work, well, I think I would like to go to Niagara Falls and then return via Montreal. Betty had the week off anyway, and I was able to call in and get an extension of the weekend for several days. So we packed our car that night."

Betty Hill's comments are similar: "This was how impulsive it was. The only money we had was in our pockets. Saturday the banks were closed so we couldn't even cash a check. I think the amount between the two of us was less than $70. So the questions they asked were interesting, mainly because we had never thought along those lines. They provoked a lot of thought in both of us, mentioning the remote possibilities of life existing on planets involved with Alpha Centauri or Tau Ceti, which was news to me. I don't think I've ever heard of them. Their questions were so far out that I just couldn't see what relationship they had to our experience. And this business of nitrates. At that time, I had all kinds of plants in the house. In fact, in the living room, I had an avocado tree that touched the ceiling. They walked around, looked my plants over and asked me what kind of fertilizer I used on them and things like this.

"And while they were here they were mentally reconstructing the whole trip. One of them said, 'What took you so long to get home?' They said, look, you went this distance and it took you these hours. Where were you? Well, when they said this, I thought I was really going to crack up. I got terrified, and I even put my head on the table. And I went back over the trip in my mind, recalling, or trying to recall that vague moment when it looked as if the moon had been on the ground. They tried to reconstruct that time sequence, and they said, 'You couldn't have seen the moon on the ground at the time, because apparently at that period . . .' they knew what time the moon had set that night. And the moon had set fairly early. It just wouldn't tie in with this time business. They suggested that we check and find just where the moon sat at the time, because it apparently wasn't the moon that we saw—or thought we saw. Then this whole lapse of time business. I really became upset about that. . . ."

"I became suddenly flabbergasted," Barney added in his words, "to think that I realized for the first time that at the rate of speed I always travel, we should have arrived home at least two hours earlier than we did. Normally, for me to travel from Colebrook to here—we know we left at 10:05 that night—actually takes less than four hours, even figuring out the period of time we stopped on the highway—and at no time did we stop for more than five minutes. I was baffled as to what the reason was for us leaving Colebrook at 10:05 P.M. and arriving back here at dawn, somewhere around 5:00 A.M.—nearly seven hours instead of less than four. Even if I allowed more time than I know we took at those roadside stops, there still were at least two hours missing out of that night's trip."

To the entire group in the Hill living room that afternoon, the missing time period became a major mystery. The Hills tried but simply could not account for it. Nor could they account for the thirty-five miles between Indian Head and Ashland, during which their recollection amounted to almost nothing. They were now more puzzled and confused than ever. For the first time it fully dawned on them that they were facing a period of simultaneous amnesia, experienced by each of them at the same time, falling roughly between the first series of beeps that emanated from the back of their car and the second series of beeps they encountered somewhere near Ashland, thirty-five miles to the south. The thought that plagued everyone at the meeting was that while it was unusual enough for one person to be struck suddenly with a temporary period of amnesia, it was very strange for two intelligent people to experience it together under such fantastic conditions.

As a hard-headed former intelligence officer in the Air Force, Major James MacDonald groped for some kind of answer to the puzzle. UFO's are constantly being discussed in the Air Force, much more so than the laconic official statements from the Pentagon indicate. Officially, the Air Force position requires that no member of the force can report any incidents to the public; all information must be channeled through the Foreign Technology Division at Wright-Patterson Air Force Base, Ohio, and in turn, any release of that information can only be made by the Office of the Secretary of the Air Force at the Pentagon. The fact remains that many Air Force pilots and radar men do talk, and those who have directly come in contact with the objects reveal stories of incredible speeds, right angle turns, and maneuvers that are impossible to duplicate by any aircraft known to the military. Even the most sophisticated weapons were said to have been used in an attempt to bring the UFO's down without success.

Major MacDonald had had no direct experience with the subject of UFO's in his Air Force career, but he had a profound respect for it. He felt that it was a subject to be viewed with an open mind, each case considered on its own merits, and that only firsthand accounts had any value. He was also aware that many reports of UFO's consisted of an observer's honest mistakes, perhaps by confusing shooting stars, Venus, shadows on a windshield, or St. Elmo's Fire, with unidentified craft. On the other hand, he was aware of the many cases involving technically qualified people of impeccable character whose close encounters with the objects were clearly observed and unexplainable in conventional aerodynamic terms. He realized the complete probability of the phenomena, that the valid reports were by no means unrealistic or absurd and that extraterrestrial life was not only possible but entirely probable. Space programs on the earth included impact landings on Venus and a soft landing on the moon—so why couldn't the reverse process be taking place?

He was fascinated by the probe that Hohman and Jackson were conducting, impressed by their attention to detail and their posing of interesting and imponderable questions. But most critical of all—what happened in the two hours when the Hills suffered double amnesia? What could have happened? What *did* happen?

When the discussion focused on this critical point, the problem narrowed down to finding a way of discovering what happened during the missing time period, a way to penetrate the unyielding curtain that began to descend when Barney Hill looked through the binoculars and came down completely when the first series of beeps sounded in the speeding car. What was missing was not only the two hours of time—but a distance of thirty-five miles, for which there was little accounting.

It was at this point in the informal gathering that Major MacDonald suggested the possibility of medical hypnosis.

He had, during his Air Force career, become somewhat familiar with the subject and was impressed with its valid use under controlled medical conditions. He was also aware of its dangers in the hands of stage hypnotists or other inexperienced people. He knew that hypnotherapy and hypnoanalysis had been used in cases involving amnesia, producing some strikingly dramatic results in the rehabilitation of servicemen suffering from war neuroses (sometimes described as "battle fatigue" or "shell shock"). In a sense, he reasoned, the Hills had experienced a violent trauma much like shell shock, a condition that often produced temporary amnesia—which had frequently been treated successfully by medical hypnosis.

When Major MacDonald suggested hypnosis, the group was immediately interested. Hohman and Jackson by now had no doubts about the character and competence of the Hills, but they were aware that this strange case needed further documentation. Major MacDonald, who had discussed the case many times with the Hills, was convinced of their sincerity and anxious to help them overcome the nagging doubts and fears. On several occasions, Barney had said to MacDonald, "Jim—how do I *know* that this thing happened? How do I *know* that I wasn't just seeing things? I'm in this terrible position where I really *do* know it happened, and I can't get myself to believe it. It's bugging me so seriously that my ulcers are kicking up, just at the point where they were getting better."

It was agreed that the idea of medical hypnosis was a good one, but the problem became one of finding the proper medical man to take the case, or if, indeed, he thought it was wise to do so. Obviously, the case should not be entrusted to any but the most competent psychiatric specialist, but no one immediately came to mind. Hohman, Jackson, and Major MacDonald agreed to make inquiries, and the Hills, both felt the idea had merit.

"I agreed with the idea wholeheartedly," Betty later said. "Because the moment they suggested hypnosis, I thought of my dreams, and this was the first time I began to wonder if they were *more* than just dreams. Then I really got upset over my dreams. I thought, well now, if I have hypnosis, I'll know one way or the other because this was, I thought—God, well maybe my dreams are something that really happened. I also thought about that strange experience while driving with Barney in the car— when he slowed down for the other car standing in the road. I really panicked at that time. And when hypnosis was suggested, I thought of this incident too. And I thought to myself, why did I react in this way? I've never done that before in my life."

"My reaction to the hypnosis idea," Barney added, "was, first, what are the effects of hypnosis? What is it about? The experience of it. What will I feel like going under? I was mildly reluctant, without saying so, to submit myself to such a thing, unless it was for someone I could have complete confidence in. But what overruled my apprehension about that was the thought: once and for all, for all times, this might clear up Betty and her nonsense about her dreams. I further thought that the hypnosis process might also explain the mental blockage I had at Indian Head— and that whole trip that seemed to be missing for the thirty-five miles from Indian Head to Ashland. So I felt that this could be something I would get a full understanding about, and of course it would clear up Betty's dreams to the point that for once and for all, I could say: 'Look,

Betty —they are *dreams*. They have nothing whatever to do with the UFO sighting.'

"You see, Betty kept wondering about what happened between the two series of beeps. I didn't think anything happened between the two. All I thought was that it would get me beyond that point of standing on the highway, looking at these moving figures in the craft, the one that kept looking back at me with those eyes. He gave me the impression— and this was dim in my memory, but there just the same—that he was a very capable person, and there can be no nonsense here. We have business to attend to. These were all thoughts going through my mind. As to how this person was affecting me, I wanted to get beyond that point. And this was the reason that Jim MacDonald's suggestion appealed to me."

It was to be some time before the Hills were able to follow up the suggestion. In the meantime, the compulsion grew in both of them that they must return to the scene of the incident, as Walter Webb had suggested, and relive the experience trying to recapture the elusive shreds of memory.

CHAPTER FOUR

It wasn't until after the holidays that the Hills were able to think about returning to the scene of the encounter. The inevitable Christmas bustle helped suspend their lingering doubts and questions, if only on a temporary basis.

Finally, in February of 1962, a series of pilgrimages began that were to continue for many months, in all seasons. At first they would go two or three times a month; later, they were to skip many weeks at a time. But always with the same questions to answer: What happened during the inexplicable blackout? Where did Barney spin the car off to a side road? And, if he did, what happened?

The idea of hypnosis was temporarily tabled. Neither Hohman, Jackson nor Major MacDonald could suggest a psychiatrist, and Betty, especially, hoped that the return trips to the area might spark a chain of memory that would suddenly bring back their recall.

Again, Barney was ambivalent about taking the trips. Betty could overcome Barney's resistance by suggesting they look for a new and different restaurant on each trip, a particular weakness of his. They would often pack a lunch to economize on the trip up, so that they later could splurge at dinner.

Or they might leave Portsmouth at three in the afternoon on a Saturday, drive along Route 4 toward Concord, then swing northerly on the expressway, planning to reach Route 3 at dusk. They reasoned that after dark the area would be as it was the night of the encounter, the landscape more provoking to their senses if they were to discover the vaguely defined road that they half recalled from the limbo period of their amnesia.

On one occasion that winter, Betty, with a flash of insight, recalled a vague vision of a diner she thought they had passed near Ashland shortly after the second series of beeps had brought them back to their senses. They had pulled up beside it, since it was the first lighted place they had come across in many miles. It had turned out to be only a night light and their hopes for a cup of coffee had been jolted. They would drive along Route 3, on several back roads branching off the main road, but they could find no sign of a diner of any kind. They would bicker about where they might have traveled, or which of the byways off Route 3 they might have made a turn on. No clear recall came back to them.

At Cannon Mountain, Indian Head and Lancaster they would reenact their frequent stops, in the hope that the repetition of the process might stimulate their memories. There was even disagreement as to where they had made road stops before the amnesia set in, although the general areas were firm in their minds. They brought the binoculars with them but had only a faint hope that they would see the object again.

Most often, they would plan the reenactment systematically, winding northward up U.S. 3 to a point above Cannon Mountain, turning around, and beginning the trip back down to Portsmouth the same night. Even with frequent side excursions to find the lost road, they could not account for the inordinate length of time it took them to reach Portsmouth the night of the incident.

On one occasion they stopped by a small restaurant near Woodstock, where several residents told them of frequent sightings of the objects hovering over Route 3, sometimes remaining suspended over an hour. (The UFO's had been reported to the Air Force, but nothing further had been heard.)

The Hills had no fear, no apprehension on these trips, the challenge of the mystery overriding the shock of the experience. They would park on a turnout, with a sweeping view of the mountain valleys during a moonlit night, and sit and look at the stars and the sky, as if some clue might arise to bring back their memories.

"During one winter night," Barney recalls, "we found ourselves on a road that seemed to go nowhere, a lonely mountain road that I cursed myself for turning on. As we got deeper and deeper into the valley, the road deteriorated into a mass of snow. About midnight I found myself trying to turn the car around, hoping that I wouldn't get stuck in the snow, and furious with Betty for suggesting driving up into the mountains. I thought, why go through all this? Why not just forget the whole thing? Or if we can't forget it, why make such an effort to relive all this or to think we can bring back the two lost hours? I don't know why we weren't apprehensive, to tell the truth. Vaguely, I hoped to see the thing again, I think. I can't even say. I *did* want to see it again. What I found most interesting about all these trips was that we never seemed to agree, completely. We would bicker and become mildly quarrelsome. Betty would insist I should take a right turn, and I would insist on making a left. But what bothers me still is the question: Why did I have so much apprehension that night at Indian Head, and yet I had none on returning to the mountains, scheduling our time to be there late at night? I don't know what the answer to that is."

*   *   *

The return trips were fruitless. Always the same curtain of darkness for Barney after the critical moment at Indian Head. Always, the blind veil for Betty after the strange series of beeps as they drove frantically away from Indian Head, with Barney, apparently in great emotional distress, at the wheel. Always the blank between Indian Head and Ashland.

The idea of hypnosis was not dormant for long. As the Hills attempted to settle down to something like a reasonable routine, they occasionally discussed the incident with a few close friends, Betty still being haunted by her graphic and startling dreams. For Betty, talking it out with close friends was helpful. Barney continued to try to ignore the subject, except on those occasions of the trips. He continued to plead with Betty to forget the dreams.

On one day in March of 1962, Betty had lunch with Gail Peabody, a friend of hers who was a state probation officer and in whom Betty had full confidence. She mentioned the idea of hypnosis, and Gail responded promptly by recommending a psychiatrist she knew of who was medical director of a private sanitarium in Georgetown, Massachusetts, only about ten miles away from Portsmouth.

On March 12, 1962, Betty typed a letter to the doctor.

52

Patrick J. Quirke, M.D.
222 West Main Street
Georgetown, Mass.

Dear Sir:

We are seeking the services of a psychiatrist who uses hypnotism, and are wondering if it would be possible to make an appointment to see you on a Saturday morning? My husband and I are both employed, but our working hours are such that this would be convenient for us. If this is not possible we could make an appointment at your convenience.

We have a unique reason for requesting this interview. The enclosed bulletin of the National Investigations Committee on Aerial Phenomena, briefly describes an experience that occurred to us last September 19–20, 1961. We have been interviewed by Mr. C. D. Jackson and Robert Hohman of (name of company withheld).

Many puzzling aspects remain, so it is believed that hypnotism could clarify these. We have handled this experience confidentially with the exception of NICAP and a few close friends.

We do have a complete story of the report written by Mr. Walter Webb, of the Hayden Planetarium, which we would be willing to send to you, for your review. If you do not have time available to see us, or would prefer not to do this, would you be willing to suggest another psychiatrist willing to undertake this.

Very truly yours,
Eunice and Barney Hill

The interview took place on March 25, 1962, at eleven in the morning.

The private sanitarium is known as Baldpate, formerly the inn that inspired the famous old play *Seven Keys to Baldpate*. It sits on the top of a mountain, with a sweeping view of the Massachusetts countryside. It has been converted into a retreat for psychiatric patients who seek a comfortable, home-like atmosphere for therapy. The Hills were impressed by the paintings, the fireplace and the cheerful atmosphere, not at all what they had expected.

"At no time did I feel uncomfortable," Barney said. "The doctor sat across from us at his desk, while we sat in comfortable chairs, and I felt relieved to talk to this man about our experience, particularly since he did not look at it as if it were two persons talking about an obvious hallucination—and he was giving his professional attention to it. He acknowledged that we had an unusual experience, but he felt that we might gradually begin to remember some of the missing things, since we had probably suppressed much of the experience as a protective

53

device. He felt that at this stage it might not be a good idea to explore this block of mine and Betty's disturbing reactions, forcibly, at least."

The ultimate, mutual decision was to postpone any action at the time, but that if problems should persist, then therapy might be indicated. The Hills felt relieved that Dr. Quirke ruled out simultaneous hallucination, a matter that had been giving them both some concern.

* * *

The long commuting drive from Portsmouth to Boston, the night work schedule, the separation from his sons who were living in Philadelphia with his former wife, the doubts about the Indian Head experience and the problem with his ulcers all began to take their toll on Barney. His condition was further complicated by the recurrence of elevated blood pressure, creating a vicious circle whereby he could not successfully remedy the last condition without the removal of the other problems, and vice versa. Another disturbing symptom began at this time, more of an annoyance than anything else, but contributing to his general problem: a series of warts began to develop in an almost geometrically perfect circular ring in the area of his groin. While they were a minor problem, they added to his concern.

By the summer of 1962, Barney's exhaustion and general malaise prompted him to seek a psychiatrist for his overall condition, entirely aside from the traumatic experience he and Betty had had in the White Mountains. He did not, in fact, associate his need for therapy with the UFO incident, feeling mainly that the conflict over his father-son relationship was at the base of his problem, the long distance to Philadelphia making it impossible to be a devoted father.

The physician treating him for elevated blood pressure and ulcers recommended a distinguished psychiatrist in nearby Exeter, New Hampshire, Dr. Duncan Stephens, and the long process of therapy began during the summer of 1962.

At first, the incident at Indian Head was ignored altogether by Barney. He did not emphasize it in his talks with Dr. Stephens because it seemed to be only a minor part of his anxiety, a sidelight to the other conditions, and he concentrated on his general emotional and social problems, with the help of Dr. Stephens.

He indicated to Barney that there were many unusual and interesting facets to his case, including the circumstances of Barney's interracial marriage in a New England town, a sociological condition that could not be ignored. He pointed out that both Barney and Betty were making a remarkably good adjustment, that their inherent good will and honesty and contribution to community life were remarkable.

Barney found him probing back through his early life to explore the experiences of his early childhood, and helping Barney to work through the conditioning influences of his early days. During the therapy, Barney became more aware of the special conflicts and problems arising from being a member of a minority race.

All through his family background was a record of interracial relationships. His mother's grandmother was born during slavery, her father being a white plantation owner. Being fair of color, the maternal great-grandmother was raised in the owner's house and cared for by his sisters, even though she was legally a slave. When she married, the plantation owner gave her and her husband 250 acres of land, to be handed down to their children.

The farm became quite profitable over the years, passing down to Barney's uncle, who assumed the care of Barney and another sister and brother when his mother became ill in Philadelphia for many months. During this time young Barney grew to feel that his aunt and uncle were his own parents. When his mother finally recovered, it was painful for him to leave his aunt and uncle and the large farm in Virginia. The feeling was reciprocal, since the couple could not have children of their own, and they offered to raise Barney and assure him of a college education.

But he returned to his parents in Philadelphia, to the hot asphalt streets and the walled-in row houses of the city. His father, though poor, was a good provider. He, too, reflected a mixed marriage; his paternal grandmother was fair—the daughter of white and colored parents. His grandfather was a proud Ethiopian freeman.

During the dismal depression years, Barney Hill's family never went without food and shelter, though many of their neighbors did.

"One Christmas stands out vividly," Barney recalls. "My father said he didn't think Santa Claus would be able to visit us that year because the newspaper stated that Santa's sleigh had been damaged in a blizzard at the North Pole. With long faces and saddened hearts my brothers and sisters and I went to bed. I woke up around five in the morning and found that the door of my room leading to the hall was tied. I went through the adjoining door to my sisters' room, and that was tied, too. I was able to squeeze through, untie the door, and the four of us ran downstairs. There in the living room were all the toys we had wanted and asked for under a beautifully decorated Christmas tree. My father and mother came downstairs, pretending great surprise. 'What do you know?' my father said. 'Santa did come. It must have been the noise we heard last night on the roof!' My father and mother derived much pleasure in giving us surprises this way."

Although Barney's parents created an atmosphere of love in the family's home life, he knew the inevitable struggle and conflicts that the Negro unnecessarily suffers. "One time in Junior High School," Barney recalls, "when the time came to select our course, I told my school adviser that I eventually wanted to become a structural engineer. He advised me to select another course because there was no future for Negroes in that field. I was disheartened. My marks suffered. I thought there could possibly be a future for me in the military service, so when America began its peacetime draft, I decided to enlist in the Army. I have always felt that it's right and proper to defend against an aggressor at all times, an attitude instilled in me by my uncle."

This attitude came in handy in the turbulent streets of Philadelphia. On one particular day, Barney learned through a friend that a gang of boys threatened to beat him up if they caught him out of his own neighborhood. Within the hour, Barney was on his bike, pedaling to the home of one of the boys, where he knew they gathered. He marched into the backyard and said: "I understand you fellows are looking for me."

One of the boys advanced, and said, "Yes, we are."

A scuffle followed, with Barney soundly trouncing the youngster. When he finished, he turned to the others and said: "I'll fight all of you together—and separately. Because I plan to leave my street any time I feel like it!"

There was no more trouble in the neighborhood.

Barney served three years in the Army, running into a similar incident of bullying, in which he succeeded in trimming down to size a soldier, thirty pounds heavier than he, in a grudge boxing match. His son from his previous marriage, Barney, was born while he was serving during World War II; his younger, Darrel, after he had been discharged.

Both in and out of therapy, Barney increasingly examined these and other scenes of his background. And as he did, his curiosity increased as to why he reacted so violently to the object as it hovered over him in the sky at Indian Head. What confused Barney most about the incident was that he was never inclined to panic, never afraid of facing a traumatic crisis. This attitude was reflected when he walked steadily across the road and out onto the field toward the enormous object, carrying his binoculars, on that night of September 19, 1961. It was not until he put the binoculars to his eyes and focused on the craft that he panicked and ran back to the car. The unexplained panic, that he knew to be foreign to his general reactions, plagued him, in addition to the curtain of absolute blankness that descended at that moment.

For a full year, from the summer of 1962 through the following summer of 1963, Barney continued working through his problem with Dr. Stephens, but never emphasizing and only briefly considering the UFO incident. Barney felt at first, and the doctor seemed to agree, this was peripheral to the case, a side issue that could only be considered as a sudden shock in a recent period of his life, rather than a deep, underlying cause of his symptoms. Further, Betty was not experiencing as much distress as he was over the incident, aside from the vivid recall of her dreams that fired up her curiosity. They had both taken Dr. Quirke's suggestion to relax for awhile and, temporarily, to put aside the idea of hypnosis as means of clarifying their memories.

One evening in September 1963, the Hills were invited by their church discussion group to relate (for the first time at any kind of gathering) their experience with the UFO in the White Mountains. They had mentioned the incident to their minister, who along with others in the church had a growing curiosity about the subject in the light of increasing Unidentified Flying Object reports throughout New England, and especially in New Hampshire and Vermont. Because of these reports, Barney and Betty felt that people might be willing now to accept their story without the usual skepticism. They had mixed feelings about the idea, as usual, although Betty was now becoming convinced that their story should be told. If it should represent a landmark in the history of the phenomenon, did they have a right to confine it to themselves?

At the discussion group meeting was another invited speaker, Captain Ben Swett, from the nearby Pease Air Force Base, who was well known in that area for his study of hypnosis, a subject which together with the story the Hills would tell might make up an interesting evening.

"After the Captain listened to our story—as much as we could tell with the blanking out of memory that took place at that moment at

Indian Head—he was interested that the account was cut off as if by a cleaver at that point," Barney recalls. "We mentioned the fact that Hohman, Jackson, and Major MacDonald had recommended hypnosis, and as a man well acquainted with it himself, the Captain agreed that this might be a good idea. Especially if it were conducted by a psychiatrist. As a layman, he didn't dream of doing it himself. We, too, were aware of the danger of indiscriminate hypnosis. But it did stimulate our interest in the idea, which had been dormant for a long time."

At his next session with Dr. Stephens, Barney brought up the subject. The doctor told him that even though the UFO incident might be a sidelight, they should leave no stone unturned in examining Barney's anxieties. Dr. Stephens also indicated to Barney that simultaneous hallucination, to say nothing of simultaneous amnesia, was highly unlikely, although there is a rare psychological phenomenon known as *folie à deux,* in which two people develop a psychotic condition in which their beliefs and delusions are similar. This also seemed unlikely, since most of the conditions for this phenomenon did not seem to be present. Except for the possibility of this one traumatic experience, there were no particular symptoms mutually reflected in their constant, day-to-day relationships as husband and wife over the entire period they had been married.

Dr. Stephens found it advisable at this point to have the opinion of Dr. Benjamin Simon, a well-known Boston psychiatrist and neurologist. Dr. Simon is a graduate of Stanford University, with a Master's degree, and received his M.D. from Washington University School of Medicine in St. Louis. While an undergraduate at Johns Hopkins University, he became interested in hypnosis when he served as a subject in some experiments conducted by the Psychology Department there. During his psychiatric and neurological training, he developed proficiency in techniques and procedures. While on a Rockefeller Foundation Fellowship in Europe in 1937 and 1938, he further extended the knowledge which was to prove so useful a few years later.

In World War II, he found it a very useful adjunct in the treatment of military psychiatric disorders, first as Consultant Psychiatrist to the General Dispensary in New York, and later on a very extensive scale as Chief of Neuropsychiatry and Executive Officer at Mason General Hospital, the Army's chief psychiatric center in World War II.

The responsibility of bringing treatment to three thousand patients a

58

month made necessary the use of all the varied types of treatment, especially those which could be used in briefer therapy and with groups. Hypnosis, and its companion therapeutic procedure, narcosynthesis (the so-called "truth serum"), fulfilled these requirements expeditiously and became well established as therapeutic agents.

When John Huston produced his outstanding motion picture documentary on psychiatric treatment, "Let There Be Light," at the Mason General Hospital, Colonel Simon served as adviser, and personally did the scenes involving hypnosis and narcosynthesis. For his work as Chief of Neuropsychiatry and Executive Officer, he was awarded the Legion of Merit and the Army Commendation Medal. Mason General Hospital and its personnel received the Meritorious Service Unit Award. After leaving military service in 1946, Dr. Simon maintained his interest in these special procedures, though their place in civilian psychiatric practice is much more restricted.

* * *

In his office on Bay State Road in Boston, Dr. Simon received a call from Barney Hill early in December of 1963. Since the referral was made by Dr. Stephens, Dr. Simon set up an appointment for a consultation on December 14.

Bay State Road in Boston is sometimes known as Doctor's Row. Formerly composed of fashionable town houses for Boston's Back Bay Brahmins, many of the structures have now been converted into pleasing and comfortable medical offices.

Barney and Betty Hill left Portsmouth well before seven o'clock on the morning of December 14, driving in and parking their car near Dr. Simon's offices with a comfortable margin of time before their appointment at eight. They approached the consultation with mingled feelings of curiosity, nervousness, and some apprehension, although these feelings were tempered with the relief that comes from taking a decisive step and action in the direction they thought would help.

Betty's anxiety was of course based on her dreams. When Hohman and Jackson had pointed out the time discrepancy to them, her anxiety had grown markedly, and the thought that they might have been more than just dreams was critically upsetting to her. Although less emotional in her general reaction than Barney, and more stoic, her fear that the dreams might be based on reality was affecting her work as well as her equanimity. At one time, not long after Hohman's and Jackson's visit, she confided in her supervisor for the State Welfare Department, with whom she frequently had dinner after Barney had left for his night-shift work. "I gave her the description of the dreams I had written down," Betty recalls, "and we used to talk them over. This must have gone on over a period of a couple of months. And finally one night she said to me, 'How do you know these dreams are *not* real?' She said that every indication and reaction I was having pointed to the direction that all this might have been reality, and that I should be willing to accept that as a possibility, but after that I began to give it serious consideration. Going into Dr. Simon's office that day gave me some confidence that I could clear this up, to remove this thing that was eating at me all the time. To get some kind of confirmation—one way or the other."

Betty, who had never been in therapy, was faintly amused at the fact that she had often escorted some of her welfare cases into psychiatric clinics, and now the tables were about to be turned. Barney, whose therapy had been continuing for many months, was curious about the possibility that they might be going to undergo hypnosis; he was anxious to see if indeed he *could* be hypnotized and what sort of method would be used to accomplish this.

Barney, at a later date, recalled his impressions of the first visit: "Walking into his office where Dr. Simon holds his consultations, I found it very impressive. It was nicely carpeted with green, along with a green pad on his desk—it was comfortable and quiet. He completely captivated me to the point that I felt this was a person I could trust. It was an instantaneous thing with me that I immediately liked him. And this was also what was to help me overcome my anxiety. Betty and I were together, of course, at the first consultation.

Betty, too, thought that the office was attractive and the doctor impressive. "I had full confidence in him even before we met, because at a recent Child Guidance Clinic I looked him up in the *Biographical Directory of the American Psychiatric Association*. The entry there convinced me of his competence and professional standing. To me, this was so important because of the unusual nature of our case."

Dr. Simon, somewhat surprised to note the interracial marriage of his patients, began with a general history of their problems, highlighted, of course, by the incident at Indian Head two years before.

Dr. Simon was aware that Barney had been undergoing therapy for his anxiety state and that it was increasingly apparent that the experience with the Unidentified Flying Object was an important facet in his failure to respond adequately to his treatment. He was similarly aware of the nightmares leading to Betty's anxiety. It became quickly apparent that both Barney and Betty needed treatment. Treatment would be centered on their anxiety reaction with the apparent amnesia for part of the experiences in the White Mountains as the point of departure.

There were practical questions, too, for both of them. The matter of cost was something they could not ignore. Their combined income was reasonably comfortable, but with two of them in therapy, they realized, there would be a severe strain on the budget. And the job of psychiatric treatment could not be accomplished over a short period of time. In addition to the fees that a competent psychiatrist would set, there was the not inconsiderable cost of driving to Boston each week for a double session. This was serious business to them, not a whim or fancy, and they accepted it as such.

The Unidentified Flying Object aspect was a secondary matter to Dr. Simon, because his first and major job was to determine the treatment, and aid the patients in overcoming their psychiatric problems. The UFO experience fell within the limits of the material he had heard and the little he had read about the subject. This secondary aspect of the case *was* most interesting, and he foresaw a rather prolonged and intensive period of therapy that might be unique.

One of the major objectives, of course, was to open up the amnesia, and since this symptom responds particularly well to hypnosis, the doctor decided to use it to initiate the treatment.

The general attitude of Dr. Simon to UFO's was neutral, tempered by a hard-headed realism that such objects could exist, as experimental aircraft or foreign reconnaissance craft not yet announced to the layman —or simply mistaken aircraft or stars. He had no personal interest in the subject and was willing to accept whatever authoritative sources said about it. He didn't realize the amount of controversy involved, even among the scientific community, nor was he familiar with the National Investigations Committee on Aerial Phenomena, whose report the Hills brought with them to give the doctor a full background on their experience, as documented by Walter Webb.

At the consultation that morning, Dr. Simon evaluated their cases and gave an outline of his treatment plan. Because the purported amnesia was a central factor in their distress, he planned to begin by using hypnosis to penetrate the amnesia, if this is what the condition turned out to be, and to proceed according to the developments. Dr.

Simon also decided to record the therapeutic sessions on tape, both for an accurate record and for probable use to bring the material into consciousness under controlled conditions.

During hypnosis, the incidents described in the trance can be wiped from conscious memory. Conversely, on instruction from the doctor, they can be recalled. For the most real reproduction of the trance experience, the patient can listen to his own voice on tape and analyze it with the doctor, step by step.

The reality or non-reality of the dreams was of course foremost in Betty's mind. For nearly two years now, the answer to this question had been gnawing away at her. For Barney, as he had already told Betty, he was hoping that for once and for all she would accept the fact that her experience in regard to an abduction was no more than an intense series of dreams. The trauma of the low-level sighting on Route 3 was enough for Barney; to carry the incident on to the possible abduction—just the thought of it—was more than he cared to think about. To the doctor, the uniqueness of the story remained nothing more than the background against which he would have to work.

Barney and Betty Hill, like most laymen, had only a smattering of knowledge about hypnosis. Dr. Simon explained to them that the process was a close relationship between the doctor and the patient, in which the Hills would be brought into a condition like sleep. There would be no danger of harm to them—they should have nothing to fear.

In a lecture some years ago to the New York Academy of Medicine, "Hypnosis: Fact and Fancy," Dr. Simon covered the entire field of hypnosis and its function in medical and psychiatric practice, pointing out that only in the last several decades has hypnosis received significant attention as a medical practice.

> Who can hypnotize? Who can be hypnotized? Who cannot be hypnotized? [Dr. Simon asked in the lecture]. Any intelligent adult with appropriate knowledge of technique can hypnotize. Any intelligent adult and most children above the age of seven can be hypnotized; in fact, children are more easily hypnotized than adults. Very psychotic individuals and the mentally retarded are very resistant to hypnosis. Most of these cannot be hypnotized. . . .
>
> Ninety-five percent of hypnotizable persons can attain the first stage, but only about 20 percent can be brought to the third or somnambulistic stage. . . .
>
> Will plays no part whatever in hypnosis, and the belief that hypnotizability is a manifestation of a weak will is false. The factors which influence

hypnotizability are the intelligence of the individual, his conscious willingness, and the degree of unconscious resistance or submissiveness. The latter are not always manifest on the surface. . . .

Contrary to the common fears of the public, termination of the hypnotic state is not generally a problem. Universally, the suggestion for waking results in waking. There need be only the added suggestion of feelings of comfort and freedom from anxiety. In the rare instances where the subject does not wake on suggestion, if left alone he will fall into a natural sleep and wake up in a matter of hours. . . .

Sometimes drugs—such as sodium amytal or pentothal—are used to facilitate induction of the hypnotic state where the patient is unduly resistant. Under these conditions, the waking period will be delayed by the effect of the drug, but the suggestions given during the induction will be carried out as post-hypnotic suggestions. The two aforementioned drugs are of some value in difficult inductions and will help relax the apprehensive patient and increase his suggestibility.

There are generally described three stages of hypnosis: light, medium, and heavy. In the light stage, catalepsy of the eyelids [inability to open the eyes at will] can be produced on suggestion, and a certain degree of general suggestibility is present. Post-hypnotic suggestions may be given, and a great deal of treatment can be accomplished. . . .

In the medium stage, paralysis of volitional control of the larger muscles of the body may be produced—major catalepsy. In this stage, analgesia, insensitivity to pain, may be successfully suggested. . . .

In the third stage, or somnambulistic stage, almost any phenomenon can be produced, and the patient will be amnesic unless he is definitely told to recall the trance state. [This was to play an important part in the treatment of the Hills.] Positive or negative hallucinations may be induced, and post-hypnotic suggestions given in this somnambulistic stage will be very effective. Activity of the autonomic nervous system manifested by blushing, constriction of skin vessels, and slowing of the pulse can be produced. There is conflict among authorities on this matter, but there are reports of actual blistering by the suggestion of intense heat. . . .

Dr. Simon closed the lecture by stating his conviction that hypnosis should not be used in any field beyond research, medical practice and dentistry. He also added:

Hypnosis has gone through many periods of enthusiastic acceptance and then ensuing rejection as have some of our "modern trends" in psychiatry. There is no doubt that these symptoms [those removed by hypnosis] tend to recur or to be replaced by more distressing symptoms, unless the underlying emotional conflict [of which the symptoms are manifestations] is resolved. Unless the physician can be sure that he will be able to continue treatment of the patient after the removal of the symptoms, the symptoms should not be removed by hypnosis. . . .

Many question whether a forceable breakthrough of resistance [such as that which is provided by hypnosis] is a desirable approach. In a variety of conditions, hysterical, psychosomatic and others, hypnosis may help to shorten the time of therapy by facilitating the approach to unconscious conflicts, as has been described. Hypnosis has dangers and yet it is not dangerous. The essential dangers lie in its use by those not bound by a professional code of ethics, and who are not adequately trained.

As the Hills were to discover, they were in cautious, medically conservative hands. With the doctor's basic attitude neutral to the UFO subject, if not prejudiced against it, they were to run into a stiff test of whatever beliefs they now had as a result of their experience at Indian Head. Betty, in spite of her growing interest in the phenomenon, was willing to accept the truth of the matter, whatever it was. Barney, hopeful to clear up the anxiety symptoms that were seriously disturbing his life, was at the point where he wanted above all for the truth to come out, regardless of what it was.

None of them were to realize that the truth was so elusive, even with the desire and the most advanced means to find it.

CHAPTER FIVE

With the Hills' story and Walter Webb's six-page report in hand, Dr. Simon found himself interested in the uniqueness of the case and the unusual data accompanying it. The story, to all appearances, seemed reliable and valid. He noted that Webb's detailed opinion was based on an interview shortly after the incident, and the impact of it on the Hills was still evident two years later. While Dr. Simon's concerns were centered around the problem of the Hills' anxiety symptoms, he was aware that the Unidentified Flying Object aspect might add a new dimension to the case. As far as the existence or nonexistence of the phenomenon itself, the doctor took a neutral position.

Since hypnosis is the method of choice for the rapid opening of an amnesia,* and may be, as Dr. Simon expresses it, the key to the locked room, he planned to use it as a part of the therapeutic procedure. The sighting of the unidentified object had built itself into one of tremendous importance to the Hills, and the condition of aroused and concentrated

---

*During World War II, hypnosis and narcosynthesis (narcoanalysis) were used rather extensively and often interchangeably in the treatment of acute psychiatric disorders. Hypnosis was most effectively used where there was a "point of departure" like an amnesia. Narcosynthesis was used most frequently to release the anxiety associated with mental conflicts below the surface of consciousness where a focal point was not so clearly apparent. This was accomplished by the slow injection of a drug, usually sodium amytal or sodium pentothal, the so-called "truth serums." They were neither sera nor did they necessarily produce the inviolable truth. They did, as did hypnosis, help in the discharge of repressed or suppressed emotional conflicts.

attention produced by hypnosis might throw some additional light on their experience.

At eight in the morning, on Saturday, January 4, 1964, the Hills arrived at the doctor's office on Bay State Road for their first regular visit after the initial consultation. It was to be the first of three sessions in which the doctor would repeatedly induce hypnosis, as a conditioning process.

During these sessions, both of the Hills responded well, and the doctor was satisfied that they would be good subjects, able to attain the depth of trance desired. The repetition of the process over the three-week period would serve to reinforce the induction and to establish specific post-hypnotic cue words to replace future induction procedures. In this way the subsequent inductions would be quick and sure. In exploring the amnesia both the doctor and the patients would be going up a blind alley, and the reinforcement of the hypnosis would make it possible to maintain good control in the face of possible emotional disturbances that can arise in such an exploration.

Barney's nervousness increased somewhat as he prepared to undergo hypnosis for the first time. Dr. Simon stood him by the large desk in the office, placed his hands at his side, and stood near him, in front of the desk and just in front of a comfortable chair.

"Dr. Simon began talking to me," Barney described the process, "telling me that I was relaxing, and he had me clasp my hands together, and that they would be tight, tight, very tight, that I couldn't open them no matter how hard I tried. And I was standing there feeling very, very foolish, because I thought if this is hypnosis, there is nothing to it. I'm just humoring the man. I didn't want to hurt his feelings. I think he stopped and placed his hands over my eyes so that they would close. I said to myself that I wasn't really hypnotized, and when he told me that I couldn't pull my hands apart, I knew that all I had to do was open my fingers, and I could do it. But I just didn't feel like opening my fingers. I didn't even feel I was asleep, but then I was aware that he was waking me up and asking me how I felt. And I felt very, very good, very calm and comfortable. And I no longer then had any fear of hypnosis."

As so often happens, the patient feels he is humoring the operator, pretending to be cooperative, and without his knowing it, he moves into a deep trance with no knowledge or memory of what happened, unless the operator tells him he can remember.

The two, simple cue words creating rapid induction were repeated several times during the early sessions, along with tests to check the validity and depth of the trance. These are some of the customary tests used for this purpose: instructing that the patient's arm be stiff as a bar of steel (it remains so); testing for insensitivity to pain (when it is suggested, the patient does not react to the stimulus given); instructing the patient that the operator's finger will feel like a hot poker when it touches (the subject will pull his hand away in pain, even though the pain is only suggestion); and others.

Since the time of Mesmer the use of hypnosis in medicine has gone through many cycles of popularity. Breuer found that his patients were able to recall specific traumatic events through hypnosis. In part because he found that not everyone could be hypnotized, Freud developed the psychoanalytic method. The present medical attitude is reflected by Lewis R. Wolberg, M.D., Medical Director of the Postgraduate Center for Psychotherapy, New York City, and Clinical Professor of Psychiatry of the New York Medical College. He has described hypnosis as a state of being suspended like a hammock between consciousness and sleep. It should be used in a treatment plan, particularly when a patient is unable to verbalize freely, or when strong repressions bottle up highly charged material. "When a patient has repressed traumatic memories," he once told a medical symposium, "he may seal these memories off so effectively that it may not be possible to get to them with traditional techniques. Sometimes with hypnosis one can cut through repression enough to bring up traumatic memories."

With Barney and Betty Hill, this aspect of the hypnotic process would be important. The opening up of amnesia requires the use of time regression, wherein the patient's memory becomes vivid and exact —details long forgotten to the conscious mind emerge sharply. It is not unusual for person in hypnosis to recall the name and color of the eyes of everyone at his fifth birthday party if so requested, even if that might have taken place decades before. There is also the tendency to relive, re-create and reenact the time segment being recalled, so that the subject again goes through emotions involved in the original experience, a process referred to as abreaction. The physician must always be cognizant that in bringing to light unconscious memories and feelings, these may be intolerable to the patient and could lead to serious after-reactions. At times, the subject may emerge from the trance if he feels threatened, he may refuse to go further, or as in

Barney Hill's case, he may plead to be taken out of the trance without emerging on his own. Often, when the emotional release, or abreaction, comes, the patient feels measurable relief. The doctor's control of the patient during hypnosis is essential. This was to be demonstrated later as the sessions continued.

Barney Hill, in spite of some apprehension, was fascinated by the process.

"After the first test," Barney Hill recalls, "a curious thing happened. As I got ready for the induction into hypnosis, I looked at my watch. It must have been five minutes after eight. And he gave me the key word, and I was hypnotized. And as far as time was concerned, I thought he was waking me immediately. But I looked at my watch, and it was after nine. I must have been without consciousness for an hour, and yet it seemed no time at all. I recalled also, just at the beginning of what must have been the trance, that he had poked my hand with something that felt like the bristle of a brush. I asked him if I could see this done. So the doctor put me in a trance again, and told me to open my eyes in the trance and that I would remember this part of it. Then he took a needle-like instrument and pushed it against my hand and there was no pain associated with this, except perhaps like a bristle of a brush. In fact, he put considerable pressure on it, and I could feel no pain at all. And I was amazed at that, because I looked at my skin, and the needle that had penetrated my skin, and there wasn't any blood. So I began to realize that there were two things that could happen here: One, I could be hypnotized and made to forget that I had been hypnotized so that I would awaken and would assume that I hadn't been hypnotized at all; two, I could be hypnotized and if I was told I could remember, I would retain a knowledge of all that had taken place under hypnosis."

In spite of Barney Hill's excellent response to the initial induction, Dr. Simon resolved to stay with his plan of two more sessions, during which Barney and Betty would become more reinforced in the process so that a deep trance would be reached quickly and the hypnosis could continue without interruption.

As with Barney, the doctor found that Betty Hill was also an exceptionally good subject. She would, he found, go into a deep trance easily and respond completely both to the trance and to the post-hypnotic suggestions without faltering.

With both subjects clearly responding to the induction, the doctor could now continue with future sessions simply by stating the established cue words that would produce the trance. He would, however, play safe by repeated deep trance inductions.

The doctor further tested the Hills during the three preliminary sessions with various posthypnotic suggestions, such as asking them, three minutes after they were awakened, to smoke a cigarette which would taste so bad that they would have to crush it out. They would be offered another and told that it would be fine, which of course it was. He instructed them (always separately, because this would be the method he would be using in the later sessions) that they would not remember anything whatever they revealed under hypnosis, unless they were directed to. Until Dr. Simon had the whole story and could assess its emotional effect, he was careful to make sure that the amnesia was reinstated after each session. This also had the desirable effect of preventing communication between the Hills after the sessions that were to follow, avoiding distortions that might arise from their discussing the material revealed under hypnosis. Later the memory of what came out under hypnosis would be made available to both, through tape recordings or by directing them to remember at a time when this would be therapeutically desirable.

The doctor planned to take Barney first, regress him to the night of September 19, 1961, and have him reveal every detail of the trip down from Canada to Portsmouth. Since the trance would provide details of marked clarity there was a reasonable expectation that Barney would bridge the amnesic gap under hypnosis, the blocking off of his memory after each session would permit Betty to give her own story in later sessions without being influenced by Barney.

Frequently, when a subject is in a deep trance, he cannot recall what has happened during the session when he is brought back into consciousness at the direction of the operator. However, he can recall the material if he is instructed by the operator to do so.

With the tests and induction period over after the third session, the Hills looked forward to the start of the therapeutic sessions, with the hope that once and for all the mystery at Indian Head would be cleared up. They were both comfortable and relaxed about the whole hypnotic process now, in fact they almost enjoyed its after effects.

"I can just describe it," Barney recalls, "as if it were like getting into a hot tub of water and soaking, as if every nerve in my body would be pleasant and tingling. It was something I had never been able to achieve before. Just a tingling, pleasant glow, just like a rubdown."

But both of them knew that the serious business was about to begin —that a long job lay ahead of them in their search for an end to the anxieties that had been upsetting their lives for so many months. The Hills arrived at the usual early morning hour at Dr. Simon's office on February 22, 1962, Betty realizing that she would merely be going to have her induction reinforced, and Barney ready to make his excursion into the unknown.

The doctor's procedure was clear for this session: after he reinforced Betty (the simple process of rehypnotizing her so that she would maintain her capacity for the deep trance state, when the time for her sessions came later), he would have Barney go back to the night of the journey and retrace it in detail. A psychologically-determined amnesia is commonly the loss of memory for painful ideas or experiences that serves to keep them out of consciousness. Through the concentration of attention brought on by hypnosis, the opposite of amnesia is often created—hypermnesia, or superlative memory. In this session, it was hoped that not only would the forgotten material be recalled, but that the accompanying emotions would be reexperienced. To bring back the recall without the emotions would not serve adequately from the therapeutic point of view.

For the tape recording of the sessions, Dr. Simon used a Revere M-2 Automatic cartridge-loading recorder at 1 7/8 IPS. The cartridges were not only longplaying, but they could be stacked ahead of time so that there would be a minimum of interruption during the sessions. Where an interruption was necessary, the procedure was simple: the doctor would simply tap Barney on the head, tell him that he would hear no sound whatsoever during the intermission period, and then tap him on the head again to continue. A subject under hypnosis has such accuracy of recall and retention that he will continue at the exact point left off, even if he is in the middle of a sentence. The recall and reliving not only approaches the accuracy of a tape recording, but it may be turned on and off at will at the instruction of the operator.

Further, the subject will take the instructions and questions of the operator in a literal sense. If asked a question: "Did you talk to this man?" the subject may respond by saying, "No, I did not talk to this man, I whispered to him." The preciseness of the response is marked.

* * *

Barney took his seat in front of the doctor's desk. He started to reach for a cigarette, but on the cue words from Dr. Simon, his eyes closed, and his head nodded. His hands were folded across his lap—he looked like anyone who had dozed over his morning paper while he sat in an easy chair. The deep trance was induced, and satisfying himself that Barney was fully in the trance state, the doctor began the session.

DOCTOR

(He is completing his reinforcement of the trance.)

You are deeper and deeper asleep. Deep asleep. You will remember everything now, and you will tell me everything.

BARNEY

Yes.

DOCTOR

And I want you to tell me in full detail *all* your experiences, *all* of your thoughts, and *all* of your feelings, beginning with the time you left your hotel. Were you in Montreal?

BARNEY

(His voice on the tape is now amazingly flat, monotonous, and trance-like in contrast to his animated tones of normal conversation. He responds to the doctor's questions with bluntness, with little inflection, in a curious monotone, and with measured preciseness.)

We did not stay in Montreal. We stayed in a motel.

DOCTOR

You stayed in a motel. What was the name of it?

BARNEY

In another city.

DOCTOR

Yes, where did you stay?

BARNEY

I can't seem to remember.

DOCTOR

It was near Montreal?

BARNEY

It was approximately 112 miles from Montreal.

(The attention to detail here is interesting—linking the word ap-
proximately with such an exact mileage figure.)

DOCTOR

Is there any reason why you can't remember it?

(There must be some reason. In such a deep trance, a subject
usually recalls many details.)

BARNEY

We arrived at night at this motel, and I did not notice any name in the
motel.

(The reason comes out, as expected.)

DOCTOR

I see. Do you know what the city was?

BARNEY

It was not a city; it was out in the country. We had been driving from
Niagara Falls through Canada.

DOCTOR

Keep right on. Tell me about your arrival there.

BARNEY

We arrived in this small area, we did not see any town marks, and my car
was making a lot of noise. It was Betty's car that we were driving. I was
driving the car.

(The precision, the almost cumbersome exactness of the phrase is
typical of the deep trance state.)

And I stopped at a service station and they told me the car had not been
properly greased. And so they greased the car and this eliminated the
noise that the car was making. We then decided we could not continue
to Montreal and that we should look for a place to sleep overnight. And
that's when I saw this motel, and did not pay any attention to the name.

(He is again explaining why he could not remember the name. He
has also been instructed to relate all his thoughts as well as his
actions.)

The thoughts that were going through my mind were: Would they accept me? Because they might say they were filled up, and I wondered if they were going to do this, because I was prejudiced . . . .

DOCTOR

Because *you* were prejudiced?

BARNEY

. . . because *they* were prejudiced.

DOCTOR

Because you were a Negro?

BARNEY

Because I am a Negro.

DOCTOR

You've run into that before, I take it?

BARNEY

I have not actually run into being denied a place of accommodation.

DOCTOR

You mean you just worry about it?

BARNEY

But I do know that this does happen, and I was concerned because I was getting tired. And when I went to this place, they immediately accepted me. It cost us $12 for the two of us, and we stayed overnight.

DOCTOR

Did you express your concern to your wife? Does she share it?

BARNEY

She does not share my concern about this matter.

DOCTOR

Did you express it to her, or did you keep it to yourself?

BARNEY

I do express them to her.

DOCTOR

Did you on that night?

I did not. I never express them to her when we are seeking a place.

I see. All right. Go on.

We had a little dog with us, and we were told it was a nice little dachshund-type dog, and we could have her in the motel unit.

(He is, of course, referring to their dog Delsey, describing her in literal terms.)

The next morning we got out bright and early, and there was a restaurant across the street. And we decided to eat breakfast. I had my grapefruit, ham, eggs, coffee. We then are driving along this wide highway. It's a new road, it's a beautiful road. It's four lanes in certain sections.

(Again, the desire shows itself to fill in every detail, inconsequential or not.)

I am coming into Montreal, and I do not particularly like the thoughts of staying here.

Why not?

It's a big city, there's much confusion, there are a lot of trucks on the road. There's quite an amount of traffic. It's building up, and I don't want to stay in Montreal with all this traffic. I have difficulty in keeping the highway route number I want . . . traffic is everywhere. And I decide that we should find a motel if we are going to stay overnight. To my chagrin, all motels are located quite a distance, or to me I think, a distance from the city. And I am riding, we are riding around, and I see a few Negroes, and I am amazed. I had not realized there were Negroes in Montreal. And I am quite a distance away from the downtown section, and all the buildings have wrought iron, like stairways, on the outside of the buildings. And I pull over to a service station, and I ask how I can get back to my route. And he doesn't understand me, and I realize he doesn't understand English.

(Barney speaks in the present tense, an indication of the full reexperiencing of the events, rather than the recounting of them.)

74

So I put two dollars worth of gas in the car and drive off. I locate a policeman directing traffic . . . .

DOCTOR

Why did you put two dollars worth of gas in the car instead of filling it?

BARNEY

I did not want gas when I stopped to ask directions.

DOCTOR

In other words, you felt you ought to repay them, is that it?

BARNEY

I felt I should do something. And I pull over to the side, and I ask the policeman: "How can I find, I keep thinking Route 3," and he does speak English very haltingly over the strong accent, but he does give me directions. I'm passing a beautiful school, it's a Catholic school. I see the priest out there. Beautiful rolling grounds, it's sitting on a hill. It's a very beautiful school in Montreal. And again, I miss my turn . . . .

(Barney continues describing the detail of the trip across Canada, and the upper part of Vermont.)

One fourteen! It's dark—it's not a good road—but it's a short distance to New Hampshire and I see the signs of Colebrook—and it is welcome. I feel alert. I feel that my trip is over and I'm on Route 3 and I see Route 3 going to the left and to the right from straight ahead, and I become confused, and I realize I want to go straight and not to the left. I decide to stop and check my map, and I turn around and go back to a restaurant I have passed—and I park—and we go in. There is a dark-skinned woman in there, I think, dark by Caucasian standards, and I wonder—is she a light-skinned Negro, or is she Indian, or is she white?—and she waits on us, and she is not very friendly, and I notice this, and others are there and they are looking at me and at Betty, and they seem to be friendly or pleased, but this dark-skinned woman doesn't. I wonder then more so— is she Negro and wonder if I—if she is wondering if I know she is Negro and is passing for white. I eat a hamburger and I become impatient with Betty to not—to drink her coffee so we can get started, and the clock and my watch say five minutes after ten, and I know I should be in Portsmouth, I think, by two o'clock.

DOCTOR

Didn't you say just a while ago it was 1:10 or 1:15?

BARNEY

I said *Route* 114.

DOCTOR

I see. All right, go on.

BARNEY

I see dark, very dark. No traffic and Betty has asked me to stop the car and let Delsey out—she's the dog.

DOCTOR

Why is she named Delsey?

BARNEY

I think the people that owned her before called her Dolce (he gives an Italian-like explosive pronunciation) — Dolce — and Betty called her Dolce—and this became her name.

DOCTOR

Go on, you stopped to take Dolce out.

BARNEY

My thoughts keep going back to Canada. I stop in Coaticook, Canada.

DOCTOR

Yes . . .

BARNEY

I can't park close to this restaurant, so I park on the street and we must walk to the restaurant. And everybody on the street passing us by is looking. And we go in to this restaurant, and all eyes are upon us. And I see what I call the stereotype of the "hoodlum." The ducktail haircut. And I immediately go on guard against any hostility. And no one says anything to me . . . and we are served.

DOCTOR

Now this other restaurant you were in—was that in Canada?

BARNEY

That was in Colebrook, New Hampshire.

DOCTOR

How is it your thoughts go back to Canada? Is this a memory you're having again?

BARNEY

I just went back. I went back because when Betty was telling me to stop the car when we left Colebrook, New Hampshire, and we are now in the country part, I was thinking that I should get hold of myself, and not think everyone was hostile, or rather suspect hostility, when there was no hostility there. It was a very pleasant restaurant. The people were friendly. And I wondered why was this so important to me? And why was I ready to be defensive—just because these boys were wearing this style of haircut.

DOCTOR

Just your thoughts went back to Canada?

BARNEY

Yes. I was thinking of that when we were in New Hampshire. When she asked me to stop and let the dog go for a walk. That's when my thoughts went back ...

(Here, shortly before the sighting, Barney reveals again his apprehension, his ambivalence with respect to his acceptance by others, his need for reassurance. The seemingly unfriendly waitress pressed him to seek a reassuring one. Colebrook, the unfriendly, perhaps by clang association—a psychiatric term involving similar sounds which conjure up associations—invoked Coaticook.)

BARNEY

(He continues to describe the drive down U.S. 3. In the vicinity of Lancaster, New Hampshire, in his recall, he first brings up the object in the sky.)

I look up through the windshield of the car, and I see a star. That's funny, but I said, Betty, that's a satellite. And then I pulled over to the side of the road, and Betty jumped out her side with the binoculars. And I got the chain, and I hook it to the dog on her collar, and I say come on, Delsey, let's get out. And she jumps out ....

(Barney is mixing present and past tenses now, varying probably with the intensity of his feelings.)

And I look towards the sky, and I look back to Delsey, and walk her around to the trunk of the car. And I'm saying, hurry up, Betty, so I can get a look. And Betty passes the binoculars to me. And I see that it's not a satellite. It is a plane. And I tell Betty this, and give the binoculars back to her. And I am satisfied.

DOCTOR

What kind of plane was it?

BARNEY

I look—and it is to the right. And it does not go where I thought it would go. It does not go past me to the right, my right shoulder. I think it will pass my right shoulder, off in the distance, going to the north. I am facing west, and my right is to the north. And it does not go to the north.

(There is a faint trace of amazement beginning to come into his voice. From his tone, you can feel him reliving, not retelling, the story.)

DOCTOR

Does it have propellers?

BARNEY

And I think this is strange. I cannot tell. I cannot hear a motor to know if it has propellers.

DOCTOR

Was your engine running?

BARNEY

My engine was running.

DOCTOR

How about the noise that it had been making before you had your car greased?

BARNEY

It was not making this noise. And I did not pay attention to my engine running. I was concerned that it would not cut off while I was standing here with all the lights on in the car, and the battery runs down. And I was concerned, and I looked at the exhaust, and could tell that smoke was still coming from the exhaust.

From the exhaust of ....

My car.

So I did not concern myself too much after that. And this object that was a plane—was *not* a plane. It was—oh, it was funny. It was coming around towards us. I looked up and down the road. And I thought: how dark it is. What if a bear was to come out? And I worried. I returned to the car and said, let's go Betty. It's nothing but a plane. And they're coming over this way. They're changing course. Probably it's a Piper Cub.

A Piper Cub would have only one or two windows, wouldn't it? You saw windows in this plane?

This is what I said, and this is what I saw when I returned to my car. A Piper Cub.

You saw a Piper Cub?

And I drive, and Betty is still looking. And she said, "Barney, this is not a plane. It is still following us." And I stop and I look and I see it is still out there. Off in a distance. So I search for a place to pull off the road. And I see a dirt road to the right of the main highway. And I think this is a good place where I can pull off. And if any car comes, it won't strike me. And I get out of the car, and I am thinking . . . this is strange.

(His tone reflects the strangeness, now. Ominously.)

'Cause it is still there. And Betty said—*I think* she said, I am mad with her. I say to myself, I believe Betty is trying to make me think this is a flying saucer.

(The tape recorder needs a minor adjustment, and he must interrupt.)

All right. Let's stop right there for now. Until I speak to you again, you will not hear any sound here. You will be comfortable and relaxed. Just rest comfortably until I speak to you again.

(The doctor adjusts the equipment, then:)

All right. You may proceed.

BARNEY

And I am wondering why doesn't it go away. And I stop and I look again. And I see where it has gone up ahead of us on Cannon Mountain. And I think when I get past Old Man of the Mountain . . .

(The stone formation that has become the symbol of New Hampshire . . .)

It will be in a good area to look and see this thing. And I am going to report it.

DOCTOR

Do you still think it was a Piper Cub?

BARNEY

I am wondering why these pilots are military. And they shouldn't do that. They shouldn't do that. They will make some person have an accident by flying around like that. And what if they dive at me. And the military should not do that.

DOCTOR

Was it a single engine plane?

BARNEY

I do not know.

DOCTOR

You still saw no propellers anywhere?

BARNEY
(Still in his dead, level voice.)

I saw no propellers.

DOCTOR

Was it light enough to see?

(Throughout the entire interrogation, the doctor is checking, double checking, challenging.)

It was just a light moving through the sky. And I heard no noise. And I think this is ridiculous. And—

(He speaks as though Betty were with him.)

Betty! This is *not* a flying saucer. What are you doing this for? You want to believe in this thing, and I don't.

(Now he returns to his level monotone.)

And it is still there. And I *wish* I could pass a state trooper or someone, because this is dangerous.

DOCTOR

What was the danger?

BARNEY

I am thinking of bathing in French Creek, with my two boys. And this plane came overhead, and dove straight for us, and pulled up just a few inches from the state park.

(The movement of the object in the sky brought to Barney's mind a similar incident with a plane some time before in which he had a strong emotional reaction. It is interesting how related reminiscences of the past are recalled with the vividness and clarity of the original experience.)

DOCTOR

In French Creek?

BARNEY

In Pennsylvania. French Creek, Pennsylvania.

DOCTOR

Was it a Piper Cub?

BARNEY

It was a jet plane. A fighter plane. And I feel it in my chest. The explosion when it went up in the air again. And my ears, they feel like bursting. And I think of that. And I become angry with this plane that is flying around, that it might do that. And it is a frightening sound, the boom.

(He is referring to the sonic boom of the jet breaking the sound barrier at French Creek. He is apprehensive of this happening again here in the White Mountains.)

DOCTOR

The jet?

BARNEY

Yes. French Creek.

DOCTOR

If there is any sound from what you call a Piper Cub, you can hear it now.

(The subject may "hear" the sounds of his past experience.)

BARNEY

I can't hear any sound.

DOCTOR

No sound whatsoever?

BARNEY

(Almost plaintively.)

I want to hear a *jet*. Oh, I want to hear a jet so *badly*. I want to hear it.

(He is referring to the sound of the motor, not the sonic boom. He is anxious to relate this mysterious object to reality.)

DOCTOR

Why? Why do you want to hear a jet?

BARNEY

Because Betty is making me mad. She is making me angry because she is saying: "Look at it! It is strange! It is not a plane! Look at it!" And I keep thinking, it's got to be. And I want to hear a hum. I want to hear a motor.

DOCTOR

How far away was it?

BARNEY

It was—oh—it wasn't far. It was about 1000 feet, I guess.

DOCTOR

A thousand feet?

82

BARNEY

One thousand feet.

DOCTOR

If it were a Piper Cub, do you think it would have been silent at this distance?

BARNEY

(Who is a practiced plane-watcher.)

I do not. I—I *know* it is not a Piper Cub.

DOCTOR

(Pressing hard for facts and inconsistencies.)

How do you happen to know so much about Piper Cubs?

BARNEY

I thought it was a Piper Cub, because I had seen Piper Cubs landing on the water at Lake Winnipesaukee. And I have seen them [with ski landing gear] landing on the ice. And I stopped my car, and Betty and I said, "Look, there's another one." And we enjoyed watching these planes. And I knew I was in the mountain area where I had seen Piper Cubs flying, and I thought this was a Piper Cub.

DOCTOR

All right.

BARNEY

But it was not. It was too fast. It moved too fast. It would go up and down. It could go back so fast . . .

(More amazement in his voice, as if he is watching the object do this.)

It could go away—and come back.

DOCTOR

Did it go back and forth, or did it go in circles?

BARNEY

It would—go toward the west. And without looking as though it turned, it would come straight back. It would go like a—

(He gropes momentarily for a simile.)

I think of a paddle and a ball and a rubber band tied to it. And you hit the ball, and the ball goes out and comes straight back, without a circle. And I think only a jet could fly that fast. And I am hoping I can find a good place where I can stop and really see this thing—whatever it is. And I see a wigwam, and I recognize this place, and I feel safe. And I feel—in the barren hostility of the wooded area . . .

(He is referring to a commercial trade wigwam, closed now for the season, but in the summer selling souvenirs of Indian Head at that time.)

DOCTOR

What is this place?

BARNEY

It is Indian Head. I had been there before. And I feel comforted that I see a familiar place. And I think I will get a good look at this thing because Betty was very annoying. She was annoying by telling me, "Look!" And I can't look. I had to drive the car.

DOCTOR

Did you think she was serious?

BARNEY

I knew she was serious.

DOCTOR

Was she excited?

BARNEY

And I know Betty only becomes excited rarely. She does not become—she does not get involved, like I do, emotionally as quickly. And so, this angered me, because I knew she was excited. It would have to be something, making her this excited.

DOCTOR

You said you thought she was trying to make you believe this was a flying saucer. Had you talked about flying saucers?

BARNEY

No.

(He is not sure about the doctor's question, so he asks for an explanation.)

Is this ever—or when?

Ever.

BARNEY

Yes. We talked about flying saucers. And no one ever said anything conclusive except that they might exist. Betty said she believed in them.

DOCTOR

Did she believe in them?

BARNEY

I felt—it wasn't that important. I didn't believe in them.

DOCTOR

But she did?

BARNEY

Yes, Betty did believe in flying saucers.

DOCTOR

Did she have any reason for believing in them?

BARNEY

Her sister. I am thinking of visiting her mother and father in Kingston, New Hampshire. And they live in a nice, quiet area. Only three houses —her two sisters' and her mother's houses are located there. And at night you can look at the sky and see millions of stars. And I think how beautiful this is. And we were talking about satellites. The Russians had sent up Sputnik. And her father was talking about, and how you could see some satellites from here at certain hours. And we talked about flying, we talked about life on other planets. And then Betty's sister said she had seen an object flying, long and cigar-shaped, and smaller objects coming to it and flying away from it.

(NICAP files record scores of this kind of report.)

I listened—and I did not criticize. But I thought nothing. I just listened and was indifferent to the conversation. So we did talk about flying saucers. But I have not talked about flying saucers since 1957, when we were talking about Sputnik. And this was 1961.

DOCTOR

Well, we're back in 1961 now. And you are looking for a place where you can stop and observe this. And Betty has been constantly egging you on.

BARNEY

(Sharply and suddenly.)

I want to wake up!

(This is an indication that the subject may be about to experience a painful recall, a memory that he cannot face even in the trance. Dr. Simon is alerted at this point to the likelihood of a strong emotional reaction.)

DOCTOR

(Firmly.)

You're not going to wake up. You're in a deep sleep. You are comfortable, relaxed. This is not going to trouble you. Go on. You can remember everything now.

BARNEY

(He is now becoming measurably excited.)

It's right over my right! God! What is it?

(His voice begins to tremble.)

And I try to maintain control, so Betty cannot tell I am *scared. God,* I'm scared!

DOCTOR

(His voice is calm, very calm, and firm in the face of Barney's mounting emotion.)

It's all right. You can go right on, experience it. It will not hurt you now.

BARNEY

(Breaks into breathless sobbing, then screams.)

I gotta get a weapon!

(He screams again in his chair, his sobs becoming uncontrollable. The doctor is faced with a hard decision now: to impose an amnesia

and bring him out of the trance, or to keep him moving through the experience for the abreaction (discharge of feeling). Further, the amnesic period would appear somewhere in this area, and it has not yet been penetrated.)

DOCTOR
(Very firmly.)

Go to sleep. You can forget, now. You've forgotten.

(He provides Barney with momentary relief.)

You're calm now. Relaxed. Deeply relaxed. You do not have to make an outcry.

(Now he brings him back again to the experience. Barney's violent reaction subsides slightly, but he is still breathing heavily.)

But you can remember it now. Keep remembering. You feel you have to get a weapon.

BARNEY

Yes.

DOCTOR

This is going to harm you, you felt.

BARNEY
(He speaks in great excitement.)

Yes. I open the trunk of my car. I get the tire wrench . . . part of the jack. And I get back in the car.

(Again, his panic is rising.)

DOCTOR

All right. Just keep reasonably calm.

BARNEY

And I keep it by me. And then I get out with the binoculars.

(Now with quiet terror.)

And it is *there*. And I look. And I look. And it is just over the field. And I think, I think—I'm *not* afraid. I'm *not* afraid . . .

(But his voice is in terror.)

I'll fight it off. I'm not *afraid!* And I walk. And I walk out, and I walk across the road. There it is—up there! Ohhh God!

(He again breaks into a scream.)

DOCTOR

(His voice very calm and firm.)

It's there. You can see it. But it's not going to hurt you.

BARNEY

(Intensely emotional.)

Why doesn't it go *away! Look* at it!

(An especially loud gasp.)

There's a man there! Is—is—is he a Captain? What is he? He—he looks at me.

DOCTOR

Just a minute. Let's go back a little now. You said it was there. Did you say a thousand feet away?

(The doctor is referring to the last time Barney mentioned the distance. In the space of time covered by Barney's recall, the object has now moved to slightly more than treetop level, and not more than a few hundred feet away from Barney, he later recalled, as he stood in the field.)

BARNEY

Oh, no.

DOCTOR

A thousand yards?

BARNEY

No, it doesn't look that far. It's very big. And it's not that far. And I can see it tilted toward me!

DOCTOR

What does it look like now?

BARNEY

(Very hesitantly, as if he is studying the object above him in the sky; but much calmer now, much more objective.)

It—looks—like a—big—pancake. With windows—and rows of windows, and lights. Not lights, just one huge light.

DOCTOR

Rows of windows? Like a commercial plane?

BARNEY

Rows of windows. They're *not* like a commercial plane. Because they curve around the side of this—this pancake. And I say to myself: My God, *no!* I have to shake my head. I've got—I've got—this can't be true. This *isn't* here.

(Sighs heavily, almost a moan.)

Ohhh, it's still there.

(There is a fatalistic resignation in his voice.)

And I look—up and down the road. Can't somebody come? Can't somebody come and *tell* me this is not there? It *can't* be, but—

DOCTOR

You're still safe. You can see it all clearly.

BARNEY

(With complete resignation.)

It's there.

DOCTOR

(Perhaps Barney is dreaming this. The doctor will press this point.)

You'd had no sleep that evening?

BARNEY

I pinch my right arm . . . it's not my right arm, it's my left arm. I'm confused.

DOCTOR

You're clear now. Relaxed.

BARNEY

(With more fatalism in his tone.)

It's still there.

(As if an idea strikes him.)

If I let my binoculars fall and dangle from my neck—and start over again, maybe it won't be there.

(Resigned, as he seems to go through this maneuver, a magical defense ritual, like crossing his fingers.)

But it is.

(Now with incredulity.)

Why? What do they want? What do they *want?* One person looks friendly to me. He's friendly-looking. And he's looking at me . . . over his right shoulder. And he's smiling. But . . . but . . .

DOCTOR

Could you see him clearly?

BARNEY

Yes, I could.

DOCTOR

What was his face like? What did it make you think of?

BARNEY

It was round.

(Pauses for a moment, then:)

I think of—I think of—a red-headed Irishman. I don't know why.

(Another pause, then:)

I think I know why. Because Irish are usually hostile to Negroes. And when I see a friendly Irish person, I react to him by thinking—*I* will be friendly. And I think this one that is looking over his shoulder is friendly.

DOCTOR

You say looking over his shoulder. Was he facing away from you?

BARNEY

Yes. He was facing a wall.

DOCTOR

You saw him through this window? You said there was a row of windows?

BARNEY

(He takes care to be extremely precise.)

There was a row of windows. A huge row of windows. Only divided by struts—or structures that prevented it from being one solid window. Or then—it would have been one solid window. And the evil face on the—

(He starts to say "leader.")

He looks like a German Nazi. He's a Nazi . . .

(There is a questioning tone in his voice.)

DOCTOR

He's a Nazi. Did he have on a uniform?

BARNEY

Yes.

DOCTOR

What kind of uniform?

BARNEY

(With a small amount of surprise.)

He had a black scarf around his neck, dangling over his left shoulder.

(He gestures in his trance.)

DOCTOR

You pointed it out as if it were on you.

BARNEY

(Half to himself.)

I never noticed that before.

DOCTOR

He had a black scarf around his neck?

(Another sharp probe:)

How could you see the figures so clearly at that distance?

BARNEY

I was looking at them with binoculars.

Oh. Did they have faces like other people. You said one was like a red-headed Irishman.

BARNEY

(Describing the scene very slowly and carefully.)

His eyes were slanted. Oh—his eyes were *slanted!* But not like a Chinese—Oh. Oh.

(Quite abruptly.)

I feel like a rabbit. I feel like a rabbit.

DOCTOR

What do you mean by that?

BARNEY

(He recalls a scene from his earlier days, a scene that flashed through his mind as he stood in the dark field at Indian Head, an example of reminiscent recall showing the persistent impact of early experience on the present when similar in emotional significance.)

I was hunting for rabbits in Virginia. And this cute little bunny went into a bush that was not very big. And my cousin Marge was on one side of the bush, and I was on the other—with a hat. And the poor little bunny thought he was safe. And it tickled me, because he was just hiding behind a little stalk, which meant security to him—when I pounced on him, and threw my hat on him, and captured the poor little bunny who thought he was safe.

(Pauses a moment, in quiet reflection.)

Funny I thought of that—right out there on the field.

(Repeats the phrase as if to himself.)

I feel like a rabbit.

DOCTOR

What was Betty doing all this time?

BARNEY

I can't hear her.

(Later, in one of their many trips to the scene, the Hills checked this to find that it was very difficult to hear at the estimated distance Barney was from the car.)

DOCTOR

Did you make any outcry to her the way you did to me?

BARNEY

I—I can't remember—I don't know.

(An effort to avoid under hypnosis but he must also remember, and he speaks again as if he realizes this.)

I did not.

DOCTOR

You would remember if you did.

BARNEY

(His thoughts seem to be on the craft, and not on what the doctor is saying.)

I did not. I know this creature is telling me something.

DOCTOR

Telling you something? How? How is he getting it to you?

BARNEY

I can see it in his face. No, his lips are not moving.

DOCTOR

Go on. He's telling you something.

BARNEY

(His voice begins to rise in emotion again. Strong emotion.)

And he's looking at me. And he's just telling me: Don't be afraid. I'm not a bunny. I'm going to be . . . I'm going to be safe. He didn't tell me I was that bunny.

DOCTOR

What *did* he tell you?

BARNEY

(As if he's quoting what he was told.)

93

Stay there—and keep looking. Just keep *looking*—and stay there. And just keep looking. Just keep looking.

DOCTOR

Could you hear him tell you?

BARNEY

Oh! I got the binoculars away from my eyes. 'Cause if I don't, I'll just stand there.

DOCTOR

Did you hear him tell you this?

BARNEY

Oh, no. He didn't say it.

(More tremor in his voice.)

DOCTOR

You *felt* he said it?

BARNEY
(Very firmly.)

I *know.*

DOCTOR

You know he said it?

BARNEY

Yes. Just stay there, he said.

(Now his voice breaks in extreme terror.)

It's pounding in my head!!

(He screams again.)

I gotta get away! I gotta get away from here!

DOCTOR
(Quickly, firmly.)

All right. All right. Calm down.

BARNEY
(Still breathless.)

Gotta get away.

94

DOCTOR

Calm down. How can you be sure he was telling you this?

BARNEY

(He speaks now with awe.)

His *eyes!* His *eyes.* I've never seen eyes like that before.

DOCTOR

You said they were friendly.

BARNEY

Not the leader's. I said the one looking over his shoulder.

DOCTOR

How did you know the other one was the leader.

BARNEY

(In careful, level tones again.)

Because everybody moved—everybody was standing there looking at me. But everybody moved. These levers were in the back . . . or they went to a big board, it looked like a board. And only this one with the black, black shiny jacket and the scarf stayed at the window.

DOCTOR

He had slanted eyes. What did that make you think of?

BARNEY

I don't know. I've never seen eyes slanted like that.

(He gestures with his hands carefully, in an attempt to describe the eyes.)

They began to be round—and went back like that—and like that. And they went up like that. Can I draw it?

DOCTOR

You want to draw it?

BARNEY

Yes.

DOCTOR

(He hands him the materials.)

95

I'm giving you a pad and a pencil. You can open your eyes, and you can draw whatever you want. You can draw it now. Go ahead.

(Under deep hypnosis, the subject can open his eyes without in any way disturbing his trance. He will have no memory of the event when he is awakened, unless the operator tells him he can. Barney Hill is no artist, nor does the trance state enhance his ability. He draws a crude, but graphic sketch, and hands it back to the doctor. Then he continues the story.)

BARNEY

I'm driving.

DOCTOR

You're back in the car now?

BARNEY

Yes.

DOCTOR

You put down the binoculars, did you?

BARNEY

I put them down.

DOCTOR

Yes. And you got into the car. Did you speak to Betty?

BARNEY

I'm getting a hold on myself. I'm saying to myself, "Remember, you've got fortitude. You can drive a car." And I told Betty to look out—and the object was still around us. I could *feel* it around us. I saw it when we passed by the object. When I got in the car, it had swung around so that it was out there. I—I *know* it was out there.

(With conviction.)

Yeah—it's out there. But I don't know where.

(With genuine surprise.)

That's funny.

DOCTOR

Yes—speak a little louder.

96

BARNEY

(He complies. The puzzlement is now mounting in his voice considerably.)

I know Route 3.

(Now another emotional crescendo.)

Oh, those eyes! They're in my *brain!*

(Very plaintively.)

Please can't I wake up?

(This is a plea to relieve him of anxiety.)

DOCTOR

(With reassurance.)

Stay asleep a little longer. We'll get through this now.

(Barney is showing signs of more emotion.)

All right. All right. You'll get through this all right. Follow your feelings. Tell me. They won't upset you so much now.

BARNEY

(Now his voice becomes dreamy and musing.)

They're *there.* Isn't that funny—all the woods. That crazy dog. She stays in the car all the time. Isn't that funny? She stays in the car!

DOCTOR

She doesn't bark at anything?

BARNEY

(Surprised at Delsey's lack of response.)

She just stays there.

DOCTOR

What about Betty?

BARNEY

(The quiet amazement in his voice is growing now, but his fear has subsided.)

I don't know.

DOCTOR

Isn't she saying anything?

BARNEY

(He is intense, reliving the scene. He doesn't seem to hear the doctor.)

I—I—don't understand. Are we being robbed? I—I—I—I—I—I don't know.

DOCTOR

What makes you think you're being robbed?

BARNEY

(A significant pause, then:)

I know what's in my mind, and I don't want to say it.

DOCTOR

Well, you can say it to me. You can say it now.

BARNEY

(In total awe.)

They're—*men!* All with dark jackets. And I don't have any money. I don't have anything.

(Now with great puzzlement.)

I don't know.

(Now back to awe again.)

Oh—oh, the eyes are there. Always the eyes are there. And they're telling me I don't have to be afraid.

(Now, as if he's peering ahead on the road.)

Is that an accident down the road? What's the red? The bright red?

DOCTOR

Bright red?

BARNEY

Yes. Orange and red.

DOCTOR

What is that? Where is that?

BARNEY

Right down the road.

DOCTOR

Down the road?

BARNEY

(Again living with the scene more than responding to the doctor.)

And I don't have to be afraid. But they won't talk to me.

DOCTOR

Who won't talk to you?

BARNEY

The men.

DOCTOR

In the vehicle?

BARNEY

No. They're standing in the road.

DOCTOR

There are men standing in the road?

BARNEY

Yes. They won't talk to me. Only the eyes are talking to me. I—I—I—I don't understand that. Oh—the eyes don't have a body. They're just eyes.

(He speaks now as if he were moving into another state of consciousness, almost catatonic. As if his eyes were fixated, concentrated completely on another pair of eyes. Then, very suddenly, he speaks with tremendous relief.)

I know. I *know.*

(He muses to himself.)

Yes, that's what it's got to be.

(He laughs very flatly, very self-reassuringly, and quietly.)

I know what it is. It's a wildcat. A wildcat up a tree.

(The relief indicated here is intense, as if he were finding something that had a basis of reality, as if he were searching for some explanation for an imponderable phenomenon. Then, he is not so sure:)

99

No. No. I know what it is. It's the Cheshire cat in *Alice in Wonderland*. Ah, I don't have to be afraid of that. It disappeared too, and only the eyes remained. That's all right. I'm not afraid.

DOCTOR

You didn't see this ...

BARNEY

No, I saw it.

DOCTOR

You saw it. You're still seeing this man?

BARNEY

(Again in his own thoughts.)

The eyes are telling me, "Don't be afraid."

DOCTOR

That's the leader's eyes?

BARNEY

I don't even see the leader.

DOCTOR

The other eyes.

BARNEY

(With certainty.)

All I see are these eyes.

DOCTOR

The eyes now.

BARNEY

I'm not even afraid that they're not connected to a body. They're just *there*. They're just up close to me, pressing against my eyes. That's funny. I'm not afraid.

DOCTOR

Now—what's happened to this vehicle?

BARNEY

I don't see any vehicle.

DOCTOR

It's gone?

BARNEY

It's there. No. It's not gone. But I don't see it. I'm just there.

(This is, of course, puzzling to the doctor, but he must stay with the patient, live with his thoughts and statements, and try to draw out from him what the patient is seeing and experiencing, without leading him too much and permitting free expression.)

DOCTOR

And where are you? Are you in the car?

BARNEY

No. I'm just suspended. I'm just floating about.

(His voice is now relaxed, relieved.)

Oh, how funny—floating about. Just floating. I—I—want to get back to the car. Just floating about.

DOCTOR

You're really floating about—or is that just the way you feel?

BARNEY

That's just the way I feel.

DOCTOR

You're still outside the car?

BARNEY

No.

DOCTOR

You're in the car?

BARNEY

I'm not in the car. I'm not near the car. I'm not in the woods. I'm not on the road.

DOCTOR

Well—where are these men?

BARNEY

I don't know.

DOCTOR

On the road?

BARNEY

I don't know.

(He persists airily.)

I'm just floating about.

(Now he seems to be suspended. He speaks his thoughts at this point as if he's speaking directly to Betty.)

Heh, heh, Betty. That's the funniest thing, Betty. The funniest thing. I never believed in flying saucers but—I don't know. Mighty mysterious. Yeah, well, I guess I won't say anything to anybody about this. It's too ridiculous, isn't it? Oh yes, really funny. Wonder where they came from? Oh, gee, I wish I had the—I wish I had gone with them . . .

DOCTOR

You wish you had gone with them?

BARNEY

Yes. Oh, what an experience to go to some distant planet.

(A pause as he reflects, then:)

Maybe this will prove the existence of God.

(Another brief pause.)

Isn't that funny? To look for the existence of God on another planet?

(Now directly as if to Betty:)

Were you scared? I wasn't. No, I wasn't afraid. I wasn't afraid, anyway. Ridiculous, just you and I here talking about it.

(Now his tone changes, as if considerable time has elapsed—something very disturbing is being passed over—this hints strongly at the amnesia gap.)

Well—it looks as if we're getting into Portsmouth a little later than I expected . . .

(His voice trails off. The doctor waits a moment, decides that this should wait for an evaluation of the effect of the session thus far.)

DOCTOR

All right. We'll stop there. You will be calm and relaxed. You will forget everything that we have had in this period together, until I ask you to recall it again. You will forget everything we have talked about until I ask you to recall it again.

(The repetition is intentional, to reinforce the command.)

It will not trouble you, it will not worry you. You will not be concerned. You will remain comfortable and relaxed and have no pain, no aches, no anxiety.

(The doctor then reinforces the cue words for future sessions.)

You will recall what I want you to recall, do what I tell you to do. You will forget what has transpired here until I ask you to recall it again. You're comfortable and relaxed now. No aches, no pains . . . no anxiety . . . All right, Barney, you may wake up now. You'll be comfortable and relaxed.

(Barney opens his eyes, a little groggy now. But he comes to full consciousness quickly.)

BARNEY

(Looks at his wristwatch.)

Wow. Nine-thirty. Didn't you bring me in here at ten minutes after eight?

DOCTOR

Yes.

BARNEY

Where was I?

DOCTOR

Right here with me.

BARNEY

Where are my cig—was I about to reach for a cigarette?

DOCTOR

Looked that way. Go ahead and have one.

BARNEY

I thought I was coming in here, and you asked me to take this seat, this chair, then I was going to reach for a cigarette. I never reached for it.

DOCTOR

(He is studying Barney's reactions to assure himself that Barney is fully out of the trance.)

How do you feel?

BARNEY

I feel fine.

DOCTOR

Good. Know what happened here?

BARNEY

You put me into a trance. I know the purpose of it, but—

(There is a pause.)

DOCTOR

That's all right. We'll continue this next week. A week from today . . .

*   *   *

The first probe into the unknown had been made. But the amnesic veil had scarcely been pierced. What was to follow, none of the three knew—and at this point, only the doctor was aware of what had been uncovered.

All through the session, Betty had been waiting, with some apprehension, in the waiting room. She made the pretense of fingering through a copy of the *New Yorker* and *McCalls,* but with little success at reading them. The waiting room is down the hall from Dr. Simon's office. Even though the offices are soundproof, Betty was aware of the emotional outbursts Barney had made at the crucial points. Anticipating that this could happen, the doctor had scheduled the Hills at a time when the offices were free of other people. Since the building was empty of all sounds, Barney's two major outbursts were intensified by the silence and Betty's own close attention to what might be happening.

"It hit me with such force that I sat there and cried all the time," Betty Hill recalls. "And I sat there wondering what kind of condition Barney would be in when he came out of the doctor's office. There were two big outbursts, the second not as loud as the first. The rest of the time it had been fairly quiet. So I waited—waited for him to come out. And when he did, both he and the doctor were smiling—pleasant, and I was quite surprised. So I didn't think I should say anything to Barney at all about my crying and things. I just played it by ear, and asked him what happened. I asked him if he was upset, and he said no, he wasn't. There was nothing to be upset about, he said."

Barney had no true recall about what had happened in the session except for some vague and fleeting impressions. It did not seem to him that he had been under hypnosis for more than a few minutes. He felt no discomfort at all, and only his watch indicated to him that over an hour and a half had gone by.

He was insatiably curious about what had happened during the session, but of course there was no way whatever of knowing until the doctor would give him the instruction to remember. There was no feeling associated with the lost time period.

On the way back to Portsmouth, they stopped by the International Pancake House, a splashy, chrome restaurant on Route 1 leading up to New Hampshire, near Saugus.

They ordered a heaping breakfast, Barney at that time unaffected by the strains of his session. Betty was pressing Barney for details about how he felt, and though she had been in hypnosis for the test sessions, she was anxious to find out Barney's full reaction to the therapeutic session. Barney reassured her that there wasn't anything upsetting about it, and Betty continued to withhold from Barney the fact that she had been in tears most of the time he was in the doctor's office.

Barney felt fully relaxed until they got back to their home in Portsmouth. He then began to have an overwhelming fear of something—something entirely vague and undefinable, something that he felt he should feel guilty about. He was very frightened about this feeling, as if he had a tremendous pressure in his head. He didn't relate it particularly to the hypnosis. He describes it as something buried in his unconscious, trying to work its way up to his conscious. He got upset enough to start to call the doctor about it, then decided to wait. The thought flickered through his mind that he might not want to go through with the rest of the program, or at least that he ask the doctor to take Betty on next, and give him a rest. But his fears gradually left him, and the anticipation and urge to know, to penetrate the mystery, took over.

CHAPTER SIX

When Barney Hill left the office after the first session that Saturday morning, Dr. Simon picked up the microphone of his tape recorder, and dictated:

> During the explosive parts of the patient's discussion, he showed very marked emotional discharge. Tears rolled down his cheeks, he would clutch his face, his head, and writhe in considerable agony. When he first described the eyes, he drew circles in the air which were in the shape of the eye that he ultimately drew. He actually drew a curve representing the left side of the face, and drew the left eye on it, without any other detail. When asked which eye this was, he showed some confusion. Then he drew the rest of the shape of the head, and also drew in the other eye and the cap and the visor. And then, as an afterthought, he drew in the scarf. Mrs. Hill was induced by post-hypnotic suggestion for reinforcement in anticipation of the time when she will be interviewed. She was in the waiting room for the entire period.

It was obvious in this first step of the procedure that Barney had only partially gone beyond the threshold that had blocked his conscious memory on that night. There was still only a vague and disconnected, dream-like description of the enormous object approaching him, the eyes of the figure aboard the ship, a bizarre floating sensation, an apparent accident down the road, and figures in the road with no explainable motive. All through the conscious period of the event, Barney's description was sharp and clear, with attention to the minutest detail. Then at the point he reexperienced Indian Head, his description became vague and fragmented—detached. There seemed to be two resistance points, one at the moment he raised the binoculars to his eyes, just after he had driven off and the object moved over the car, and the other at some point farther down the road, a roadblock. Here the account Barney gave leaped to a comment about arriving home at Portsmouth later than he had expected.

All through the account under hypnosis, Barney had indicated his deep-set resistance to the idea of Unidentified Flying Objects. As Barney later said, the likelihood of the object being a product of wishful thinking on his part seemed very slim, indeed. His strong objections to the existence of the phenomenon were deeply set, although his ambivalence about the experince was puzzling.

Dr. Simon was orienting his treatment to the recall of the patients' experiences and their accompanying thinking, and feeling—not to the establishment of the reality or nonreality of unidentified objects. Whether the experiences were true in the absolute sense was far less important to the doctor than their existence as a part of the patients' past or present mental life. Throughout the investigation, tests to establish reality were, of course, in progress, but no preliminary conclusions were possible at this time. A great deal of evidence remained to be obtained, particularly from Betty Hill, who had not yet been heard from.

The incident had little or no precedent. The roadblock, the figures Barney recalled in the road, and the strange reactions Barney had in the latter part of the session would need further exploration, as well as any possible distortion or fantasy.

Barney's pleas to Dr. Simon to let him wake up came at those moments when emotions were resurgent and memories were probably painful. Many recorded cases indicate the subject's resistance to the operator as he attempts to push past the block holding back the conscious memory. Only the operator's patient persistence can overcome the resistance.

The doctor's decision to keep Barney in the trance in spite of the intense abreaction, or emotional outburst, was based on the doctor's judgment of how much he could be safely permitted to endure.

*   *   *

On February 29, 1964, the Hills arrived punctually for their appointment, Betty being reinforced again, and Barney remaining in the office for his second therapeutic session. Before putting him in the customary trance, Dr. Simon asked him a few questions in review.

DOCTOR

Well—how have you been, Mr. Hill?

BARNEY

I've been fine. Physically, I've been fine, at least. But I have been upset . . .

DOCTOR

Tell me about it.

BARNEY

Well, last week after I left your office, I began having what I thought was remembrance of what had taken place in the office, and this became quite disturbing to me.

DOCTOR

And what did you remember?

BARNEY

I remembered "eyes." And I thought these "eyes" were telling me something. And I became alarmed because I thought my very sanity was in jeopardy. I considered calling you after reaching home, but I did not. And my wife and I went out to visit friends, and that relieved the tension.

DOCTOR

Is that the only thing you remember?

BARNEY

Basically, yes. Another interesting thing that seemed to happen, I began to pick out little details about my trip, which I thought was interesting, because I never thought of these things before. I had given no thought to them. Such as stopping in New York State and buying a six-pack of beer and Betty and I taking it to a motel. I thought of how when we were told we could take the little doggie in, and I put her in the bathroom and tied her with a long chain because the bathroom was tiled. In case she made an accident, it wouldn't soil the rug. And these things seemed to come back to me . . .

DOCTOR

They seem to be things you hadn't told me, but of course you wouldn't remember that. But I had told you to remember *everything*. And these seem to be things that you skipped.

BARNEY

Oh. I see.

DOCTOR

Because when you are in a trance you are told to remember everything. And these seem to be irrelevant details. But you hadn't mentioned them, the ones you mentioned now, so maybe you felt a little guilty that you hadn't although they are probably, irrelevant. Speaking of that, had you had much to drink on this trip?

BARNEY

That was the only thing.

DOCTOR

The six-pack? The two of you?

BARNEY

Yes. We each had a can of beer Sunday evening, and then we retired. And we brought back the four cans left.

DOCTOR

I see. You hadn't been doing much drinking on the trip at all?

BARNEY

No.

DOCTOR

Did this anxiety fade away as the week went along?

BARNEY

It more or less did. Yes, it did. It became sharpened last night. Last week, Saturday morning, when I got up I felt a little nauseous as if in anticipating, in anticipation of this. Last night, this occurred again.

DOCTOR

You are quite concerned about this experience. You'll begin to feel all right about that. You'll be all right. You won't have to worry about your sanity.

(This reassurance may have hypnotic force since repeated contact with the doctor at times increases suggestibility. Here was a warning that the repressed material would have to be dealt with carefully. It was threatening to break through prematurely in the absence of the doctor. He would make future instructions for amnesia more compelling until things had been worked through to a greater extent.)

But tell me—what do you think about this "eye" business? What do you think of? Does it connect up with anything? Does it suggest any thoughts to you?

BARNEY

No, it doesn't. Well, yes—I might say the only connection it does have is a foreboding type of effect. Of betraying. Of having been given a warning. This is the only kind of effect it has on me.

DOCTOR

You feel you have been given a warning?

BARNEY

Yes.

DOCTOR

Ever have that thought or feeling before?

BARNEY

No, I've never had anything like that before.

DOCTOR

About hypnosis—do you feel the eyes play a part in that?

BARNEY

No, I don't think so.

DOCTOR

Well, you wanted me to take Betty, and take you off the hook for a while. Is that it?

(The doctor refers to a brief mention of this Barney had made as he entered the office.)

BARNEY

Well, that's what I thought.

110

Do you recall the eyes as part of the session we had? Or was it something that just hung over with you?

The eyes just seemed to hang over from that.

Well, that was the last thing we got to. It was last Saturday, and it did carry over a bit. I'll see to it that you don't have that anxiety. We'll resume.

(He is now preparing to put Barney in the deep-trance state again.)

You don't remember now where we left off. We'll go back and I can probably take some of that over again. Let's go back a bit before the eyes came into the picture.

(The doctor gives the cue words. Barney's eyes close immediately, and his head nods forward on his chest.)

You are deeper and deeper and deeper asleep. Fully relaxed, and deeper and deeper and deeper asleep. You are in a deep sleep. You have no fear, no anxiety. And now you will not be troubled by anything you remember. But you will remember *everything*. You will remember everything. All your feelings and all of your actions. They will not trouble you now, because they are here, with us. They will not trouble you, and I am here.

(The repetition is to reinforce the instruction. It may or may not be needed.)

Your sleep is deeper and deeper, you are completely relaxed. Far, far asleep. Deeper and deeper asleep. . . . Now you will remember everything that we have gone over about your trip from Montreal. You will go back a bit, *before* you had the experience with the eyes. And you can begin to tell me about the experience with the unidentified object. You can start a little before we left off. Wherever you feel you freshly remember something.

(His voice is again flat and colorless; he is fully in trance.)

I'm remembering being in the woods, parked. And I have Delsey. And I'm walking her around the back of the car. And Betty had asked if I would leave Delsey out. And Betty is standing off to the left of the car with the binoculars, and she is looking at this unidentified flying object. And I am standing there looking up and down the highway, because I am looking for other cars. And I give Betty the dog's chain, and I ask her to let me see with the binoculars. And I only see a plane, flying in the sky. And I tell her this is a plane, and it is on its way to Montreal, where we just left. And I want to hurry and get back to the car and return to Portsmouth. And Betty gets into the car, and she says, "Isn't that strange?" And I'm driving along, and she said, "It's still out there." And I think it's strange, and think it must be a Piper Cub. And it's not making any sound. And I want to hurry up and get away, because this is *strange,* this strange thing flying around. And I believe very strongly that it can see us. And it is late at night, and I feel I am exposed.

DOCTOR

In what way do you feel exposed?

BARNEY

I feel I am in an exposed situation where my car lights are very bright. And it's dark where I am. And I know this object is flitting around in the sky. I think of a fly flitting aimlessly in the sky, with no pattern, as it is hovering over something it is about to light on. And I think this thing out there is just hovering around. And Betty is telling me to stop again. And I do. And I said, "Betty, what are you trying to do? Make me see something that isn't there?" And I became very angry with her. Because I think this is a plane, something that we can explain. And I believe, rather feel, that she is trying to make me think it is not. And this irritates me.

(In his normal conversation, Barney seldom starts his sentences with and. *Yet here, he seems to do so constantly, almost in Biblical style.)*

DOCTOR

What was her reply to this?

BARNEY

Betty's reply was, "Well, why is it doing what it is doing? Why doesn't it go away? What is it doing?"

112

DOCTOR

Now this will not upset you. You can tell me your feelings, but you will not be upset about it. Go ahead.

BARNEY

I said, "Betty it can't—" I was thinking—I did not say that to Betty. I was thinking, my mind was thinking, it cannot be a plane.

(Note the concern for truth and accuracy here, making sure that he does not make any misstatements to the doctor.)

This is why I became upset because Betty was telling me it wasn't acting like any type of conventional flying craft. I somehow knew this and did not want to be told this.

DOCTOR

Did you feel that it wasn't acting like a conventional flying craft?

BARNEY

Yes, I did.

DOCTOR

In what ways?

BARNEY

Well, it flew very peculiarly. It did not fly in a definite straight line. It would go up suddenly ...

(This is a very common UFO report.)

DOCTOR

Just rise vertically.

BARNEY

Just rise in a very straight-up position, and then fly for a short while horizontally. And then it would dip down. And as it did this, I noticed that the row of lights on it seemed to tilt and level off, as I imagined the body of this thing, of the position of this thing would be in.

DOCTOR

As if it were banking?

BARNEY

As if it were banking. But banking didn't fit, it doesn't seem to fit what I'm trying to describe. Because if it had banked, I could think of a plane, and know it would be a plane. It just tilted. It did not bank in a swooping bank. It just, from a horizontal line, became a vertical line.

(Another common UFO report.)

DOCTOR

How would you describe the shape of it?

BARNEY

I could not outline the shape.

DOCTOR

An ordinary plane, even a Piper Cub, has to be somewhat cigar-shaped. Even big helicopters.

BARNEY

Yes. The row of lights was like a row in a cigar-shaped pattern, only that it was a straight line that I saw, and it was elongated.

(Many reports of UFO's in the Air Force and NICAP files indicate a cigar-shaped object in the distance, but as it draws nearer, it becomes discernible as the lateral profile of a large disc.)

DOCTOR

You didn't surmise that this thing was round, like a so-called flying saucer?

BARNEY

No, I didn't see that.

DOCTOR

It did have some resemblance to ordinary planes, then?

BARNEY

At this time, yes.

DOCTOR

You imply that it changed shape later?

BARNEY

Yes. As I continued down the highway, I had a peculiar feeling that it was spinning.

DOCTOR

Like a top?

Like a top.

DOCTOR

Now, when you spoke of this before, you spoke of some lights down the highway. Red lights, I believe. Does that ring any bells? Lights down the highway—as if some men were working down there?

BARNEY

Yes. But that is further on.

DOCTOR

I see. Go on then, in your own way.

BARNEY

So I continued to look, and I would stop and leave and go. And Betty would insist that I stop. And we did this several times.

DOCTOR

Was this all to stop and look again?

BARNEY

To stop and look. And when I can see the tramway on the mountain up ahead, and I knew where I was, and I knew I would eventually pass by the Old Man of the Mountain. And the object seemed to have speeded up, and to go to the right side of the Old Man of the Mountain. And I was going around the left side of the base. And when I got to where the Old Man of the Mountain figure was, I stopped again and got a good look. And I knew that this object still seemed to be out there. And it was stopped when I stopped. I thought this was strange.

(His voice becomes more and more intense as if he were watching what he describes.)

And it moved—oh, I did not see it move. I started driving the car, and Betty said it is moving behind the mountains again. And I was approaching a clear spot where I saw two wigwams on my right. And I knew I was close to Indian Head. And I saw this object far off even as I approached this spot by slowing down and looking. And then I returned to looking down the road to drive, and Betty became very excited. She said, "Oh, Barney, you must stop the car. Look what it is doing!"

115

(The doctor is encouraging the repetition of the story, to check for inconsistencies.)

And I became slower in my driving. And I looked through the windshield. And on her side the object looked as if it were right out there in front of the windshield, only I had to look up to see it. And I must have been driving five miles an hour, because I had to put the car in low gear so it would not stall. And I said, "Oh, this is funny." I thought of all the thoughts I had back since I first saw this thing. I thought it was a Piper Cub, I thought it was an airliner, I thought it was a military craft and that the military was having fun with us. And I came to a complete stop, and I reached down on the floor of the car to my left and picked up the tire wrench and kept it in my hand.

DOCTOR

You had already got the wrench from the trunk of the car?

BARNEY

Yes. And I kept hold of it and stuck it through my belt. And I got out of the car with my binoculars, and I stood with my arm on the door, and my right arm partly on top of the hood, the roof, of the car. And I look. And before I could get the binoculars up to my eyes, even as I did get them up there, the car was vibrating from the motor running. So I stepped away. And the object shifted, in an arc. And I thought, "How remarkable, it was a perfect arc." But it continued to have a forward look, facing me, as if it swung and did not move from a position, but just swung from a position with the front facing me.

(Again, a typical pattern of many low-altitude UFO reports.)

And it moved to my left. And I continued to look and begin walking across the highway, shaking my head and blinking my eyes that this was just some kind of something that I could not explain.

(He is now at the moment when he reached his emotional crisis in the first session. But he is calm now, not at all as he was then, partially due to the doctor's suggestion in the trance induction.)

And I hoped if I looked down the highway and looked back, it would be gone. And I continued to walk across the highway toward the front of my car down the road. And I continued to look with my binoculars each time I would stop, and look up. And I would walk further toward it, and stop and look up. And I thought, "How interesting, there is the military pilot, and he is looking at me." And I looked at him, and he looked at me. And there were several others looking at me, and I thought of a huge dirigible, and I thought of all the men lined up at the window of this huge dirigible and were looking down at me. Then they moved to the back and I continued to look at this one man that stood there, and I kept looking at him and looking at him.

(The contrast in his description here, steady and unemotional, compared to the previous session is marked.)

Is this the man you call the leader?

BARNEY

He was dressed differently. And I thought of the Navy and the submarine, and I thought the men that moved back were just dressed in blue denims. But this other man was dressed in a black shiny coat, with a cap on.

DOCTOR

When you spoke of the hoodlums back on your trip, did they wear these black, shiny coats that they often do?

BARNEY

No, they did not.

(The doctor is checking to see if there was any influence on Barney's mind from the Montreal experience. Could the echo of the hoodlums Barney saw be reflected in what he pictures here? Both represent potential danger, resulting in fear, the common denominator.)

DOCTOR

There is no resemblance between them and this leader?

BARNEY

No. These Canadian men in Montreal were dressed in conventional dress, but the hair was in duck-bill style. And I thought of them as hoodlums because of their hair style.

DOCTOR

You can get back to this leader.

I looked at him, and he looked at me. And I thought, "This is not going to harm me." And I wanted to get back to Betty and discuss this interesting thing we were looking at. And I kept looking and he looked at me, and then I came back to the car. And Betty was flopping in the front seat. And I said, "Betty, were you excited?" And she said, "Why didn't you come back? I was screaming for you to come back. I could not understand why you were going out across the road."

DOCTOR

You hadn't heard her scream?

BARNEY

No, I did not hear her scream. And I just thought she was flopping on the seat. But she said she had leaned down across the seat so that she would be able to be closer to open the door and holler for me to get back in the car.

(The reassurance at the beginning of the trance appears to have reduced the terror of this recollection.)

I returned to the car and began driving down the highway. And I drove quite a few miles and noticed I was not on Route 3. . . .

(Here, for the first time, the door to the forgotten time period begins to swing open. His block had always been on the field at Indian Head, followed by blurring of consciousness after he had begun to drive away from the object. Betty, also, had never been able to bridge this point, except, she thought, the possibility that her dreams might be reality.)

BARNEY

And I could not understand that, because it is a straight highway. And I looked and I was being signaled to stop. And I thought, I wonder if there has been an accident. I do have the tire wrench. I'll put it near my hand. . . .

DOCTOR

Let me interrupt again: What was it you saw down the highway?

BARNEY

I saw a group of men, and they were standing in the highway. And it was brightly lit up, as if it were almost daylight, but not really day. It was not the kind of light of day, but it was brightly lighted. . . .

(Another description typical of many low-altitude UFO reports, including those of police officers and technical men.)

And they began coming toward me. And I did not think after that of my tire wrench. And I became afraid if I did think of this as a weapon, I would be harmed. And if I did not, I would not be harmed. And they came and assisted me.

DOCTOR

Who assisted you?

BARNEY

These men.

DOCTOR

They assisted you out of the car?

BARNEY

I felt very weak. I felt very weak, but I wasn't afraid. And I can't even think of being confused. I am not bewildered, I can't even think of questioning what is happening to me. And I am being assisted. And I am thinking of a picture I saw many years ago, and this man is being carried to the electric chair. And I think of this, and I think I am in this man's position. But I'm not being carried to the electric chair. And I think of this, and I think I'm in this man's position. But I'm not, but I think my feet are dragging, and I think of this picture. And I am not afraid. I feel like I am dreaming.

(This again, is a denial of fear. Later, when Barney listened to the playback of the tapes, he likened this event to the feeling he had when he went into hypnosis with the doctor. The questions have since been on his mind: If this is true, was he being put into hypnosis by these "men," and if so, was his amnesia caused by this?)

DOCTOR

Are you asleep at the time?

BARNEY

My eyes are tightly closed, and I seem—disassociated.

119

DOCTOR

Disassociated? Is that what you said?

BARNEY

Yes.

DOCTOR

(Checking Barney's definition.)

What do you mean by that?

BARNEY

I am there—and I am not there.

DOCTOR

Where is Betty through all of this?

BARNEY

I don't know. I'm trying to think, where's Betty? I don't know.

DOCTOR

Are these men part of your dream?

BARNEY

(Firmly, and with conviction.)

They are there, and I am there. I know they are there. But everything is black. My eyes are tightly closed. I can't believe what I think.

DOCTOR

Is there anything else that you think that you haven't told me?

BARNEY

Yes.

DOCTOR

You can tell me now.

BARNEY

I am always thinking of mental pictures, because my eyes are closed. And I think I am going up a slight incline, and my feet have stopped bumping on the rocks. That's funny. I thought of my feet bumping on the rocks. And they are not going up smoothly. But I'm afraid to open my eyes, because I am being told strongly by myself to keep my eyes closed, and don't open them. And I don't want to be operated on.

DOCTOR

You don't want to be operated on. What makes you think of an operation?

BARNEY

I don't know.

DOCTOR

Have you ever been operated on?

BARNEY

Only for my tonsils.

DOCTOR

Does this feel like that time?

BARNEY

I think like that, but my eyes are closed, and I only have mental pictures. And I am not in pain. And I can feel a slight feeling. My groin feels cold.

DOCTOR

Is that like any feeling with the operation?

BARNEY

I'm not being operated on. I am lying on something, and I think of the doctor putting something in my ear. When I was a boy. The doctor put something in my ear, and I looked up at it, and he explained to me that you could peek into the ear and light it up with this thing. And I think of that. . . . And I feel like the doctor did not pain me, and I will be very careful and be very still and will cooperate, and I won't be harmed.

(He pauses.)

DOCTOR

Yes. Go on.

BARNEY

I can't remember.

DOCTOR

You were thinking about this when you were on the road?

BARNEY

I was thinking about this when I was lying on this table.

DOCTOR

Where were you lying down?

BARNEY

I thought I was inside something. But I did not dare open my eyes. I had been told to keep my eyes closed.

DOCTOR

Who told you that?

BARNEY

The man.

DOCTOR

What man?

BARNEY

That I saw through the binoculars.

(He speaks matter-of-factly, as if the doctor should certainly know all about this.)

DOCTOR

Was this one of the men in the road?

BARNEY

No.

DOCTOR

These men in the road—what part did they play?

BARNEY

They took me and carried me up this ramp.

DOCTOR

Carried you up the ramp?

BARNEY

I know I was going up something, and my feet were dragging. And this man spoke to me, and I knew I had heard his voice, and he was looking at me when I was in the road.

DOCTOR

This happened after you were in the road?

BARNEY

This happened after I was in the road at Indian Head. I thought I had driven quite a distance from Indian Head when I got lost and found myself in the woods.

DOCTOR

You got lost after Indian Head, is that it?

BARNEY

I was not on Route 3, and I couldn't understand why.

DOCTOR

Was Indian Head before or after you saw this object?

BARNEY

I don't understand the question.

DOCTOR

Well, was it after you were at Indian Head that you saw this object?

BARNEY

It was at Indian Head that I saw the object standing in the sky. And it is after Indian Head. I have driven several miles, I think I have driven a lot of miles. And the road is not Route 3. But is in a heavily wooded area. But it is a road. And this is when I am flagged down.

DOCTOR

You are flagged down?

BARNEY

Yes.

DOCTOR

These men flagged you down?

BARNEY

Yes.

DOCTOR

How many were there?

BARNEY

I thought I saw a cluster of six men. Because three of them came to me, and three did not.

123

DOCTOR

How were they dressed?

BARNEY

I was told at that time to close my eyes. And I closed my eyes.

DOCTOR

But before you closed your eyes, didn't you see them?

BARNEY

They were all in dark clothing. And they were all dressed alike.

DOCTOR

Were they white men?

BARNEY

I don't know by the color. But it did not seem that they had different faces from white men.

DOCTOR

Were they in a uniform of any sort?

BARNEY

I thought of a Navy pea jacket, just before I closed my eyes.

DOCTOR

Did they say anything else besides "Close your eyes?" Did they tell you why they were stopping you?

BARNEY

They didn't tell me anything. They didn't say anything.

DOCTOR

Was there any vehicle around?

BARNEY

I didn't see any.

DOCTOR

You didn't see any vehicle?

BARNEY

I was told to close my eyes because I saw two eyes coming close to mine.

(The fragment in the first session where he thinks of a wildcat, or the Cheshire cat, perhaps.)

And I felt like the eyes had pushed into my eyes.

DOCTOR

Were these the same eyes of the leader that you saw from the binoculars?

BARNEY

Yes.

DOCTOR

Do you think it was the same man?

BARNEY

I didn't think of anything. I didn't think of the man in the sky in the machine that I saw. I just saw these eyes, and I closed mine.

(His voice becomes rather awed each time he mentions the eyes.)

And I got out of the car, and I put my left leg on the ground and two men helped me out. And I did not walk. I felt like I was being supported. And I did not go very far, I thought, before I felt I was going up, going up a ramp of some kind. My eyes were tightly closed, and I was afraid to open them.

(Another pause, then:)

Oh, that doesn't say what I mean.

DOCTOR

Well, try again.

BARNEY

I didn't want to open them. It was comfortable to keep them closed.

(Barney reflects the desire to shut out the experience.)

DOCTOR

Were these men holding you?

BARNEY

They were by my side, and I had a funny feeling, because I knew they were holding me, but I couldn't feel them.

DOCTOR

Is this what you mean last time when you spoke of floating?

125

BARNEY

I felt floating, suspended. I am thinking of getting out of the car, and I had not thought that these men when they helped me out of the car—I could not feel them. And I only became aware that I could not feel them when we were going up an incline. And then I felt I could not feel them. My arms were in the position of being supported. But I was not walking. And I want to peek. I want to look. I want to look.

(This was the feeling in the first session, now clarified.)

DOCTOR

Yes, go on. This won't trouble you now. You can tell me.

BARNEY

I opened my eyes.

DOCTOR

You opened your eyes. What did you see?

BARNEY

I saw a hospital operating room. It was pale blue. Sky blue. And I closed my eyes.

DOCTOR

Do you remember the operating room when you had your tonsils out?

BARNEY

I remember the hospital, and I was in there because they thought I had appendicitis. And I stayed there for thirteen or fourteen—No, it was thirteen days.

(Again, the insistence on absolute literal accuracy, even on irrelevant details.)

And I used to walk down the corridor and peek into the operating room. And I thought of that. It wasn't when I had my tonsils out.

DOCTOR

Was that operating room in the hospital blue?

BARNEY

No. It was bright lights.

DOCTOR

Bright lights?

126

BARNEY

Bright lights. Like electric bulbs. But this room was not like that. It was spotless. I thought of everything being so clean. And I closed my eyes.

DOCTOR

Did you feel you were going to be operated on?

BARNEY

No.

DOCTOR

Did you feel you were being attacked in any way?

BARNEY

No.

DOCTOR

Did you feel you were *going* to be attacked in any way?

BARNEY

No.

DOCTOR

You said your groin felt cold . . .

BARNEY

I was lying on a table, and I thought someone was putting a cup around my groin, and then it stopped. And I thought: How funny.

DOCTOR

Speak a little louder, please.

BARNEY

I thought how funny. If I keep real quiet and real still, I won't be harmed.

(Again the magical ritual.)

And it will be over. And I will just stay here and pretend that I am anywhere and think of God and think of Jesus and think that I am not afraid. And I am getting off the table, and I've got a big grin on my face, and I feel greatly relieved. And I am walking, and I am being guided. And my eyes are closed, and I open my eyes, and that is the car. And the lights are off, and the motor is not running. And Delsey is under the seat. And I reached under and touched her, and she is in a tight ball under the seat, and I sit back. And I see Betty is coming down the road, and she gets into the car, and I am grinning at her and she is grinning back at me. And we both seem so elated and we are really happy. And I'm thinking it isn't too bad. How funny. I had no reason to fear. And we look and I see a bright moon. And I laugh and say, "Well, there it goes." And I'm happy.

DOCTOR

You mean this object was gone?

BARNEY

Yes.

DOCTOR

It had gone?

BARNEY

It was going.

DOCTOR

Going. Could you still see it?

BARNEY

It was a bright, huge ball. Orange. It was a beautiful, bright ball. And it was going. And it was gone. And we were in darkness, and I put on the lights of the car and looked down the road. And I thought there is a bend in the road. And we begin driving, and I could see a slight incline, and then I drove and came back to Route 3, because I was on a cement road. And I thought, oh boy, if I could only find a restaurant and get a cup of coffee. And Betty and I feel, I feel real hilarious, like a feeling of well-being and great relief.

DOCTOR

What were you relieved about?

BARNEY

I am relieved because I feel like I've been in a harrowing situation, and there was nothing damaging or harmful about it. And I feel greatly relieved.

DOCTOR

And the flying object was gone?

128

Yes.

And it didn't come back?

Betty is giggling, and she said, "Do you believe in flying saucers now?" And I said, "Oh, Betty, don't be ridiculous. Of course I don't." And we heard a beeping and the car buzzed, and I kept silent.

You heard a beeping.

It was a beeping sound. Beep—beep—beep—beep—beep.

Was your radio on?

No. My radio was not on. It was so late, and I did not think I could get a station. So when I left Canada, I cut my radio off. I played my radio in Quebec, because I thought it was funny, humorous to get the Canadian stations, and every word was spoken in French. And the music sounded different to my ears. When I left Montreal I became determined to drive home, and I cut my radio off. I don't play my radio when I am driving.

Now these beeps. You heard these beeps again. Did they sound like some of these beeps you get on a radio, when you have code signals? Or what did they sound like?

(Rapidly and sharply.)

Beep—beep—beep. They sound like beeps.

Well, what did you do? What did you think about them?

I thought it was strange, the beep—beep—beep. And at the first beep or two, I touched the steering wheel with my finger tips, because I

129

thought I felt a vibration when I heard the beep. And as it continued, Betty looked to the back, and I slowed the car down and stopped. And I said to Betty, "Is there something shifting in the car?"

DOCTOR

Did she say anything about hearing the beeps?

BARNEY

She said, "What is that noise?" And we looked in the back, and Delsey had climbed up on the back seat, and her ears were popped up, and the beep, beep, beep. And we said, "Oh—oh, do you think that thing is still around?" I called it a thing, Betty called it a flying saucer. And we had no answer, and we both thought, how strange. And I thought, that's very peculiar. I wonder if I can make the car do that. So I drove the car fast, and then would decelerate, rapidly. And I swerved over to the left of the highway and back to the right. And I came to a complete stop and accelerated rapidly. But I could not seem to get that sound. And we drove down the highway. And I saw the road for the expressway: 17 miles to Concord. And I drove to Concord and down Route 4.

DOCTOR

Did the beeping follow you there?

BARNEY

No. I did not hear any more beeps.

DOCTOR

After you got on the Concord road, is that it?

BARNEY

No, I did not hear any beeps quite a distance before I reached the main highway. Because Route 3 was also concrete, where I heard the beeping. And I heard it two times: when I got into the car, and when I returned to the car and started down the highway. And I thought, "What is that, Betty?" And we did not hear it anymore.

(He is referring back to Indian Head.)

DOCTOR

But she heard it too?

BARNEY

She heard it, too. And we did not hear it again until after we had been in the woods and had returned to Route 3. And she asked me, did I believe in flying saucers? And I did not want to say what I really believed.

DOCTOR

What did you really believe?

BARNEY

I believed that we had seen and been a part of something different than anything I had ever seen before.

DOCTOR

You mean also with the experience with these men in the operating room?

BARNEY

Yes.

DOCTOR

Did you fear you had been kidnapped?

BARNEY

I didn't use that word. I can only use that word intellectually. I did not feel that I had been kidnapped. But I think of kidnapping when you are being harmed.

DOCTOR

And you weren't harmed?

BARNEY

No.

DOCTOR

You had no idea why this was done?

BARNEY

I was anxious to get home and look at my groin.

DOCTOR

You wanted to look at your groin. Afraid that they had done something harmful?

I wanted to look. I thought, this is proof that something happened to me. And I was unsure. And I would waver, feeling that it can't be. And then I would think, but it did happen. And I would think when I get home and look at my groin, I will touch whatever touched me, and see if there is a mark. And this is what I thought.

(But this thought was completely gone when he reached full consciousness. When he arrived home, he did examine himself, but had no memory whatever of the reason he did so.)

DOCTOR

All right. Go on.

BARNEY

I drove home and I walked into the house. And I was too tired to bring in the luggage. And Betty got out of the car, and she took Delsey, and she let her relieve herself on the grass and brought her in. And I went into the bathroom and examined myself and saw nothing wrong. And I went into the bedroom, and I kept thinking that something is around me. I went to the window, and I looked up into the morning sky, and I went to the back door and opened it and looked at the sky. And I thought, something is around, somewhere. And Betty and I retired, talking. Wasn't that strange, whatever happened. And I could not remember anything that happened except that I was at Indian Head. And I went to bed. And when we woke up, we decided we would not ever tell anyone. And would only talk about it to each other. And I said, "But Betty, will you draw a picture of what you think you saw? And I will." And we drew pictures, and they were identical. And Betty called her sister and told her sister.

DOCTOR

You mentioned something about spots on the car.

BARNEY

Betty came away from the telephone, and she said, "Where is the compass, where is the compass?" And when Betty does that to me, I immediately get angry. And I said, "I don't know what you're talking about, Betty." And she said, "The compass! The compass! Where's the compass?" And I said, "In the drawer, where it always is." And she got it, and I was irritated because when she got excited like this, she didn't think to open the drawer and find it. And she went out of the house, and I went to the bedroom window, which is the front window of our house, and I thought, this thing is getting the best of Betty. And we'd better forget this as soon as possible. And stop remembering it. And she stormed into the house, and said, "Barney! Come here! Come here, quick!" And I walked out, and I looked at the compass when she placed it by the car. And I said, "Oh, this is ridiculous, Betty. After all, the car is metal, and any metal will attract and cause a compass to react this way." And she said, "Look what it does. And look at the spots on my car!" And I looked, and there were large spots, shiny spots, on the trunk of the car. And I thought, what caused that? And I started to wipe one off, and she said, "Don't touch it!" And I said, "How can you know if it isn't anything?" And then I put the compass close to it. And the compass would spin and spin, and I could move the compass a few inches to a spot, to a part of the trunk and that did not have a spot, and the compass would drop down. And I could not understand this. And I knew I did not know anything about compasses. And I told Betty , "It is nothing at all. The compass is a cheap compass. It is nothing to get alarmed about."

DOCTOR

What gave her the idea of getting the compass?

BARNEY

I did not know at that time.

DOCTOR

What did you find out?

BARNEY

She told me later that while she was talking with her sister, her sister had suggested that she get a compass and check and see if the car was magnetized or something or other. And this why she . . .

DOCTOR

You say these spots made a compass needle spin?

BARNEY

When we would place a compass anywhere but on the spots, the needle would just flop down.

133

DOCTOR

You say these were shiny spots. What did you mean by that? Were there changes in the color of your car, or dust removed, or what?

BARNEY

Highly polished.

DOCTOR

As if the car had been highly polished?

BARNEY

Yes, in those spots.

DOCTOR

How big were they?

BARNEY

About the size of half dollars, silver dollars.

DOCTOR

Did you try to remove them? Or did you try to wipe the rest of the car off?

BARNEY

I never bothered with the spots.

DOCTOR

Was the rest of the car dusty?

BARNEY

Yes, it was.

DOCTOR

And you didn't try to polish it out and see if it would duplicate those spots?

BARNEY

There had been a rain . . .

(It rained the afternoon and evening after they arrived back in Portsmouth.)

and where the rain had washed some of the dust off, the shiny spots were still there, and I didn't try to dust them off.

134

DOCTOR

Could these spots have been caused by the rain drops hitting and taking the dust off?

BARNEY

No. The spots were shiny and in perfect circles.

DOCTOR

Well, what did you do? Just leave the spots?

BARNEY

I did.

DOCTOR

Did you wash or polish your car at some reasonable time afterward?

BARNEY

That was Betty's car, and she washes her car. I suppose she did. I didn't pay any more attention.

DOCTOR

You don't know. How long did those spots stay, then?

BARNEY

I shut them out. I don't know. I just stopped thinking about those spots.

DOCTOR

You don't know when they disappeared—or did they?

BARNEY

Yes, they're gone.

DOCTOR

All right. We'll stop with this now. You will no longer think about what we talked about today, until I ask you to recall it. It will not trouble you at all. The eyes will not trouble you. You will not even think about them. Everything is comfortable, everything is relaxed. No need for anxiety, and nothing to worry about. Is that clear?

BARNEY

Yes.

DOCTOR

You are comfortable, aren't you?

Yes, I am.

And relaxed. And you are not worrying, and you will not worry. Every-thing will be quite all right. And you and Betty will come back a week from today, just as you did today. You feel all right, now?

(The doctor is doubly assuring that Barney will not have the same problems he had during the week before.)

Yes, I do.

You are very comfortable. You will not worry at all. It is not going to affect your mind. It's an experience we'll talk about more, get it all cleared up. So you will have no fear, no anxiety. You will not think about this; it will not come to you any more. Anything we talked about in these sessions, you will not think about; it will not trouble you. You'll be com-fortable and relaxed. No pains, no aches, no anxiety. You'll be all right.

Yes.

You may wake now.

(Barney immediately wakes, feeling calm and refreshed. He has no memory whatever of what has gone on during the session.)

*   *   *

At the start of this session on February 29, Barney was not certain if the doctor was going to go along with his request to take Betty and give him a rest after the reaction he had had to the first session. In fact, he half expected, at the moment he went into the trance, that the doctor was merely doing it for the purpose of reinforcing him for further treat-ment. When he looked at his watch at the end of the second session, he was totally surprised to find that it was nearly ten—almost two hours later. He was even more startled at this, because, although he had reached the point where he could accept the loss of contact with any sense of time for an hour or so, he was sure that he would have some consciousness of a lapse of time that long.

He felt very relaxed and comfortable as he came out of the trance and thought that he could remember talking about everything up to Indian Head, even within the trance. He seemed vaguely to be aware of the doctor's voice, but there was no clear remembrance of this.

"Actually," Barney later said, "I did not have any recall as to the actual sessions under hypnosis. But I seemed to develop a tremendous recall apart from the sessions of hypnosis, as if suddenly, I could say, 'Betty, do you know the color of the rug at the motel we stayed at before we got to Montreal? It was pale blue.' Things of that sort. And tying the dog to the radiator in the lavatory. I could remember things like that. And also, I remembered—consciously, that is—details of all the route numbers we had traveled. And after the second session, I recalled that we stopped at this quaint, farmhouse-type restaurant before Montreal. And the picture that came to my mind was so vivid. It was very quaint and attractive, lovely. Large fireplace, the side of the entire wall was a fireplace. We had a delightful breakfast there on the trip, the kind you would feed lumberjacks. Large chunks of ham, three or four eggs, if you wanted them. The picture came back so sharply. In other words, the picture of the conscious part of the trip was sharpened, even though I had no idea what I had said about the missing segment.

"Then, after this second session, I began having dreams. I had peculiar dreams, where I began dreaming about UFO's for the first time in my life. And I read a book about a doctor in a concentration camp in Germany who was in great distress, and I began to picture him as Dr. Simon, and this made the book acutely distressing to me. Because somehow, Dr. Simon had become sort of a close friend. He had become more than a close friend. He had become someone I loved, and I didn't want any harm to come to."

CHAPTER SEVEN

With the second session over, Dr. Simon reviewed the case in the first real light that had been thrown on the amnesic period. The case was breaking down into two separate phases: the first encounter, which was described as happening at Indian Head, and the second encounter, which apparently took place in a wooded section of a road off Route 3, involving a roadblock, and the bizarre description of an abduction aboard a space ship.

The evidence revealed in the two sessions with Barney seemed to indicate that he had undergone a severe emotional upheaval with an experience with an unidentified object, either real or interpreted to be real. The second experience—the abduction—had much less support from established reports of the UFO phenomenon and had to be considered as far less probable or unreal. Much more data would have to be available to weigh the scales convincingly as far as this was concerned. At this stage of the treatment, it appeared that part or all of the first encounter could be real. The second encounter had no valid precedent and appeared to be unreal, consequently reflecting back on the first experience.

Before proceeding further with Barney, Dr. Simon decided to begin with Betty and probe her recall. The doctor was working with facts, data, and logical conjecture, which he would test and add new data to to confirm or reject as he went along. A physician must be skeptical but should have some working hypotheses to help evaluate the material revealed.

The doctor was not interested in the UFO aspect, per se, except as an integral part of the Hills' experience. His presumption as he prepared to continue with Betty Hill on the following week was that the first encounter could have happened; the second encounter was unlikely.

*　　*　　*

On her way in to her first session, Betty Hill found herself actually looking forward to the experience. She had sat through two long sessions waiting for Barney, with some discomfort. She could not imagine herself getting as emotional as the first confused noises she had overheard during his first session seemed to indicate, and which she still had not mentioned to him.

At Dr. Simon's office on March 7, 1962, the procedure was reversed. Barney was reinforced, and Betty remained in the office for the session to begin. She was not sure whether the doctor would put her in a trance or conduct a conscious interview.

She had with her in her pocketbook a copy of the paper she had written out describing her dreams in detail. Driving in with Barney, she asked if she should show them to the doctor, but Barney suggested that she wait until the doctor asked for them. Barney's feeling about Betty's dreams was always one of extreme discomfort. He didn't like to think about them—didn't approve of Betty's preoccupation with them—didn't believe they had any basis in reality. Although he had not directly told Betty, he didn't want Dr. Simon to be influenced by her dreams. Consequently, the detailed description of the dreams remained in Betty's pocketbook as she prepared for her session.

She distinctly remembers hearing the cue words, as they were spoken by the doctor at her first long session on March 7.

"When he said them," Betty recalls, "it was always with the feeling of complete surprise to me. It's like suddenly someone slaps you. He says the words, and whatever you're doing immediately stops. I was in the middle of putting a cigarette out and was conscious for a brief moment that I was trying to do this, and I couldn't do it. I actually think when you're going into a trance, you just don't immediately go. It's like going to sleep. Sort of like drifting. You slide into it. I think you really couldn't stop yourself if you tried."

Betty heard the words distinctly. But almost immediately, she thought, she heard the words from the doctor: "You may wake up, Betty." In between the phrases, for over an hour, Betty reexperienced in full detail

139

the incident at Cannon Mountain. What she revealed would not be known to her for weeks later.

DOCTOR

(Her eyes close; her head nods.)

You are in a deep, deep sleep. Deep asleep. Fully relaxed and far asleep. Very comfortable, fully relaxed, deep asleep. Far asleep, deep, deep sleep.

(With the repeated reinforcement of the induction she has experienced over the weeks, this was all that was required to put her into the trance state.)

Now we're going to go back, back to your vacation in September of 1961 as you were coming from Niagara Falls to Montreal. You will remember what you did, and you will recall everything, all your experiences, all of your memories, all of your feelings, and you will give me all of this in full detail. Now you're coming from Niagara Falls to Montreal. You're on your way home from vacation. Now tell me all that you experienced, all that you felt. You and your husband.

BETTY

(Her voice is less monotonous compared to Barney's flat and vacant tone but she is in a deep trance, as he was.)

We're driving along, and the streets were wide, sun was shining. There were quite a few people in the streets. And I was looking at the houses and stores and windows . . .

(She speaks, however, with longer pauses, as if she waits for the scene to pass by her eyes before she relates it.)

We stopped at a gas station to get directions, and the attendant spoke French and couldn't understand us. So we went to another garage, and they told us how to get back into the center of Montreal. And I saw a mink coat in the window for $895. Then we decided we'd find a hotel, but then we didn't know if they'd allow Delsey to be in a hotel. So then we thought we'd look for a motel somewhere outside of Montreal. And we passed a place with a sign I thought said "potato fritters," and the woman in this little drive-in restaurant came out and started speaking in French. And I said I didn't understand French, and she kept saying she was sure I was French. But I'm not. And then I found out it wasn't potato fritters, it was potato chips. So we had the potato chips and coffee, and I can't remember if I had a hot dog or a hamburger, or one of each . . .

(Again, the struggle to remember minutiae, even if not significant. If she were instructed to, she could remember. Also, different details of the trip are selected for description by Betty than Barney chose to relate. She continues with her description of the basic story of the trip down through Canada to Colebrook and then on to Lancaster, her story paralleling Barney's account of this portion of the journey. Then:)

And we kept driving and looking around. The moon was bright, but not quite full, but very bright and large. And there was a star down below the moon, on the lower left-hand side of the moon. And then right after we left Lancaster I noticed that there was like a star, a bigger star up over this one. And it hadn't been there. And I showed Barney, and we kept watching it. It seemed to keep getting brighter and bigger looking. And we watched it for quite awhile. And I was puzzled by it. Also curious. And while I was watching it, Delsey was getting somewhat restless. And then we went by a mountain that obstructed the view. And when I got to where I could seee the star again, I thought it had moved . . .

(Again, Betty Hill rarely begins her sentences, in ordinary conversation, with and. Yet, like Barney, she persistently does so in trance.)

But I wasn't quite sure, so I kept watching it. And it seemed so it did move, and Delsey was restless. So I told Barney we should let Delsey out. And it would give us a chance to look at this star through the binoculars. We drive along, and we came to a parking space off the highway, one that had been built there. And I guess it was so people could drive off and look at the view. And there were woods all around. And there were a couple of trash barrels. And Barney said we should look out for bears. I got out of the car and put—let's see— yes, I got out of the car and put Delsey on her leash and started to walk her. And I noticed that the star was definitely moving, so I went back to the car and got out the binoculars. And Barney took Delsey, and I was looking through the binoculars at the object. And Barney was saying it was a satellite, but it wasn't. It was moving fast, but it went in front of the moon, and I saw it. I saw it travel across the whole face of the moon, and it was odd shaped. And it was flashing all different colored lights.

DOCTOR

How far away would you say it was?

BETTY

It looked at the time it wasn't close to us. But I could see it outlined in front of the moon. And there were like searchlights rotating around it.

DOCTOR

Like those lights you see on police cars?

BETTY

No. You know what a searchlight looks like?

DOCTOR

Yes.

BETTY

And how it's sort of in a pencil line of light, and it swings around. They were like that.

DOCTOR

You could see those long beams?

BETTY

Of white—and they were different colors.

DOCTOR

Were they usual colors that you know, or were they—?

BETTY

Yes, they were bright colors. Like a bright orange light, almost a reddish beam. And there was like a blue, well, you said like a light on a police cruiser. You know, it was something like that because when the cruiser light turns around somehow, and it flashes. Even though they seem to come out into a ray thing, somehow. All these different kinds of lights seemed to be that same flash, flash, flash.

DOCTOR

There were colors other than red, amber and green?

(The doctor of course is referring to conventional lights used in this country on planes, vehicles and for traffic control.)

BETTY

Like a blue and like a flash. Flash, flash, flash. And I had never seen anything like it before. And it was moving quite fast. But I've never seen a satellite, but I've always thought of a satellite as traveling almost like a shooting star, maybe not quite as fast. But this wasn't traveling that fast. Well, when I saw it go in front of the moon, I was sort of fascinated, and I kept watching. But then I tried to get Barney to look, I wanted him to see it before it got away from the face of the moon. But he kept saying, "Oh, it's a satellite."

DOCTOR

Are you referring to Telstar or Echo—that sort of thing?

BETTY

Yes. And Barney said it was just a satellite, and he was over by the car, and by the time he got back it had gone from in front of the moon. But he did look at it, and then he looked at it for a few seconds and gave the binoculars back to me.

DOCTOR

You said it had an odd shape, did you?

BETTY

Yes.

DOCTOR

How would you describe this shape? Round? Shaped like anything you know? A plane?

BETTY

No. Not like a plane. All I could think of, like a cigar.

DOCTOR

Like a cigar?

BETTY

Yes. It was long, and there weren't any wings. And it was going side-ways. You know, like a cigar. It was going from the left to the right. It

143

was just like holding a cigar up in front of the moon, with all these lights flashing around it. So then Barney looked at it, and I took the binoculars and looked again and gave them back to him. And then I went over and put Delsey in the car and got in the car myself and shut the door. And then Barney came over and got in the car, and he said, "They've seen us, and they're coming this way." And I laughed and asked him if he had watched Twilight Zone recently on TV. And he didn't say anything.

DOCTOR

Why did you mention Twilight Zone?

BETTY

Because the idea was fantastic.

DOCTOR

Had there been anything like this on Twilight Zone?

BETTY

I don't know. I never see Twilight Zone. But I had heard people talk about this program, and I always was under the impression that it was a way-out type of thing. And so when he said that they had seen us, and that they were swinging around and coming in our direction, I thought his imagination was being overactive.

DOCTOR

Did he have binoculars at the time?

BETTY

I left him standing on the edge of this parking area, looking at this thing when I took Delsey, and she and I got in the car. And I sat down and waited for him to finish looking. And this is when he came back and said that it had turned around and was coming toward us.

DOCTOR

Did you look to see if it was doing that?

BETTY

Not at that moment. I thought this was sort of, I didn't know. Well, Barney kept saying that it was headed toward us. So I thought, well, I don't know what gave him this idea, but I was beginning to get a little curious why he felt this. So I picked up the binoculars, and at first I couldn't find it, couldn't find the object. But then I did see it. And I could see it was getting closer to us and was coming in. And it was still far, far away, and even when it was coming in, it still looked like a star. It was a solid-light type of thing. And then, when I would take the binoculars down and look at it, it was just like a star coming in closer.

(An echo of many more reports in NICAP and Air Force files.)

But then when I looked at it through the binoculars, it would, of course, appear to be much bigger. But it was flying in a very odd way. And this is what I was all excited about.

DOCTOR

What do you mean by odd way?

BETTY

Well, you know how an airplane flies along in a straight line? It wasn't flying like that. It was turning, it was rotating. And it would go along in a straight line for a short, just a short distance, and then would tip over on its side, and go up.

DOCTOR

Well, let's see. It was shaped like a cigar, you say.

BETTY

Yes.

DOCTOR

Did it fly like it was a cigar going along? Like an arrow?

BETTY

This is the way it looked.

DOCTOR

When it tipped over, what did it do? How did it tip?

BETTY

Well, all right. You take a cigar and you lay it flat on the desk. Now you stand the cigar up on one end. Right straight up and down. This is what this did. And in the meanwhile, it gave the appearance of spinning all the time.

(Other reports of this nature indicate that the cigar shape, as in Barney's case, is an indication of a disc that is seen in profile.)

Was it turning on the long axis?

BETTY

Yes. It would go along straight, and then it would suddenly go right up straight. And then it would flatten horizontally. And then it would drop down straight. This seemed to be the overall pattern. It wasn't done in an exactly precise way. It would jerk out. It would flatten out. So it was sort of, it wasn't smoothly done. And as they got closer, there seemed to be more of this jumping back and forth in the sky. And then it followed us for a long time. And Barney was driving, and I was watching this almost completely—and the way it was flying, I thought maybe it was the vibrations of the car that was causing it to look this way.

DOCTOR

You mean this jumping effect?

BETTY

Yes. I thought maybe the vibrations of the car was giving the effect. And so, I was keeping asking Barney to stop the car and look at it. And he would stop and say he couldn't see it flying this way, while I could. And so then I would look at other objects, like a star, to see if it would give this appearance. And it wouldn't. I kept trying to figure out, I kept saying, "Nothing flies like this, so it's something I'm doing to make this idea that it's flying like this." Everything else I looked at was all right. It didn't jump around. It was just this one object. We kept starting and stopping and looking at it. And we would drive along. Now when we got by Cannon Mountain, this is where the tramway is . . .

DOCTOR

(He needs to make an adjustment of the tape recorder.)

All right, we'll stop there now. You will not hear anything further until I speak to you again. You will be perfectly at ease . . .

(He completes the adjustment.)

All right Betty. Continue now where you left off.

(She continues at exactly that point.)

UFO as seen by Betty Hill in first encounter.
From sketch by Betty Hill.

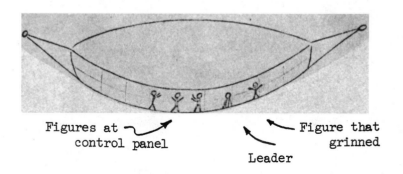

Figures at
control panel

Figure that
grinned

Leader

UFO as seen by Barney Hill showing figures,
"fins," and red lights. From sketch by Barney Hill.

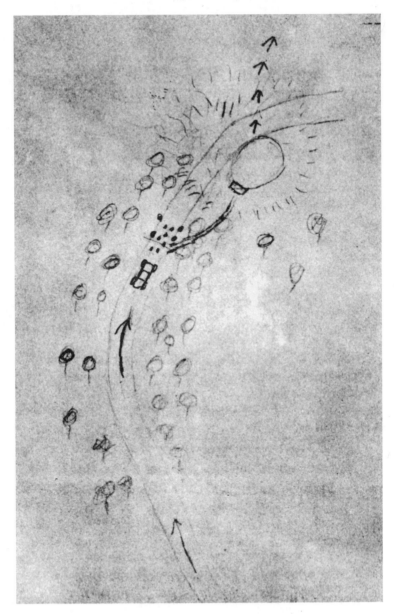

Sketch by Barney Hill, drawn after the therapy had released the repressed material, of his recollection of the actual site of the possible abduction. Dots represent his recollection of the "men in the road." Round object in clearing is his recollection of the approximate position of the object.

Barney Hill, under hypnosis, drew the above sketch of the "leader" of the alleged abductors. Later, while he was listening to the tape recording of his own account of the incident, he seemed to go into a trance-like state, and drew the more finished sketch below. The eyes were elongated, he said, and the lips appeared to have no muscles.

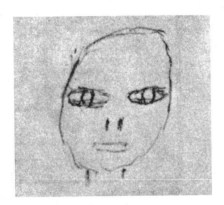

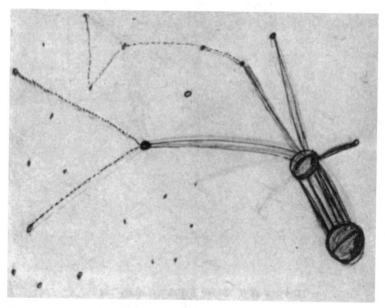

Under hypnosis, Betty Hill described a map she was shown "by the leader aboard the ship." Later, she sketched it. She said she was told that the heavy lines marked regular trade routes, and the broken lines recorded various space expeditions. The following year, the map seen below was published in the New York Times. (Note the caption.)

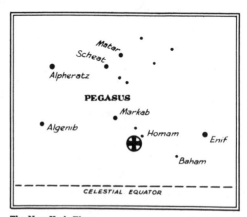

The New York Times   April 13, '65

FROM DEEP IN SPACE: Radio source called CTA-102 (cross), in direction of constellation Pegasus, may be sending intelligent radio emissions, Russian believes.

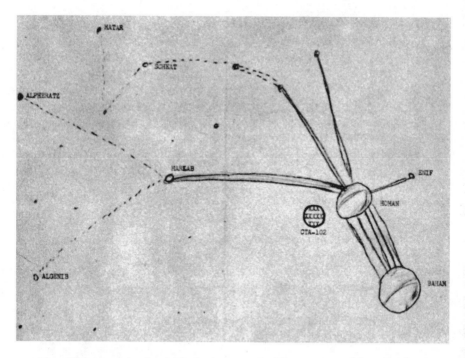

Mrs. Hill, struck by the similarity between the Times map and her sketch,
then added the corresponding names.

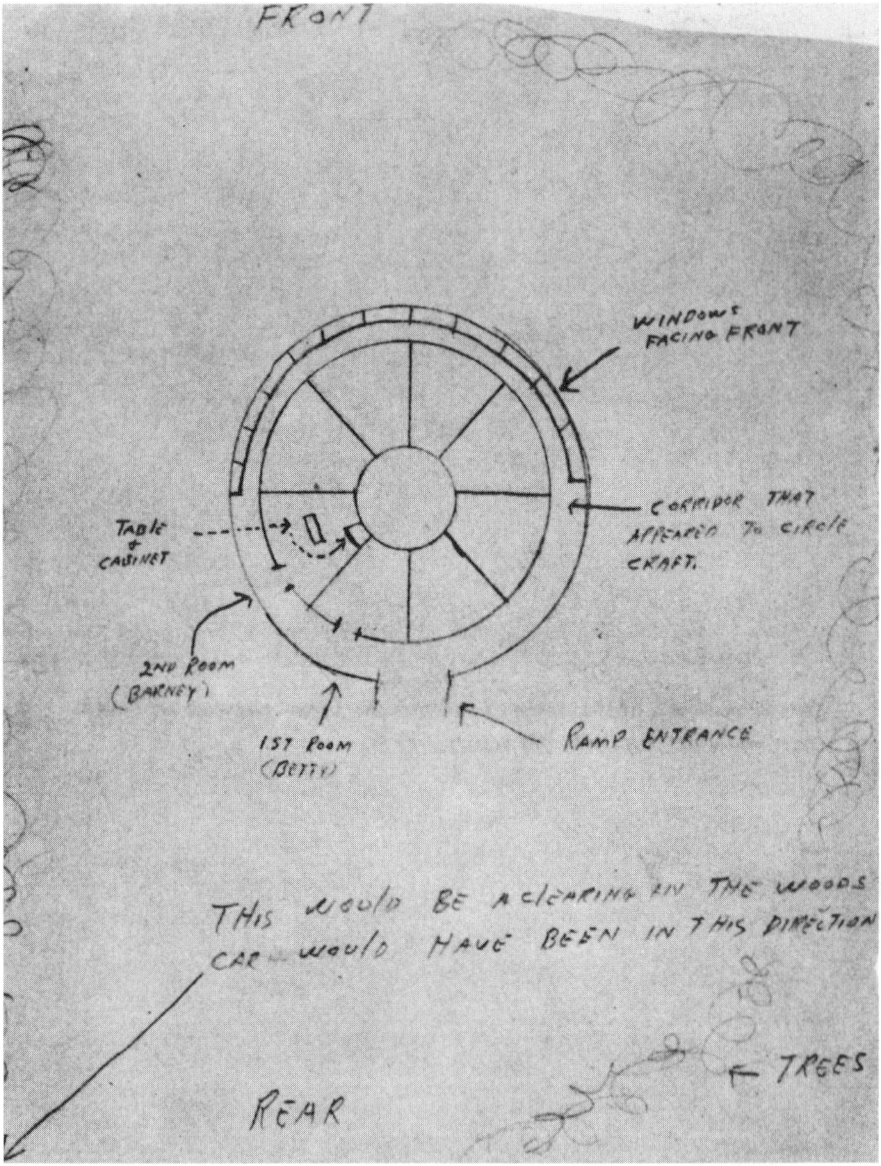
FRONT
WINDOWS FACING FRONT
CORRIDOR THAT APPEARED TO CIRCLE CRAFT.
TABLE & CABINET
2ND ROOM (BARNEY)
1ST ROOM (BETTY)
RAMP ENTRANCE
THIS WOULD BE A CLEARING IN THE WOODS
CAR WOULD HAVE BEEN IN THIS DIRECTION
TREES
REAR

Sketch by Barney Hill, drawn for the writer four years after incident, in an attempt to reconstruct his impression of the craft. Hypnosis sessions penetrating the amnesic period tended to bring out more memories after the formal therapy was concluded.

DR. BENJAMIN SIMON

Jeeves Studio

Barney and Betty Hill with their dachshund, Delsey,
who was with them on their interrupted journey

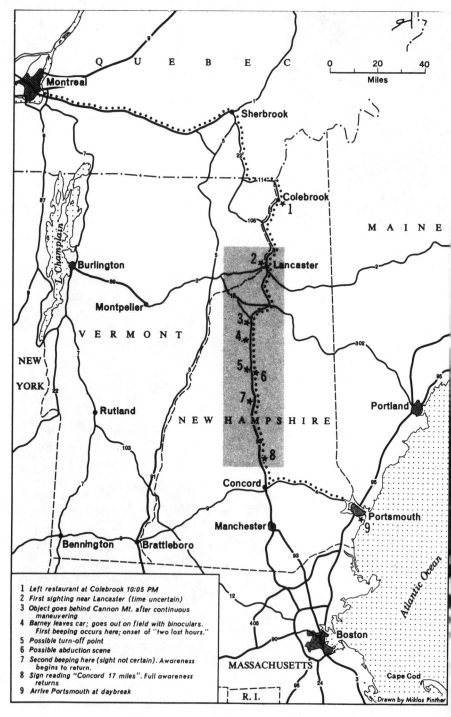

1 Left restaurant at Colebrook 10:05 PM
2 First sighting near Lancaster (time uncertain)
3 Object goes behind Cannon Mt. after continuous maneuvering
4 Barney leaves car; goes out on field with binoculars. First beeping occurs here; onset of "two lost hours."
5 Possible turn-off point
6 Possible abduction scene
7 Second beeping here (sight not certain). Awareness begins to return.
8 Sign reading "Concord 17 miles". Full awareness returns
9 Arrive Portsmouth at daybreak

Drawn by Miklos Pinther

Route taken by Barney and Betty Hill on the night of Sept. 19, 1961.

. . . we came by the tramway at Cannon Mountain, and there's a lighted area on the top . . . I think the lights might have been from a restaurant. And as I was watching, the lights went out.

(There are many reports of electrical disturbances by UFO's, including lights, auto ignition, headlights, radio and television.)

I don't know if it went down in the valley between the two mountains, or if it turned its lights off. And this puzzled me, because I kept looking for it. And then I thought, well maybe they're going away, they aren't interested in us. But then we came out by Old Man of the Mountain, and there it was. But it looked almost as if it were bouncing along the top of the mountain, the ridge. And it would go down a little bit on the other side, and I would lose sight of it. And I kept wondering why they were following us. And I would figure that, I was wondering if they were as curious about me as I was about them.

DOCTOR

You speak of "they"?

BETTY

I mean, well, I figured there must be somebody inside of the object, you know, someone directing its flight. And so, whoever was inside, this is "they." I was very curious, and I had the feeling that someone might be there, and they saw us. In a way, it was all very intriguing. And I didn't know what was going to happen, but I wasn't afraid. I was just curious. And I just had a feeling that something is going to happen, and I don't know what it is. And I hope I won't be too afraid when it does happen. And so we kept riding along, and we stopped at one place, there were too many trees, we lost sight of it there. When we got to the Flume, Barney drove in on the parking area on the right-hand side. And we stopped there and tried to really get a good look at it again. But there were too many trees there, too. But we would go along and there would be areas where we could get, it would be fairly clear. And then we went past the Flume, somewhere between the Flume and Indian Head, or it was just beyond the Flume, or just beyond Indian Head, there was a motel. It was like cabins, these small, neat-looking cabins, and the sign itself wasn't lighted, but there was one cottage on the end that had a light on. And there was a man standing in the door. And I saw this, and I thought, if I want to, I can get out of this whole situation right now. All we have to do is drive in here, and this object will go away. And that will be the end of it. I mean, this is our escape from it, if I want this. And I was thinking this, and I didn't say anything to Barney, I didn't say anything. All I could think of was, I don't know where we're going, but I'm ready for it. And Barney was sort of irritating me, because he wanted to, his whole attitude was that I was trying to wish something on him. I got the impression that he was trying to deny what was actually happening. That he didn't want to know that it was there, even though he would stop and look at it. He didn't have any realization of what was going on. Now it was fairly close, and I could see that it wasn't spinning, because I could see that there were lights on one side, and this gave it a blinking and twinkling effect. But then all of a sudden, it stopped doing this. And I got the idea that there were lights only on one side. And then all of a sudden, the object shot ahead of us and swung around in front of the car. Well, I was watching it when it did this. And it was on my side of the windshield, directly in front of me. And I looked at it through the binoculars, and I could see a double row of windows. And then, as I was watching it, I was thinking this side has the windows and the back of it must be dark. And this is why it twinkles. And while I'm sitting there, I'm amazed by all this. Then all of a sudden on one side, on the left-hand side, a red light came out. And then on the right-hand side, a light came out.

DOCTOR

You say left- and right-hand side?

BETTY

I was facing the object.

DOCTOR

You're looking through the windshield?

BETTY

I was looking through the windshield, right up at it.

DOCTOR

How far away would you say it was?

BETTY

Oh, I couldn't estimate. You couldn't see it too clearly without the binoculars. I could see a band of light without them. And when I saw the second red light, I kept telling Barney to stop. "Stop the car, Barney, and look at it!" And he kept saying, "Oh, why it's nothing. It'll go away." And I kept saying, "Barney! You've got to stop! Stop the car, Barney, and look at it. It's amazing!" And he said, oh, he was going to humor me then so he said, "Oh, all right. Give me the binoculars." And he looked at it, and I kept saying, "Do you see it? Do you see it?" And he said, "It's just a plane or something." And I kept saying, "OK, it's a plane. Did you ever see a plane with two red lights? I thought planes had one red and one green light." And he kept looking at it, and then he gave the binoculars back to me, and I'd watch it. And then he said he couldn't see very well. He opened the car door—no first, he put down the window in his car door, and he tried to stick his head out and look up over the roof of the car at it.

(Betty's voice has become increasingly animated now, but still quite matter-of-fact.)

But the motor of the car was running, and he said, well, he got out. He opened the car door and stepped out. He put one foot on the highway, and one was inside the car. And he was standing with the car door open, but he was leaning against the body of the car. He kept looking at it, and then he didn't say anything. He just stepped outside. And he stepped outside, and he kept going away from the car. And I thought, well now, this isn't a very bright place for us to have stopped the car, because we're right on the main highway. We're not on the right side or the left side. We're right directly in the middle. And there should be traffic on the highway. So I thought, well, while he's out getting a good look at this, I'll watch if any cars come in either direction, in case I have to get the car out from the middle of the street. So I'd look out the back window and out the front window. And it seems as though I sat there and sat there and waiting and waiting and Barney didn't come back. And I was sitting there waiting. And I'd look. It was dark there. There weren't any street lights or anything. I noticed when I looked out, he was quite a distance from the car, and he was still going away from the car.

(Now, for the first time, emotion begins to come into Betty's voice. Oddly enough, it occurs at just about the same time and place that Barney's intense emotional outburst occurred.)

So I leaned over the front seat, and I was saying, "Barney! Come back here!

149

(Now her voice breaks in emotion. She begins to sob as she speaks.)

Barney! You damn fool, get back here! Barney, come back!"

(She is reliving the incident now, calling directly to Barney, rather than describing it.)

If that damn fool doesn't come back, I'm going after him! "Barney! What's *wrong* with you?"

(Her profanity is more affectionate than condemnatory. All of their bickering is rather congenial.)

And I'm calling, "Barney! Barney! Barney. Get back here! What's wrong with you?"

(Now back to description, but still breathless.)

I started to slide . . . I was going to get out his side of the car because that door was open all the way. I started to slide across the seat, because I was going to go out and get him. Just as I started to slide, and I got the door most of the way open, he came to the car. He was running like mad down the street.

(A New Hampshire colloquialism for "road.")

And when I heard him coming, I sat up. I was lucky I did, afterwards. Because he threw the binoculars in the car, and they landed on the seat beside me. He was hysterical.

(And now she almost is.)

He . . . he . . . he . . . he . . . he was. I don't know if he was laughing or crying. But he was saying that they were going to capture us. We had to get the hell out of there. They were going to capture us. Because the car motor was running, he put the car into first, and he stepped on the gas. And we started to take off very rapidly. He kept saying to me, "Look out! Look out! You can see them. They're right overhead. They're right directly over our car. . . ."

And so, I did want to see them again and I was sort of afraid—but I wasn't that afraid. And so, we were moving, we were going quite fast then. And so I wound down, I turned down the window on my side of the car, and I tried to put by body out through the window and look out. And I kept looking and looking, and I couldn't see them.

150

I couldn't see the light. I couldn't even see the sky. I couldn't see anything. And so I told Barney, "I don't think they're out there. I don't see anything. It's all black. I don't see them." So then I pulled my head in, and I wound up the window of the car. And I thought, well, maybe they're out the back, because I kept looking for the lights. And I looked out the back window, and I didn't see anything. And the, all of a sudden, there was this: Beep, Beep, Beep, Beep, Beep. And Barney said, "What's that? What's that? What's that noise?" I said, "I don't know." All I could think of, is some kind of electrical signal. You know—beep, beep, beep, beep-beep . . .

(Now she is rather matter-of-fact in her tone, analyzing what this might possibly be all about.)

I wondered, oh, darn. Why didn't I learn the Morse code, cause maybe this is the Morse code, and I don't know it. Then I thought, maybe it's electrical. Maybe it's a shock. So I put my hand on the metal of the car, and I kept feeling and feeling, and I didn't feel a shock, no kind of electrical shock. But the whole car was vibrating. You know, little vibrating. And I thought, well, that's funny. The—the—there was no—well, I don't know. There was a beeping, and there wasn't any electrical shock. What happened next?

(The sharpness of detail, of minutiae, leaves her, at the same point in time and location as with Barney. She continues to speak, but in puzzlement, as if she is probing, searching for a lost memory.)

We're riding along . . . and I kept waiting for Barney to tell me about what he saw on the highway. . . .

(She stops talking. Her groping at this point is unavailing.)

DOCTOR

(After waiting a considerable length of time.)

How long would you say he was away from you when he was on the highway? Actually, how long was it?

BETTY

Oh, it seemed a long time.

DOCTOR

Well, how long was it?

151

I don't know. I would say, for some reason I don't know why, I would say four or five minutes.

Four or five minutes.

Yes. I don't remember looking at my watch, and it was dark anyway. And I heard the beeping sound.

Did you see this object anymore?

I kept trying to see it. Every once in a while, I would look out the window for it, but—my mind's a blank.

(Another pause. She is groping.)

But I can almost remember . . .

Yes, you can.

(She is obviously straining to remember.)

Right at this point, I can't get beyond that beeping.

(Nor could Barney, at this point.)

You can. It's all right now. You can get beyond it.

(Now a very long pause. Betty is breathing heavily, but she makes no other sound.)

Yes, go on. It's all right.

(Now Betty begins to cry, in short, rapid sobs, as if she were trying to hold herself back.)

All right. You needn't be too upset.

(Another long pause. Then she draws a sharp breath, as if she has made a forced resolution in her mind. She speaks very rapidly, breathlessly, as if she doesn't want to say this.)

We're driving along . . . I don't know where we are . . . I don't even know how we got here . . . Barney and I, we were driving, I don't know how long . . . I don't know how long. . . .

(The words come out between sharp, short sobs.)

And we haven't even been talking . . . I've just been sitting here . . . feeling that something is going to happen . . . and I'm not really too afraid . . . except right now I am . . . at the time I didn't feel afraid . . .

(She stops talking, then cries.)

DOCTOR

(After a long pause.)

Why are you crying if you're not afraid?

BETTY

I'm afraid now . . . but I wasn't . . . I don't . . . I wasn't . . . I wasn't afraid . . . I was afraid when I saw the men in the road . . .

DOCTOR

Men in the road?

BETTY

(Now she breaks out with an anguished cry.)

I've never been so afraid in my life before!

DOCTOR

(Very calmly.)

Tell me about the men in the road. It's all right now.

BETTY

(She begins to say something, but she is sobbing too much to get it out.)

DOCTOR

You're safe here. Tell me about the men in the road.

BETTY

(Her voice is trembling, her breath rapid.)

We're driving along . . . we're on a tarred road . . . and all of a sudden . . . without any warning or rhyme or reason or anything . . . Barney made a—he always—the brakes squealed, he stopped so suddenly . . . and made this sharp left-hand turn off the highway . . . and we went on to this narrow road . . . I was wondering what he was doing, to turn down here . . . He wasn't saying anything, and I wasn't either . . . so I figured, well, maybe we're lost . . . But so what, we'll come out somewhere . . .

(She is still having difficulty in speaking.)

And we're going along . . . and there was a sharp curve . . . there were trees . . . there were a lot of tall trees on my side . . . I don't know about Barney's side of the road . . .

(Again, the desire for complete accuracy in reporting.)

But—there were these men standing in the highway . . . and I wasn't too afraid when I saw them . . . they were standing there, and I thought, well, you know, they weren't so awful . . . there was, oh, I don't know . . . and they were just . . . I wasn't too afraid when I saw them. And they were just—I couldn't get a good look at them . . .

(She reflects a moment, then:)

But then I thought, well—they in a car? A car broken down? What are they doing here? And Barney of course had to stop. And then he stopped the car, and these men started to come up to the car. They separated. They came in two groups. And when they started to do that, I got real scared. And the car motor died. The car stalled. And then they started to come toward us.

(A brief pause, then:)

And when they started to do that, I got real scared. And the car motor died, the car stalled. And when they started to come up to us, Barney tried to start the car. And you know how a motor of the car will just turn over, and it won't fire? He couldn't start the car . . . he couldn't start the car!

(She bursts into tears again. The last words are muffled.)

154

He did what?

BETTY

He tried to start the car, and it won't start! And the men are coming toward us! And I thought, well, I can get away from them if I get the car door open, I can run in the woods and hide! And I'm thinking of that, and I just put my hand on the car door to open it, and the men come up, and they open it for me!

(She sobs profusely.)

And they open the car door . . . and this . . . this man . . . two men behind us . . . and . . . and . . .

(Her words are again muffled by her crying.)

DOCTOR

I didn't hear that.

BETTY

(Trying to get herself under control.)

Two men at the car door . . . and there's one . . . two . . . three men . . . and there's one . . . two more behind them . . . and one man puts his hand out . . .

(She stops again.)

DOCTOR

Go on.

BETTY

(A long pause of deep breathing.)

I—I don't know what happens . . .

DOCTOR

You can remember everything now. What do these men look like? Did you see their faces?

BETTY

No.

DOCTOR

How were they dressed?

155

BETTY

Alike. Somehow or other.

(More sobbing, a little more controlled.)

DOCTOR

Do they have a uniform, or ordinary clothes?

BETTY

More like a uniform.

DOCTOR

A uniform. Did it resemble any uniform you already know?

BETTY

I couldn't say.

(And she lapses into silence again.)

DOCTOR

(He waits a considerable length of time, then:)

All right, your memory is very sharp. You needn't be worried. You remember everything now. Tell me what happened.

(Another long pause.)

What are you thinking now?

BETTY

I'm thinking I'm asleep.

DOCTOR

You're asleep in the car?

BETTY

(This is the same point at which Barney became vague and diffuse . . . when he felt he was "floating about" . . . when he saw "the eyes.")

I'm thinking I'm asleep . . . I'm asleep, and I've got to wake up! I don't want to be asleep. I keep trying . . . I got to wake myself up . . . I try . . . and I go back again . . . I keep trying . . . I keep trying to wake up . . .

(Long pause, then:)

Then I do! I open my eyes! And I'm walking through the woods . . . And I just open my eyes quick, and I shut them again . . .

(She begins sobbing intensely.)

But even though I'm asleep, I'm walking! And there's this man on this side, and a man on this side . . . and there's two men in front of me. And I look all around . . . and it's a path . . . and there's trees . . .

(More words come out, but the sobbing completely obscures them.)

And I look at these men . . . and I turn around . . . Barney's behind me . . .

(She stops short again.)

DOCTOR

Barney's behind you?

BETTY

There's a couple of men behind me, and then there's Barney. There's a man on each side of him. And my eyes are open . . . but Barney's still asleep. He's walking, and he's asleep . . .

(She is still sobbing, but then gets under control.)

And then I begin to get mad! And I say to myself, "Who the heck are these characters, and what do they think they're doing?" And I turn around, and I say, "Barney! Wake up! *Barney!* Why don't you wake up?" And he doesn't pay any attention. He keeps walking. And going a little bit further, and I turn around, and I say his name again, *"Barney!* Wake up!" And he still doesn't pay any attention. And then the man walking beside me here says, "Oh, is his name Barney?" And that's where I looked at this man, and I figured it's none of his business. So I didn't speak to him. Then we keep walking, and I try to wake Barney up again. I keep saying, "Barney, Barney, wake up!" And he doesn't, so the man asks me again, "Is Barney his name?" And I wouldn't answer him, so he says, he said, "Don't be afraid. You don't have any reason to be afraid. We're not going to harm you, but we just want to do some tests. When the tests are over with, we'll take you and Barney back and put you in your car. You'll be on your way back home in no time." I mean he was, he was sort of reassuring in a way, but I can't say I trust what he said. And I wasn't sure what was going to happen. And we kept walking and walking, and Barney was still asleep . . .

(Although she has her sobs under control, they are still punctuating all this.)

DOCTOR

You mean he was walking in his sleep?

BETTY

Yes, he was like sleep-walking.

DOCTOR

These men spoke good English?

BETTY

Only one spoke, the one who was on my left. Then he was more or less . . . he had an accent. He had sort of a foreign accent . . . but he was, you know, very businesslike. So then we kept walking, and we came to a clearing. And there was—I wish it were lighter so I could get a better picture of it—there was a ramp to the door. The object was on the ground . . .

(She pauses.)

DOCTOR

The object was on the ground?

BETTY

(Very matter-of-factly now.)

I think it was the same one I was watching in the sky. And there were trees and a path, and there was this clearing. And they're taking me up to the object. I don't want to go on it. I don't want . . . I don't know what's going to happen if I do. I don't want to go. Barney's no protection . . . he's sound asleep. And I don't want to go on it.

DOCTOR

He's sound asleep. What was he doing? Walking along, or was somebody supporting him?

BETTY

Yes. There's a man on each side. One has each arm, and they're sort of . . . well, he's sort of . . . his eyes are shut, and he doesn't hear anything I say. But he's standing on his own two feet. But he's in a daze, and they're sort of directing him, helping him along. And he's quite a bit taller than the men.

DOCTOR

He's taller than the men?

BETTY

Yes. Yes, he's way above them. So when we get to the object, I don't want to go on. And so the man beside me says to go on. He's a little angry with me. He said, "Oh, go on. The longer you fool around out here, the longer it's going to take. You might as well go on and get it over with, and get back to your car. We haven't got much time, either." So he, and one of the others, each take my arm, and I get sort of a helpless feeling. There's not much I can do at this point, but to go on with them. I go up the ramp, I go inside, and there's a corridor to the left. We go up the corridor, and there's a room. And they stop to take me in the room.

(She is calmer now, much calmer.)

I'm standing in the doorway, and I turn around, and I'm waiting for them to bring Barney in. But they don't do this. They lead Barney right past the door where I'm standing. So I said, "What are you doing with Barney? Bring him in here where I am." And the man said, "No, we only have equipment enough in one room to do one person at a time. And if we took you both in the same room, it would take too long. So Barney will be all right, they're going to take him into the next room. And then as soon as we get through testing the both of you, then you will go back to your car. You don't have to be afraid." And so I watched them take Barney into the next room, and I go into this room. And some of the men come in the room with this man who speaks English. They stay for a minute—I don't know who they are, I guess maybe they're the crew. But they only stay for a minute, and the man who speaks English is there, and another man comes in. I haven't seen him before. I think he's a doctor. And they came in the door . . .

(As with Barney, under hypnosis she tends to mix the past and present tenses.)

. . . and in one corner, there's a stool, a white—is it white? I don't know if it's white or chrome, but there's a stool, there's a stool, and they put me on it. I sit on the stool. And they—I have a dress, my blue dress on, and they push up the sleeve of my dress, and they look at my arm here. They both look at my arm, and then they turn my arm over and they look at it on here . . .

(She indicates a portion of her arm.)

. . . and they . . . they rub, they have a machine, I don't know what it is. They bring the machine over and they put it, I don't know what kind of machine, it's something like a microscope, only a microscope with a big lens. And they put—I don't know—they put, I had an idea they were taking a picture of my skin. And they both looked through this machine here, and here—

(She gestures.)

And then they were talking. I don't know what they were saying. I couldn't understand this part, what they were saying. And then they took something like a letter opener—only it wasn't—and they scraped my arm here . . .

(She indicates again.)

and there was like little—you know—how your skin gets dry and flaky sometimes, like little particles of skin? And they put—there was something like a piece of cellophane or plastic, or something like that, they scraped, and they put this that came off on this plastic.

(She has fully recovered her calmness now, is very matter-of-fact.)

And then he, the man who spoke English, they both spoke English here, the man who brought me on this contraption is the one who took this, he took this plastic, and he rolled it all up, and he put it in the top drawer. And then they put my head, there was like a dentist, not like a dentist, something like, you know, the brace of a dentist's chair. You have this thing that holds your head, I don't know, it seemed to pull out the back of the stool, somehow or other, and they put my head in that.

(Again the doctor has an adjustment to make. He stops her for a moment, then she continues right on.)

So I'm sitting on the stool, and there's a little bracket, my head is resting against this bracket. And the examiner opens my eyes, and looks in them with a light, and he opens my mouth, and he looks in my throat and my teeth and he looks in my ears, and he turned my head, and he looked in this ear. And then he takes like a—oh, a swab or a Q-tip I guess it is—they use it on babies—and he cleans out, he puts it in my left ear, and he puts this on another piece of this material. And the leader takes it and rolls it all up and puts it in the top drawer, too.

(She stops a minute, as if to recall the picture more clearly.)

Oh, and then he feels my hair down by the back of my neck and all, and they take a couple of strands of my hair, and they pull it out, and he gives this to the leader, and he wraps that all up and puts that in the top drawer. Then he takes something maybe like scissors, I don't know what it is, and he cut, they cut a piece of it, and he gives that to him. And then he feels my neck, he starts feeling behind my ears, under my chin, and down my neck and in and through my shoulders, around my collarbone, and—

(Again, a pause to recollect.)

Oh—and then they take off my shoes, and they look at my feet, and they look at my hands, they look my hands all over. And he takes—the light is very bright so my eyes aren't always open. I'm still a little scared, too. I'm not particularly interested in looking at them. And so I try to keep my eyes shut. But no, I do open, not all the time, just to give myself a little relief. When I'm not looking at them, I shut my eyes. And he takes something and he goes underneath my fingernail, and then he, I don't know, probably manicure scissors or something, and he cut off a piece of my fingernail. And they look my feet all over, they keep—I don't think they do anything to them, they just feel my feet and my toes and all. And then the doctor, the examiner says he wants to do some tests, he wants to check my nervous system.

(Now she speaks with firmness.)

And I am thinking, I don't know how our nervous systems are, but I hope we never have nerve enough to go around kidnaping people right off the highways, as he has done! And, oh, he tells me to take off my dress, he tells me to take off my dress, and then before I even have a chance hardly to stand up to do it, the examiner—my dress has a zipper down the back? Yes, it has a zipper down the back. And the examiner unzips it, and so I slip my dress off. And I don't have my dress or shoes on. And there's next, over the stool and sort of in the middle of the room, there's a table, some kind of a table. It's not up very high, I'd say the height of the desk. So I lie down on the table, on my back, and he brings over this—oh, how can I describe it? They're like needles, a whole cluster of needles, and each needle has a wire going from it. I think it's something like a TV screen, you know. When the picture isn't on, you get all kinds of lines. Something like that. And so, he puts me down on the table, and they bring the needles over, and they don't stick them in me. No, not really like sticking a needle into a person, but they touch me with the needles. It doesn't hurt . . .

(At times, she pauses, as if waiting for the process to be completed.)

Except—where was it? Someplace. He just touches, and I feel just the needle touching, that's all. It doesn't hurt at all. But then he does it all up in the back of my ears, and in here somehow . . .

(She points to different parts of her head.)

and up here. Up in all different spots of my head. And then he probes more of my neck here and in through here somehow or other.

(She indicates her arms.)

And then down here . . . I don't know, then he puts it on my knee, and when he did, my leg jumped. And then on my foot, too. He did it around my ankle, somehow or other. And then they have me roll over on my stomach, and they touch all along my back. They touch with these needles, somehow or other. I don't know what they're doing, but they seem to be so happy about whatever they're doing. So then they roll me over on my back, and the examiner has a long needle in his hand. And I see the needle. And it's bigger than any needle that I've ever seen. And I ask him what he's going to do with it . . .

(She is beginning to get upset again.)

It won't hurt me. And I ask him what, and he said he just wants to put it in my navel, it's just a simple test.

(More rapid sobbing.)

And I tell him, no, it will hurt, don't do it, don't do it. And I'm crying, and I'm telling him, "It's hurting, it's hurting, take it out, take it out!"

And the leader comes over and he puts his hand, rubs his hand in front of my eyes, and he says it will be all right. I won't feel it.

(She becomes calmer.)

And all the pain goes away. The pain goes away, but I'm still sore from where they put that needle. I don't know why they put that needle into my navel. Because I told them they shouldn't do it.

(Another pause.)

DOCTOR

Did they make any sexual advances to you?

BETTY

No.

DOCTOR

They didn't?

BETTY

No. I asked the leader, I said, "Why did they, why did they put that needle in my navel?" And he said it was a pregnancy test. I said, "I don't know what they expected, but that was no pregnancy test here." And he didn't say any more.

DOCTOR

All right. We'll stop here now. You'll be relieved, relaxed and at ease. Perfectly at ease, comfortable and relaxed. When I wake you up, you will not remember anything that has transpired here. You will not remember anything that has transpired here until I tell you to recall it.
(He repeats the last phrase for emphasis.)

But it will not trouble you, and you will not be worried about it. You'll be comfortable and relaxed and at ease. No pains, no aches, no anxieties. You have no fear, no anxiety; you are comfortable and relaxed . . . You may wake now. . . .

(Betty opens her eyes slowly.)

BETTY

Am I all the way awake?

DOCTOR

You are awake completely. What happened?

Waked—awake—waked up? Head feels fuzzy.

(She laughs lightly.)

DOCTOR

Feel all right now?

BETTY

Yes.

DOCTOR

That's good. We'll continue next time. A week from today. Same time.

(Betty is dismissed by the doctor.)

*   *   *

Betty woke up from her long session feeling drowsy, much as if she had been awakened from a normal night's sleep. She found herself looking around the office, a little startled, and was vaguely aware that she had been slightly upset.

"Somehow I had the feeling I had been crying," she recalls, "You've heard of people crying in their sleep, and the person wakes up, and they're sort of conscious that they've been crying in their sleep. I had this feeling. I really didn't have the feeling of actually awakening completely for about two days. I felt sort of in a daze, a shock, and it was difficult for me to concentrate. I felt that if I just closed my eyes, I would go right back to sleep again." In the car, Barney kept asking Betty about her reaction. She explained that she felt all right, but that she didn't feel up to talking about it. They spent Saturday night with some friends near Boston, but most of the time Betty felt exhausted and was not very good company.

However, she was more composed after a few days, and, as the doctor had suggested, calm and relaxation took over.

She did not know at the time, nor did Barney, that her recall was almost identical with the long report she had written about her dreams.

CHAPTER EIGHT

After Betty's first extensive session, Dr. Simon dictated in his notes:

> This interview went on rather smoothly until the areas of fear in the latter part of the sighting of the flying object, when she began to show marked disturbances. Tears were running down her cheeks; she squirmed in her chair. The same occurred with very marked agitation during the procedure that appeared to be taking place in the strange object. During the apparent medical examination, tears were running down Mrs. Hill's cheeks, her nose was running. Although she accepted a Kleenex quite readily, it was felt best to stop at this point, even though she was still in the "operating room," because of the degree of agitation which ensued. Both were given appointments to return a week from today.

They did, on March 14, 1964. Just before the Hills came into the office for Betty's second session, Dr. Simon made a few preliminary remarks on the tape:

> The Hills are expected at 8:00 this morning. And the examination of Mrs. Hill will be continued from the point at which it was stopped a week ago, just after the instrument had been removed from her navel for the "pregnancy test."

Before putting Betty into trance, however, the doctor chatted with her informally.

BETTY

I think I ought to tell you before we start that I had two nightmares since I was here last week.

DOCTOR

Would you say they were dreams or nightmares?

BETTY

I'd say they were nightmares.

DOCTOR

And the first one was when?

BETTY

On Tuesday night.

DOCTOR

The Tuesday after you saw me? What was it about?

BETTY

I can't remember what that one was about. I can remember water, a lake, I think, and a shoreline. But I can't remember any more about it.

DOCTOR

Make you think of anything? Any particular lake?

BETTY

No.

DOCTOR

What about the other dream then?

BETTY

The other one was that—I don't know where I was—there was a light, and it was bouncing all around. And I could see this light. It would bounce toward me and then away. And I felt as though I was in great danger from the light, and that it was going to touch me. It was going to shine on me, and I didn't want this to happen. And just as it was coming toward me, I woke up. I was trying to scream, I don't know if I did scream or not. But I woke myself up.

DOCTOR

Did Barney know about it?

BETTY

Well, it frightened me so much, I woke him up.

DOCTOR

You sleep in twin beds?

166

BETTY

No, double bed.

DOCTOR

You deliberately woke him up?

BETTY

Yes.

DOCTOR

Apparently you must not have screamed, then.

BETTY

I don't think I did.

DOCTOR

Did this resemble anything—you remember your UFO experience—where you had this vehicle coming close to you. Was it anything like that, or was it different?

BETTY

This was like the light of a flashlight. This type of thing. And then it was bounding around, it was small.

DOCTOR

It was small. Not like a spotlight somewhere?

BETTY

It would seem like a spotlight.

DOCTOR

Like an operating-room light? Or something like that?

BETTY

Smaller than that.

DOCTOR

Anything like a light that some doctors would wear on a head mirror?

BETTY

I think it would be larger than that. I would say probably about six or eight inches in diameter.

167

DOCTOR

All right. Outside of that, everything has been all right? You haven't been worried or upset about our last session? Or don't you remember anything about it?

BETTY

I think I do.

DOCTOR

What do you think you remember?

BETTY

I remember crying, and I could remember, well, I think I remember sitting in the car and watching Barney out on the highway. And seeing men in the road.

DOCTOR

You saw men in the road? Can you envision them now?

BETTY

Yes.

DOCTOR

What do they look like?

BETTY

Not clear enough to make anything out.

DOCTOR

They look like ordinary American men?

BETTY

No. They're different somehow.

DOCTOR

Different in what way?

BETTY

I don't know.

DOCTOR

Was there a vehicle in the road? A car, motorcycle?

BETTY

No.

168

DOCTOR

Just men in the road? Dressed in any special sort of clothes? Uniforms, or some standard form of dress?

BETTY

I think they were all dressed alike, but I couldn't see, couldn't describe how they were dressed.

DOCTOR

Do you have any idea of why you were crying? You say you remember, you think you remember, crying?

BETTY

Why do I think I was crying? Because I was scared.

DOCTOR

What were you scared of?

BETTY

Because I knew something was going to happen, and I didn't know what it was.

DOCTOR

All right. Now we'll continue.

(The doctor gives the cue word; Betty's eyes close immediately.)

Deep, deep asleep, deep asleep, far asleep. You're fully relaxed, very, very deep asleep. Deeper and deeper asleep. Deeper and deeper, very, very, deep asleep. You're comfortable and relaxed. No fear, no anxiety, very deep asleep. We will go back to where we were a week ago, just where we left off in your experience. Just exactly where we left off. Where are you now?

BETTY

(In deep trance now.)

I'm on the table and the leader, they had hurt me by putting a needle in my navel. And the leader had run his hand in front of my eyes, and when he did this, all the pain . . . I didn't have any more pain. It went away. And I felt very relaxed, and I felt grateful to him because he stopped the pain.

169

DOCTOR

About this needle, is there anything attached to it? Like a wire or tube?

BETTY

Yes.

DOCTOR

What did it look like?

BETTY

It was a long needle. I would say it looked like a regular needle used for injections. Or maybe to take blood out. I don't know.

DOCTOR

Was there a syringe attached to it?

BETTY

There was something. And I don't know why they did it. It was some kind of test. And I didn't want them to do it. I said it would hurt, and the leader said it wouldn't. When his hand went over my eyes, the pain stopped.

DOCTOR

How far in did he stick the needle?

BETTY

Oh, it was a long needle. I don't know, I thought it—I didn't look, but I would say the needle was four inches long—six, maybe.

DOCTOR

Did you say something was attached to it. Like a wire or a tube?

BETTY

Like a tube. And they didn't leave it in very long. Just for a second.

DOCTOR

What kind of pain was it? Was it like the pain you get when you put a needle in your arm? I guess you have given blood, or something like that.

BETTY

No, it wasn't like that. It was—all I could think of was a knife.

DOCTOR

Like a knife.

BETTY

Because it was such, so much pain. I was—I think I was moaning and couldn't lie still.

DOCTOR

Was there a light there?

BETTY

The room was brightly lighted.

DOCTOR

Was there any kind of spotlight?

BETTY

Yes. There was a light behind my left shoulder. Like a spotlight.

DOCTOR

How big was it?

BETTY

Oh, it was like a desk light. I don't know. Six inches.

DOCTOR

All right. Go on.

BETTY

Then, I was grateful to the leader for stopping the pain. And he seemed to be very surprised. And so they said that was the end of the testing. And the leader helped me sit up. He took hold of my arm, and I swung around on the table.

DOCTOR

What sort of table was this? Was this an examining table? An operating table? As in a doctor's office?

BETTY

Like a regular examining table. It wasn't like the examining tables that some doctors—I don't know if all doctors have the same type of examining tables or not. This was more like a—it was a long table, but it wasn't awfully long. I guess it was like a regular examining table. It was light, well, I don't know. White or metal. It was metal, I know; it was hard. It wasn't soft in any way. That type of thing. So the examiner was helping me. He helped me get off the table, and I swung around. And he gave me my shoes, and I put those on and got down on the floor. And my dress was there, and I put my dress on. And I was going to zip it up, and he took hold of the zipper at the top and zipped it up. And then— oh, I said, "I can go now. I can go back to the car." And he said, "Barney isn't ready yet." And so then I begin to get worried, and I asked him why it was taking so long with Barney. And he said that they were doing a few more tests with him, but he'd be right along in a minute. And, gee, there was a cabinet there, and the doctor—the examiner—he had gone out of the room. There was just me and the leader there.

DOCTOR

So there was a doctor there, you say?

BETTY

The man who did the examining; he did the testing. And he left. So there was just the leader and me. I felt, I was grateful to him because he stopped my pain, and now I wasn't afraid at all. And so, I started talking with the leader. And I said to him that this had been quite an experience. It was unbelievable. That no one would ever, ever believe me. And that most people didn't know he was alive. And that what I needed was some proof that this had really happened. So he laughed, and he said what kind of proof did I want? What would I like? And I said, well, if he could give me something to take back with me then people would believe it. And so he told me to look around, and maybe I could find something I would like to take. And I did—and there wasn't much around—but on the cabinet there was a book, a fairly big book. So I put my hand on the book, and I said, "Could I have this?" And he told me to look in the book, and I did. It had pages, it had writing, but nothing like I had ever seen before. It looked almost like a—I don't know—it wasn't a dictionary—maybe a—it had the—the writing didn't go across, it went up and down.

DOCTOR

Did it look like any language that you know, or was it in English?

BETTY

No, it wasn't in English.

172

DOCTOR

Did it look like—what language do you know that goes up and down?

BETTY

I don't know it, but I can recognize it. I can't read it: Japanese.

DOCTOR

Japanese. Did this look like Japanese? This writing.

BETTY

No.

DOCTOR

Was it writing or printing?

BETTY

It was different. I don't know, because it was—I mean, I couldn't tell. Even though I have seen Japanese written, it had sharp lines, and they were, some were very thin and some were medium and some were very heavy. It had some dots. It had straight lines and curved lines. And the leader laughed and he asked me if I thought I could read it. And I told him no. I laughed too. I said no, but I wasn't taking it to read. But this was going to be my proof that this happened. That this—this was my proof. And so he said that I could have it. I could have the book if I wanted it. And I picked it up, and I was delighted. I mean this was, this was more than I had ever hoped for. And I'm standing there and I'm saying that I had never seen anything like the book and that I was very pleased that he had given it to me. And that maybe some way I could figure out in time how to read it. And so then I said, I asked him where he was from. Because I said that I knew he wasn't from the earth, and I wanted to know where he did come from. And he asked if I knew anything about the universe. And I told him no. I knew practically nothing. That when I was in graduate school we were taught that the sun was the center of the solar system, and there were nine planets. And then later, of course, we did make advances. And I told him about seeing, I think I met him at one time, Harlow Shapley; he wrote a book, too. And I had seen photographs that he had taken of millions and millions of stars in the universe. But that was about all I knew. So, he said that he wished I knew more about this, and I said I wish I did, too. And he went across the room to the head of the table and he did something, he opened up, it wasn't like a drawer, he sort of did some-

173

thing, and the metal of the wall, there was an opening. And he pulled out a map, and he asked me had I ever seen a map like this before. And I walked across the room and I leaned against the table. And I looked at it. And it was a map—it was an oblong map. It wasn't square. It was a lot wider than it was long. And there were all these dots on it. And they were scattered all over it. Some were little, just pin points. And others were as big as a nickel. And there were lines, there were on some of the dots, there were curved lines going from one dot to another. And there was one big circle, and it had a lot of lines coming out from it. A lot of lines going to another circle quite close, but not as big. And these were heavy lines. And I asked him what they meant. And he said that the heavy lines were trade routes. And then the other lines, the other lines, the solid lines were places they went occasionally. And he said the broken lines were expeditions . . .

So I asked him where was his home port, and he said, "Where were you on the map?" I looked and laughed and said, "I don't know." So he said, "If you don't know where you are, then there isn't any point of my telling where I am from." And he put the map—the map rolled up, and he put it back in the space in the wall and closed it. I felt very stupid because I did not know where the earth was on the map. I asked him would he open up the map again and show me where the earth was, and he again laughed. And I thought, well, I still have the book—it's a big book. I went back to the cabinet and put the book down and started to look through it again. All of a sudden, there's this noise in the hall. Some of the other men came in and with them is the examiner. They are quite excited, so I asked the leader what's the matter with them. Did something happen to Barney? It has something to do with Barney. The examiner has me open my mouth, and he starts checking my teeth. And they are tugging at them. I asked them what they are trying to do.

DOCTOR

What are they doing with them?

BETTY

They were tugging, pulling at them. They were very excited.

(She laughs.)

The examiner said that they could not figure it out—Barney's teeth came out, and mine didn't. I was really laughing, and said Barney had dentures, and I didn't, and that is why his teeth came out. So then they asked me, "What are dentures?" And I said people as they got older lost their teeth. They had to go to a dentist and have their teeth extracted, and they put in dentures. Or a person sometimes—Barney had to have dentures because he had a mouth injury. He had to have his teeth extracted. And the leader said, "Well, does this happen to many people?" He was—uh—he acted as if he didn't believe me. And I said, "Yes, it happens to almost everyone as they get older." And he said, "Well—older. What is older?" I said, "Old age." So he said, "What is old age?" And I said—"Well, it varies, but as a person gets older there are changes in him, particularly physically. He begins to sort of break down with age." So he said, "What is age? What did I mean by age?" And I said, "The life span—the length of time people lived." He said, "How long was this?" And I said, "Well, I think a life span is supposed to be about a hundred years at the most. People can die before that—most of them do—because of disease, accident, this type of thing. And I think the average length of time—I don't know—was sixty-five or seventy." So he said, "Sixty-five or seventy what? What did I mean?" I said, "Years." He said, "What is a year?" And I said I did not know exactly how it was figured out, but it had to do with how many days, and the days had so many hours, and the hours had so many minutes, and the minutes had so many seconds. And I thought that in the beginning time had—depended on the rotation of the earth and the position of the planets and the seasons and all. And I had my watch on, and I showed him from twelve to twelve could be from midnight to noon to midnight. I tried to explain, but he did not understand what I was saying. And I couldn't—I don't know—

DOCTOR

But he did understand English?

BETTY

Yes. So then he asked me, well what did we eat? And I said, we ate meat, potatoes, vegetables, milk. And so he asked me, "What are vegetables?" And I said that this is a broad term and could cover a great variety of certain kinds of foods we eat. But I couldn't just explain what vegetables are, there were too many. And he said was there one kind I liked. I said that I ate a great many, but my favorite is squash. So he said, "Tell me about squash." So I said that it was yellow, usually, in color. And he said, "What is yellow?" So I said, "Well, I will show you." And I started looking around the room, and I couldn't find anything yellow at all. And I wasn't wearing anything yellow. I told him I couldn't show him what the color was, but it was a bright color—something like—we consider sunlight yellow. And there was no sense talking about vegetables, because I couldn't explain what I meant. And —oh! I said, "I can't—I don't know how to do this. I can't tell you where the earth is on the map, I don't know. All these things you ask me—I am a very limited person, when trying to talk to you. But there are other people in this country who are not like me. They would be most happy to talk with him, and they could answer all his questions. And maybe if he could come back, all his questions would have answers. But if I did, I wouldn't know where to meet him." And he laughed, and said, "Don't worry, if we decide to come back, we will be able to find you all right. We always find those we want to." And I said, "Well, now what do you mean by that remark?" And he just laughed. And then Barney is coming. They are bringing Barney out. I hear the men out in the corridor. And I said, "Barney's coming." And he said, "Yes, you can go back to the car now." And I got the book, and Barney is coming up—and his eyes are still shut!

(She laughs again.)

He missed an awful lot. I wonder if they are making him keep his eyes closed. And so it is time to go back to the car, and the leader said, "Come on, we will walk back to the car with you." So I said, "All right, but I do wish I really knew if you were going to come back." And he said, "Well, we will see."

(She pauses a moment, then:)

And we are out in the corridor. Barney is behind me, with his eyes shut and a man on each side of him. And I am all ready to go down the ramp when some of the other men—not the leader—but some of the men are talking. I don't know what they are saying, but they are very excited. And then the leader comes over and takes my book. And I say—ohh— I'm furious.

(She is very intense, almost crying.)

And I said, "You promised that I could have the book." And he said, "I know it, but the others object." But I said, "This is my proof." And he said, "That is the whole point. They don't want you to know what has happened. They want you to forget all about it."

(Now she speaks as if talking to the leader.)

"I won't forget about it! You can take the book, but you can *never, never, never* make me forget! I'll remember it if it is the last thing I do." And he laughs, and says, "Maybe you will remember, I don't know. But I hope you don't. And it won't do you any good if you do, because Barney won't. Barney won't remember a single thing. And if you should remember anything at all, he is going to remember it differently from you. And all you are going to do is get each other so confused you will not know what to do. If you do remember, it would be better if you forgot it anyway."

(Again on the verge of crying.)

And I said, "Why? Are you trying to threaten me? Because you can't scare me, because I won't forget. I will remember it somehow." And then he said, "All right now, let's get back to the car." And I was standing there by the side of the ramp, and I'm not so mad now. They have taken Barney ahead, while we were talking. I said, "I do wish I could have some proof of this, because it is the most unbelievable thing that ever happened." We were walking, and the path—just a short distance—it doesn't seem as long as it did going in. Going in seemed awfully long. And he said, "I am going to leave you here. Why don't you stand by the side of the car and watch us leave?" So I said, "All right. I would like that. If we are not in danger from it." He said, "No, you will be far enough away from it." And he said he was sorry that I was badly frightened in the beginning. And I said, "Well, this has been a new experience, and I didn't know what was happening. But I certainly wasn't afraid now." It has been an amazing experience, and I don't know—maybe I would forget it. And I hoped that somehow we would meet again. Maybe he would come back, and there would be people who could answer his questions. And he said, well, he would try. And then they all turned around and started to go back. And I get up to the car, and Barney is inside. I open the car door, and I say, "Come on out and watch them leave." Barney is still in a fog, but his eyes are open, and he is acting more normally now. Delsey is sitting on the seat where I sit, so I felt Delsey, and she is trembling all over. I pick Delsey off the seat, and I'm patting her, and I say, "Don't be afraid, Delsey. There's nothing to be afraid of." I am leaning against the fender of the car, and Barney comes out and stands beside me. And we are going to watch them leave. Delsey won't look, she is still shaking. And it starts glowing—it is getting brighter and brighter.

DOCTOR

What is getting brighter?

BETTY

The object.

DOCTOR

This is the object you saw in the sky before?

BETTY

Yes. Only now it is a large ball, a big orange ball, and it is glowing, glowing, rolling just like a ball.

(Later, Barney and Betty were to recall this as what they felt was the huge moon that appeared to them to be on the ground.)

Now it does and goes down, and there is a dip, and then—zoom—it keeps going away farther and farther. And I say, well, Barney, there they go, and we are none the worse for the experience. Let's get in the car and head back to Portsmouth. And he goes around and gets in his side, and he is driving. I get in the other side. I put Delsey over in the back seat, on the floor, and pat her on the head and tell her she is a good dog. And Barney starts the car, and we start to ride. And I'm just so happy, and I said, "Well, Barney, now try to tell me that you don't believe in flying saucers." And Barney said, "Oh, don't be ridiculous!" And I think he is joking. But then all of a sudden we get this beep-beep-be—beep-beep on the trunk of the car again.

DOCTOR

This is the second time you are getting the beep?

BETTY

Yes. And I said, "Well, I guess that is their farewell. They are off, wherever they are going. And I don't know, it is just so fantastic I suppose we should forget all about it."

178

DOCTOR

What did you say to each other now?

BETTY

Well, when Barney said, "Don't be ridiculous," I don't know whether he is kidding me or not. So I don't say anything. And he says—so I know he is conscious of this—he said, "Look and see if you can see it around anymore." How can he look out and see something around, if he's going to deny its existence? So I do. I look around, and every once in a while, all the way home, I keep looking for it. And I keep wondering, have they gone? How far away have they gone? But I still have the feeling that they are very close. I keep looking for them. I look through the binoculars.

(Another long pause, then:)

Outside of Concord, north of Concord—we did not stop, but we slowed down very, very slowly and I was watching with the binoculars, and I didn't see them again. But I kept looking all the way home. We kept riding along, and I said, "We won't believe it—no one will. What the heck, let's forget about the whole thing. It is too fantastic. People will think we are crazy. I mean—just to talk about flying saucers, people will think—you know—way out." But this is so much more than seeing something go through the sky. I think I wanted to forget about it. I might as well. What could I do about it? But I wonder if they ever will come back. I go around looking for them. And I look out the window in the kitchen at home.

(Betty repeats the details about arriving home in daylight, un-
packing, taking a tub and going to bed exhausted. Then:)

DOCTOR

Your memory is sharp now. Did you at some time tell Barney about your experience? About being in the vehicle?

BETTY

No.

DOCTOR

And he didn't speak to you about being in the vehicle?

BETTY

I can't remember any time he mentioned being inside of it.

DOCTOR

Well, go on.

BETTY

I'm puzzled now as to why we didn't talk about it.

(Months later, after the therapy was over, the Hills summarized their thoughts on this question by comparing it to their hypnosis sessions, where they had no memory whatever about what they said, until they were instructed to remember by the doctor.)

Because you would assume that we would. I don't understand it myself. We just said, well, it is an amazing experience, and that is all I said.

DOCTOR

You had two experiences, you say. One of having sighted this thing and seeing the recognizable people. The other experience of being in the vehicle. These were two different experiences.

BETTY

But to me, well, the first one was so small. Actually, all I did was to see it flying through the air and over the front of the car. And you know, I didn't get too much of a look at it. The other part was so overwhelming in comparison.

DOCTOR

Why would you want to keep it a secret?

BETTY

Because I wanted to please the leader, because he told me to forget about it.

DOCTOR

You wanted to please the leader?

BETTY

He told me to forget about it. This had been their decision.

DOCTOR

Why did you want to please this leader so much?

BETTY

I don't know.

DOCTOR

Then you might wonder why Barney didn't talk about it. Do you think he wanted to please the leader?

BETTY

Maybe. Because I am quite sure that he was—well, his eyes were closed. But I think he had some consciousness of it, of what was going on.

DOCTOR

What had they done to him?

BETTY

They had done something that made him keep his eyes shut. And they had to help him along, walking out to the object. And before we left, they were guiding him somewhat. But I think he was walking mostly under his own power.

(She pauses again.)

DOCTOR

Yes, go on.

BETTY

Maybe it was the fear of remembering it, too. It was something about the way he said it was better to forget it. Almost like a threat. And then I think maybe I wanted to forget it myself. I don't know—I was going to say I wanted to forget it myself, but that sounds like a rationalization. Because I really don't know if I wanted to forget. I just couldn't remember it. I can remember parts, but I couldn't remember other parts. It seems to be the part between the beepings.

(Again, after the therapy, in talking to the writer when their conscious minds were allowed to review all the data revealed on the recordings of the sessions, the Hills concluded that the original series of beepings seemed to put them in a trance-like state, which later became deeper on encountering the roadblock. The second series of beepings seemed to restore them to consciousness, although they recall remaining in a dazed condition most of the way home to Portsmouth.)

181

BETTY

It's very hard to understand. There seems to be the part between Indian Head and where we were stopped on the road. The part where I felt it should be forgotten.

DOCTOR

Why should it be forgotten?

BETTY

I don't know. But there was this beep in the beginning, and then I didn't remember anything. I remember somehow Barney turning off the main road, until we saw the men standing there in the road . . .

DOCTOR

How could you see? Did they have lights?

BETTY

I could see the shapes. I could see, you know, when you're driving at . . . along at night, and there's a group or something in the highway, and your headlights on, they show up. We couldn't get by. But I don't remember anything from then up to that time. I don't know how far we rode, or anything. Something must have happened in between in that period. Even if I was just looking at scenery.

DOCTOR

(Pursuing the dream possibility.)

Did you stop to sleep?

BETTY

To sleep? No, I don't think so. I mean I think I would know if we did. I don't have any knowledge of what happened until we saw the men in the road. And then all this happened. Yet we saw the men. Then there was the beeping again. I know I wanted to forget about it.

DOCTOR

When Barney took Delsey out of the car before all this, were you worried?

BETTY

I wasn't worried then. I was watching out for other cars coming along the road.

182

Could you have gone to sleep in the car when Barney was out with the dog?

BETTY

No.

DOCTOR

What about when Barney walked away from you, and you stayed in the car?

BETTY

Oh, this was when the object was over us, when Barney was walking away from the car towards it . . .

DOCTOR

Did you go to sleep when he was out there?

BETTY

No.

DOCTOR

All right. Now, the next morning, you wished you had a Geiger counter. What happened then?

(Betty repeats in detail the long story of seeing the shiny spots on the car, calling the Pease Air Force Base, watching the compass needle react to the shiny spots, calling her sister. She recalls that when she waxed the car some time later, the spots did not disappear, but actually became shinier. She recounts how she wrote NICAP in Washington and her desire to find out every-. thing she could about the subject of UFO's. At the conclusion of the story, the doctor closed her portion of the session and brings Barney in to check his experiences against some of the material Betty had given him.)

DOCTOR

(After he puts Barney in a trance. Betty, of course, has been dismissed at this point.)

Now Barney, I want to review with you a few points of your experience when you were apparently taken aboard this unidentified object. You are back now, you are comfortable and relaxed. But you are back—back when you were in the road. Tell me about these men.

BARNEY

(In his usual monotone. It is important to remember that neither Barney nor Betty is aware of either his own or the other's story.)

We're coming down the road, and they're waving to me . . .

DOCTOR

Waving to you?

BARNEY

Yes. Their hands were not up, but down. In a motion that indicated for me to stop.

(He later described it as a sideways, swinging motion.)

DOCTOR

Was there a vehicle there?

BARNEY

No, there was no vehicle.

DOCTOR

What light was there? Headlights?

BARNEY

It was just an orange light.

DOCTOR

An orange light.

BARNEY

And I could see this orange glow. And I started to put—to get out of my car, and put one foot on the ground. And two men were standing beside me, helping me out. And I felt very relaxed, yet very frightened.

DOCTOR

Did they identify themselves in any way?

BARNEY

No. They didn't say anything.

DOCTOR

Did they indicate what they wanted?

BARNEY

They didn't say anything. And I knew I was walking, or moving down the road from the position of where my car was parked. And I could see the ramp that I went up. And I closed my eyes.

DOCTOR

Where was this ramp going?

BARNEY

To a doorway. A doorway of a very, very funny shape. Like a doorway into a very strange looking craft. And I stepped inside. And I heard a voice, just like the voice I heard on the highway back at Indian Head, telling me that no harm would come to me. And I keep my eyes closed.

DOCTOR

You didn't actually hear it at that time?

BARNEY

That was what I couldn't understand.

DOCTOR

You thought the leader in the vehicle was talking to you?

BARNEY

Yes.

DOCTOR

That was the voice you thought you heard?

BARNEY

Yes.

DOCTOR

You didn't actually hear it, then?

BARNEY

That was what I couldn't understand.

DOCTOR

You think it was transmitted to you, or something?

BARNEY

Yes. I went down this corridor, just a few steps, and into another door.

DOCTOR

They were leading you?

BARNEY

They were holding me on both sides. And I went in. And I thought my foot stumbled over a bulkhead right at the base of the door.

DOCTOR

Was Betty around?

BARNEY

No. Betty wasn't with me. And I saw this table, and knew I would go over to it. I was carried . . . walked over to it. And I just knew I was to get on this table.

DOCTOR

What did this table look like? An operating table? examining table?

BARNEY

It looked like an operating table.

DOCTOR

An operating table. What is the difference between an operating table and an examining table?

BARNEY

Or an examining table. I don't know. I just knew that I could be supported fully on it. And it was very plain. Nothing elaborate. Just that I could lie on it. And my feet extended out from the bottom of it, overlapped it from the position I was lying in. And I felt my shoes being removed. And I could hear a humming sound that they seemed to be making. I was very afraid to open my eyes. I had been told not to open my eyes, and it would be over with quickly. And I could feel them examining me with their hands. . . . They looked at my back, and I could feel them touching my skin right down my back. As if they were counting my spinal column. And I felt something touch right at the base of my spine, like a finger pushing. A single finger.

DOCTOR

Did they speak at all to you?

BARNEY

I could only hear this low, humming sort of sound . . .

186

(He demonstrates it. It sounds like mmm-mm-mm-mm-mmm-mm.)

And then I was turned over, and again I was looked at. And my mouth was opened, and I could feel two fingers pulling it back. And then I heard as if some more men came in. And I could feel them rustling around on the left side of the table I was lying on. And something scratched very lightly, like a stick, against my left arm. And then these men left. And I was left with what I thought were three men. But the two who had brought me in and the other one who seemed to follow these two men—there were more than one person in the room. But only one man seemed to be moving around my body all the time. Then my shoes were put back on, and I stepped down. And I think I felt very good because I knew it was over. And again, I was led to the door where my feet kicked against this thing at the very bottom of the door, like a high door jamb. And I stepped over it and went back toward the ramp. And I went down and opened my eyes and kept walking. And I saw my car, and the lights were out. And it was sitting down the road and very dark. And I couldn't understand. I had not turned off the lights. And I opened the door and felt for Delsey and got in. And I sat on the tire wrench, and I took it, removed it from the seat and put it on the floor. And Betty was coming down the road, and she came around and opened the door.

DOCTOR

Was she alone?

BARNEY

She was alone. And she was grinning. And I thought at that time she must have made a road stop in the woods. And she got into the car, and said, "Well, no one will believe this." Or I might have said it, because I said, "No, no one. This is so ridiculous. No one will believe it." And I was thinking what had happened and that we were sitting there, looking down the road, and I could see this glow get brighter and brighter. And we said, "Oh, my God, not again." And away it went. And then I put on the lights and started the car up and drove silently down the road. And I thought I must have driven twenty miles, and I came back to Route 3.

DOCTOR

What did you say to Betty?

Betty said to me, "Well, do you believe in flying saucers?" And I said, "Oh, Betty, don't be ridiculous."

DOCTOR

Did you tell her about your experience in this vehicle?

BARNEY

I had forgotten the experience.

(Both Betty and Barney maintained under the stiffest questioning that their memories for these experiences were immediately wiped out after they left the vehicle . . . until the hypnosis restored them.)

DOCTOR

You had forgotten.

BARNEY

Yes.

DOCTOR

Did she tell you about her experience?

BARNEY

No. She did not.

DOCTOR

Then neither of you spoke about your experiences in the vehicle?

BARNEY

No.

DOCTOR

(He is fully aware that they have consciously claimed that they had no memory of their joint experience, but he is continuing to test under hypnosis.)

Why not?

BARNEY

I didn't remember it.

DOCTOR

I see. This memory had just been wiped out? Do you think that she had seen the vehicle?

188

BARNEY

I didn't know.

DOCTOR

And you don't know it today?

BARNEY

No.

DOCTOR

All right, then. We'll stop there.

* * *

Dr. Simon woke Barney from his trance, and the session was terminated for the day. Out of it had come the confirmation that Betty's recall under hypnosis paralleled her dreams almost exactly. Dr. Simon did not know at the time that Barney, because he was embarrassed about Betty's dreams and wouldn't consider their basis in reality, had persuaded Betty not to talk out her dreams with the doctor until he asked about them. Betty had agreed not to bring them up until she was asked, in order not to unduly influence the doctor. He was to explore the dreams later as the therapy progressed, along with other aspects of the puzzling case that had to be reexamined.

First, there was the nature of the experience. What was real? What was not? Barney might have certain anxieties on a trip away from home because of his racial sensitivity. Certain fears might be exaggerated under these conditions, making Barney excessively sensitive.

The question marks were obvious: How could two people describe similarly a complex phenomenon in detail, both in the conscious state and under deep hypnosis? How could they recount remarkably similar details of an abduction by humanoid intelligent beings which defied any encounter documented in history, when neither was aware of what the other had seen or reported under hypnosis to the doctor? Did this or did this not happen?

If a person were a believer that hypnosis is absolute, that the individual under hypnosis cannot produce anything but the truth, and if both the Hills were fully under hypnosis, then he would believe their story. The weight of authoritative evidence indicates that in hypnosis what the subject believes determines what is truth to him. Consequently, the truth of the Hill's experience was determined by the strength

189

of their conviction. Where the likelihood of lying is slim, the possibility of reporting a fantasy, fully believed by the subject as true, was a possibility. The probability of two similar fantasies, reported by two different people is slight. What is the answer?

The story at this point could be assessed from two polar points of view: the Hills were lying or the experience was true. An outright lie on one hand and the truth on the other. But what about in between? One possibility: hallucinations. A person may have a temporary hallucination in a period of extreme fear.

In spectrum form, the possibilities at this stage might be considered as follows:

1. The incident was a complete lie.
Dr. Simon did not accept this possibility. He felt the Hills were sincere, credible people, telling what they believed to be the truth both consciously and in the trance state.

2. The incident was a dual hallucination.
The doctor also felt this was improbable. Throughout the sessions, there were no indications of this.

3. The incident was a dream or illusion.
This would be explored in detail as a possibility, that an actual experience had taken place on a sensitized background. A background existed on which could be imprinted illusions or fantasies, later to be reexperienced in dreams.

4. The incident was a reality—the abduction took place.
This type of experience had never been documented reliably with any convincing evidence. The doctor believed this to be too improbable, and much material was similar to dream material.

The conscious sighting of UFO's, in the light of reports from scientists, technicians, Air Force personnel, airline pilots, and radar men all over the world remained a distinct possibility, if not a probability. Further, the Hills' honesty seemed sure. They corroborated each other's story both consciously and under hypnosis.

By substantially ruling out lying and hallucinating, the doctor began to weigh the evidence of illusory elaboration, especially an examination of the dreams involved.

Betty did have dreams. Elaborate dreams. Dreams that were repeated in detail under hypnosis. The doctor had examined in Barney's session whether he, too, fell asleep on the road and dreamed the abduction. Barney was convinced that he did not fall asleep on the trip, and the doctor was willing to accept this.

After the first sessions with Barney, Dr. Simon began to assume that the illusions and fantasies were his—and that Betty had absorbed them from him. But in the following sessions, Betty, under hypnosis, confirmed Barney's experiences to a remarkably close degree. This might have been conscious collusion. But here were two people, neither aware of what he was saying, who were telling identical stories (which the Hills weren't permitted to know until later). If the story couldn't be accepted as truth, a rational alternative, given every kind of test, was needed. The doctor would be alert to absurdities and incongruities in finding an explanation that would either support or refute.

With the completion of Betty's second trance, it appeared that the reverse of the doctor's initial assumption might be true. If the total experience were not true, a dream of fantasy initiated by Betty might have been absorbed by Barney, who appeared to be more suggestible. Dr. Simon noted that the things Barney experienced in the abduction portion of the incident were in Betty's story. On the other hand, very little of Betty's abduction sequence was included in his story. His recall of being taken through the woods was vague compared to hers. The details of the examination aboard the craft were much more extensive in Betty's story than in his.

If this assumption were true, then the question of how Betty's dreams were absorbed by Barney would have to be carefully examined.

By the time of the next session on March 21, 1964, the following Saturday morning, Dr. Simon planned to work on the theory that somehow Barney had absorbed and been influenced by Betty's dreams, and that Betty's dreams had developed into convictions that seemed real to her. This possibility had been suggested by a friend.

As with Betty on the previous week, the doctor conversed with Barney before putting him into a trance. At the beginning of the conversation, Barney told the doctor that for the first time in his life he had dreamed about UFO's, on three different nights over the past week—on Sunday, Tuesday and Wednesday. The dream was a recurring one: Barney was standing on the ground looking at UFO's in the sky, and Betty was screaming about them.

The discussion continued for several minutes, with Barney reviewing how he had casually brought up the UFO story to Dr. Stephens, which in turn had led to the Hills' visit to Dr. Simon.

191

DOCTOR

(Barney is still fully conscious—has not yet been put into trance.)

Also—Betty had been troubled with dreams and nightmares.

BARNEY

Yes. She had been.

DOCTOR

Is that right?

BARNEY

Yes. That's correct.

DOCTOR

(He is going to press hard on the dream aspect now, both in conscious and trance parts of the session.)

And she told you about these things. She told you about these in ordinary conversation?

BARNEY

Yes.

DOCTOR

Did you ever witness any of her nightmares?

BARNEY

No, I had not.

DOCTOR

You were always asleep.

BARNEY

Yes.

DOCTOR

Now, you two sleep in a double bed?

BARNEY

Yes. We do.

DOCTOR

Does Betty talk in her sleep?

BARNEY

No. She doesn't.

DOCTOR

As far as you know, she doesn't.

BARNEY

I know she doesn't.

DOCTOR

She does not.

BARNEY

Or when I am awake sometimes, and she's asleep. I've never heard her.

DOCTOR

You've never heard her talk in her sleep.

BARNEY

No.

DOCTOR

Now—when she described these dreams, how much did she tell you about them? What did she tell you she had dreamed?

BARNEY

She would tell me that somehow she is wondering if there is a reference or relationship of her dreams to the missing time period up there in the White Mountains.

DOCTOR

This missing time period—it was pointed out by Mr. Hohman?

BARNEY

He thought it was interesting that the distance between Ashland and Indian Head, which is about thirty-five miles, he thought it was interesting that we just couldn't recall anything about that part of the journey. And I just couldn't seem to recall. And I thought I was just probably driving my car.

DOCTOR

You hadn't been aware that the trip took an excessively long time?

BARNEY

No.

Only when Mr. Hohman pointed it out did it seem to be the case?

BARNEY

Yes. He thought it was interesting when we said we heard these beeping sounds at Indian Head, and then we picked up the story by saying, "And then when we reached Ashland, we heard this beeping sound again." So he said, "Well, what happened in between the period of time, those thirty-five miles?" And I just couldn't seem to recall. Then I realized that I had been driving for a period of time with no knowledge of passing anything, or going down Route 3 in this section.

DOCTOR

Did you pass any cars? Meet any people?

BARNEY

No. We did not.

DOCTOR

So you were particularly impressed by this lapse of time?

BARNEY

No, I wasn't.

DOCTOR

And Betty wasn't. All right.

(The doctor now proceeds to put Barney in a trance, with the usual instructions.)

And now you recall fully all the experiences that we have talked about in this office. All of them—and all of your feelings. But they will not upset you any more. You will recall all of your feelings and all of your experiences. I want to go back and talk about the experiences you had being stopped in the road by some men in dark clothes. Now: from whom did you learn about this experience? You didn't really have it, did you?

BARNEY

(Now in full trance.)

I was hypnotized.

DOCTOR

You were hypnotized. By whom?

194

By Dr. Simon.

*(Barney disassociates the present Dr. Simon in a hypnotic relation-
ship from the Dr. Simon of a past session.)*

Yes, that's true.

*(The doctor now begins to test the extent of Betty's influence over
Barney. He must be careful, though, of unduly influencing the subject, because of the high suggestibility hypnosis creates.)*

But somebody told you something else about it. Who was that?

Betty.

And how did she tell you about it?

She said that she had a dream and that she had been taken aboard a
UFO. And that I was also in her dream and taken aboard.

How did she tell you this?

Usually when someone was visiting. And I just told her it was a dream
and nothing to be alarmed about. She told me a great many of the details of the dreams. She would tell me that she had gone into the UFO
and talked to the people there on board. And she was told that she
would forget. And she told these people in the UFO that she would not
forget. And I told her they were only dreams and that I can't believe
that, whatever these things are. But she says no. That somehow she
feels there is a connection between these dreams and what happened.
Because she has never dreamed of UFO's before. And she would tell
me that they stuck something in her navel. And she was not telling this
to me, but I would be listening as she told this to Walter Webb, as she
told about the UFO sighting that we had had. And then I would hear
her dreams. But never did she tell me directly about her dreams.

*(Barney is now correcting himself from the statement that Betty
told him her dreams directly.)*

DOCTOR

But she did tell you something about them?

BARNEY

Only that they had come into the room with my teeth, and they were
quite startled that my teeth would come out and hers would not.

DOCTOR

How about the other things you described to me, about what happened
to you when they were examining you. Did she tell you about that?

*(Again: Was Barney's recall only that which Betty had put into
his mind?)*

BARNEY

No. She never told me that. I was lying on the table, and I felt them examining me.

DOCTOR

Is this part of Betty's dream?

BARNEY
(Firmly.)

I am telling you what actually happened. At the time Betty was telling
about her dream, I was very puzzled, because I never knew this happened. Now I have found out that it did.

DOCTOR
(More testing, more challenging.)

Now all this dream about being taken aboard—and all the details about it,
this was all told to you by Betty, wasn't it?

BARNEY

No. Betty never told me. Only about my teeth.

DOCTOR

Only about your teeth.

DOCTOR

How do you know this happened?

BARNEY

I was hypnotized by Dr. Simon. He has made me go back to September
19, 1961, when I left Montreal, and I told what was happening to me

196

each time he asked. And I talked to people I had never seen before. And I knew that I had seen a UFO, and I came to Indian Head and had gotten out of my car and walked toward this UFO, and I could not believe it was there. And yet I could not make it go away.

(Now Barney becomes emotionally upset again.)

And I felt compelled to go closer—and I prayed to God to make me—
(He breaks down in sobs.)

DOCTOR

This won't trouble you now. Just take it easy.

BARNEY

(A little calmer now.)

And I prayed that I could get away and run back to the car. And I did. And the eyes kept following me back to my car. And I felt very, very upset. . . .

(The doctor lets him go on to recount the Indian Head part of the story again. There are no inconsistencies revealed; it is the same as he has always related it. Then Barney continues into the amnesic period.)

And I kept driving and driving. And I made a turn, and I never knew the reason—and—well—I made that turn. I turned to the left, and I found we were in a strange area where I had never been before. And I was very uncomfortable, and somehow the eyes were following me, telling me that I could be calm, that I would not be harmed, that I should relax. And I saw these men coming down toward me.

DOCTOR

Now what about these men on the road. Are you sure they were there?

BARNEY

(Very firmly.)

They were there. And I never knew this. I never knew this. Because I was hypnotized by Dr. Simon, and he told me I would relate this, and I related this . . .

DOCTOR

(Bluntly.)

Did you dream this?

197

BARNEY

No. I did not dream it.

DOCTOR

You mean these men actually stopped you?

BARNEY

Yes.

DOCTOR

All right. Go on from there.

BARNEY

And I started to get out of my car. And I felt myself supported by two men, and my eyes were closed . . .

DOCTOR

(It is obvious that Barney is going to stick to his previous story.)

Just a minute. Didn't Betty tell this to you while you were asleep?

(It is possible sometimes to give a strong hypnotic suggestion to a person when he is in certain stages of normal sleep.)

BARNEY

No. Betty never told me this.

DOCTOR

Didn't she have dreams of this and talk to you in her sleep?

BARNEY

She has never told me this. I have never heard her tell me this. Betty said that we were inside a UFO in her dreams. Not how we got there.

DOCTOR

Yes, but didn't she tell you that you were taken inside?

BARNEY

Yes, she did.

DOCTOR

Then she told you everything that was seen inside and about being stopped by these men?

198

BARNEY

No. She did not tell me about being stopped by the men. She did not have this in her dreams.

(He is correct in this.)

This is only when I was hypnotized . . .

DOCTOR

Only when you were hypnotized.

BARNEY

Yes. I saw this.

DOCTOR

How do you account for this? How do you account for this happening? Do you think it really happened?

BARNEY

It did happen. I don't know what to say. I don't want to remember it. I suppose I won't remember it.

DOCTOR

Who told you you won't remember it?

BARNEY

I was told in my mind that I would forget that it happened. It was imprinted on my mind.

DOCTOR

Imprinted on your mind? Who told you?

BARNEY

I thought it was the man I saw looking down at me, and I was looking back at him. And I thought it was him. And he told me that I should be calm and that I should not be afraid. And that no harm would come to me. And that I would be left alone to go on my way. And that I would forget everything, and I would never remember it again.

DOCTOR

How do you account for the fact that you know nothing about Betty's experience, yet she seems to know everything about yours?

199

BARNEY

I was not in the same room with her. I don't know where she is. I—somehow felt relaxed. I thought it would soon be over and that no harm would come to us.

DOCTOR

You said before you don't know what happened—but you also said that Betty told you a lot about what happened in her dream.

BARNEY

She told me about herself. I did not know about what happened to Betty on the highway, but I never believed her dreams.

DOCTOR

If you don't believe her dreams, why do you believe yours?

BARNEY

I never dreamed about UFO's until last Sunday . . . I had them on Sunday night and on Tuesday night and on Wednesday night. And this is the first time I have ever dreamed of UFO's.

DOCTOR

You told me some time ago that you felt disassociated when you saw this UFO. What did you mean by that?

BARNEY

I felt that I had never known what this feeling was like. And I felt disassociated. As if I had my body moving, and yet my thinking was separate from it. And I had never felt like this before in my life. And I felt disassociated. And I never experienced this feeling again until I was in your office. And you made a little doggie come into the room. And I got hypnotized, and it made it seem as if the little doggie was there.

(He is referring to the test the doctor made with him.)

DOCTOR

This was an hallucination then, was it?

BARNEY

That was an hallucination.

DOCTOR

Then how about this story of being kidnapped. Couldn't that have been an hallucination, too?

BARNEY

(The doctor cannot shake him.)

I wish I could think it was an hallucination.

DOCTOR

(Pressing hard.)

Why couldn't it have been?

BARNEY

I don't know.

DOCTOR

How about Mr. Webb suggesting to you that something must have happened with that time?

BARNEY

Mr. Webb didn't suggest that. Mr. Webb did not suggest that something happened to me.

(Again, the strict adherence to literal truth under hypnosis. It was Hohman who had made this suggestion.)

DOCTOR

Well, he pointed out that some of your time was not accounted for.

BARNEY

There was a period of time from Indian Head to Ashland, and I kept thinking that all I could remember was getting out on the highway at Indian Head. I could never remember except to run back to my car and drive away. And I did not know what I was doing from Indian Head to Ashland. Mr. Hohman suggested that some of my time was not accounted for.

DOCTOR

Did you feel "disassociated" about this part of the experience?

BARNEY

I did not feel disassociated. I just didn't think about it. I did not feel anything except I had to have driven, and that is all I felt.

DOCTOR

And you're sure this actually happened?

                              BARNEY

I feel very sure it happened.

                              DOCTOR

Did these men speak to you?

                              BARNEY

Only the one I thought was the leader.

                              DOCTOR

The one you thought was the leader in the space ship?

                              BARNEY

Yes.

                              DOCTOR

What kind of language did he use?

                              BARNEY

He did not speak by word. I was told what to do by his thoughts
making my thoughts understand. And I could hear him. And I could
not understand in that I *could* understand him. And I was told that
I would not be harmed.

                              DOCTOR

Was this some kind of mental telepathy?

                              BARNEY

I am not familiar with this term.

                              DOCTOR

Mental telepathy is being able to understand someone else's thoughts
or having your thoughts understood by someone else.

                              BARNEY

I could understand his thoughts. His thoughts came to me, like I feel
your thoughts—when you talk to me, that is. And I know you are
there, and yet my eyes are closed. And you ask me questions. And I
know you are there, but I don't know where. And this is how he told
me that I would not be harmed. And that I would be let alone to go
as soon as they had taken me to this room. And then I did not see

     202

him or hear his thoughts, telling me I would not remember any of this because I was not harmed, and I wanted to forget. And he helped me to forget by telling me that this is what I wanted to do. And I did not remember anymore.

DOCTOR

You told me that Betty tried to hypnotize you at one time.

BARNEY

When we were standing on the highway in the White Mountains, and we stopped the first time to get a better look at this light that was moving through the sky coming toward us, I could see this happening. And I said, "It's a plane." And Betty said, "Look how it is flying . . ."

(Barney continues with the long detail of their first stop on Route 3, in which Betty tries to influence him that this is something strange, and not a plane. And how he felt strange about it, because there was no sound. But he indicates that he would not let Betty influence him unduly. His recall is again identical to his previous statements. When he mentions that he hoped to see some traffic, or a State Trooper, the doctor interjects with a question:)

DOCTOR

You wanted to see some men in the road?

BARNEY

I didn't want to see these men.

DOCTOR

When no harm came to you—did you feel better?

BARNEY

I felt funny. And I could not remember. And yet I *knew* something had happened. And I was confused that I was off Route 3. I was driving back to Route 3, and I just could not understand why I went off it . . . And shortly after that, we heard the beep—beep—beep—beep. And I kept quiet after that.

DOCTOR

Didn't Betty hypnotize you?

203

No. Betty did not hypnotize me. I wanted to think she was wrong about the object to make me feel better. Because I kept seeing this object in the sky . . .

(Now he repeats again the details of his stop at Indian Head, indicating that he thought the object would have to be a helicopter to stay suspended in the air. Yet there was no sound, and he knew it wasn't a helicopter. Barney reaches the point in the description where he is going to run back to the car.)

And I ran back to the car. And yet I knew it wasn't there . . .

DOCTOR

You knew it wasn't there . . .

BARNEY

I knew it couldn't be real; to have something like these eyes in my head . . .

DOCTOR

In your head?

BARNEY

Yes. These eyes.

DOCTOR

This whole thing was in your head then?

BARNEY

No.

DOCTOR

Why couldn't it be?

BARNEY

I remember it just like I remembered everything up to when I stopped at Indian Head. I remember everything I did. Then I drove down the highway, and I went through North Woodstock and then made a left turn. And Betty was looking at me sort of puzzled. And yet she did not question what I was doing. And I could sense what she was thinking. And I said, "I know what I'm doing all right. I know we're on the right road."

DOCTOR

What do you think she was thinking? You said you sensed what she was thinking.

(Again, the possibility of Betty's beliefs transferred to Barney.)

BARNEY

I thought she was thinking that I had gone off the highway, and that . . .

DOCTOR

Do you often sense her thoughts?

BARNEY

Yes, we sometimes do this. We sometimes try to see if we can sense what the other is thinking. It's not too effective.

DOCTOR

You've actually tried this? To see if you can sense each other's thoughts? You practice at it?

BARNEY

Well, when I was in Philadelphia, she would say that she would want me to call her. And she said that many times, she would lie there in her room, and say, "Call me, Barney." And then I would call her. Not that I thought that she had asked me to call. But I had already planned the call anyway. But she would say, "You must have read my thoughts, because I was lying here hoping you would call."

DOCTOR

Could she have planted all these thoughts about the UFO in your mind? You said that she wanted to hypnotize you.

BARNEY

I know Betty didn't hypnotize me. I wanted to think she had hypnotized me. I wanted to think that the object wasn't there. And that's why I said, "What are you doing, Betty? Trying to hypnotize me?" And since I kept saying it was a plane, I wanted her to say, "Yes, it's a plane." And then we'd drive on. But it kept following us, and I did not like that. I knew it was very peculiar that a plane would follow a car down the highway like that. And I hoped it was not there. And I did not want it to be there. And yet it kept staying and going down the highway with us . . .

(Again, with full detail Barney recounts what happened at Indian Head, indicating that he could not believe this thing possibly would be there, but it was, and that it seemed as if it were going to capture them.)

DOCTOR

How did you know that it was going to capture you?

BARNEY

I could see this thing coming very, very much closer. And I, too, was walking closer. And I saw like a—it was not like a ramp—but a low object coming down from the bottom of it. I could see this through the binoculars . . . I thought of a ladder, but I didn't really know what it was. Except that something was coming down from it. And the wings that slid out were not like the wings of a plane, but they were like a military bat-type of wing. It slid out.

DOCTOR

You mean the wing slid out from the fuselage?

BARNEY

It did not have a fuselage-type shape. And as the wings began sliding out, the red lights began moving away. And I noticed that they were an extension of these wings. And I was able to break away and run back to the car.

DOCTOR

What was the shape of this? If it wasn't a fuselage shape, what kind of shape was it?

BARNEY

It had more of an oval, pie-plate-type shape.

DOCTOR

Betty described it as cigar-shaped.

BARNEY

When it was soaring in the sky, it gave the appearance of a cigar, because I thought it was a passenger plane because of the longness of it. But then it was off in the distance. And only when it came close did I notice what I thought was a straight row of lights of a plane, turned out to be a curved type of series of lights.

206

DOCTOR

All right now. We'll stop there unless you have anything further, and this will not trouble you.

(For the first time now, the doctor is going to permit Barney to recall some of the things he has recounted under hypnosis—a major step in the therapy.)

And now—you will remember these experiences to the extent that they will not trouble you. You understand me? After I awake you, you may remember whatever doesn't trouble you about that. You will remember that they are not going to trouble you, they are not going to harm you, everything is past now, and gradually, gradually as we continue to see each other, you'll be remembering these things . . .

(It is important for the instructions to be absolutely clear because of the tendency of the subject to take things quite literally.)

But they will not cause you any nightmares, cause you any trouble, and you will know more and more about it as we go along. Is that clear?

BARNEY

Yes.

DOCTOR

You will have no fear, no anxiety; you will be comfortable and relaxed. And we will continue to talk about these things in this way. The same will be true for Betty. You will remember these things to the extent that you can remember *without being upset, without being bothered.* I will see you again a week from today. That all right?

BARNEY

Yes.

DOCTOR

All right. You may wake now.

(Barney wakes up on the command.)

How do you feel now?

BARNEY

I feel fine.

(A pause, then:)

Uh, I'm puzzled about something. I can remember being hypnotized. Usually when I come in here, I know I have been hypnotized, but I wouldn't remember. And I would look at my watch, and a couple of hours might have gone by. And I would think only about ten minutes had passed. And—and—uh—I can remember things that—about this today's session that I couldn't remember about any session that we had.

DOCTOR

What do you remember now?

BARNEY

About the UFO sighting that I was talking about and—uh—certain things puzzled me that I could not quite understand. Uh, I could never understand—I used to talk to Walter Webb when he would pay us a visit, and we would talk about our sighting, my sighting and Betty's sighting. And I would always talk and would come right up to the men in the craft turning to the panel. And I never could go further than that. But now I can almost see just what that fellow looked like that was looking down at me. And he was not frightening—not frightening in a— a—horrible sense, like a distorted, unhuman type of creature. He was more—the frightening part was the military precision of—as if a person who knew what to do, could do it, and was willing to carry it out. And when I said that he was going to capture me, uh, I used to remember that—but never could remember why I felt he was going to capture me.

DOCTOR

Well—why was he going to capture you?

BARNEY

I don't know why. Why was he going to capture me?

DOCTOR

Well, why did you think he was?

BARNEY

Well, now. I was forced out there. And I never could understand what caused me to walk out to that object when all my senses—uh—would not do a thing like that. And—it's very strange. Almost unbelievable.

DOCTOR

Well, now, some strange things from here on out will occur to you, as we go along. And you're going to become more and more conscious of what was going on in hypnosis than you have remembered. It won't trouble you, and you will remember it more and more as you get used to it and won't be thrown off guard.

BARNEY

Yes—uh—you know, Betty and I used to go to the White Mountains after this sighting, this would have been in 1962, occasionally in 1963. And we would drive around in these different back roads of the mountains. We could never seem to understand what we were doing off the main highway, because I just couldn't seem to understand why I felt I was on Route 3. And yet I wasn't sure I was on Route 3. But now I know that I turned off the highway.

DOCTOR

Now you remember, don't you, you and Betty talking about these things. About her dream?

BARNEY

Yes, yes. Betty would mention those.

DOCTOR

You know a lot more about her dreams than you remembered?

BARNEY

Well, no. Some of the things she told me about her dreams, where I was part of them, was my teeth being taken out. And I said, "Well—what was I doing?" And she said, "You weren't doing anything." Because she really didn't know, other than that.

DOCTOR

You didn't stop to rest any time on this trip, did you?

(The possibility is being explored of a dream along the road, while Barney was asleep.)

BARNEY

Yes. We stopped—oh, it was quite—I'd say approximately twenty miles out of Montreal.

DOCTOR

Yes, but I mean after the sighting.

BARNEY

No. We didn't stop at all.

DOCTOR

You didn't stop for a steak, or take a nap, or anything like that?

BARNEY

No. It was just a continuous drive down. And I felt in good spirits. I felt in high spirits. I was well-rested from the night before. And we spent a delightful day, and I knew I could drive from the White Mountains down to Portsmouth, so I didn't stop. I didn't feel too tired. But that's puzzling—because vaguely, I could remember a red glow in the highway, and I always thought someone was doing something like that—flagging me down.

DOCTOR

You mean like swinging a lantern?

BARNEY

No. No. Well—yes—if he had had a lantern in his hand.

DOCTOR

Well, that would have given a red glow, wouldn't it?

BARNEY

No—the glow wasn't coming from an object in his hand.

DOCTOR

I see from somewhere else?

BARNEY

The glow was just a large glow. I—I thought, oh, my God, it can't be in the daytime.

DOCTOR

You had a pretty large moon that night, didn't you?

BARNEY

Oh, I thought about the moon. But the thing was right there on the highway. I could never seem to understand. I have looked for that spot, and I looked for it. I said, "Now, how can the moon be on the highway in that kind of position?" And I could never seem to find any terrain up there that would fit what I sort of dimly remembered. This thing was sitting there was like—and I kept remembering this man flagging me down. And then I sort of don't remember. And now I remember.

DOCTOR

All right, then we'll continue next Saturday. I'll talk to Betty for a while now.

BARNEY

All right.

*   *   *

Barney's part of the session had come to an end. For the first time, the things he had forgotten were beginning to come back into his conscious mind. Betty, too, would be permitted to recall those things that would not trouble her after her session on that same day.

But still the questions remained unanswered, and an ultimate solution to the puzzle seemed quite distant.

CHAPTER NINE

The session of March 21 continued, after the discussion with Barney, and Betty was brought back into the room. Betty went into the trance again quickly and easily, as usual. Again, the instructions were given to recall not only the details of what happened, but the feelings Betty experienced about these details.

DOCTOR

(Betty is now fully in trance.)

Now, I want to ask you about your experiences when you thought you were taken aboard this flying object. When you sighted this thing, Barney saw men in the object at the time of the sighting with his binoculars. Did you see any men?

BETTY

This is when he got out and walked toward it?
(She is referring to the Indian Head portion of the experience.)

DOCTOR

Yes. You never saw any men in this object?

BETTY

No. I didn't.

DOCTOR

He described them to you, did he?

212

BETTY

Yes.

DOCTOR

How did he describe them?

BETTY

He said they were wearing uniforms. He thought they were uniforms. And he said that their leader looked down at him and frightened him. And there was another man and it looked as if they were pulling levers in the wall in back of the leader.

DOCTOR

This wasn't later that he told you this? It was at that time, was it?

BETTY

No. Not at that moment.

DOCTOR

Was it at some time after you got home?

BETTY

It was after we got home.

DOCTOR

At the time, he didn't tell you anything about it?

BETTY

No. He didn't.

DOCTOR

Well, go on.

BETTY

He did say that they . . . I had the idea that there was someone, he must have seen someone, even though he didn't say so. Because he kept saying, "THEY are going to capture us."

DOCTOR

I see.

BETTY

He didn't say IT was going to.

DOCTOR

He was quite frightened, then?

BETTY

Yes.

DOCTOR

And you were frightened?

BETTY

No, I don't think so. Not at that time. I was more curious and interested. And I had the feeling of being sort of helpless. That something was going to happen, and I didn't have too much control over it. But I wasn't really afraid. I guess I was looking forward to it.

DOCTOR

You were looking forward to something happening?

BETTY

Yes.

DOCTOR

What sort of thing did you look forward to happening?

BETTY

I didn't know what was going to happen.

DOCTOR

A new experience?

BETTY

Uh-huh.

DOCTOR

Now, when you were supposedly on board, and you say he put this needle into your navel . . .

BETTY

Yes.

DOCTOR

Was there any blood?

BETTY

Not to my knowledge.

214

DOCTOR

Did you find anything after you were home to indicate something had been put into your navel?

BETTY

I don't remember looking.

DOCTOR

You didn't think of looking?

BETTY

No.

DOCTOR

So you wouldn't know. And now—there is no indication, I take it?

BETTY

I don't think so.

DOCTOR

When the leader was talking to you, he spoke in English, you said, and yet he seemed to be of foreign origin.

BETTY

Yes.

DOCTOR

And he didn't know a good many things.

BETTY

And he had an accent.

DOCTOR

And he had an accent. Are you familiar with the accent? German? French? Japanese? Some other?

BETTY

No, I don't know what kind it was. One of the men had a worse accent than the leader.

DOCTOR

Did you ask these people their names?

BETTY

No.

DOCTOR

Why not?

BETTY

I didn't think of it. They didn't ask me my name, either. But I kept saying Barney's name, so they knew this.

DOCTOR

And you and Barney did not talk about these experiences afterward?

BETTY

Right afterward?

DOCTOR

Well, at any time. You did say, I believe, that you didn't talk about it on the way home.

BETTY

No. We didn't.

DOCTOR

But you did tell it to him afterwards, did you?

BETTY

Well, when I had the dreams, I told him I was having nightmares, well not really nightmares, but strange dreams. But I didn't tell him about my dreams at that time. And then, when Mr. Hohman and Mr. Jackson came to the house, and we were trying to recall—I think it was Mr. Hohman asked us why the trip took so long to come home. And that's when I said that I remembered about the moon being on the ground.

DOCTOR

Is this that big yellow object, or light, you saw?

BETTY

Um-hmm. It was just like a big moon. And it was on the ground. I could see sort of right through the trees in front of us.

DOCTOR

Barney heard you describe all these things, I suppose?

BETTY

Well, when they said, "What took so long?" I said, "We didn't know what took so long." But then I started to think about the moon being

216

on the ground. And I mentioned seeing it. And Barney said, "Yes. I saw it too." Then we thought that we should check and see, try to find out what time the moon set that night, to see if it were the moon, or what it was. And, when we were talking about this, I got quite upset —I don't know if I showed this or not—when this happened, I thought of my dreams. And I thought, well, maybe there was some basis to the dreams I'd been having. Maybe this is what took us so long.

DOCTOR

Now your dreams—

BETTY

Yes?

DOCTOR

Were they the things that happened in this experience you thought you had had? The dreams were of being placed aboard this vehicle?

BETTY

The dreams were something like it, but not. There were still a lot of differences.

(Betty goes on to recount the story of how she told her supervisor, who suggested that this might have happened, might have been the dream of an actual experience.)

DOCTOR
(Referring to Betty's supervisor.)

She is the one who said this actually might have happened to you?

BETTY

Yes. She said this must have happened to you, because if it had not happened, then you wouldn't be acting this way. That I wouldn't have this concern about it. I'd say, "Well, it was a dream, and I should forget it." And then I began to feel that something had happened, I wasn't sure what it was. There was something more than what I could really, actually, truthfully say I could remember.

DOCTOR

Now—was she the only one you told your dreams to?

BETTY

No. I told my sister Janet.

DOCTOR

How about your upstairs neighbor?

BETTY

No.

DOCTOR

Did you tell anyone these dreams in Barney's presence?

BETTY

I think he must have heard me talk about them.

DOCTOR

So he really did know about your experiences, didn't he?

BETTY

He knew some of it. I think he must have heard me saying something to somebody.

DOCTOR

Didn't all these things that you feel happened—didn't they happen in your dreams? Couldn't this *all* have been in your dreams?

BETTY

No.

DOCTOR

Why do you feel sure of that?

BETTY

Because of the discrepancies.

DOCTOR

Now tell me about the discrepancies that make it clear that it couldn't have been your dreams. Now—we know your supervisor told you it must have happened. Up until then, you couldn't believe it. Now after she told you that, you believed it happened. What were the discrepancies? You didn't know about the discrepancies because you couldn't remember about this experience, you told me.

BETTY

I knew what I had dreamed and that it was different. This was different.

DOCTOR

What makes the difference?

BETTY

There's so much more. And—

DOCTOR

Suppose that "so much more" had been parts of dreams that you couldn't remember? One doesn't always remember all of his dreams. Isn't that possible?

BETTY

I don't know.

DOCTOR

In other words, the dream that you can remember did not have everything that you were able to tell me. Is that right?

BETTY

That's true.

DOCTOR

But if you were able to tell me all of your dream, including the part of it you couldn't remember, would that fit in?

BETTY

No. Because some things were different.

DOCTOR

Some things were different.

BETTY

Yes.

DOCTOR

Well, could it be then that when you remembered the dream, some things were different? You just remembered differently because you were afraid to remember everything.

BETTY

You mean in my dreams, I would be afraid to remember?

DOCTOR

No. If you remember dreams, sometimes you forget parts of them. Because you're fearful. You know that, I think, from your own training as a social worker.

BETTY

Uh-huh.

DOCTOR

And yet there might be some parts of a dream that are misremembered, for the same reason. Is that possible?

BETTY

Well, I dreamed in my dreams I walked up steps. And here, I didn't walk up steps. I walked up a ramp.

DOCTOR

Is that a very significant difference, do you think?

BETTY

I don't know.

DOCTOR

The way you walked up?

BETTY

But the map—I could almost—in here . . .

(She is referring to her recall under hypnosis when she says "in here.")

in here, I could almost draw it. If I could draw, I could draw the map.

DOCTOR

You want to try to draw the map?

BETTY

I'm not good at drawing. I can't draw perspective.

DOCTOR

Well, if you remember some of this after you leave me, why don't you draw it, try to draw the map. Don't do it if you feel concern or anxious about it. But if you do, bring it in next time, all right?

BETTY

I'll try to.

DOCTOR

But don't feel as if you're compelled to do it.

(Sometimes a post-hypnotic suggestion can be very distressing. The doctor is guarding against this by leaving it up to Betty's volition.)

BETTY

Okay.

DOCTOR

Now—what other discrepancies. You mentioned the ramp and the stairs.

BETTY

There's always so much more. Here.

(Again, here *means under hypnosis.)*

DOCTOR

There's always so much more in what you've told me than there is in the dream. Is that right?

BETTY

Yes.

DOCTOR

It could be that all that extra that you remember could be the part of the dream that you didn't remember. Couldn't it?

BETTY

No. I don't think so.

(Like Barney, she is unshakeable.)

DOCTOR

Again—why don't you think so?

BETTY

Because—I know that you can dream, and not remember. But—

DOCTOR

How can you account in this experience for these men who seemd to speak our language and yet didn't know a lot of things about it. Like dentures. And aging. And things like that. And you felt they came from another world, I take it. Didn't you?

BETTY

Ummm—yes.

DOCTOR

Then how would they know all about this? How could it happen? Have you tried to explain all this to yourself?

221

BETTY

How could they speak English?

DOCTOR

Yes. How could this happen? That they could communicate with you in this way? And yet they were not of this world?

BETTY

Maybe they've been studying us.

DOCTOR

That would mean they would have to come here and know us, and everything else—wouldn't it?

BETTY

Umm, yes. And maybe they picked up some radio stations.

DOCTOR

But in a dream, this could all happen. Things don't have to be explained in a dream. Did you feel that they could communicate with you in any other way than words? Were they able to transfer thoughts?

BETTY

I don't know about thoughts.

DOCTOR

Do you believe that thoughts can be transferred?

BETTY

Yes. To a certain extent.

DOCTOR

Have you been able to transfer your thoughts to anyone, or receive someone else's thoughts?

BETTY

Barney and I are always saying the same thing at the same time. That type of thing.

DOCTOR

Well, do you communicate in any other ways? Could you have communicated all this to Barney through thought transference?

BETTY

(She laughs.)

No. I don't know as I could believe to that extent. Like, sometimes I used to have a teacher in college, and I would sit in the front row, and I might be bored. I would sit there, and I would think, "Scratch your face, you know, scratch your leg." And then wait to see how long it would take him to do it. You know—play around like this.

DOCTOR

Then you wanted to see how much power there was in thoughts?

BETTY

Yes.

DOCTOR

But you had no such communication between yourself and these strangers?

BETTY

(She pauses a long while, as if thinking this over.)

I don't know if I did hear them in English.

(Is she trying to please Dr. Simon by giving him the answer she thinks he wants? This is common in hypnosis.)

DOCTOR

Oh? You didn't hear them in English?

BETTY

I don't know.

DOCTOR

How do you think you heard them, then?

BETTY

I've been telling myself I heard them in English, with an accent. But I don't know.

DOCTOR

Well, did you hear them in any language? Or was it by thought transference?

BETTY

I knew what they were saying.

DOCTOR

You knew what they were saying—

BETTY

And they knew what I was saying—

DOCTOR

(As Betty begins to show signs of emotional strain.)

All right. This won't trouble you. You're all right.

(She is calm now.)

Well—do you think that was some form of thought transference?

BETTY

(Musingly.)

It could have been. But if it was, I knew what they were thinking.

DOCTOR

You knew what they were thinking. You rather liked this leader, didn't you?

BETTY

I was afraid of him at first.

DOCTOR

But afterwards?

BETTY

I—you know—began to feel that they weren't going to harm me.

DOCTOR

So it all works out that you're not harmed, and everything is all right.

BETTY

Yes.

DOCTOR

All right, now. After this, it will not be necessary for you to forget everything that goes on here. But you will remember only that part that you can remember without being upset and without being worried and bothered. Do you understand?

(Again, as with Barney, the important step of permitting Betty to slowly filter in to her consciousness the material she has revealed under hypnosis.)

BETTY

Yes.

DOCTOR

And it will not trouble you, any of it. As you go along, it will bother you less and less. And you will be able to remember those things that you can remember without anxiety and without fear. You will be able to talk more and more about it in that way. But, in the meantime, you will not be troubled by any of the things that you do remember. And gradually, it will come back more and more clearly. And you will talk about it more and more. Is that clear?

BETTY

Yes.

DOCTOR

You will have no fear, no anxiety. You'll be comfortable and relaxed, and we will continue to recall these things and discuss them together. You'll have no fear, no anxiety. I'll see you again a week from today. All right. Wake, Betty. You may wake.

(Betty wakes from her trance.)

How do you feel now?

BETTY

All right.

DOCTOR

Do you know more about what happened?

BETTY

Yes.

(The doctor reassures her that she'll be all right, and plans are made for the appointment the following week.)

After the Hills had left, the doctor dictated his brief summary:
There seem to be indications that a great deal of the experience was absorbed by Barney Hill from Betty, in spite of his insistence that this was his own. And there are definite indications that her dreams had been suggested as a reality by her supervisor. The implications are self-evident, and it is planned now to continue these interviews at a more conscious level. Both of them appear to have been remembering more now after the sessions.

CHAPTER TEN

By March 28, the following Saturday, the recall of what had been taking place in the sessions had increased progressively on the part of both Barney and Betty. Dr. Simon explored this aspect when the next session began. He spoke first with Betty before putting her in trance.

DOCTOR

Do you recall much of your experience now?

BETTY

Yes, I think so. I've also had a couple of nightmares again.

DOCTOR

Is that so?

BETTY

Yes. And Barney's been having nightmares all week. He seems to have the feeling right now, we were talking about this last night, trying to figure this out: Are they going to come back?

(The doctor reviews Betty's dreams in detail, comparing them with the recall of what she feels is the actual experience, as revealed under hypnosis. The session continues with Betty now in trance.)

DOCTOR

You seemed in some ways to anticipate, in spite of your anxiety, to look forward to these men coming back and taking you on some adventures. Is that the way you feel?

BETTY

Frankly, I wouldn't be surprised to see them.

DOCTOR

Would you like to see them?

BETTY

Not right now.

DOCTOR

Not right now. When?

BETTY

If I could get over being afraid. Right now I think I'd die of fright if I saw them again.

DOCTOR

All right. This will not trouble you. You will as during the past week be able to remember more and more as you lose your fright, fear, and you will not recall any more than you can tolerate and live with. You will be relaxed and comfortable and have no anxiety, and your memory will continue to improve for everything as you can remember without anxiety. You will be comfortable and relaxed, no pain, no anxiety. You may wake now. How do you feel?

BETTY

All right. Fine.

DOCTOR

Well, I'm going to see Barney, then I'm going to see the two of you together afterward.

BETTY

All right.

DOCTOR

Do you remember what happened?

BETTY

I think so, if I think about it.

DOCTOR

You don't feel like thinking right now?

BETTY

(Laughs)

I could think about it, maybe, in about five minutes.

*   *   *

To both Barney and Betty, now that the doctor was permitting their revelations under hypnosis to filter back to consciousness, the strange experience became in their eyes a definite possibility, this in spite of Barney's previous stout resistance to the whole idea of UFO's and Betty's dreams.

To the doctor, much was unresolved, even though the Hills had resisted his challenges both in and out of hypnosis. By working with them consciously now, with only occasional periods of hypnosis as might be indicated, he hoped to achieve alleviation of their anxiety, which in spite of the mystery of the reality or nonreality of the abduction story, was the main purpose of the therapy.

It was after this session that Betty gave the written dreams to the doctor to read. Of significance was the fact that these, too, were identical in detail both to the dreams she had just described, as well as her recall of the amnesic period under hypnosis.

Barney's discussion on that morning of March 28 reflected what had been going on in his mind during the week since Dr. Simon had instructed him that he could recall some of the material revealed in the trance state.

DOCTOR

Well, how've you been, Barney?

BARNEY

Not bad, Doctor. Uh, very interesting. So many things I had to talk about all this week, and I was quite amazed, last week, particularly, it's interesting how I know these things I want to say, and then when I get here I am not reluctant to discuss them, but I seem not to be able to put them in proper words. What I'm trying to say is that I just can't seem to believe—well, I'm just flabbergasted, if this is any explanation of what I'm trying to say.

DOCTOR

Flabbergasted about what?

228

At what I remembered from our sessions last week.

Uh-huh.

This business of seeing a UFO, an object, and personal contact with it seems to stretch my imagination as to the incredibility of the whole thing. Last Sunday, Betty and I were so concerned at this point that we made a trip up to Indian Head where we turned around and slowly drove back. And I said that what I shall do is whatever more or less my instincts direct me. Maybe I'm using the wrong term when I say *instinct,* these are the turns I will take. And we traveled just south of North Woodstock where I made, as if I had done this before, a sharp left turn onto Route 175.

North Woodstock, you say?

Yes. And I made a left turn at Route 175 from Route 3. Well, it was during the daylight so things would look different in the day than they would at night, but we both were saying, gee, this looked just like something we'd seen before. We had, to our conscious knowledge, never been in that particular area of New Hampshire, and there was a sharp right turn which would have carried us in a large circular drive toward a town called Waterville. What happened is that as we traveled a short distance, oh maybe three miles, we suddenly ran into a barricade, a barrier which would have indicated snows in the area. And in backing out we saw a fellow in the area that lived there, and I asked him about getting through. And he said not until the next month can you get through there, that area it's snowed in. But to reach Waterville you could go and approach from another area, but it is a continuous road that circles around this, in this particular location. And, we are now determined to travel that road when the snows thaw, and it's negotiable. Now, these were some of the thoughts that went through my mind. Another thought that I thought of was that Betty will say, "You don't accept or you can't, or are unwilling to accept things." And my answer to her is that it is not a matter of really accepting, but that I'm so flabbergasted by the entire thing that I find it difficult to accept it. I told her I wanted to ask you, What are the elements, what are the chances of a person uh, hallucinating something? I want to know the answers to these things. There are peculiar things that happened with Betty and me that we had never discussed prior to coming here and being hypnotized by you.

DOCTOR

Such as, what?

BARNEY

One is that the door of this thing that we went into had a bulkhead—well, that may be the wrong thing to describe it—but at the door jamb there seemed to have been an obstruction. And I tripped going, and I tripped coming back. And I mentally had the picture of the type of doors on naval crafts, of naval crafts or ships at sea—the type of door that swings.

DOCTOR

Have you been in the military service?

BARNEY

In the Army, not in the Navy.

DOCTOR

World War II?

BARNEY

World War II. And Betty realized that. And there was something else, too.

DOCTOR

She realized what, that there was an obstruction?

BARNEY

Yes. And there's something else that disturbs us both. And this has disturbed me greatly. Many times I was tempted to call you, but that inner mechanism of mine that causes me to fight things out, I guess, prevented me from disturbing you if it could have been prevented, knowing you are busy. But Betty said that somehow now she cannot believe she communicated with these creatures, if there had been these creatures, by word of mouth. And I was always aware that somehow there was something peculiar, which is the absence of a mouth. And I had no doubts about getting out of my car, walking toward this large thing hovering in the sky and staring down at me. In my conscious mind I always knew that this is what had actually happened. But then I would become confused when I said it would talk to me, or rather it had communicated something to me, and that was very frightening to me, and I ran, and I saw this through binoculars, 7 x 50 binoculars. So that next question would have been by someone hearing this is: What did they look like?

DOCTOR

Do you always carry binoculars with you when you travel?

BARNEY

Always in my car. I just always carry binoculars because Betty and I love traveling on weekends.

DOCTOR

It is relatively uncommon for people who are just traveling. They usually carry cameras.

BARNEY

Well, we also have a camera. But we didn't own a camera at that time.

DOCTOR

Well, go on.

BARNEY

So that, I always knew that I had looked up at something. I had seen figures looking down at me, in what I thought was a smile by our conventional method of smiling with the lips going up. It was more of a twinkling or a recognizing an eye as being a part of the smile. And I just can't remember any mouth.

DOCTOR

Uh-huh.

BARNEY

I just can't recall any mouth. And in a faint way of hearing these things talking, which is very confusing to me, it was like a mumbling when they were, when it was not anything addressed or directed to me. It was a mumm, mumming type of a thing. Less than a mumm mumm, but more of a mmmmmm. And this is baffling to me, particularly when

Betty said well, last week, she realized that she was *not* talking to them. There is something else I want to say before I forget to mention it. Betty mentioned to me that at the time that this sighting had taken place, I was working nights. And we did not sleep together; only on weekends because it was the type of situation that I would sleep in the day and she at night. And when she had told me these dreams of hers, to be polite I listened. Well, she was not really telling them to me, but telling them to others. And I would never offer any opinion, because I had my own private opinion about dreams, that they were dreams. Because I dream, and dreams don't have any particular significance other than that you dream of something that you have associated somewhere in your past or in your life or in your present, and this stimulates your mind to dream when you are asleep. And this is the way I put Betty's dreams. Not that I was a physical part of her dreams, but only a part of her dreams in her mental capacity to dream. And so I never put any great emphasis on her dreams, I had never dreamed consciously of a UFO in my life until here recently. And I wanted to ask, "Is it possible I could have dreamed of a UFO unconsciously and not have had—?" To clarify what I am saying, I have had many dreams over many periods of times of my life and in many instances I can't recall what I dreamed about. But I do know that it was along a certain particular line. If I had dreamed of being in Philadelphia, I would waken and forget the dream. But I would know that somehow the dream content was somewhere in Philadelphia, and I would not be totally unaware. But, I had never, to my knowledge, dreamed of a UFO until recently.

DOCTOR

By recently, you mean last week?

BARNEY

Sunday before last, which would have been a week ago last week.

DOCTOR

You dreamed that before you saw me last time.

BARNEY

Yes.

DOCTOR

You didn't tell me about that.

232

BARNEY

I did mention that to you, that I had dreamed of a UFO—

DOCTOR

Yes, oh, yes. You said you dreamed of a UFO, but you didn't have any details.

BARNEY

No details were associated with it.

DOCTOR

In other words, you feel that you dreamed of a UFO, but you couldn't remember the dream, is that it?

BARNEY

You mean in the past?

DOCTOR

No, at that time, in the way we were talking about. You asked me if one could dream, say, unconsciously.

BARNEY

Well, what I meant is: Could I after 1961 have dreamed of a UFO, and then under hypnosis my dream is coming out?

DOCTOR

Now, what you're talking of, what do you think it might have been?

BARNEY

Repeat that question?

DOCTOR

You say, now your dream is coming out. To what part of the things that you recall are you referring?

BARNEY

Well, the only part of my dream that I had recently that made any sense was the structure and walking up to the object. It was just a distorted dream, but the physical structure of the craft itself fitted in with my conscious attitude of what a craft like this would look like. And, last night, I dreamed again of being on a UFO. And this could have been a result of Betty having drawn a picture, what she was attempting to do was to draw a picture of a map with, she calls it perspective, and I call it a map in dimension. But this is what she was attempting to do. And this is what could have stimulated me to a dream of this type. But I dreamed that I was on aboard this UFO, and I was questioning the people there, where did you come from? And they were telling me that they had come from a planet . . .

(Barney continues to describe his dream, in which he reflects his growing preoccupation with the possibility that something strange and weird happened in the interval: talking with intelligent human-oid beings, etc. As he concludes, the doctor speaks.)

DOCTOR

Now, you and Betty have been talking to each other about what's been going on, you've been remembering things?

BARNEY

Yes.

DOCTOR

So, she's now told you about her experience on the object.

BARNEY

Yes.

DOCTOR

And you've told her.

BARNEY

Yes.

DOCTOR

About being on board, being examined, and all those things?

BARNEY

Yesterday, at the breakfast table, we were talking about it. And, gee, I get chills. I get chills even now. Ugh.

DOCTOR

So it's something you don't want to remember too strongly now?

BARNEY

Well, I do remember what we were talking about. I was telling her I can see it so clearly. This much I had always realized: that somewhere, this is prior to coming here for hypnosis, that I had always realized that somehow there were someone stopping us. But I never could put any sense to it. So I dismissed it completely from my mind.

DOCTOR

Could someone have flagged you down? Just someone, anyone who might flag you down?

BARNEY

I would have—I'm quite sure I would have remembered.

DOCTOR

Well, you were pretty frightened at the time.

BARNEY

I would have remembered someone flagging me down. Particularly a group of men.

DOCTOR

Well, now, about this experience. How do you feel about it? You have a lot of doubts about it. You're asking me, could it have been a dream?

BARNEY

Yes, I'm asking these kinds of questions.

DOCTOR

What do you think, could it have been?

BARNEY

Well, now, in the truthful answer, trying now not to conceal my feelings of being ridiculed, I would say it was something that *happened*. But I—I—I put a protective coating on myself, because I don't want to be ridiculed.

DOCTOR

You and Betty appear to have had somewhat similar experiences, but also different. It seems to me that Betty knew about everything that happened to you, but you know nothing about what happened to her.

BARNEY

Well, Betty didn't know. All she knew about me is that I had gone into a room and then had come from this room. And that they had come running out of it.

DOCTOR

That you heard from Betty telling her dreams?

BARNEY

Yes, I have heard of these dreams.

DOCTOR

And all these things were found in her dreams, weren't they? These things that happened to her?

BARNEY

The things that happened to her?

DOCTOR

Yes, that she said happened in the object.

BARNEY

I would say there is a similarity.

DOCTOR

You heard all this?

BARNEY

I had heard all that. Yes. The difference is that though I had heard her dreams, and Betty would talk about them, I never would talk about the idea of having or believing I had been stopped on the highway. I knew I saw a large object. I knew this, but I didn't think much of it.

DOCTOR

Well, you were pretty well convinced of having sighted something. But you have some doubts in mind about the rest. Of whether it was reality, or dream, or what it was.

BARNEY

Well, it is because of my unfamiliarity with hypnosis, what it can do.

DOCTOR

Never mind about hypnosis. How do you feel? You have, you were expressing some doubts about it. You asked me, could this have been an hallucination and a dream?

BARNEY

Yes, talking to you as a professional man.

236

DOCTOR

Then, why would you and Betty have the same experience? If you could give me some possible explanation there?

BARNEY

Uh, these are the questions I'm asking. Could she have influenced me?

DOCTOR

Well, you were always afraid she would influence you, weren't you?

BARNEY

That's interesting, because I knew she *wasn't*.

DOCTOR

You accused her of trying to hypnotize you to make you believe something you didn't want to believe. I'd rather reserve diagnosis of that for a while. I want to go through more material yet.

BARNEY

Yes. Well, at the time I would like to say this: that when I was standing out there, I knew she *wasn't* influencing me. What I was thinking is that I would rather not talk about it. Okay, we see something, now let's get in our car and drive about our business. And this irritated me when she kept saying, "But look, it's right over there!" And even as I would slow down to take a peek, I would see this object out there. And this greatly irritated me. And so I said, "What are you trying to do? Make me see something that isn't there?" Knowing that it *was* there and not wanting it to be there. And I think this is a part of why I'm confused.

DOCTOR

Now, Betty had a nightmare or two before she saw me last time. She tells me she woke you up and told you about it. Do you remember that?

BARNEY

Yes, she did wake me up.

DOCTOR

She thought she had possibly screamed. But if she had, you would've heard. But she said then she woke you up and told you about it.

BARNEY

I didn't hear her. And then she said she had this dream.

DOCTOR

Did she tell you what it was?

BARNEY

That I'm trying to remember. Whether she told me what the dream was or not. Uh, it had something to do with being on the craft and that. She had discovered that she wasn't talking to these people.

DOCTOR

This she told you was a dream?

BARNEY

This is what she told me was her dream.

DOCTOR

It's not what she told me was a dream. She told me that there were two dreams, really. One of them was sort of like a moonbeam down on a lake, something like that, or over a body of water.

BARNEY

Yes, she told me about that.

DOCTOR

And then of a yellow object, this great lighted object taking off, which both of you have experienced.

BARNEY

Well, that, yes. If this was a dream that she had, it is only an extension of something I do know and did see. But eliminating the water from what I'm saying, is this large object sitting there, and then it started moving off and going very rapidly away. This, too, I always knew about before hypnosis. But much of this I wanted to forget very badly.

DOCTOR

Why were you so anxious to forget it? You've been worried this week, haven't you?

BARNEY

Well, I don't know whether I can say this is the typical, or rather this is more of the typical manifestations of the male who likes things solid and explainable. I don't know whether this would be my answer as to why I wanted to forget.

DOCTOR

Are you afraid of something?

BARNEY

Am I afraid of something?

DOCTOR

Yes.

BARNEY

Yes, this is something else I'm grateful you brought out. Because somehow I always had a fear, after this sighting, that a great disaster—now how I could explain this disaster? There was harm that could come to Betty and me by pursuing this.

DOCTOR

I see.

BARNEY

By even trying to investigate. See, I've always been the reluctant person.

DOCTOR

What sort of harm, from where would it come?

BARNEY

From a position that I best can describe it that a person would know if ever I had gone too far by revealing something.

DOCTOR

You mean then that you had a secret of somebody's that you were afraid of revealing? Or do you feel you had been told that—

BARNEY

To forget.

DOCTOR

You had been told to forget these men?

BARNEY

Yes.

DOCTOR

At least, this is the way you feel about it, whether it was a dream or reality.

BARNEY

Yes.

DOCTOR

And this is part of a dream.

BARNEY

I know it *wasn't* a dream.

DOCTOR

That you were told to forget by the men?

BARNEY

Yes. That this is something that can really serve no purpose, and you have to forget it, you will forget it, and it can only cause great harm that can be meted out to you if you do *not* forget.

DOCTOR

You say you were told this?

BARNEY

Yes. As if this is a conclusion to an event. That now it is over, you forget.

DOCTOR

In other words, it is a feeling about the event.

BARNEY

Yes.

DOCTOR

That you mustn't speak of it.

BARNEY

Yes.

DOCTOR

There is a danger in speaking of it.

BARNEY

Yes.

DOCTOR

And the danger is going to be, what? Any notion about that?

240

BARNEY

Well, there is a reluctance on my part to be abroad with Betty up in the mountains at night. Not during the day, or not necessarily in the mountains, but in any isolated area. It was as if when I was walking out to this craft, and now I'm going back prior to hypnosis, the same type of effect that was drawing me to it. Before I broke and ran back to the car. It was the same type of power as I tried to describe, a force that was causing me to continue to come closer to it, even when I wanted to run away.

DOCTOR

A fascination in spite of your fear?

BARNEY

Well, fascination was there. I was amazed.

DOCTOR

All of this was a feeling in yourself. Wasn't it?

BARNEY

Being out there on the highway?

DOCTOR

No, the feeling of power, and so on.

BARNEY

Yes, yes, this was very, very—

DOCTOR

This was a feeling in yourself, wasn't it? As if it were being produced from something stronger than yourself.

BARNEY

It was being produced by something stronger than me, outside of me, that I wasn't creating this.

DOCTOR

I see. This power.

*　　*　　*

As the discussion continued, Barney brought up the fact that the small circle of warts that had developed in an almost geometrically perfect circle around his groin some four months after the incident at Indian Head had become inflamed after his therapy with Dr. Simon had begun. As the conscious memory of what he had revealed under hypnosis came back to him, he became aware of the recollection that in the examination on the craft, a circular instrument had been placed at exactly the same point where the warts had now appeared. He wondered: Had these been caused by the examination and the instrument used? Barney was also intelligent enough to realize that the reverse could be true: The warts might be a psychosomatic symptom connected with the feelings experienced under hypnosis. And yet, Barney reasoned, they had initially appeared back in 1962, when he had no conscious memory of the events aboard the craft. Now, in 1964, during the sessions, they became inflamed.

Neither Dr. Simon nor the skin specialist Barney visited appeared to be concerned about the warts, which were easily removed by electrolysis. But to Barney, the gnawing thought remained that this could be evidence—if indeed there was anything to this totally incredible story.

DOCTOR

Well, do you have any other thoughts?

BARNEY

Well, I haven't been answered one way.

DOCTOR

How's that?

BARNEY

Well, I was thinking, when I speak of hypnosis and its effect and the possibility of dreams. Yet I know I *did not* dream this. I know this for a certainty. I think all I am trying to do is be reassured.

DOCTOR

To be reassured of what?

BARNEY

Uh, I *know* it happened. I talk to people, not that many people, but I'm thinking of those I have talked to about it. And I only feel that I have to face the possibility of this happening. I know, unfortunately, the person who is listening to me cannot know what I do know. That these things did happen to me, particularly when I was out there on the highway and walking toward the—the hovering craft there. I also knew that something very strange had happened immediately afterwards. Yet, when I talk to a person, it is almost as if I had been given an A on a report card, and I keep asking others to look at it and tell me is it really there.

DOCTOR

When did you first have that feeling that something else had happened besides sighting the object and everything connected with that?

BARNEY

Uh, surprisingly, when I first arrived home in Portsmouth the same day. I had this feeling of foreboding, something would happen. I'd say, "Betty, let us forget this thing. Let us forget even the portion of having seen the sighting from Lancaster all the way down to Indian Head. Because no good can come of it."

DOCTOR

Yes, but when did you get the feeling that something else had happened? Aside from the feeling of foreboding.

BARNEY

I had that. I can only think that that was a private part of what I knew.

DOCTOR

Wasn't this after Mr. Hohman brought up the question of what happened?

BARNEY

That might have been when Betty believed that, when she became interested after her dream and talked with Mr. Hohman. But I felt there was more to this. And what caused me to do that, is that I was talking to Walter Webb. And I had gotten as far as being out on the highway. And I had gone right up to the point of looking at the object with my binoculars, and it's looking back at me. Then suddenly it was almost as if a fleeting revelation that something happened. And now I can't even remember, and was brought up to a standstill, and I couldn't go any further.

DOCTOR

That's when you were talking with Mr. Webb?

243

BARNEY

This is when I was talking with Walter Webb, yes. I found that there was something very strange about this whole thing. Now, I can go right up to this point. I can remember walking back, running back to the car, but just what I had done, but I didn't pursue this any further with Walter Webb, because I felt a tremendous pressure, a tremendous pressure to say, "Let's drop this thing, Betty." Now you have your report, Mr. Webb, let us forget it. This was the extent of that. I used to privately think about this. That Betty was in the car with me, we were together, when after she asked me, "What did you see? What did you see?" I only said, "It's going to capture us. . . ."

DOCTOR

You were afraid it was going to capture you.

BARNEY

Yes, I knew that.

DOCTOR

You knew that; what do you mean? You knew it was going to capture you?

BARNEY

Uh, yes, if this can be an explanation of something you know is about to happen. I knew if I had stayed out there on that highway—

DOCTOR

I see, if you had stayed there, you would have been captured?

BARNEY

Yes. So I could only go up to that part and never go any further. Betty and I didn't talk about it, it seemed so fantastic, something happening at that point, and we not talking about it.

DOCTOR

But Betty talked a lot about it to everybody else. She called her sister, she called—

BARNEY

Well, I was thinking of that night—from the time I returned to the car, we didn't talk about it. She just said, "Well, what did you see?" And I didn't answer her. Other than I said, "It's going to capture us." And

244

then I didn't answer her, or I didn't pursue the conversation further. And the next thing, as I could always remember, is seeing this big object sitting in the road, and my first remark was, "Oh, my God, not again." And Betty was saying, "It's the moon." And I was saying, "Yes, it's the moon." And we both thought how peculiar that the moon was going away. And then I didn't say anything else, and she didn't say anything else about it while we drove toward Portsmouth.

DOCTOR

Had there been any peculiarities in the road, hillocks, valleys, or things where the moon might look as if it's on the ground? You sometimes see that.

BARNEY

That's what I wanted to think, yes. But the moon wouldn't be moving. What was so surprising was that we weren't moving.

DOCTOR

You weren't moving?

BARNEY

No.

DOCTOR

What had stopped you?

BARNEY

Well, nothing had stopped me. I just wasn't driving ahead at the time. I thought afterwards that the reason I wasn't moving is apparently I had brought my car to a halt to negotiate some kind of a turn, or something or another. And this I accepted. And as we drove further on, Betty then remarked to me, "Well, now do you believe in flying saucers?" And I said, "Don't be ridiculous, Betty."

DOCTOR

Well, now what's the question you say I hadn't answered?

BARNEY

Uh, hypnosis and dreams, and am I hallucinating or giving an event of a dream, thinking it a part of reality. Yet, even as you could answer this question, I basically *know* what had *happened, happened.* And this is why I think the whole thing's ridiculous, to even ask the question.

DOCTOR

Well, as I've said before, I don't want to go into any great detail of the answer at this time. All these things can happen, let me say that. Anything can happen, when you come down to it.

BARNEY

Yes.

DOCTOR

But, I can reassure you that you have nothing to fear and everything is all right. But I want to reserve any more concrete answer for some time in the future.

BARNEY

Yes.

DOCTOR

As we develop this thing more and more into consciousness.

BARNEY

Yes.

DOCTOR

And I'm going to continue to work with you now, both of you more and more in consciousness. As you continue to remember the things that came out only under hypnosis, and you won't have to resort as much to hypnosis. And at the proper time I think then we will go into more of it.

BARNEY

I think the only explanation as to how we would go into such detail about this, is that for the last three years Betty and I have both been puzzled greatly by this discrepancy or failure on our part to talk about a situation in Indian Head and not resume our conversation until Ashland. And I think this is where we have rather been more attuned to remembering these two incidents, these two locations rather. Because we wrestled with this problem so many times as to just what could we have been doing, and we never were able to conclude anything.

DOCTOR

Well, we'll hope that you will open up more and more about that as to what you were doing as these things begin coming back, as there comes a point where there's no gain in constantly repeating a thing in the hypnosis until we can bring it into consciousness. We want it to get into consciousness to the extent that you can tolerate it, without any anxiety, and this will come.

*   *   *

The session continued with a discussion of how Webb, Hohman, and Jackson had been influential in encouraging the Hills to consider hypnosis as a means of relieving their growing concern about the incident. While Dr. Simon emphasized that the therapy would be involved primarily with their conscious thinking and feeling, he would still use hypnosis when it seemed necessary.

For the purpose of reinforcement, however, he put both the Hills into a trance and reemphasized that they would continue to remember various aspects of their experiences that were tolerable to them without their being upset.

He also indicated that in the near future, if the Hills were willing, they would be permitted to hear the playback of the recordings, so that complete experience—not just fragments—would be relived on a conscious level.

To Betty and Barney, the chance to hear recorded experiences marked a milestone in their treatment. They reacted with a combination of intense curiosity—and some apprehension.

CHAPTER ELEVEN

April 5, 1964, the day of the next session, found the Hills leaving Portsmouth at an earlier hour than usual. Prompting this was the possibility that they might be permitted to hear some of the playbacks of the tapes, the contents of which were, of course, a total mystery to both Barney and Betty.

The Hills usually left their house at 6:45 on the morning of their sessions; this day it was 6:15. Arriving in Boston early, they found a luncheonette a short distance from Bay State Road, taking time to have coffee and doughnuts and to talk about their feelings if the doctor should let them listen to the tapes. Barney found himself repeating the question to Betty, "Are you curious? I certainly am," while Betty would tone him down with the suggestion that they might not hear the tapes after all, and there was no sense in overanticipating the event.

In discussing this period of therapy two years later, Barney Hill is not exactly sure what he felt at the time. But he recalls to some extent that the fragments of the sessions that began to come through to his consciousness brought him to the point that he felt, in spite of his resistance to the idea, that an extremely unusual experience had taken place that night in the White Mountains—that he could consider the possibility that Betty's dreams might be more than dreams. Further, he recalls that what stood out most in his mind as he became aware of what had taken place in the hypnosis sessions was the sharpness of the image of the men in the road. He even speculated that this might not be a fantasy, but could conceivably be an actuality. "When I look back at the therapy at this stage," he said, "I found that, in contrast to my former skepticism and resistance to the entire UFO idea, that what I thought was the moon was not the moon at all, but the object itself."

However, he recalled at that later date two years after the therapy that no major portion of the repressed material came through. There seemed to be only leaks or flashes of recall.

Betty remembers being extremely curious about what might come out of the playback, but she seems to think that she was less emotional and more pragmatic than Barney. She remembers that she finished both her coffee and doughnut.

Barney hardly touched either.

*   *   *

As the Hills left the luncheonette and started toward the office, Dr. Simon was dictating his customary brief preface to the session which was to follow:

Mr. and Mrs. Hill are expected at eight o'clock for a continuation. Mrs. Hill revealed in the last conscious interview, not under hypnosis, that she had been walking in the woods and had been asleep. This was not pursued, but will be followed up at this time.

The doctor was still not certain whether he would begin the playback of the tapes but would reserve judgment on that until further on in the session. The material was emotionally strong and would have to be offered in small doses, under careful observation of the reaction of both the Hills.

Dr. Simon took Betty into his office first, and they talked informally.

DOCTOR

Well, Betty, have you both been feeling all right?

BETTY

Yes.

DOCTOR

I want to ask you one thing. When I talked to you last time, and you weren't under hypnosis, I asked you what you remembered about the experience in a general way. And you said that you remembered about seeing the object come down. And that just before you were beeped,

Barney asked you to look out, and you did. And you said something like, "I looked at it, and I kept thinking I didn't see it, because I was expecting to see the lights. And I didn't see the lights." You went on to say that you saw the bottom of it, right over the car. And you couldn't see the bright lights or the stars. That you knew that this big, dark mass was moving right over the top of the car.

BETTY

Yes. That's right.

DOCTOR

And I asked you if it was going away, and you said it was directly over the car.

BETTY

Yes.

DOCTOR

Then I asked how about the period of time you couldn't account for. Did you remember any of that? Did Mr. Hohman point it out? You remembered that. Then I asked you what happened. And you said something about going around the corner on a side road. And the men in the road. Do you remember that?

BETTY

Yes.

DOCTOR

Then after that, you said you could remember being asleep. And walking in the woods and going on a ship. What about this sleep? You had never mentioned about being asleep.

BETTY

Well, I seem to remember that when the men who were in the road came up to the side of the car, I went to sleep.

DOCTOR

When they came up to the side of the car, you went to sleep?

BETTY

Yes.

DOCTOR

Yes, and then what?

BETTY

And then I don't know what happened during this period of time. But it seems as though I was asleep and that I was really forcing myself to wake up.

DOCTOR

I see. Now—is it possible that you actually had fallen asleep while Barney was in the road?

BETTY

No. No, I don't think so.

DOCTOR

Well, under what circumstances would you be asleep then?

BETTY

Well, in thinking about this, I would assume that they did something that would make me not conscious of what was going on.

DOCTOR

But you never mentioned at any time before, either in or out of hypnosis, anything about being asleep. You don't think it's possible that while you were in the car, you were tired enough so that you might have fallen asleep?

BETTY

No, I didn't fall asleep in the car. No.

DOCTOR

Then it was a feeling that you were asleep, rather than any knowledge of it, is that it?

BETTY

Yes.

DOCTOR

That you must have been asleep?

BETTY

Yes.

DOCTOR

Well, how could that be? You mean that the men had put you to sleep and then taken you through all this procedure?

They must have. Because when I saw them coming toward the car, my impulse was to open the car door and to get out and to run and hide in the woods to get away from them.

But you didn't.

No.

And everything that followed after that you think might have been after you were put to sleep?

Yes.

Is that right?

(Betty nods.)

Do you remember anything else now? Anything that you feel you want to talk about before I get into the more general discussion with both you and Barney?

There is one thing that puzzles me.

What is that?

This happened after all this was all over, and we were on the way home. I suppose this has nothing to do with anything, but after all, this had happened. We were driving home, we were looking for some place that was open, so we could see people and get a cup of coffee. And we drove, we were driving along, and we saw a diner. The lights were on in the interior, and we assumed it was open. So we drove into the yard and found that it was closed. And I always felt that if I could find this diner, it might be a clue to what actually happened.

Yes.

252

BETTY

And I still haven't been able to find that diner.

DOCTOR

So there is a possibility later on that you might locate it, is that right?

BETTY

Yes. I'm still looking for it.

(She laughs.)

DOCTOR

All right. I think I'll talk to Barney for just a minute, then I think I'll talk to you together about the overall picture and what we might plan to do.

BETTY

All right.

(The doctor dismisses Betty and summons Barney to the office.)

DOCTOR

(To Barney.)

Anything special that you should like to discuss?

BARNEY

(He gives the doctor a sketch of what he recalls to be the abduction area.)

This is something that I drew. I don't know if it makes much sense, but this is the way the road looked. The arrow points up in the corner there. At the top is the direction this so-called moon had taken off.

DOCTOR

When did you draw this?

BARNEY

When I returned home last Saturday.

DOCTOR

Good. I'll keep this. Now, in my talk with Betty last time, she said something about she could remember the men in the road, walking in the woods, and going on a ship—and something about being asleep. Did you have any feeling of being asleep at any time?

BARNEY

Of being asleep? No, I did not. Or is this under hypnosis, or what?

DOCTOR

It doesn't matter which way.

BARNEY

Well, prior to hypnosis, I had no knowledge at all about this missing period.

DOCTOR

No, I mean as part of your experience there, you had no feeling of being asleep, or of being put to sleep, or of anything like that?

BARNEY

No. I have no recall of that.

DOCTOR

You were just dazed, I take it. Well, I think now we want to talk to the two of you together a bit and see where we go from there.

BARNEY

Very good.

(Betty is called back into the office to join Barney and the doctor.)

DOCTOR

(To both Barney and Betty.)

I think we've gone far enough in the situation now, and while we haven't got every point clarified nor every detail clarified, it would take a pretty good deal of extensive repetition to do it. But much might come out if we proceed now on the general plan I have in mind. I want to go over everything in great detail. And of course I want to keep you from having any unnecessary amount of anxiety. What I'd like to do is to get this into consciousness and discuss it freely. Now there are two things involved. I mean each of you have had a common experience, and you have had separate experiences. I can take you each individually, and then together, or just take you two together. How do you feel about it?

BARNEY

I think that we can work together, don't you, Betty?

(Betty agrees.)

DOCTOR

So you can get a complete sharing of this thing and see it from each other's side. All right. Number two: I can talk about it, and give you the experiences. Or we can take a certain amount of risk in terms of your anxiety by going over all this together and playing it back.

BARNEY

Yes.

BETTY

Playing it back?

DOCTOR

Yes.

BETTY

(Emphatically.)

Play it back.

DOCTOR

There is quite a bit of it, and it's going to need quite a few sessions. But I think it's probably the better way, and I think that I would rather not discuss the realities and fantasies until you've really gotten all the material that I have, of which you are unconsciously aware but consciously are not. Now, do you want to do it that way?

BARNEY

I think that would be good.

DOCTOR

And at any time, let's discuss. You are willing that we play back the tapes involving each of you together?

(Barney and Betty both agree.)

All right. Then we'll do that. Now if this thing gets hard to bear—and some of it isn't going to be easy to take—I want to know it. Let me know right away, and I can always help ease you.

Right.

What we had better do is listen and then at the end of say ten or fifteen minutes, or whatever we want for discussion, we'll stop for a moment. If you feel we should have more discussion, we'll be able to stop the tape and talk freely at any time while playing this. Is that satisfactory?

(Barney and Betty both agree again.)

*　　*　　*

Dr. Simon pushed the button of the recorder, and the first session, the tape containing Barney's recall of the trip through Montreal and down through New Hampshire, began.

When the tapes started, a strange thing happened. In his general reinforcement of the hypnosis with the Hills, the doctor had taken the precaution to make sure that no other person than he could put them into hypnosis by using the cue words.

When Barney's tape began, the induction procedure was the first material that came out over the speaker. Barney, glancing in Betty's direction, was startled to see her sink back in her chair. As Barney was finishing the discussion with Dr. Simon, he hadn't listened to the first part of the tape; Betty had. She remembers going under, while she was still aware of what was happening. She tried to stamp her foot to alert Barney and the doctor that she was slipping into a trance, but she couldn't move it. After waking Betty, Dr. Simon reinforced both so they would not respond to any cue words unless *he* gave them face to face. They continued.

"When I first began hearing my voice under hypnosis," Barney later describes it, "I was lifted out of my seat. I couldn't believe it. I knew it was my voice, but it was difficult for me to really understand that this was me, saying that this has actually happened. It was as if I had been asleep and had talked in my sleep. I just couldn't believe it. I wasn't too concerned about the first part of the tapes—coming down through Canada, and the first part of our leg through upper New Hampshire. I had remembered practically all this detail consciously. But as the tapes moved along toward Indian Head, I didn't know what was going to happen. I could feel my ulcer. I mean I could feel my stomach churning, my muscles tighten. I just didn't know what to expect. I know I sat on the edge of my chair, shifting my position frequently.

"The tone of my voice was interesting, because it didn't sound a bit like me. And also, the way I slurred my words."

Betty's reaction was similar: "I thought he sounded as though he were asleep. But then, I began to get scared. I said to myself, 'Oh, good lord—I'd just as soon go home and not hear them!' And then I began to wonder. Everything was building up to the part that I had heard all the way out in the waiting room, when I heard Barney's outcries. I was anticipating that and wondering what my reaction would be."

Slowly, the tape approached the portion involving Indian Head. "I knew I was getting to the point in which I had no complete memory," Barney continues in describing his reaction at a later date. "I felt quite secure being with the doctor in his office, and I had complete confidence in him. I knew that if the going got too rough, he could take me out of it. Then I was suddenly startled. When I put the binoculars up to my eyes, I couldn't believe I had reacted that way. And the eyes. The eyes that seemed to come toward me. Then I heard myself saying that the eyes seemed to be burning into my senses, like an indelible imprint. And I began, in the doctor's offices, to feel the pieces unfolding. I was beginning to remember. Suddenly the lost pieces began coming together. Even while listening to the tapes, I felt this. I suddenly realized how I had broken my binocular straps. And I remembered that for days after Indian Head, I had an intense soreness in the back of my neck. Listening to the tapes, this came back to me sharply—the violent thrust of my arms breaking the binocular strap. All of this was unfolding—not just on the tapes, but beginning to unfold in my mind, my conscious mind.

"I did not feel too much shock there in the doctor's office, perhaps because he had fortified me by posthypnotic suggestion that I would be able to tolerate this in relative comfort. But I noticed that Dr. Simon kept watching us very closely as he was playing the tapes. He was apparently conscious of any pressure being built up in us. And he would stop the machine, and talk with us several times.

"Every once in a while, I would look over at Betty. And she has a way of looking at me and being reassuring. It's sort of a look that she can give, almost to say 'I'm in love with you, Barney.' And I felt this reassurance. And it helped.

"I think you can say the best description was that I was numb, as I listened. Information was flooding back into my mind, but my emotions were numb. I continued to feel that if it became too distressing, the doctor would be able to control it.

"And then, as the tapes went deeper and deeper into the part I had never remembered, there was the feeling as if heavy chains were lifted off my shoulders. I felt that I need no longer suffer the anxieties of wondering what happened.

"I felt mainly that I was actually reliving the experience. It was a bright clear morning as we listened to the tapes. The sun was filling the doctor's office, but as the tape was played, it was as if a pall had descended, and I was sitting there out on that mountain road at night. I could actually *see* what I described as the Cheshire cat. This growing, one-beam eye, staring at me, or rather not staring at me, but being a part of me. I could turn my eyes, and I did while sitting in the doctor's office there listening. I blinked my eyes and shut the lids as if to get this from my mind. I was certain now, on listening to the tapes, that I had never really understood before. Suddenly, lo and behold, I could actually describe things beyond Indian Head. There are many emotions and reactions that occur within a fleeting second, so that I was running a gamut of these emotions and reactions. And I think this is why it never became too distressing for me to listen to the tapes. I could hardly wait to talk to Betty alone about it. I wanted to tell her my thoughts, my feelings. To tell her that this was just too much to digest at one time. I had to observe and study this more. It would take time to get used to it—listening to that person who was representing me on the tapes. I kept saying to myself, 'Is that *me* on the tapes saying this?' And then the word *incredible* kept coming up in my mind. It was just incredible, completely unbelievable that this was me.

"And I think I really felt in two minds about it. Maybe one reason I wanted to talk to Betty in the car was that it camouflaged my real meaning—I wanted to be rid of listening to the tapes so that I could quickly go back and join my full conscious mind, and forget it.

"At the part of the tapes where my voice said that I was just 'floating about,' I then knew that I wasn't really floating about. I was being half-dragged to the ship. I could actually feel the suspension—rather of being suspended with the arms holding me. And what was so curious is that I could feel the pressure of the arms. When I talk about this, I feel chills about the whole thing, the pressure of the arms, of these small men holding me and dragging me along.

"And then I thought of my shoes—the tops of them being scraped, literally scraped, that I noticed the day after Indian Head. How else would the *tops* of the shoes be scraped? And I was able to realize that these men made me forget what happened. They told me to. They told me to forget, and I wanted to forget. And I think this is why it wasn't too difficult for me to put this whole thing out of my mind for so long. I knew, I felt, I was almost sure as I listened to the tapes that this was no fantasy or dream. It was a matter of little doubt to me. It seemed without any doubt that this 'man' *could* communicate with me, and he did. I also know that I wasn't anxious to communicate with him. I was listening to this—being reassured by him that no harm was going to come to me, but I didn't accept it. I also took out a pencil and sketched from memory what the man might have looked like. I never had seen the sketch I drew under hypnosis at this point. They were fairly similar.

"And if we had heard no other session on tape beyond this, I would have had all this in my mind. I began to anticipate what was going to come out on the tapes the second session. I would have all this on my mind. I would have been highly confused as to why it was there, but it would have been there."

Betty, in recalling her further reactions as they listened to the tapes for the first time said: "When the tapes came to the part where Barney was standing there on the highway, I felt very sorry for him. I had sort of a feeling of being somewhat devastated. That—why had we bothered, now that we had gone so far? What was the reason to find out about the whole thing? Let's forget hypnosis ever happened. Maybe we would have been better off just to leave things as they were. Maybe it was better just to wonder. And suddenly I became aware that all through this, I had never really stopped to think of what Barney's experiences were. His having separate experiences alone. And listening to Barney's voice made me relive the incident too. It was just like being right back out there on the highway."

*   *   *

With frequent stops, the first tape was completed. Both Barney and Betty were somewhat stunned.

In the elevator going down, they were alone for the first time, with a measurable recall of the incident now thoroughly in their minds.

The first thing that Betty could say was in reference to Dr. Simon. "I certainly," Betty laughed, "hope that Dr. Simon isn't really a spaceman!"

And again Barney said, with the same whimsy, "Don't be ridiculous!"

Driving back to New Hampshire, Barney found himself rubbing the back of his neck, where back in 1961 the burning sensation from the leather strap of the binoculars seemed to have inexplicably appeared and disappeared.

His overall reaction to the tapes he summed up succinctly: "I felt so overwhelmed and relieved. Now parts of my life that had been missing were added to it again. Parts of my life were being put back together."

CHAPTER TWELVE

In summarizing the session of the first playback of the tapes, Dr. Simon dictated:

> The first interview with Mr. Hill was now played back to Mr. and Mrs. Hill together and carried to the point of the sighting and the outburst of extreme anxiety that Mr. Hill had. He showed considerable distress at this, but seemed to manage it quite well. And as it proceeded, he took out a piece of paper and began to draw. In this drawing, he sketched out again a head, with some very staring eyes, of almond shape, but not slanted. At the end of this, he seemed to be very well composed and wished to be assured of its fantasy nature. Both wish to continue in this fashion, and a date was set a week from today to continue the playback of the hypnotic sessions. It is of interest when the playback was begun and the cue word was used, Mrs. Hill went into a trance. Both were then intentionally put into another trance and were told that they would not respond to the cue word when they heard it on the playback, but only when it came directly from me.

During the week that followed, Barney tried to analyze the incident from the point of view that it might have been a fantasy, but so many details came flooding back as a result of hearing the recording that he found himself seriously doubting this theory. Both he and Betty were vacillating constantly, at one moment feeling that perhaps this could be a dream—at others becoming convinced of the reality of it.

The playback of the recordings stimulated release into the Hills' consciousness of further details, some which had not been expressed during the hypnotic sessions. This release of new material is a product of the "working through" process in psychotherapy, either with or without hypnosis.

Later, at his home in Portsmouth, Barney found himself remembering how he opened his eyes fleetingly on entering the craft. "I remember I had passed the outer door where my feet scraped against the bulkhead," he recalled some time later, "and I got a good look at the three men who were standing by the door of what would have been the room where they examined me. I saw them just as I was about to enter this. So that I could see the curved contour of the corridor just fleetingly. And I was quite upset about that, because they were talking to each other. Yet I was also being understood and was understanding someone else who was continuing to tell me that we were not going to be harmed.

"The interior of the craft was filled with this bluish light—and by that I mean a fluorescent kind of light, which didn't cast any shadows. The men had rather odd-shaped heads, with a large cranium, diminishing in size as it got toward the chin. And the eyes continued around to the sides of their heads, so that it appeared that they could see several degrees beyond the lateral extent of our vision. This was startling to me. And something that I remembered, after listening to the tapes, is the mouth itself. I could not describe the mouth before, and I drew the picture without including the mouth. But it was much like when you draw one horizontal line with a short perpendicular line on each end. This horizontal line would represent the lips without the muscle that we have. And it would part slightly as they made this mumumumming sound. The texture of the skin, as I remember it from this quick glance, was grayish, almost metallic looking. I didn't notice any hair—or headgear for that matter. Also, I didn't notice any proboscis, there just seemed to be two slits that represented the nostrils.

"Betty and I went to hear a lecture one time by Dr. Carleton S. Coon of the Department of Anthropology at Harvard, and he showed a slide of a group of people who lived around the Magellan Straits. We both had quite a reaction when we saw it, because this group of Indians, who lived in an extremely cold atmosphere high in the mountains where there was little oxygen, bore a considerably close resemblance to what I'm trying to describe. And the professor was telling us how this group of people had, in the course of many generations, shown considerable physiological changes to adapt to the climate. They had Oriental sort of eyes, but the eye socket gave an appearance of being much larger than what it was, because nature had developed a roll of fat around the eye and also around the mouth. So it looked as if the mouth had almost no opening and as if they had practically no nose. They were quite similar, in a general way, to the men I'm trying to describe.

"When I was in the corridor, I was surprised that the leader didn't follow me into the room. But again—the eyes seemed to follow me. It was as if I knew the leader was elsewhere, but his effectiveness was there with me. Wherever he was, he was still able to convey messages to me, such as recognizing when I would become more fearful or needed calming down. I know how ridiculous this sounds, but it's the only way I can describe it. He was able to do this. There was another person in the room with me beside the three men at the door. And he was the one who scraped my arms and did the examining, checking my spinal column and that sort of thing.

"I only got a very brief glance at the room, through the door. It was very barren, and the only furniture I could see was this table. The walls were smooth and barren, just this plain bluish-white color. No pictures or ornaments. The room was pie shaped, but as if the point of the pie had been cut off. I couldn't see any windows. The ceiling and floor and walls all seemed to be made of the same material, but I didn't notice what the texture was. Also, I didn't notice where the light source was.

"The main thing I was impressed by was the table that I was to lie on, because it was so much shorter than anything that would ordinarily hold a human being. So that when I got on the table, my legs dangled over the end. And I thought this was peculiar.

"I was escorted, sort of dragged I guess, both in and out of the ship. There was a slight difference in temperature, so that I knew I was in an interior as they took me over the bulkhead or whatever it was. I didn't notice any odor particularly. And I could breathe all right inside. There wasn't any struggle for breath. And as I was escorted out, I was still being held, and I could feel the night air rush toward me. There was a difference between being inside there and outside, and I could feel it.

"I bumped my feet again on this bulkhead on the way out, and I could feel myself being taken down the ramp. Then I found myself walking on rough ground, and I still thought that the people who had taken me out were still with me. But I opened my eyes, and I was standing there alone. And I thought, 'Oh, that's interesting.' And suddenly, I forgot what had happened completely. I had absolutely no memory of it. I thought, 'Oh, I must have walked into the woods to take a break in the trip. That's what must have happened. I'll go to the car,' and it was sitting there on the road, and I walked up to it. I was curious why the motor was off, and the lights were off. I wouldn't usually do this just to jump out of the car for a rest stop. And I sat down on the front seat on top of the tire wrench. I thought, 'That's interesting. What's this doing here?' And I pulled it from under me and placed it in the well between the door and the seat itself.

"Then I heard Delsey whimpering. I thought, 'Oh, Delsey—you're under the seat. I thought Betty was taking you for a walk.' I was sort of foggy—my mind was unclear. But I took Delsey out of the car after I had started up the motor and put the headlights on. Then Betty started walking out of the woods, and I thought, 'Well, that's what I'm doing. I'm sitting here waiting for Betty.'

"She came down the road from an angle, as if from the woods on the other side of the road. So to me it seemed that I had obviously stopped on Betty's request. And she almost casually said, 'Come on out, let's watch it leave.'

"Then I thought, 'That's ridiculous. Watch *what* leave?' But I thought I'd humor her, I'll get out. And then I saw the moon—I immediately thought of it as the moon, and then we both were amazed, because the moon was moving. I was sure it was the moon setting. But I was curious about it, because it just didn't seem to be a normal moon. Then everything seemed to go blank again, this fog, this haziness set in until I saw the sign: Concord—17 miles. I do remember vaguely wondering how this enormous disc, that had been very orange in color, could change so quickly to a brilliant, silvery color."

During this week Betty thought often about her reaction to Barney's description on the tapes. "It seemed as if I were reliving everything again," she recalls. "When he was out on the highway, there, just before the beeping sound, I could recall how I flew across the front seat and yelled for him to come back. A lot of other detail kept coming back to me, so vividly."

As the other sessions of the playback continued, the recall of both Barney and Betty accelerated, filling in more detail, with many half-remembered fragments falling into place. They became more acclimated to hearing their own somnambulistic voices but still found it hard to believe that these were their own stories.

To Betty, the moment the men came up to the door of the car at the time of the roadblock, she now felt that she had gone into a hypnotic trance of the same type she experienced in the sessions in the doctor's office. She felt as if both she and Barney had in some way been mesmerized by the beeping sounds to a quasi-hypnotic state, which deepened at the point where she began to open the car door to run into the woods and hide. At the moment that one of the men in the road opened the car door for her, he put his hand out, and she felt as if her consciousness were slipping away, just as she had so many times during the sessions. She noted that both she and Barney on the tapes had to struggle to remember at identical points, first at Indian Head and shortly after at the roadblock. To Barney, the sensation was one of floating. To her, there was the long period of haziness after the series of beeps, then a feeling of falling into a trance-like state that she forced herself to come out of by sheer will power.

"Hearing my portion of the experience on the tapes," she recalls, "I could feel the struggle I was making to get myself to wake up again after the men seemed to put me into a trance. I could remember shaking my head and feeling as though I were trying to climb out of a well. I was really struggling. I could remember saying to myself, 'I've got to wake up, I've got to wake up.' And each time I would say this, I would force myself a little more awake.

"When they took me out of the car, I wasn't very cooperative. When we got to the ramp, I think I probably braced my feet against it. Then I remember either this voice or this thought—whatever it was—saying to me that I wasn't going to be harmed. I did see the exterior of this craft as they were walking me up to it. I got the impression that it was sitting in some kind of depressed area in the ground. There was something underneath it, a gully or something, and I didn't know if the object itself was sitting there or if there was some kind of support. But there was this kind of rim that went around the craft. And I don't know why, but I had the idea that this rim was movable, that it would spin around the perimeter, maybe. Like a huge gyroscope of some kind. I don't know for sure, and this is just my impression.

"Well, the ramp took us up on this rim, and I guess they took us just a couple of steps along the rim to this door. In the part we entered, there was a curved corridor that appeared to go around the craft on the inside. I don't know where it stopped or ended. The entrances to the rooms were on the inner side of the corridor. And I kept looking for windows, but I couldn't see any. I got the impression that the craft was metallic, entirely metallic, and there was a light coming through the doorway, like that of a light coming out of a front door at night, sort of the quality of a fluorescent light.

"Then they started to take me into this room. And I wasn't going. I stopped and told them to bring Barney in, too. Because they were walking Barney past me. And they kept right on going with him. That's when they told me not to worry, he'd be all right.

"I got the impression that the leader and the examiner were different from the crew members. But this is hard to say, because I really didn't want to look at the men. It seemed to me that these two were taller, but maybe that's because I wanted to make them taller. I was sort of scared of the crew members, and I had the feeling that the leader and the examiner were keeping them back, away from us. I could see them out in the corridor, and they seemed to be going back and forth from Barney's room to mine.

"In a sense, they looked like mongoloids, because I was comparing them with a case I had been working with, a specific mongoloid child—this sort of round face and broad forehead, along with a certain type of coarseness. The surface of their skin seemed to be a bluish gray, but probably whiter than that. Their eyes moved, and they had pupils. Somehow, I had the feeling they were more like cats' eyes. And I couldn't remember any buttons or zippers—but then I really didn't want to remember.

"The room was triangular, with the point cut off. Barney and I both agree on that. The table was sort of in the middle, but down near the cut-off part. It was far enough out so that anyone could walk around it. Over beside it was a white stool and different kinds of equipment, gadgets, all over the wall. When they looked at my arm, they took this thing out of the wall, and then sort of put it back in. Then on the wall where the entrance was, there were these storage cabinets, built in. Thinking back, I think everything seemed to look as if it were made of metal or plastic, but there was a white tone to everything. The surface of the table was hard and smooth and cold.

"When they talked among themselves, they made a noise that had no meaning to me at all. And I had this impression that the leader seemed to look differently from the others, but again I might have been distorting on this. Their bodies seemed to be a little out of proportion, with a bigger chest cavity, broader chest. Now, if I remember correctly, I first insisted that they were talking to me in English, with an accent. Then Dr. Simon and I spent a lot of time on this, and I think my final conclusion is that while they weren't speaking English, I could understand what was being said to me as if it *were* in English. But whether it was English or not English, verbal or nonverbal, I understood clearly what they were trying to get across. This was when they were communicating with me. As I mentioned, when they talked among themselves, they were entirely impossible to understand."

The Hills were unable to agree on this point. Barney's recollection is: "It was much like being put into hypnosis by Dr. Simon. I knew this leader was there, yet I felt there was a complete separation of his words and his presence. Only that what was there was a part of my knowledge. I did not hear an actual voice. But in my mind, I knew what he was saying. It wasn't as if he were talking to me with my eyes open, and he was sitting across the room from me. It was more as if the words were there, a part of me, and he was outside the actual creation of the words themselves."

One reason why Betty felt that the communication might have been verbal is that she thinks that she spoke verbally to them. Both the Hills were aware of many inconsistencies of their recall, and these were constantly coming up in the exploration of the incident with the doctor. Among these was the impression Betty got that the humanoid beings seemed to have no concept of time. Barney pointed out, and Betty agreed, that it was a paradox for the leader to say "Wait a minute" when he had asked her what *time* was.

"When we were going out of the room with this book," Betty recalls, "the leader definitely said 'Wait a minute,' whether this was out loud or not, I don't know. I had been in a discussion with him about old age, too, trying to explain what a hundred years was, that sort of thing. And I found it hard to explain. I think we got into this discussion when he asked about Barney's false teeth. They were puzzled why Barney's teeth were able to be removed and mine were not. Then I said that people often have dentures when they get older. He asked me, 'What's older?' And I said, 'Old age.' This is when we also went into a discussion of diet, what do you eat? There was no way of getting across to them what I was trying to say, like meat, potatoes, vegetables, and so on. When I tried to tell them about squash, I said it was yellow, and that's when he said, 'What's yellow?' "

Barney feels Betty made a mistake in this, both from the point of view of time concepts and vocalizing the communication. "I still question whether Betty actually conversed with these people," he says. "It was communication, but it was nonverbal. Several things Betty has said have caused me to question it. The slip of whether this was time,* yet she said they didn't understand time as we understand it. I feel Betty has created other distortions in her mind. She referred to the so-called leader and examiner as different from the others, and I believe they were all basically the same."

Betty replies to this by saying, "When I was being taken aboard this thing in the beginning, I knew they indicated to me that if we cooperated and didn't waste too much time, they would take us back to the car and let us go on our way. But I don't know if the word *time* was used or not."

*   *   *

Inconsistencies and paradoxes like these were examined as the playback sessions continued over the next several weeks. The bizarre and unusual qualities of the case continued to be puzzling and challenging.

Primarily, the sessions were a long, detailed review, with the information on the tapes stimulating further recall and comment from both Barney and Betty. Other aspects, both in and out of the mainstream of the therapy were brought to light and considered. Barney's ulcers flared up at the beginning of the playback sessions, but gradually subsided again. With Walter Webb, the Hills retraced the route of the journey, filling in further details, and were convinced that they had found the exact spot of the roadblock on a side road two or three miles east of Route 3.

Both Barney and Betty were overwhelmed by the massive detail that came out on the recordings, much of it entirely unknown to them consciously. "I never had any idea of the extent of this material coming out on the tapes. I never realized how much of this I was trying to put out of my mind. The tapes seemed utterly incredible," Barney commented.

Barney still wanted to deny that this ever happened. "I was thinking I was ready to stop the entire seeking of the recall of the incident," Barney told the doctor in one of the sessions after they had listened to a long portion of the playback. "Betty asked me why. And I thought because I cannot explain what came out under hypnosis, and I hate to think I'm nuts. I also noted last week while listening to the playback of

---

*Betty recalls that the "leader" said, "Wait a minute." Both Barney and Betty saw at once the strange paradox of his saying this and then asking what a year and other time elements were.

Betty, I wanted to close my eyes very much. It became almost an obsession. That's why I got up and moved over and looked out the window."

By May 30, nearly two months after the playbacks of the tapes began, Barney felt a definite relief from his tensions. "I haven't felt as tense this week as I have in previous weeks," Barney told the doctor. "Haven't had to take any medication for the ulcer at all."

On June 6, the doctor utilized hypnosis for some further exploration with Betty.

DOCTOR

(He completes the induction of Betty into a trance.)

. . . you are now in a deep sleep, deep, deep, sleep. I want you to think back to the time you told me you were asleep. Think back on that . . .

(He is referring to the moment of the roadblock.)

Were you asleep?

BETTY

No.

DOCTOR

Why did you think you were asleep?

BETTY

(Again the literal answer above to the first question.)

I had been asleep.

DOCTOR

You had been asleep?

BETTY

When I was in the car. The men put me to sleep.

DOCTOR

The men put you to sleep.

BETTY

Somehow.

269

DOCTOR

How did he get to the car?

BETTY

I opened the door. I was going to get out and run.

DOCTOR

Why?

BETTY

Because I was afraid.

DOCTOR

Where was Barney?

BETTY

In the car.

DOCTOR

You were both in the car?

BETTY

Yes.

DOCTOR

And these men came from where?

BETTY

From the middle of the road.

DOCTOR

Did they have lights with them?

BETTY

No, they didn't.

DOCTOR

How could you see them?

BETTY

From the headlights of the car.

DOCTOR

And he said he would put you asleep?

BETTY

He didn't say anything.

DOCTOR

How did you know he was going to put you asleep?

BETTY

I didn't know he was going to put me asleep.

DOCTOR

What made you say then that you think you were asleep?

BETTY

Because I woke up.

DOCTOR

You woke up where?

BETTY

When I was walking.

DOCTOR

Do you think they put you asleep?

BETTY

Yes.

DOCTOR

How?

BETTY

They did something. I couldn't remember. The man put his hand out. I was sitting in the seat. I was turning. I had the door open. And then I turned and I was going to run, because I was afraid. Then, when I opened the door, the man opened it wider. There were three men. And the one nearest me, nearest the handle of the door—I was going to get out—and he put his hand up. And then I didn't know anything.

(She later compared this to the experience of undergoing hypnosis.)

DOCTOR

Until when?

BETTY

Until I was walking. I made myself come awake.

DOCTOR

Now, you said they examined your skin. Was it something like a microscope?

BETTY

Yes.

DOCTOR

Why do you think they were examining your skin? Were they interested in the color of it?

(The interracial implications here are obvious.)

BETTY

I don't think so. I think they were interested in the structure of my skin.

DOCTOR

What about the structure?

BETTY

Well, they kept looking at it, and I guessed that from the way they reacted. I mean they all, you know, the examiner and the leader, they took one look, and then the other one would look. They looked two or three different times.

DOCTOR

Why this unusual interest in your skin? Do you have any thoughts about it?

BETTY

No. I don't.

DOCTOR

Do you think it might be because your skin and Barney's were of a different color?

BETTY

I don't know, but I think they were interested because their skin and mine were different.

DOCTOR

In what way was it different?

BETTY

In color.

272

DOCTOR

What was the color of their skin? Were they different—these men who were examining you?

BETTY

The leader and the examiner were more alike.

DOCTOR

In what way?

BETTY

They looked taller than the crew members.

DOCTOR

That's all?

BETTY

They were taller and their skin was of a different color.

DOCTOR

Well, what was the difference in the color? What was the color of the crew members' skin?

BETTY

Uh—

DOCTOR

Why do you have so much trouble telling me the difference?

BETTY

Because I keep thinking that the crew members are Oriental, Asiatic. Only they were not as—they're short.

DOCTOR

And the leader is not short?

BETTY

He's more, the leader and the examiner are taller. They're about as tall as I am.

DOCTOR

You mean the crew members are much shorter than you?

BETTY

The crew members were shorter.

DOCTOR

How much shorter?

BETTY

I'd say they were not—uh—five feet. I think the leader is about as tall as I am.

DOCTOR

Were you afraid of these people?

BETTY

I wasn't afraid of the leader. I was at first, but I wasn't afterwards.

(The doctor then asks Betty about her general background, her early days, her family influence, and her experience with an interracial marriage. Under hypnosis she reveals a better-than-average adjustment to the problems of the mixed marriage and the fact that she is unable to have children because of an operation. The doctor then goes on to explore Betty's general reactions the night of the incident.)

DOCTOR

You don't always express your fears so readily, do you? During these experiences with the flying object, you weren't afraid at first, and then you realized later how afraid you'd been?

BETTY

Well, I think maybe I'm the type of person if any emergency occurs, everybody else might be going to pieces, and I go to work until it's all over with. And then after it's all over, I have sort of a delayed reaction. But this is the type of person I am. When I saw that object out in the sky there, though, I don't think I had too much fear about it.

DOCTOR

When you had all these experiences with your dreams—why would you have dreamed all these things? The dreams were the same as the experiences that you felt you had.

274

I figured that in my dreams, I remembered what actually happened.

*   *   *

This final session in which hypnosis was employed seemed to sum up the dilemma that had carried through the entire six months that the therapy took place in. Was the experience dream or reality? Where did the truth lie? Who could certify what the truth was? How were all the puzzling inconsistencies to be resolved—regardless of which solution to the question was assumed?

In a sense, among the principals, there were three points of view. Dr. Simon felt that from the available evidence from all sources, and our present knowledge of mental functioning, he could accept the probability that the Hills had had an experience with an unusual aerial phenomenon, a sighting that stimulated an intense emotional experience in both of them. While anything is conceivable, he felt that the abduction was improbable. Betty felt that the hypnosis had demonstrated marked evidence that her dreams were a reflection and remembrance of reality. Barney vacillated between these points of view, although his ultimate conclusion was that he could not distinguish between other known reality and the sequence of events that finally came out under hypnosis. In other words, once the amnesia was overcome, he could sense no difference between what he remembered consciously and what he re-called under hypnosis: The entire journey had been a complete, uninterrupted continuum, including the abduction sequence.

In the last three sessions, up through the final one on June 27, 1964, the three points of view frequently came out in the discussions. A healthy sign was that both Betty and Barney were less anxious after the recordings were played back.

"When we got to the end of the tapes," Barney recalled later, "I had an overwhelming sense of relief, a feeling of unburdening. Betty and I became more amiable than ever. My blood pressure condition eased up, as well as my ulcers."

Betty agreed. Even though the mystery was by no means completely solved, her anxiety lessened because she had done all she could to probe into the unprecedented story of their encounter. Her dreams grew less disturbed.

By June everyone recognized that there would be no full conclusion, either to the therapy or the incident which played so big a part in it.

Both the doctor and the Hills regretted that it would be impractical to continue into deeper therapy over the long period of time that would be necessary. Summer had arrived, the long round trip would be more taxing than ever. It was a good stopping place, at least for a time. More important was the Hills' awareness that they were feeling much better—and less disturbed, even though everything had not been completely resolved.

As a scientist, the doctor tested a varying series of hypotheses as they developed and changed, testing against what phenomenon presented itself and what knowledge he could use to integrate it. At the place where the therapy was discontinued, the situation could rest with the minimum of danger. Short of acceptance of the whole experience as reality, which contradictory evidence prevented the doctor from doing, his best alternative lay in the dream hypothesis. "Anything beyond that," the doctor commented later, "would seem to stretch the limits of credulity too far. But I'm not absolutely convinced. I had to come to my conclusion. If you can call it a conclusion. It never really was one. Therapeutically, we had reached a good place to stop under the practical conditions existing, and the Hills' basic improvement. It was acceptable in my judgment to leave it not fully answered. I knew that we would be remaining in contact, and that perhaps time would bring a more complete answer."

In considering the theory that Betty's intense dreams were transferred to Barney, to become part of his reality, Barney stated his feelings to the doctor in one of the later sessions in this way:

"Doctor, if I can draw an analogy, let's say that yesterday morning I drove down from Portsmouth to Boston to work. And if somehow, I had been told that this had *not* happened to me, I'd be a bit curious. Particularly if this was said several months later, I would say, 'I'm not quite sure I drove that day,' but I'd get a calendar and check it. Then if this person kept insisting that I didn't drive there, in the face of my knowing that I did, I would have to terminate the conversation and leave it at that. I'd reach the point where I'd say to myself, 'I cannot convince this person, and he cannot convince me. There's no issue. I can drop it.'"

As the sessions drew to a close, the question of illusion or reality dominated the discussions. The doctor pointed out that he was not going to say it was either—that he and the Hills together would both

276

have to grope for the truth, but that ultimately the acceptance or non-acceptance of the occurrence would have to rest with them.

In attempting to analyze his thoughts, Barney told the doctor, "Prior to coming to your office, I had, and still do have, complete acceptance of the fact that I had driven down to Indian Head, and the object was there, and these things did take place. I also am well aware that at Ashland we received a series of beeps. These things are not a matter of the dream world or of fantasy. I am also well aware of my attitudes after arriving back in Portsmouth, which is to say, this is such a ridiculous thing. We can never tell anyone about it. Yet, so many months have passed that they have finally become years, two or three years. It is still an annoying issue with us. Now we come to hypnosis, where the technique allegedly will take us back and bring us through this period of apparent amnesia. And I can only say, 'Well, why would amnesia have existed to begin with? Why would there be this period between Indian Head and Ashland?' "

In reply, the doctor said, "Well, actually you have a partial explanation for the reason for amnesia. Psychological amnesia exists for the purpose of repressing or wiping out intolerable emotional experiences."

"So the intolerable emotional experience," Barney said, "has been the experience at Indian Head?"

"I have been going over this," the doctor replied, "and kind of separating this into two experiences. One is the experience of the sighting. I feel I have not been able to obtain out of hypnosis, data that will wipe that out. That, I'm willing to leave. The sighting itself. But the abduction, if we'll separate these two, by which I mean the experience of being taken aboard and examined, is another matter. I'm separating that out. No, you might say the whole sighting was a frightening experience. Therefore, why didn't the amnesia wipe out both? Why isn't there an amnesia for the whole thing? You remember that you were consciously, almost from the beginning, trying to have an amnesia. That is, you said, 'We won't talk about this.' You were producing amnesia in various ways. And then there came the amnesia for the other experience.

"Now, the question evolves here: Is this an amnesia in the sense of wiping out of a real experience, or an amnesia related to the wiping out of a fantasy—an intensely painful fantasy?"

The doctor indicated that he hoped there would be more light thrown on this in the closing sessions. Barney was puzzled that his reaction at Indian Head had been out of character with previous emergency experiences. He related one incident that he and Betty and two friends had encountered on a lonely highway in New Hampshire, in which two teenagers had followed their car, harassing them for nearly thirty miles before they found a state trooper, who apprehended the youths. All during this harrowing experience, Barney had remained cool and had planned to force the car off the highway and confront them himself if he had not found the police officer. "I'm only mentioning this," he told the doctor, "to illustrate the point that this is the way I usually function in the time of a crisis."

"The fact that you face these things with a clear-cut, definite plan," the doctor said, "even one that could cost you your life, is good—but what else would you do? Either, as they say, scream and go blind, or do something. And in the situation where there is no other alternative, you do well.

"Your anxiety," the doctor continued, "increased more powerfully as you were relieved of this whole UFO business, very much as the rate of psychiatric breakdowns in the First Marine Division, which took Guadalcanal. Their breakdowns increased very markedly not while they were taking the island from the Japanese, but when they were relieved by the Army. One may then afford the luxury of permitting one's anxieties to take over—to be sick. When action is necessary, action takes place.

"The rules that operate for the conscious mind won't operate for the unconscious. In the unconscious mind, consistency means nothing. Past and present don't exist. Everything is now. The past is now; the present is now; the future is now. Opposites exist together without any incongruity whatsoever. Things *are* and *are not* all at the same time. This, of course, is a fragment of the structure of dreams, too. I'd say that shortly, we can get this thing pretty well crystallized. Then I'm going to leave it in your hands as to how far you want to take the discussion. I think you must understand that I have kept focused on this experience. You can both see now that this experience cannot be seen as an isolated thing. I've kept it isolated to the greatest extent possible. This is part of the continuum of your lives. It's a stop in the roadway, and there's a great deal of material here we will not get to, which is strongly involved. Your whole past history—this is one reason why I wanted to have this session with Betty. I wanted to get into a little bit more of her life. Now any type of reasonable exploration for either or both of you would take a tremendous amount of time. And I don't know if you would want to go on to that extent. So I've been keeping ourselves focused on the best possible illumination of this whole experience. And so I would say that within a short time, we could probably bring this to a close.

"From there on, you yourself will see what might or might not be gained in continuing, depending on how acceptable the explanations. The hypnosis is not going to give us the absolutely final answers, as you can now see. It is subject to the same rules as the rest of the unconscious of a human being. But I think it's giving us enough with the mark of authority behind it, to the extent that you can have authority in anything. So that your capacity for reason, your reality-testing apparatus itself, can fill it out enough. So far as I have planned, a couple of sessions or so will be it. You may want to go one other session or two, but I'll have to leave that in your hands.

"Now, you are very active in your community work, Barney. Your energies are going into that, and I have the feeling that you're going into it better."

Barney agreed. He reported that his anxieties had been considerably reduced and his physical symptoms vastly improved; "I think this is a remarkable change, in just a brief period," he said. Betty also agreed.

*   *   *

During the closing sessions, both Barney and Betty were relieved that they had done everything possible to remove their anxieties about the experience. They felt that some kind of permanent record should be established in the event that future happenings should confirm what they both now were willing to consider as possible: the reality of the experience.

"I suppose I should say," was the way Barney put it to the doctor, "that what I've been thinking is that this is such an incredible thing— I don't know how it can ever be proven through any definite techniques —it isn't like mathematics, where you can use a definite equation to either prove or disprove it. What I was wondering is, What do you think of the idea that these tapes that we have accumulated over the months be placed in some secure place so that in the event of our deaths, or yours, and if, say, twenty or thirty years from now it's established that this experience is true and did happen, we would then have the tapes so at least we could protect ourselves from being considered eccentrics? You see, twenty or thirty years from now, we'll be sixty or seventy, and it's quite possible that some people will look on us as if we were really a bit eccentric."

The doctor agreed that the tapes would be preserved, and Barney added with a smile, "But you know, I just can't conceive of playing these tapes for anyone, and I can't help feeling, now that we're almost through, I become quite apprehensive thinking about what might have happened if we had foolishly permitted an unqualified person to hypnotize us, with the emotional impact that did come out, just what damage might have been done."

"You went pretty much on the brink of danger," the doctor said. "You can see what your reactions were in this thing. What the emotions of a human being can be when they are unleashed. Betty, with her calmness and all, still had plenty of emotion working through. This is the unconscious of the human being. And it's an area where the human protects himself by—repressions. And he wants to be very careful indeed about releasing repression. People think about repression as bad. Actually, repression is an essential of our mental lives. If we didn't repress a great percentage of our feelings, we would be chaotic human beings."

* * *

Six full months of sessions were over.

The Hills, puzzled but relieved, drove back to Portsmouth with the confused vacant feeling that comes at the end of a long, arduous job, a feeling that they would miss the doctor, the sessions, and the search for the solution to a mystery that still remained unsolved.

Dr. Simon, in his office some weeks later, opened his mail to find a letter from the organization that provided hospital and medical coverage for the Hills. At the Hills' request, Dr. Simon had submitted a brief summary of the Hills' treatment, indicating that they had suffered severe anxiety reactions after an experience with a UFO. Not surprisingly, the medical director of the organization wrote to Dr. Simon that he found it hard to accept a claim based on the diagnosis of a "UFO experience."

Dr. Simon replied in part:

"I can hardly quarrel with your unwillingness in your letter of August 4 to accept a diagnosis of 'emotional disturbance created by an experience with an Unidentified Flying Object' with respect to the claim of Mr. and

Mrs. Hill. This was not made as a diagnosis, but as a statement of the circumstances under which these two people had come to me for treatment—and with the expectation that you would send me forms for a medical statement. I have always had such when there have been insurance claims but Mr. Hill said I must only write to your office, without being able to tell me what information I would have to give you.

"Mr. and Mrs. Hill were referred to me in December, 1963. During the course of previous treatment of Mr. Hill, it was discovered that this had followed an experience in September, 1961, when Mr. and Mrs. Hill had witnessed an unidentified flying object at night while returning from their vacation.

"This was a harrowing experience for both of them and led to a very considerable anxiety for some time to come. Mr. Hill began to suffer from insomnia, apprehension and persistent anxiety. Mrs. Hill suffered from repeated nightmares, apprehension and anxiety. More recently, Mr. Hill has had symptoms of duodenal ulcer. Mr. Hill was under treatment for some time before it became apparent (during the treatment) that this experience with the unidentified flying object had played an important part; in fact, the story of this encounter came out during Mr. Hill's treatment.

"Eventually, there was brought to light the fact that both Mr. and Mrs. Hill were suffering from amnesia for a part of that night's events in September, 1961. Ultimately, both Mr. and Mrs. Hill were referred to me. Hypnosis was the obvious method, and I undertook the treatment of both of them. Treatment involved induction of a deep hypnotic state in each, and for this purpose it was necessary to carry them to the state of somnambulism.

"Treatment was accompanied by violent emotional abreaction in both patients. Because of this, treatment had to be delicately controlled and introduction into consciousness only as anxiety permitted. A tape recorder was used to record the unconscious material, and then to assist in its ultimate review and integration into consciousness. During the treatment, Mr. Hill had severe symptoms of ulcer which abated as the treatment progressed. Anxiety abated in both Mr. and Mrs. Hill. . .

"On their discharge from treatment, both were considered as recovered . . ."

"I hope that this information is adequate, and I will be glad to answer any further questions."

The insurance claim was settled promptly, probably for the first time involving a UFO case.

The therapy was at a safe and practical resting place at which the doctor felt it best to stop, even though many questions were unanswered. The relief from anxiety was significant, and sustained. There could be more discomfort for the Hills in pursuing the experience further than in letting it remain at the present state. Further, the doctor encouraged the Hills in their desire to keep in contact with him, as they continued "working through" on their own, a normal, continuing process after formal therapy is concluded.

The treatment had begun with the opening up of an amnesia, an amnesia that produced many problems of its own.

"I began," the doctor commented to the author two years after the sessions were over, "by utilizing hypnosis to get the story separately from each of the Hills. The major part of the amnesia appeared to encompass an incredible experience on the part of both of the Hills. This was not only significant, but the two people shared both the experiences, and were amnesic for these same experiences. Persistent investigation produced more problems than solutions. I had started with the thought that Barney was somewhat more suggestible than Betty, and that the story had derived from him. The story was quite improbable in the basis of any existing scientific data, but on the other hand it appeared as the case went on that the Hills were not lying, and I felt convinced of that. After getting Betty's story and noting that her dreams were identical to her recall under hypnosis, the idea occurred to me that my original assumption might be wrong: that much of Barney's recall was contained in Betty's description, though little of Betty's recall was included in Barney's story. My assumption then was that Barney had absorbed Betty's dream story. On that basis I went on more intensively to examine this possibility with Barney and to probe Betty's story further.

"I was ultimately left with the conclusion that the most tenable explanation that the series of dreams experienced by Mrs. Hill, as the aftermath of some type of experience with an Unidentified Flying Object or some similar phenomenon, assumed the quality of a fantasied experience.

"But the whole thing could not be settled in an absolute sense. The case could be safely left as it stood, especially in view of their improvement. We would remain in contact, and time might eventually bring out a more complete picture."

*   *   *

In a brief follow-up session in the spring of 1966, the doctor had a chance to check the impact of the sighting some five years after the incident at Indian Head and two years after the sessions had terminated. Barney went quickly into the trance as usual. Dr. Simon asked him some general review questions, to which he responded objectively and accurately. In the latter part of the session, the doctor reviewed Barney's feelings again, in considerable detail:

DOCTOR

What is your feeling now about the experience? Were you abducted—or weren't you?

BARNEY

(His voice, as usual, is flat and expressionless.)

I feel I was abducted.

DOCTOR

Were you abducted. Not "how do you feel." *Were* you abducted?

BARNEY

Yes. I don't want to believe I was abducted.

DOCTOR

But you are convinced you were?

BARNEY

I say "I feel" because this makes it comfortable for me to accept something I don't want to accept, that has happened.

DOCTOR

What would make it comfortable?

BARNEY

For me to say "I feel."

DOCTOR

Do you mean it would be worse to say: "I actually *was* abducted"?

BARNEY

It is not worse.

DOCTOR

You're more comfortable the other way?

BARNEY

I'm more comfortable the other way.

DOCTOR

Why are you uncomfortable about it?

BARNEY

Because it is such a weird story. If anyone else told me that this had happened to them, I would not believe them. And I hate, very badly, to be accused of something that I didn't do, when I know I didn't do it. Or if I am not believed about something I did, and I know I have done it.

DOCTOR

Well—suppose you had just absorbed Betty's dreams.

BARNEY

I would like that.

DOCTOR

You'd like that. Could that be true?

BARNEY

No.

DOCTOR

Why not?

BARNEY

Because—

(He quite suddenly becomes extremely tense and emotional, almost as much as during the first session when he recalled being drawn toward the object in the field at Indian Head.)

I—I didn't like them putting their hands on me!

(His breathing becomes fast and excited.)

DOCTOR

All right. Take it easy. You don't have to be upset.

BARNEY

(Begins to sob heavily.)

I didn't like them putting their hands on me! I don't like them touching me!

284

DOCTOR

All right. All right. They're not touching you now. They're not touching you at all. We'll let that go. You can relax.

(The doctor begins bringing him back out of the trance, with full reassurance. Barney's sobbing subsides. The review session—two years after the regular sessions—comes to an end.)

CHAPTER THIRTEEN

With the active treatment discontinued, Barney and Betty Hill settled down to their routine life, managing to put the incident at Indian Head into the background and to concentrate on their absorbing interest in community life, the activities of their Universalist-Unitarian-Church, and civil rights work. Betty Hill's schedule as a social worker for the state of New Hampshire was both demanding and rewarding; Barney's work for the post office department became more smooth and efficient now that he had been transferred to Portsmouth and was no longer working nights. His activities on the Board of Directors of the United States Civil Rights Commission, the NAACP, and the Anti-Poverty Program kept him inordinately active and occupied in his spare time. The overwhelming sense of relief and unburdening from the sessions strengthened his work, helped him to function better.

The experience of both the incident and the therapy, even if in the background, were of course far from forgotten. The Hills discussed these events both with close friends and family, hoping that more information on the elusive subject of UFO's would come to the foreground to illuminate their own experiences and to ease the feeling that they might be regarded as eccentrics. They would correspond at intervals with Hohman and Jackson and occasionally visit with Walter Webb at the Hayden Planetarium in Boston, or he would visit them in their home.

They assiduously avoided any publicity about their experiences, and by confining their discussions on the subject to their close circle of friends, they avoided any such problems. They were relieved to discover, in fact, that they could talk about it without any emotional disturbance now, and as long as this was done in private, they found it helpful.

They had almost forgotten that back in September 1962, they had been invited to tell their experience informally to a UFO study group in Quincy, Massachusetts, some months before they had begun their therapy with Dr. Simon. They had been unaware that at that meeting a tape recording had been made of their talk, which described in detail the experience and Betty's dreams resulting from the sighting. They were also unaware that this discussion later provided the basic information for the reporter who detailed the partial story in the series of articles in the Boston newspaper, appearing in the fall of 1965. Neither the Hills nor Dr. Simon had provided any direct information for this.

The Hills were both depressed and frustrated by the articles. They had turned down a request for an interview by the reporter and made it clear to him that they were not interested in putting their experience on public display. Dr. Simon, of course, had refused to discuss the subject with the reporter.

On reading the articles, Barney Hill's immediate reaction was that if he were reading this story about someone else, he would refuse point blank to believe it. Both he and Betty felt that a fragmented story like this would do nothing but place them in a position where they looked ridiculous. The story was too complex to be told superficially; there were too many cross-currents, too many involved factors that had to be taken into account. The Hills sought legal advice, but discovered that as long as the story was treated as a one-shot newspaper account and was not libelous, they could do nothing unless the story was carried beyond that.

When the Universalist-Unitarian Church in Dover, New Hampshire, extended an invitation to the Hills to speak at a Sunday evening meeting shortly after the newspaper articles had run, the Hills decided that in the talk they would try to correct the sensationalism of the news story and to convince the public that the articles were not anything to be sought or desired. The Hills would not discuss the hypnosis or therapy at all. Before the meeting, they were dinner guests of Admiral Herbert Knowles, USN Retired, one of the leading ex-military officers who was attempting to penetrate the UFO mystery in the face of the confused reports coming from the Pentagon. Here, some of the nervousness the

Hills were experiencing about the idea of the meeting was overcome.

One interesting aspect of the Dover meeting was that the co-speaker of the evening was a Public Information Officer of the Pease Air Force Base. Although his talk was noncommittal, he was by no means deprecatory either of the Hills and their story or of the flood of UFO reports that had been building up all through 1965 in that area. The meeting was held on November 8 of that year, and hundreds of people were turned away from the church, in spite of a raw and chilly rain.

The turnout for the meeting and the reaction to it indicated to the Hills that the subject of UFO's was of extreme public interest, and possibly of historical importance in the light of increasingly competent reports of sightings throughout the world. The impact on their own lives was profound and far-reaching. While further reflection on their own part brought them to the conclusion that their experience with the abduction might possibly be real, they were acutely aware of how its strangeness could not be accepted by others easily, any more than they themselves could uncritically accept their own stories as revealed to them on the recordings of their therapy sessions.

The Hills' ultimate conclusion was, after considerable reflection, that a book should be written that would tell the story in complete detail, leaving it up to the reader to decide on its importance on the basis of the facts revealed.

"Philosophically, it has given me a broader appreciation of the universe," Barney Hill sums up his feelings. "After the incident happened, Betty and I would many times visit the Hayden Planetarium, listening to the lectures. The more we learned, the more fascinating the universe became to us. We bought books on the stars and planets, and our outlook broadened considerably. I became more open-minded about the possibility of life on other planets or in solar systems that might have planets.

"I tried to speculate on our own experience as to possibilities other than an extraterrestrial craft. I had to reach the conclusion that this theory was as valid as any other. At one time, I gave a great deal of thought to the possibility that this object might have been an advanced foreign reconnaissance craft, but I didn't get too far in my own mind with this. I can't believe that other human beings would be so interested in Betty and me, that they would have conducted the type of physical examination they gave us if they had been human. They could have used their own people for that kind of examination.

"While Betty and I don't at all like the idea of being considered eccentric, we still are not too concerned about the opinions of other people about us. If we were outer-directed people, our lives would have been changed a lot more than they now have been. I might be trying to convince people by saying, 'Look—believe me, this happened.' But I'm not too interested in trying to convince anyone against his own judgment. As far as talking to someone who is interested in listening, I'm glad to do this, and they don't have to agree with me. I realize this case, until further proof comes along, will be controversial, and I accept that. I'm convinced now—against my own former beliefs—that we had an experience that is going to be extremely difficult to be believed. The only thing I can say is I have a strong feeling that this experience might have happened; you form your own opinion. If you want to believe it, you can. If you don't, that's fine too. But respect the fact that I've given this long thought, in the face of my own resistance to the idea, and I've had to come to the conclusion that there is a distinct likelihood that all this might have happened. I would much prefer it if I could be absolutely sure that none of this took place. But I can't fall back on that, much as I'd like to. I simply say that it cannot be ruled out that this happened, as it came out to me when I heard my own voice on the recordings.

"The period before the amnesia hit us both is a matter of full reality to me, and to Betty too. But just before the amnesia hit, I felt sure I saw persons of some kind aboard the craft. At that time, Betty did not. I felt this odd form of communication at that time; Betty didn't. This makes it a little difficult for me to accept the transference of Betty's dreams as an explanation—although the problem with this whole story is that *any* explanation of it seems as difficult as another to accept.

"When Betty was telling her dreams to Walter Webb or to friends, I resisted the whole idea of her telling them, because they seemed so absurd to me. Now—after listening to the recordings, I'm not so sure. When I heard my own voice describing what had happened, it seemed to me, at least, that there was no difference between what I was saying and what might have actually happened. Right or wrong, the whole story seemed to come together—both amnesia and pre-amnesia—as one stream of continuity.

"One thing I'm sure of is that I don't have that fear, that apprehension any more that I had after the experience at Indian Head. This was a vague thing, that fear, that I never had in my life before. And

I'm glad that the therapy seemed to relieve me of it completely now.

"I guess this about adds up my convictions about the story. They are still only my convictions, and anyone is free to disagree with them. The main thing I can say is that they were not arrived at easily, and only after a lot of painful and costly self-examination."

"I think the most important thing to me," Betty Hill summarizes her feelings, "is that I've taken a broader look at the world. Where are we going from here? And to look ahead at the future, you've got to know the past. I've become very interested in anything that has to do with theories or ideas about man's past. We thought man was fairly recent on the earth, but now we're finding that he's been around quite a few, maybe millions of years more than we thought. I keep wondering about what caused us to suddenly begin so much progress. In the last forty years, we seem to have broken through more barriers than it has taken us all through history.We seem to be really just on the threshold of a new science and will move ahead even more rapidly than ever, if man doesn't destroy himself first.

"I was brought up to believe in what I suppose is called the scientific method: You don't believe in anything unless it can be dissected or put in a box. I don't believe in ghost stories. Before this experience, my attitude was that anybody who believed in anything I don't understand, anyone who seemed too far-out, I considered sort of a kook. Now I think I have more tolerance toward new ideas, even if I can't accept them myself.

"When Dr. Simon first suggested the idea that maybe it could be possible that I had converted the dreams about the amnesia period into a false reality, I thought, 'Well, this is wonderful.' I was perfectly willing to go along with it. In fact, I wanted to believe this, because this whole experience isn't easy to live with. I mean, it's really a tremendous pressure on a person. And so after the session in which the dream theory was presented, I came home and I said, 'This is wonderful.' I could compare it with thinking that I had a bad experience, like an auto accident, and then somebody says, 'Forget it, it's only a dream.' You know—you're greatly relieved. You can deny the whole thing ever happened. And so I went through a stage like that. Every time I'd think of it, I'd say, 'It's just a dream, so forget it.' I could get rid of the whole thing. This will be the end of it.

"And so every night when I went to bed, I'd say to myself, 'It's only a dream.' And I was able to do this for about two weeks, I guess, after the therapy was over. Then all of a sudden one morning, I woke up with the thought, 'Whom do I think I'm trying to kid?' Zoom—it was back again. And I haven't been successful in telling myself it was a dream ever since."

Both of the Hills are aware that others will interpret some of the dream content in various ways. "This is to be expected," Barney Hill says. "And I'm far from an expert. In my case, no dreams were involved in relation to the experience until well after the therapy sessions began. My recall of the incident is not related to dreams or dream symbols. It's related to the strong feeling that what I recalled under hypnosis could be one distinct possibility of having happened. This is a lot more than I could admit for several years. I like to consider myself a realist, and I would be less than one if I tried to interpret what went on in the amnesic period as only being in the nature of dreams or dream symbols."

In her studies in sociology and psychology, Betty Hill is well aware of the varied interpretations of dreams, but she points out that even the theorists of dream structure disagree among themselves. "What interests me is that the incidents in my dreams and the incidents of the story that came out under hypnosis were almost identical. I don't feel that in this case the interpretations of dream symbols can help determine whether our experience was real or not, and this is the part of the circumstance that is most important to us now—now that our anxieties are relieved."

* * *

If the experience of the Hills at Indian Head was a totally isolated incident, it would still be important and worthy of further scientific study, even if only to clarify it.

But it is far from isolated. Reliable reports from competent observers of increased UFO sightings—many of them reported as structured crafts similar to the Hills' description—have been building up constantly since the early spring of 1965, with police, military, technical and scientific observations prominent among them. The change of attitude toward the subject by scientists from skepticism to one of interested inquiry has been noted from the beginning of 1966 on. It is no longer fashionable to be skeptical. Some scientists have argued that if the phenomenon is purely psychological, then the story should be considered even more startling than if it were an indication of extraterrestrial visitors.

At a quiet scientific meeting in June of 1966, Dr. J. Allen Hynek,

Chairman of the Department of Astronomy of Northwestern University, made a cautious talk to a regional meeting of the Optical Society of America on UFO's that had far-reaching implications as far as the scientific attitude toward the phenomenon was concerned. He lost no time in getting to the core of the speech.

"Unidentified flying objects demand serious and immediate scientific attention," he said. "I say this at the start so that you are not misled by the kooks, the nuts, and the gullible who have made this subject so difficult to explore rationally. UFO's are a real puzzle. The myth is *not* put to rest. And the scientific fraternity must now take cognizance of them. We can no longer dismiss the subject."

In addition to his astronomy post, Dr. Hynek was in charge of the optical satellite tracking program of the Smithsonian Astrophysical Observatory in Cambridge, Massachusetts, and scientific director of the U.S. Air Force balloon astronomy project *Stargazer*. For eighteen years, he has been scientific consultant to the Air Force on UFO's and has screened over ten thousand cases in their files, investigating many of them personally.

In the talk to the scientists, engineers and technicians of the Optical Society, he went on to say: "I thought the whole thing would go up in smoke, like eating goldfish or seeing how many people could be jammed into a phone booth. But the phenomenon has stayed with us—and more than that—there are far more persons of status and competence who are reporting these UFO's in extremely articulate form. To those who don't know the background—which you're not likely to get from the press—these conclusions of mine might seem very strange. But I have given them long thought."

Dr. Hynek further revealed that a leading scientist of a top-ranking university had reviewed some of his data on UFO's, and berated him soundly for not coming out boldly with a statement that the objects *had* to be extraterrestrial. "How can you *not* accept this as a fact?" the scientist asked him. Dr. Hynek reminded his colleague that he was in a lonely position among other scientists.

"After eighteen years as a skeptic," Dr. Hynek said in the speech, "I have finally been bowed down by the sheer weight of *competent* evidence. As far back as 1953, I recommended that the subject be given definite scientific study, but I have never before made a categorical proposal. This program will include recommendations for: (1) An immediate study in depth by university teams; (2) a pattern analysis by computer of existing data; (3) the establishment of a UFO Research Center staffed by competent scientists. When a phenomenon has the potential capacity of a possible scientific breakthrough, we are neglecting our responsibilities by not at least exploring every facet. Ridicule is no longer appropriate."

*　　*　　*

In the light of the overall accelerated activity in UFO reports, the experience of Betty and Barney Hill indicates the necessity of further scientific study in an attempt to solve the mystery.

There are many unanswered questions precipitated by the case as it unfolded both consciously and under therapy. The Hills' story has come to public attention with their extreme reluctance, five years after the event, and only because of a leak that resulted in a series of local newspaper articles. The Hills sought no publicity and were successful in holding back the story for several years before it became public under their protests. Their views on the experience are the result of a long and painful period of intelligent examination and study, both in and out of therapy. Their approach to the subject has been rational and cautious.

The greatest mystery about the experience is that *any* assumption on the basis of the material revealed is hard to conceive or understand. An abduction by humanoid intelligent beings from another planet in a space craft has always belonged to science fiction. To concoct a science fiction story of this magnitude would require an inconceivable skill and collaborative capacity. It is as hard for the Hills to accept the possibility that the abduction took place as it is for any intelligent person. In fact the attitude of the Hills is: We did not expect or look for the sighting to take place. Barney resisted and persistently tried to deny its existence. We did not know what happened in the missing two hours and thirty-five miles of distance until we heard voices coming out on the tape recordings. What came out on the recordings was as difficult for us to believe as for anybody else. We only know that after the pieces began coming back together, our general feelings and convictions grew on us that these experiences seemed to be reality—as real as our other recollections of any valid, factual memories.

The assumption that Betty's dreams were absorbed by Barney to create his recollection of the abduction sequence is also hard to conceive or understand. If Betty's dream had been the sole source of information about the humanoid beings, what about Barney's glimpse of persons

293

aboard the craft, recalled in full consciousness, just before the beeping sound occurred? What about other portions of the apparent abduction that Barney recalled and Betty did not? How could the couple concoct the enormous amount of detail, strikingly similar, and stick to it so consistently?

From the long and intensive exploration of the case, however, certain nearly irrefutable points emerge:

1. A sighting of some sort took place.

The two major alternatives to this point are substantially refuted:

1. To concoct the elaborate stories, matched in detail, a month after the sighting, and again more than two years later, would have required an inconceivable precision of planning, memory, and prevision of an imponderable future. Judgments from many sources as well as from two psychiatrists attested to the Hills' probity and integrity.

2. No evidence was ever brought out that either of the Hills had at any time experienced psychotic hallucinations.

Any theory (including the dream hypothesis) which excludes these alternatives is predicated on a sighting of some object or phenomenon.

2. The object sighted appears to have been a craft.

As perceived by the Hills, the craft was similar to many previously and since reported by others who have sighted unidentified flying objects.

3. The sighting caused a severe emotional reaction.

Much of the direct emotional response was repressed and suppressed, attaining conscious expression in diffuse anxiety, dreams of nightmarish quality, and physical symptoms—until released and discharged during treatment. Some of the inner emotional experiences came to consciousness only under hypnosis.

4. The anxiety and apprehension engendered by Barney Hill's racial sensitivity served to intensify the emotional response to the sighting.

Throughout the entire trip from Montreal to the "sighting," Barney Hill suffered from increasing apprehension and fear of hostile reactions to his race, though none materialized. This oppressive feeling could sensitize him to any unusual or strange experience and intensify his reactions to such an experience.

5. The Hills had no ulterior motive to create such a story. They had confined their experience to a small group of people for four years.

The Hills had kept their story restricted to a few intimates, and to interested scientists and investigators. Treatment was sought for their emotional disturbances, and they decided to release their story only after it had been publicized without their permission five years after the incident.

6. The case was investigated by several technical and scientific persons who support the possibility of the reality of the experience.

The investigations by Hohman, Jackson, and Webb, based on their experience with other cases, supported the possibility that the Hills' case could be a valid experience justifying scientific attention.

7. There is a measurable amount of direct physical circumstantial evidence to support the validity of the experience.

No explanation has been found for the shiny bright spots on the trunk of the car which caused the compass to oscillate nor for the failure of the Hills' watches to run after the sighting experience. Barney Hill's broken binocular strap and sore neck could attest to his extreme agitation.

8. Under hypnosis by a qualified psychiatrist, both the Hills told almost identical stories of what had taken place during their period of amnesia.

A dual identical psychosis (folie à deux) is substantially excluded by the absence of other characteristics of this rare psychosis, nor was there any other evidence of psychosis. A joint fabrication is also substantially excluded. The two remaining possibilities would appear to be:

1. A totally real and true experience.

2. An experience which had been so affected by the accompanying emotional state as to produce some perceptive and illusory misinterpretations—as embodied in the dream hypothesis.

*   *   *

There are no final answers. Where one question existed before, several others have come up to take its place. But if it can even momentarily be speculated that the event is true, the far-reaching implications concerning the history of the world are obvious.

Such an event would demand a reexamination of religion, politics, science and even literature. International relations would have to be thoroughly reexamined. An urgent need for a study and extensive scientific report on the subject would be quickly indicated, both national and worldwide. There is, in fact, evidence already extant that the United Nations is seriously considering a major scientific world-wide study of the subject.

Neither Barney nor Betty Hill had any thought that they might be involved in such an event when they left the little restaurant at Colebrook, New Hampshire, at 10:05 P. M. on the night of September 19, 1961. They are not crusading to convert nonbelievers or skeptics into the acceptance of the phenomenon, although they are hopeful that some new evidence might come along to clarify without question the strange circumstances of their experience. They are content now to let whatever facts that have come out of their story speak for themselves.

But as Tennyson has said: "Maybe wildest dreams are but the needful preludes of the truth."

APPENDIX

The following is the recall of Betty's dreams, which she wrote down as notes to herself after the incident had taken place. It will be noted that they are substantially the same as the recall she describes as having actually happened during the amnesic period. It is not uncommon for dreams resulting from an experience of shock to be literal; i.e., a complete re-enactment, so to speak, of an event that actually took place. On the other hand, such a dream neither proves nor disproves such an event.

Betty Hill's detailed notes are printed here for those readers who would like to compare in detail the content of her dreams with her recall of the amnesic period as it came out under hypnosis.

The similarities are marked.

*   *   *

(Dreams that occurred following the sighting of the UFO in the White Mountains on Sept. 19–20, 1961.)

Two events happened of which we are consciously aware; these are also incorporated in my dreams. First, we sighted a huge object, glowing with a bright orange light, which appeared to be sitting on the ground. In front of this, we could distinguish the silhouette of evergreen trees. Our reaction was to say, "No, not again," and then we consoled ourselves with the self-assurance it was the setting moon. At this point in the highway, we made a sharp turn to the left. Second, at the termination of this, I asked Barney if he believed in flying saucers now? He replied, "Don't be ridiculous. Of course not." I will attempt to tell my dreams in chronological order, although they were not dreamed in this way. In fact the first dream told was the last one dreamed. My emotional feelings during this part was of terror, greater than I had ever believed possible. [Betty Hill recalls almost bolting out of bed during this dream.]

We were driving home from the sighting, when we saw the bright orange glowing shape; we saw a very sharp left-hand turn in the road and found that the road curved back to the right. At this moment, I saw eight to eleven men standing in the middle of the road. Barney slowed down to wait for them to move, but the motor died. As he was trying to start the motor, the men surrounded the car. We sat there motionless and speechless, and I was terrified. At the same time, they opened the car doors on each side, reached in and took us by the arm.

(This is the first dream I had.) I am struggling to wake up; I am at the bottom of a deep well, and I must get out. Everything is black; I am fighting to become conscious, slowly and gradually I start to become conscious, I struggle to open my eyes for a moment, and then they close again; I keep fighting, I am dazed and have a far-away feeling. Then I win the battle and my eyes are open. I am amazed! I am walking through a path in the woods, tall trees are on both sides, but next to me on both sides is a man; two men in front; two men in back; then Barney with a man on each side of him; other men in back of him. I become frightened again, and I turn to Barney and say his name, but he is "sleep-walking," he does not hear me and does not appear to be conscious of what is happening. The man on my left speaks to me and asks if his name is Barney; I refuse to answer. Then he attempts to reassure me: that there is nothing to fear—Barney is all right; no harm will come to us. All they want to do is make some tests; when these are completed in a very brief time, they will take us back to the car and we will go safely on our way home. We have nothing to fear.

During this time I become conscious of several things [She is referring to her dream, as all through this account]. First, only one man speaks, in English, with a foreign accent, but very understandably. The others say nothing. I note their physical appearance. Most of the men are my height, although I cannot remember the height of the heels on my shoes. None is as tall as Barney, so I would judge them to be 5′ to 5′4″. Their chests are larger than ours; their noses were larger (longer) than the average size although I have seen people with noses like theirs—like Jimmy Durante's.

Their complexions were of a gray tone; like a gray paint with a black base; their lips were of a bluish tint. Hair and eyes were very dark, possibly black.

298

The men were all dressed alike, presumably in uniform, of a light navy blue color with a gray shade in it. They wore trousers and short jackets, that gave the appearance of zippered sports jackets, but I am not aware of zippers or buttons for closing. Shoes were a low, slip-on style, resembling a boot. I cannot remember any jewelry, or insignia. They were all wearing military caps, similar to Air Force, but not so broad on the top.

They were very human in their appearance, not frightening. They seemed to be very relaxed, friendly in a professional way (business-like). There was no haste, no waste of time.

After reassuring me that there was no cause for fear, the "leader" ignored me, and we continued to walk. I would turn back to Barney, and he still was not aware of what was happening. Incidentally, he remained in this state until we were returned to the car at the end.

We reached a small clearing in the woods. In front of us was a disc, almost as wide as my house is long. It was darkened, but appeared to be metallic. No lights or windows were seen, and I had the impression that we were approaching from the back of it. We stepped up a step or two to go onto a ramp, leading to a door. At this point I became frightened again and refused to walk. The leader spoke, firmly but gently, reassuring me that I had no reason to be afraid, but the more delay I caused by my uncooperativeness, the longer I would be away from the car. I shrugged my shoulders and agreed that we might as well get it over with; I seemed to have no choice in this situation.

We entered the disc. I found a corridor, curving to the contours of the ship. We started to enter the first room, leading from the corridor, but then I found that Barney was being taken further down the hall. I objected to this, and questioned why we both could not be examined in the same room. The leader showed some exasperation with this question and my objections, and explained, as though I were a small child, that the exam would take twice as long this way, as they only had equipment to test one person at a time in a room, and he thought that I wanted to be on my way as quickly as possible. So I agreed.

About four or five men entered the room with us, but when another man came in, they left. This man was the examiner and also spoke English. He was very pleasant, reassuring. He asked questions; some I had difficulty understanding, as his English was not as good as the first man's. My answers puzzled him at times. He asked my age, also Barney's. He shook his head as though he doubted me. He asked me what I ate; when

I told him, he asked questions, what did vegetables look like? My favorite one? Squash—what did it look like; how do we eat it? I told about peeling it, cooking it, mashing it, putting salt and pepper, butter on it. He was puzzled. I tried to explain the color of it—and looked for some yellow coloring in the room, but could not find any. I tried to tell about meat, milk, but he did not understand the meaning of the words I was using.

Then the examiner said that he wished to do some tests, to find out the basic differences between him and us; that I would not be harmed in any way and would not experience any pain. Also he would explain what he was doing as he went along. Just a few simple tests. The leader returned and remained in the room the rest of the time I was there. He was an observer during the testing. First, I sat on a stool, the examiner in front of me, with a bright light shining on me. My hair was closely examined, and he removed a few strands and then cut a larger piece on the back left-hand side. I was not able to see what he used for cutting purposes. Then he looked in my mouth, down my throat, in my ears, removing some ear wax or something. They examined my hands and fingernails, taking a piece of my nail. They removed my shoes and looked at my feet. They showed much interest in my skin and pulled out some type of apparatus which they held close to my arm on the top and inside. He seemed to be adjusting this, and I wonder if he was getting a magnified view or taking a picture. He took a slender long instrument, similar to a letter opener, and scraped along my arm. As he took these samples, he would hand them to the leader, who carefully placed these on a clear material like glass or plastic, cover with another piece and wrap them in a piece of cloth. Very similar to a glass slide.

Next he pulled a machine over, and asked me to lie down on an examining table. This machine resembled the wires of an EEG [an electroencephalograph, which records electrical brainwaves], but no tracing machine was seen. On the end of each wire was a needle. He explained that he wanted to check my nervous system. He reassured me that there would be no pain. Very gently he touched the ends of the needles to different parts of my body. He started with my head, temples, face, neck, behind my ears, back of my neck, all my spine, under my arms, around my hips, and paid particular attention to my legs and feet. Sometimes only one needle would be held against me, then two, then several. A few times he would touch a spot on my body, and I would jump, or my arm or leg would jerk; a slight twitch. Both men were highly interested in this test; and I feel that a recorder was being used, although I did not see one. Also during this exam, my dress was removed, as it was hindering the testing.

They said the next test was a pregnancy test. The examiner picked up a very long needle, about four to six inches long. I asked what he planned to do, and he said that it was a very simple test, with no pain, but would be very helpful to them. I asked what kind of pregnancy test he planned with the needle. He did not reply, but started to insert the needle in my navel with a sudden thrust. Suddenly I was filled with great pain, twisting and moaning. Both men looked very startled, and the leader bent over me and waved his hand in front of my eyes. Immediately the pain was completely gone, and I relaxed. At that moment I became very grateful and appreciative to the leader; lost all fear of him; and felt as though he was a friend. I kept repeating my thank-you's to him for stopping the pain, and he said that they had not known that I would suffer pain from this test; if they had known, they would not have done this. I could feel his concern about this, and I began to trust him.

They decided to end the testing. The examiner left the room, the leader gathered up all the test samples and put them together in a drawer, and I put on my dress and shoes. Upon questioning where the examiner had gone, he told me that he was needed to complete the testing on Barney, that his was taking longer than mine, but soon we would be going back to the car.

I spent the time waiting, by talking with the leader and walking around the small room. There was an absence of color in the room, and it was of a metal construction—like stainless steel or aluminum. Cabinets and one door were on the curved side; the remaining two walls were intersected like a triangle. There was a bright overhead light of bluish shade. Together in one corner was the equipment used in the testing. After the leader had put away all the things, we stood on the right-hand side of the door and talked. I mentioned that this had been quite an experience and I had never had anything like this happen before. He smiled and agreed and said that of course in the beginning I had been badly frightened. They regretted this fright and had wanted to do all they could to alleviate it. I admitted that I had completely recovered and was now enjoying this opportunity to talk with him; and there were so many questions I wanted to ask. He volunteered to answer all that he could.

At this point, some of the men came hurriedly into the room. Their excitement was apparent, and they were talking with the leader, but I could not understand what they were saying. They were not using words or tones with which I was acquainted. The leader left the room with them, and I became frightened that something had gone wrong with Barney's testing. The leader was gone only a short period of time; he opened my mouth and was touching my teeth, trying to move them. When he stopped, very puzzled, he said they were confused. Barney's teeth were removable, mine were not. This was an amazing discovery! The examiner returned and checked my teeth. I was laughing most heartily about this, and went on to explain that Barney had dentures, the reasons for this, while I did not need these yet, but I would as I became older; that all people lose their teeth with old age. All were very amazed, and all the men were going back and forth to Barney and then me, to look at our teeth, and to see the difference. They were unbelieving, shaking their heads.

After they left, the leader asked what was old age. I said that a life span was believed to be a hundred years, but people died at age sixty-five to seventy from degeneration and disease usually; some died in accidents and illnesses at all ages. I attempted to explain aging—the skin wrinkles, the graying hair, etc. He asked what was a hundred years, and I could not tell him, only a way to measure time.

Then I broached the subject again of this whole experience being so unbelievable to me; that no one would ever believe me; that they would think I had lost my mind; I suggested that what was needed was absolute proof that this had happened; maybe he could give me something to take back with me. He agreed and asked what I would like. I looked around the room and found a large book. I asked if I could take this with me, and he agreed. I was so happy and thanked him. I opened the book and found symbols written in long, narrow columns. He asked jokingly if I thought I could read it, and I said that this was impossible, I had never seen anything like it. But I was not taking this for reading purposes, but this was my absolute proof of this experience and that I would always remember him as long as I lived.

Then I asked where he was from, and he asked if I knew anything about the universe. I said no, but I would like to learn. He went over to the wall and pulled down a map, strange to me. Now I would believe this to be a sky map. It was a map of the heavens, with numerous sized stars and planets, some large, some only pinpoints. Between many of these, lines were drawn, some broken lines, some light solid lines, some heavy black lines. They were not straight, but curved. Some went from one planet to another, to another, in a series of lines. Others had no lines, and he said the lines were expeditions. He asked me where the earth was on this map, and I admitted that I had no idea. He became slightly sarcastic and said that if I did not know where the earth was, it was impossible to show me where he was from; he snapped the map back into place. I said that I did not intend to anger him but had told him that I knew nothing of such things. But there were many people here who did have knowledge of these things, and I knew that they would love to talk with him and would understand him. Then I suggested the possibility of arranging a meeting between him and these people, that this would be a momentous meeting; a quiet meeting with scientists or top people of the world. While I was saying these things, I was wondering if I could do this, but felt that it could be worked out some way. He asked why, and I said that most people did not believe that he existed; he would have a chance to meet us and to study us openly. He smiled and said nothing. I was in the middle of trying to sell him this idea, when several men appeared with Barney, who was still in a daze. I spoke to him, and he did not answer. I asked when he would be fully awake, and the leader said as soon as we were back in the car.

We started to walk out the door, when one of the men said something, not understood by me. They all stopped and were talking excitedly. The leader went back and talked to them. A disagreement had occurred, and the leader seemed to be in the minority. He came up to me and took the book. I protested, saying that this was my only proof; he said that he knew this, and this was the reason why he was taking it. He said that he could see no harm in my having the book, but that it had been decided that no one should know of this experience, and that even I would not remember this. I became very angry and said that somehow, somewhere, I would remember—that there was nothing he could do to make me forget this. He laughed and agreed that I might possibly do just that—to remember, but that he would do his best to prevent me from this, as this had been the final decision. He added that I might remember but no one would ever believe me; that Barney would have no recollection of any of this experience; in case Barney might ever recall, which he seriously doubted, he would think of things contrary to the way I knew them to be. This would lead to confusion, doubt, disagreement. So if I should remember, it would be feasible to forget. It could be very upsetting.

We left the ship and walked through the woods. This time it seemed like a very short time. I spent the time saying that I would always remember and asking that they return; please, please return. The leader said that it was not his decision to make; he did not know if he would come back. I said that I was very happy about meeting him, and honored, and thanked him for being kind. All the men accompanied us.

We came to the car, and the leader suggested that we wait and see them leave. We agreed. Barney seemed to wake up as we approached the car, and he showed no emotion, as if this were an everyday occurrence. We stood on the right-hand side of the car, Barney was leaning against the front fender, and I was by the door. As we were waiting, I thought of Delsey. I opened the car door and Delsey was under the front seat. She was trembling badly, and I patted her for a moment. She came out, and I picked her up, and held her, again leaning against the car door.

Suddenly the ship became a bright glowing object, and it appeared to roll like a ball turning over about three or four times and then sailing into the sky. In a moment it was gone, as though they had turned out the lights. I turned to Barney, and I was exuberant. I said that it was the most marvelous, most unbelievable experience of my whole life. I patted Delsy and said, "There they go. And we are none the worse for the wear."

We got in the car and Barney started driving. He said nothing during this whole experience, so I turned to him and asked, "Do you believe in flying saucers now?" He replied, "Don't be ridiculous." Then we heard the beeping on the car again, and I thought, good luck, good-by, and I am going to forget about you. If you want me to forget, I will, and I will not talk.